Part I

LANGUAGE

Chapter 1

At the end, he sat in the hotel room and counted out the pills.

He did not do this with words, nor mathematics, nor did his hands move, nor could he especially blame anyone else.

It didn't occur to him that Death would come; not in the conscious way of things. Death was, Death is, Death shall be, Death is not, and all this was the truth, and he understood it perfectly, and for all those reasons, this ending was fine.

Tick tick tick.

The world turned and the clock ticked

tick tick tick

and as it ticked, he heard the countdown to Armageddon, and that was okay too. No point fighting it. The fight was what made everything worse.

He was fine.

He picked up the first pill, and felt a lot better about his career choices.

Chapter 2

At the beginning . . .

The Harbinger of Death poured another shot of whiskey into the glass, lifted the old lady's head from the dark blue wall of pillows on which she lay, put the drink to her lips and said, "Best I ever heard was in Colorado."

The woman drank, the sky rushed overhead, dragged towards another storm, another thrashing of the sea on basalt rock, another ripping-up of tree and bending of corrugated rooftop, the third of this month, unseasonal it was, unseasonal, but weren't all things these days?

She blinked when she had drunk enough, and the Harbinger returned the glass to the bedside table. "Colorado?" she wheezed at last. "I didn't think there was anything in Colorado."

"Very big. Very empty. Very beautiful."

"But they have music?"

"She was travelling."

"Get an audience?"

"No. But I stopped to listen. This was student days, there was this girl who ... People won't be booking her for a high school prom any time soon, but I thought ... it was something very special."

"All the old songs are dying out."

"Not all of them."

The woman smiled, the expression turning into a grimace of pain, words unspoken: just you look at me, sonny, just you think about what you said. "A girl who?"

"What? Oh, yes, I was, um ... well, I hoped there'd be a relationship, and you know how these things sort of blur, and she thought it was one thing and I never really did say and then she was going out with someone else, but by then we'd booked the plane tickets and ... look, I don't know if I should ... I'm not sure I should talk about me."

"Why not?"

"Well, this is ... " An awkward shrug, taking in the room.

"You think that because I'm dying, I should talk and you should listen?"

"If you want."

"You talk. I'm tired."

The Harbinger of Death hesitated, then tapped the edge of

the whiskey glass, held it to her lips again, let her drink, put it down. "Sorry," he murmured, when she'd swallowed, licked her lips dry. "I'm new to this."

"You're doing fine."

"Thank you. I was worried that it would be ... What would you like to hear about? I'm interested in music. I thought maybe that when I travelled, I mean, for the work, I'd try and collect music, but not just CDs, I mean, all the music of all the places. I was told that was okay, that I was allowed to preserve ... not preserve, that's not ... Are you sure you wouldn't rather talk? When ... when my boss comes ..." Again his voice trailed off. He fumbled with the whiskey bottle, was surprised at how much had already been drunk.

"I know songs," she mused, as he struggled with the top. "But I don't think they're for you to sing. A woman once tried to preserve these things, said it would be a disaster if they died. I thought she was right. I thought that it mattered. Now ... it's only a song. Only that."

He looked away, not exactly rebuked, but nonplussed by the moment, and her resolve. To cover the silence, he refilled her glass. The tumbler was thick, clean crystal, with a clouded band at the bottom where the base was ridged like a deadly flower – one of a set. He'd carried all four up the ancient flagstone road from Cusco, even though only two would ever be used, not knowing what he'd do with the remainder but feeling it was somehow wrong to part one from the other. He'd also carried the whiskey, stowed in the side of his pack, and the mule driver who'd showed him the way across the treeless road where sometimes still the pilgrims came dressed in Inca robes and carrying a blackened cross had said, "In these parts, we just make our own," and looked hungrily at the bottle.

The Harbinger of Death had answered, "It's for an old woman who is dying," and the mule driver had replied, ah, Old Mother Sakinai, yes yes, it was another thirty miles though, and you had to be careful not to miss the turning; it didn't look like a split in the path, but it was, no help if you get lost. The mule driver did not look at the bottle again.

They had camped in a stone hut shaped like a beehive, no mortar between the slabs of slate, a hole in the roof for the smoke from the fire to escape, and in the morning the Harbinger of Death had watched the sun burn away the mist from the valley and seen, very faintly in the dry stone-splotched grass, the tracings of shapes and forms where once patterns miles wide had been carved to honour the sun, the moon, the river and the sky. Sometimes, the man with the three surprisingly docile mules said, helicopters came up here, for medical emergencies or filming or something like that, but no cars, not in these parts. And why was the foreigner visiting Mama Sakinai, so far from the tarmacked road?

"I'm the Harbinger of Death," he replied. "I'm sort of like the one who goes before."

At this the mule driver frowned and sucked on his bottom lip and at last replied, "Surely you should be travelling on a feathered serpent, or at the very least in a four-by-four?"

"Apparently my employer likes to travel the way the living do. He says it's good manners to understand what comes before the end." Having said these words, he played them back in his mind and found they sounded a bit ridiculous. Unable to stop himself, he added, "To be honest, I've been doing the job for a week. But ... that's what I was told. That's what the last Harbinger said."

The mule driver found he had very little to give in reply to this, and so on they walked, until the path divided – or rather, until a little spur of dark brown soil peeled away from the stones laid so many centuries ago by the dead peoples of the mountains, and the Harbinger of Death followed it, not quite certain if this was indeed a path used by people or merely the track of a wide and possibly hungry animal, down and down again into a valley where a tiny stream ran between white stones, and where a single house had been built the colour of the dry river bed, timber roof and straw on the porch, a black-eyed dog barking at him as he approached.

The Harbinger of Death stopped some ten feet from the

dog, crouched on his haunches, let it bark and dart around him, demanding who, what, why, another human, here, where no people came except once every two weeks Mama Sakinai's nephew, and once every three months the travelling district nurse with her heavy bags not heavy enough to cure its mistress.

"You'll want to learn how to deal with dogs," the last Harbinger had said as he shadowed her on her final trips. "Ask any postman."

Charlie had nodded earnestly, but in all honesty he wasn't bothered by dogs anyway. He liked most animals, and found that if he didn't make a fuss, most animals didn't seem to mind him. So finally, having grown bored of barking, the dog settled down, its chin on its paws, and the Harbinger waited a little while longer, and when all was settled save the whispering of the wind over the treeless ground and the trickling of the stream, he went to Mama Sakinai's door, knocked thrice and said, "Mama Sakinai? My name is Charlie, I'm the Harbinger of Death. I've brought some whiskey."

Chapter 3

In a land of forests . . .
   . . . in a land of rain . . .
There had been an aptitude test.
Reading, writing, general knowledge.

Q1 Rank these countries in order of population, from most populated to least.
Q2 Who is the director of the United Nations?
Q3 Name five countries that were previously British colonies in the period 1890–1945.

Q4 "Man is no more than the sum of his experience and his capacity to express these experiences to fellow man." Discuss. (500 words.)

And so on.

Charlie did better at it than he'd expected, not knowing what he should have studied in advance.

There weren't any other candidates in the room as he answered the questions. Most of the time it was a classroom for students learning to teach English as a foreign language. On one wall was a cartoon poster explaining how adverbs worked. An overhead projector had been left on, and whined irritatingly. He finished with twenty minutes to spare, and wondered if it would be rude to just walk out before the time was done.

There weren't any other candidates in the reception room for the psychiatrist either, as he sat, toes together, heels sticking out a little to the sides, waiting for his interview.

"Associations. I say a word, you say the first thing that comes to your mind."

"Really? Isn't that a little—"

"Home."

"Family?"

"Child."

"Happy."

"Sky."

"Blue."

"Sea."

"Blue."

"Travel."

"Adventure."

"Work."

"Interesting."

"Rest."

"Sleep."

"Dreams."

"Flying."

"Nightmares."

"Falling."

"Love."

"Music."

"People."

" . . . People. Sorry, that's just the first thing that . . . "

"Death."

"Life."

"Life."

"Living."

When he got the job, the first thing he did was phone his mum, who was very proud. It wasn't what she'd ever imagined him doing, of course, not really, but it came with a pension and a good starting salary, and if it made him happy . . .

The second thing he did was try and find his Unique Taxpayer Reference, as without it the office in Milton Keynes said they couldn't register him for PAYE at the appropriate tax level.

Chapter 4

And the world had turned.

. . . in a land of mountains . . .

. . . in the land of the vulture and the soaring eagle . . .

. . . the Harbinger of Death ordered another coffee from the café across the street from his Cusco hotel, and looked down at the black-eyed, black-eared dog that had followed him out of the mountains, and sighed and said, "It's not about what I want, honestly, but there's no way you're getting through customs."

The dog stared up at him, sitting stiff and patient on its haunches, no collar round its neck, ungroomed but well fed. It had followed him from Mama Sakinai's cabin without a sound, waited in the pouring rain outside the stone hut where he slept, until at last, guilt at its condition had made Charlie push open the wooden door to let it inside, where it had sat a few feet off from him without a whimper, to follow after him as he walked back down the ancient way to the city.

"Look," he had said, first in English, then in cautious Spanish, not knowing Mama Sakinai's favoured tongue. "Your mistress isn't dead." He'd stopped himself before adding "yet". Somehow the word felt unclean.

The dog had kept on following, and the next night, as they lay together by the ancient path, Charlie thought he heard a figure pass in the dark, bone feet on ancient stone, heading deeper into the mountains, following the paths carved by the dead, walked by the living. And he had shuddered, and rolled over tight, and the dog had pressed its warm body against his, and neither had slept until the moon was below the horizon.

The next day he'd come to Cusco, and wasted the best part of a day when he should have been sorting transportation trying to find a home for the persistent animal. He finally succeeded by chance, bequeathing it to a car repairman and his teenage daughter, she already dressed in mechanic's blues over her football shirt, face coated in grease, who at one look at the dog had exclaimed, "I got your ear!" and grabbed its ear, and it had pulled free, to which she had laughed, "I got your tail!" and grabbed its tail, and it had pulled that away, at which point she got its ear again, then tail, then ear, then tail, then ...

... until the pair of them were rolling on the ground, panting with delight.

"Who did the animal belong to?" asked her somewhat more circumspect father, as he and the Harbinger of Death watched them play.

"An old woman in the mountains."

"Ah – she is dead?"

"Yes. She is dead. Old age took her."

"You were her family?"

"No. I was sent as a courtesy. She said that she was the last of her people, and spoke a language that no one else knows. My employer likes to show respect."

"I see!" Understanding bloomed in the mechanic's face. "You are an anthropologist!"

The Harbinger of Death nodded and smiled, briefly relieved, and filed that excuse in the back of his mind in case he needed it later.

"Your T-shirt," he said to the mechanic, as the girl laughed on the floor with her new best friend. "Local team?"

"Yes, just a small side, but we're doing all right. Runners-up in Region VIII national division last year."

"Where would I find the shirt?"

Chapter 5

"Problem about supporting Arsenal is they play great first half of the season, then blow it and finish fourth . . . "

"Cricket fans aren't like your rugby lads . . . "

"*The train will be delayed. This is due to a shortage of crew.*"

"Do you have anything vegetarian?"

"Proud to announce my new transport policy, fairer prices for a more environmentally friendly and socially conscious London!"

"It's now been four months of emergency powers. *Four months.* Remind you of any other great political coups in world history much?"

"Darling, you're making a scene."

" . . . humidity in the winter when you're drying your clothes, and then you get the black mould and that's really the one to look out for, the black one, it's the one which can . . . "

"A man dies twice. Once when he dies, and once when he is forgotten."

"How's the new job? Oh, I see. So . . . not really like insurance at all?"

On the plane from Lima to LA, a woman sat next to Charlie in premium economy class (Death didn't think it proper that his Harbinger travel economy, but neither did he believe in business class) and said, "Oh wow, oh Jesus! And you've been doing this job for how long?"

"A bit over a week."

"And have you seen people *die*?"

"No."

"You're the Harbinger of Death and you haven't seen people *die*?"

"No. I go before."

"And isn't that terrible? Isn't that the worst thing ever, meeting all these people and knowing they're going to *die*?"

Charlie thought about it for a while, airline wine rolling around the plastic cup in his hand, airline pretzels stuck between his teeth. Then he said, "So far, no. So far it's been . . . I think it is . . . So far it's been okay."

Her jaw dropped, and then she turned away, and deliberately didn't look at him for the rest of the flight. That made Charlie a little sad, but it was, he supposed, a not entirely unfair reaction, all things considered.

As must be, as was foretold, Death came unto Mama Sakinai. He sat by her side, and they talked a little while, and Death said,

Of course I've had many Harbingers in the past. It is appropriate that the Harbinger is mortal, a bridge between this world and the next. In the old days I used eagles, but people stopped paying attention to them after a while – just birds in the sky – and I went to this party in Ithaca where the eagles soared and the prophets spoke and the suitors thought they knew better. But Odysseus had been through some tough times and it seemed polite to lend him a hand, though to be honest, it was at Penelope's bidding I came, though not her commandment that I obeyed. By the

12

shores of Te Waipounamu the whales surfaced and rolled their bloody eyes before the coming storm – but the priestly classes, you see, the priestly classes always do feel the need to interpret a perfectly well-established sign the newest way, and never like speaking truth to power, and so these things strayed off message. Do you mind if I . . . Thank you. Terrible habit, I know, but . . . You're very kind.

I switched to humans a few thousand years ago. One must move with the times. There were some good days. Egypt, the rain of blood, the frogs, the locusts – I was impressed, it was a spectacular piece of work. The four of us stood by the shores of the Red Sea and were just like, wow, seriously, that's taking the job to the next level, but Pharaoh ignored it as always and so night fell and where there was not fresh blood by the door, I came, just like the guy said. When the Mongols rode west, my messenger came before on a black horse, and said, "When I say big, I mean *really big*," but there's a listening issue with the human race, who have never understood when such things are fair warning and when they're merely courtesy before the storm.

One quit the job when they burned the books, saying that before it had only been people, and now it was all of humanity that died. Another refused to leave Nagasaki, saying it was apt that this was his end, and I suppose it was, and I was careful to ensure that he lodged at the centre of the blast, and stayed with him until he was ash on the wall. There was one who had a blue tattoo on her arm from the camps in the north, but people didn't want to listen, didn't understand what it was she had to say, and another who said, "The war will begin for greed, but it will become murder in the name of God," and they laughed in her face and I don't like that sort of behaviour, not when I am showing such . . . courtesy.

The desert can either preserve a body for millennia, or turn it quite to dust, depending on its condition. I am never sure which outcome I prefer, until the moment comes. Sometimes even I am surprised by who you meet again, when the sands move.

He took another drag on his cigarette, flicked ash into the tray and, stretching, said, I hope I don't bore you with all of this, but as you asked . . .

"No," croaked Mama Sakinai, her breath wheezing through her cracked and curling lips. "You aren't boring me."

Death nodded, his great red horns scraping the ceiling above his head, his bright scarlet face and spinning yellow eyes opening and closing into something that might have been a smile. She had not imagined that Death might smile upon her, but in all other respects he was the figure she had known would come, the god of the underworld, exactly as the stories had said he would be.

She said, "Your Harbinger – Charlie – gave me whiskey and talked about music."

Ah, he is fond of music, yes. I'm told he also collects obscure football T-shirts.

"T-shirts?"

He likes the odd clubs, the fourth division of the Calabrian league kind of teams. I believe he used to support Aston Villa, mused Death, rolling the cigarette between a great talon of boiling bloody skin and shifting paint, dots of white rolling like maggots over and into his flesh, sometimes bursting into new patterns, sometimes vanishing altogether into the churning colours of his flesh.

Supporting Aston Villa can induce resentment in almost anyone, even a man as phlegmatic as Charlie. The game changes; one form dies and another is born. But the game goes on.

Mama Sakinai nodded slowly at this, her liver-spotted skull resting deep back into the pillows when the motion was finished, never to rise again, and with her last few breaths whispered, "He wanted to hear the songs of my people, but they are not the same when sung in a stranger's mouth. It was good of you to send him ahead. I haven't had much conversation . . . for a very long time."

Death smiled again, and leant in close, holding the old woman's hand gently within his taloned grasp, twisting his head to the side a little so that his mighty horns might not tear the window above her head. Then, in her language – in the ancient tongue of her peoples, the ones who had hunted until the settlers came, the ones who had died in the human hunts, the ones who had forgotten their names – he murmured in her ear, There is a place waiting for you behind the setting moon, Mama Sakinai. There are the spirits of your ancestors, living anew in the rivers of the sky. They call to you, they call to you, in your own tongue; they are waiting to tell the stories again, the stories that will never more be told in this land of burning sun. They hear your footsteps on the golden way, they catch you as you fall. Your people all are dead, Mama Sakinai, and your language too, and your stories and your lives, but only the world of the living is changed, never the world of the dead.

So saying, he kissed her gently on the lips, to seal up the last of the language that would never again be heard on the surface of the Earth, and Mama Sakinai died, and her body was given to the vultures, to be buried in the sky.

Part 2

ICE

Chapter 6

"Scottish independence . . ."

"The needs of the Irish are not the same as . . ."

"Catalonia, ah, Catalonia!"

"The offside rule states that if a ball is passed to an attacker who is within the defensive line . . ."

"The unrest in Xinjiang province . . ."

"When I went to Tibet . . ."

"Don't talk to me about Kashmir!"

" . . . as in already closer to the goal than the defenders . . ."

"Look, without wanting to be unreasonable . . ."

"Georgian separatists today declared . . ."

"Do you do it with soy?"

"Went there last year, lovely people, just such wonderful hosts . . ."

"The people of Crimea . . ."

"I've got some superglue for the soles of your shoes, if you like?"

"Bury my heart in the Falkland Islands . . ."

"The Governor, number one, the Island, the Street, the South Atlantic. Do you really need a postcode?"

"Argentina of course use this to great effect by pushing their defensive formation towards the halfway line, thus creating an offside situation for . . ."

"Prevents Alzheimer's!"

"It really changed the way I think."

Chapter 7

Four months after Charlie started as Harbinger of Death, his girlfriend dumped him.

It had been a long time coming, even before he started in the new job, and though he was a bit down about it, he understood why and knew, regretfully, that in a little while he'd feel okay. He wondered if that made him a bad person.

"It's not just that you're always travelling," she explained, "and it's not about the job, it's not; I get it, like, I get it. But my next seat is in patent law and I really want to do well and there's only a couple of positions coming up at the firm and I need to get this, like, I have plans, I know where I want to live and where I want to be, and all my friends are getting on and you're getting on too, I know that, it's just . . . Look, it's been great, okay, but you're not . . . I don't think this . . ."

"It's okay," he replied. "I understand."

Two months later, she was going out with someone from the office whose area of expertise was employment law. For a brief moment Charlie hoped they'd be very unhappy together; then he met them at a party held by a mutual friend, one of the very, very few he seemed to share these days, a fluke, he hadn't thought he'd make it, and neither had the friend who'd invited him. And his ex and her new bloke were very happy together, and he was remarkably nice, for a lawyer.

"Has anyone sued Death?" he asked, a sudden thought striking from the dark, fuelled in no small part by cheap beer and chocolate brownies made with certain herbal additives.

"I think someone tried to, once."

"What happened?"

"The cancer got him before the case went to court."

"Oh. I see. Well. I suppose sometimes these things are beyond litigation."

*

Ten days later, in a hospital room in Salisbury ...

"He said that?"

"Yes. 'Beyond litigation'."

"Bless him."

"Is that ... "

"It's only slightly a joke."

"Sorry," he muttered to the nun in her pale blue gown, oxygen pumped into her nose, fluids into her arms, neither enough to save her. "I'm talking about me, and you're ... It's unforgivable."

"Not at all," tutted the old woman, last of her convent, no new blood joining, no old blood left. "I enjoy hearing about people."

He smiled limply. "That's what the woman in the mountains said, but I came here to honour you, not to bore you."

"You don't bore me. By my age, death is boring; life is wonderful. Tell me more. Tell me about living things."

"Well. I'm thinking of trying internet dating."

"Ah yes. I've heard of this."

"It's just, my line of work ... the travel ... "

"Always heard that air stewardesses had a lot of sex."

Charlie's jaw briefly dropped. The nun smiled faintly through the tape and tubes across her face. "What?" she wheezed. "Once the mother superior went, it's only been me, God, the holy word and daytime TV."

In a tower high above the scurrying streets ...

In a city that never sleeps ...

Plate-glass windows all around, a 360-degree view as the sun came up. An architect once remarked that buildings should have fewer windows, that natural light was a privilege to be enjoyed by the few, earned by the hard labour of the many. Men and women should work to have light in their lives, and if that principle was taken to heart, then Patrick Fuller was indeed a worker ...

He leaned back in his chair and exhaled, puffing out his cheeks, then, not quite believing it, leant forward to read the email again, just in case he'd missed the point the first time.

Repetition did not alter meaning.

He called his assistant into the office. Every time she came through the door, he wondered if he'd chosen her for her appearance. He had made every effort not to, and had deliberately interviewed as many male as female candidates for the job. Maybe her beauty – her now rather distracting beauty – had influenced an animal part of his brain that he had mistakenly thought he'd overcome.

Maybe she was just damn good at her job, regardless of the genetic lottery.

"Is this a joke?" he asked.

"No, sir," she replied. "We had it verified."

He stared at it one more time, then said, "I want to know everything about this. Everything. Who sent it, who received it, what it means. Also, I want a full security check of this office, a bomb sweep, and get me an appointment with my cardiologist for tonight." He thought about it a little longer, then added, "And get me a plane to Nuuk."

And the world turns . . .

"You do what?"

"I'm the Harbinger of Death."

"You're kidding."

"No."

"You're the actual Harbinger of Death?"

"Yes."

"As in . . . "

"Yes."

"That's . . . that's kinda weird, actually. I mean like, I know you said . . . your profile said 'personal assistant'."

"Well, in its way . . . "

"Yeah, but to Death."

"I didn't lie about anything on the site, just in the drop-down menu they didn't have an option for . . . "

"You don't look much like your picture."

"I don't?"

"No, I mean, not that it's lying or nothing, just that ... well, just in life, I mean, your face is different; it's more ... Look, I mean, I'm not, but ... So do you like your work?"

"It's a good job."

"That's not what I asked."

"I like travelling. I like meeting people, going to places I wouldn't ever go, seeing ... things change."

"Change?"

"Death isn't just about dying."

"That makes no sense. But you live in Dulwich – you weren't lying about that, right?"

"No, but I'm not home very much."

"So the online dating ... "

"Ah. Yes. I mean, a serious relationship ... "

" ... whatever that means ... "

"Meeting people ... "

"I think you should know I've just come out of an unhappy—"

"That's fine."

"And I'm weirded out by your job."

"I guess ... that's okay, if you're okay with it."

"I don't know. I don't know."

"I think you're kinda wonderful. Sorry, that sounded ... sorry, I was ... "

"Do you know how many dates I've been on this month?"

"I ... don't really know what you're meant to say. I thought I'd just tell the truth. Um ... I've screwed this up, haven't I?"

"No. I don't think so. Like you said, you told the truth. Let's have another drink. Let's ... talk some more."

And in a frozen land ...

... where the cracks spread beneath the snow ...

A figure walked along the ice, and thought for a while that he didn't walk alone.

Once, as a boy, he had walked along this ridge, only then it had looked different, less stone, more snow. In those days, he wore woollen gloves, and the wool froze to his hands and blood

23

seeped through the fibre and then the blood froze too. Once, the man on the ice had guided a group of explorers down the Snorgisford, the most dangerous glacier in the world, they said, but it had melted and something else had taken its place, and besides, these things were only dangerous if you were a bloody idiot who decided to climb one, not if you left them alone; if you just left them alone it'd be fine, it'd be beautiful, not frightening, it would be . . .

"You know," he said to the whiteness, "I didn't think it would be this easy."

The sky, the snow, the ice, the stone; there was no answer. There was no horizon either. There was no end to the sphere of white in which he was walking. There was no sun, there was no north, there was no magnet to point him home. He felt the weight of the bag upon his back and wondered why he'd packed so much in it. He threw it away, and felt young again, light on his feet; was tempted to run, resisted, wondered why. An old man, he thought to himself, you've become an old man wearing expensive boots. Live a little, surprise yourself, and he didn't, and he kept on walking into the white.

Chapter 8

The Harbinger of Death's phone lit up in the night, and he was immediately awake. It buzzed, vibrating without ringing across the bedside table. Next to him, the woman whose name had genuinely turned out to be Emmi – "It's like Emma, but better!" said her online profile – rolled over, pulling the pillow tighter against her head, a sure sign that she was awake, feigning sleep, chiding him with her body for having his phone on at three in the morning. He hesitated, caught between her skin, ebony against the pale sheets that covered her slumbering form, and the

24

light of the still buzzing phone. Her breathing was so slight, for a moment he wondered if she was dead, then reproached himself for something so silly. He pulled his fingers away from the curve of her back, and picked up the phone.

A calendar update, and an email.

He ignored one, opened the other, and read, quiet and alert, his face lit up moon-white in the darkness.

In the morning, Emmi said, "Dulwich is all very posh and that, but there's no decent buses to anywhere."

"There's a train to London Bridge," he replied, scraping the last of the eggs off the bottom of the pan, laying them on top of a slice of toast. "Or a bus to Canada Water."

She wrinkled her nose at this, a tiny flat protrusion on a round, warm face. Through the gentle alcoholic haze in which the two of them had staggered home last night, falling into bed in a fumbling cacophony of "you're sitting on my arm" and "hold on, I just need to put my contacts in the . . . " – even then he had felt she was stunningly, besottingly amazing. Daylight moderated that perception, making it at once less profound – she was of an average height, blunt as a mallet when she needed to be and unfashionably soft around the belly and bum – and also more thrilling than anything he could have imagined, for, sober at last, he saw a face looking back at him bursting with intelligence and life, sexier than any pouting fashion icon.

He blurted, and didn't understand why he said it, save perhaps for a desire to speak before her presence muted him for ever, "I've got to catch a plane this evening."

Her fork froze, a mouthful of egg dripping off the end. "You didn't say . . . "

"I got the message last night."

"I suppose . . . Is there a disaster happening?"

"I don't think so. I don't know. Probably not."

"Where are you going?"

"Nuuk."

"Where's Nuuk?"

25

"Greenland."

"Why?"

"I . . . It's my job."

She laid the fork back down on the plate, sat up a little straighter, folded her fingers in front of her face, rested the tips against the delicate end of her nose and said, "It's okay for this to be a one-night stand. You're nice. It's been fun. That's cool. I'm not about to go investing in things where there aren't things. It's fine. We good?"

The Harbinger of Death nodded, slow, eyes fixed on some other place.

"It is what it is. You've got to fly this evening, you said?"

"Yes."

"You got cold-weather clothes?"

"Yes. Some. And I'm sure I can get more."

"You quick at packing?"

"Yes."

"Good. We'll have breakfast, you can walk me to the station, and after that . . . whatever. Also, Charlie?"

"Yes?"

"The gas is still on."

Charlie looked down at the pan on the hob, the last crispy remnants of the morning's meal turning charred black above the hissing blue flame.

Chapter 9

There are four horsemen of the Apocalypse. The world disagrees on what they look like, for everyone sees the end in their own way, but as they are perceived by people, so they like to move with the times. And thus . . .

The Harbinger of Famine stood in the departures lounge of

Frankfurt international airport, pressed her phone to her ear and barked, "So how long will the lorries be delayed . . . ?"

The Harbinger of War slammed her fist into the horn of her little white Ford and screamed, as the one-way system into Washington DC caught her in its net and pulled her back across the Potomac, "*Fucking Beltway! If I want to fucking turn right then don't put the fucking sign five yards before the fucking* . . ."

The Harbinger of Pestilence walked down the aisles of the battery chicken farm, smelt the shit and the dust, saw the mangled limbs of the compressed birds in their grey cages and said, a smile fixed on his patient old face and a clipboard in his hand, "And how many exactly went down last weekend?"

And in a leafy suburb of London, the Harbinger of Death walked Emmi to the railway station. She kissed him on the cheek, and he waited by the gate until her train came, and then went home alone to his one-bedroom flat with magnolia walls, in a red-brick house in a part of the world where the schools were good, where people raised families and played football in the park, and got out his travel bag, only three days since it was put away, and pulled down his box of sub-Arctic gear, and began to pack, and felt the excitement of something new.

Chapter 10

The man said, why are you here?

The Harbinger of Death replied, I have a calendar, the calendar fills with appointments, my boss puts the appointments in my calendar and then I go to where it says.

The man said, how did you get here?

I flew to Reykjavik. Once there was a pilot who flew over the dormant volcanoes – I gave him a new pair of sunglasses. He wore them proudly, and his wife cried. You get reactions like that sometimes. Sometimes, you see, these things are a warning, and sometimes they are a compliment.

A warning?

That you may yet amend your ways. That you may not fly over that volcano, or you may stay at home when you should have flown or . . . Well, it depends. And Death may pass you by. I saw him again, the pilot, when I changed planes in Iceland. He smiled at me, and didn't say anything new. That's the first time that's ever happened to me, meeting someone I've met before. It's not usually . . . It was nice. It was really good. I hadn't fully understood the possibilities.

So you are here so that Death doesn't come?

Perhaps I am.

But you doubt it.

I really couldn't say.

And you flew from Reykjavik?

On a very small plane.

Only small planes fly out here.

I was beginning to get that feeling. I'm looking for this man.

Ah – Professor Absalonoftsen.

You know him, then?

This is Nuuk, biggest city in all Greenland. Everyone knows everyone around here.

Do you know where I might find Professor Absalo . . . Where I might find him?

Ule.

Ule? Where's that?

It's his name. His name is Ule.

Ah. Thank you, that's certainly easier. Do you know where Professor Ule has gone?

North.

Do you know where?

No. Just north. He took the boat up the coast.

Which boat?

A fishing boat.

Not a ferry?

No – that runs every other Thursday, but the fishermen will take passengers north for not very much. Or you can take the helicopter, but it mostly carries cargo.

Do you know which boat?

Ask down at the port, they'll tell you.

Thank you.

Is he going to die? Professor Ule? Is that why you're looking for him?

I really don't know. I have to give him something.

What?

Tea.

You're the Harbinger of Death, and you're tracking a man across the Greenland Sea to give him ... tea?

Yes.

What kind of tea?

Indian chai mixed with dates and pepper.

Sounds disgusting.

Apparently he likes it.

And this is what you do?

Yes.

Not for me to tell another man ...

You've been very helpful, thank you.

Any time! Any time. It's always nice to have visitors.

Chapter 11

In the treeless land

in the land where no trees grow

once the mayor of Nuuk tried to plant some trees, lining the little streets of his city with child-high greenery. But the summer was too cold and grey for the leaves to open, and in winter the sap inside the branches turned to ice, and they

29

dropped off in the spring thaw, splat, at the barest touch of the breeze off the sea.

There's a patch of ice behind the house of old Mrs Arnadottir that she swears has never melted. It's ridiculous, of course – in summer, temperatures have been known to get to fourteen degrees above freezing on warm days, and the youngsters go out in T-shirts and tiny skirts to soak up its gentle rays – but she claims that the shadows are thick behind her house, and the stones hold the cold well, and that once, in the years after Krakatoa blew, there was a summer when the snow never melted, and in that time this tiny blob of ice grew thicker and thicker, and now will never pass away, and what's more, the patch of ice resembles the face of Jesus.

People stop arguing with Mrs Arnadottir at that point, reasoning that it's rude to question another person's deeply held spiritual beliefs.

When you have seen the whole world, the old words said, there is always Greenland left.

The hotel on the edge of the sea had a flat-screen TV on one wall, excellent Wi-Fi, a hot tub on the roof, exposed to the elements, and a Gideon Bible in the bedside table. Charlie tried using the hot tub. Beneath a slate-grey sky he wobbled across frozen, sleet-stained timbers and lowered himself, gasping at the shock, into the shimmering blue water. Once in, getting out seemed impossible.

Charlie believed in trying everything at least once. In the ten months since he'd started this job he'd eaten sheep's brains (not his thing), been ostrich riding (many bruises), scuba diving (one of the best experiences of his life) and climbed down the inside of a volcano. He'd been in the volcano to give an icon of a strange, deformed deity, carved from bone, to one of the men who mined sulphur there. He had a feeling the bone was human, but had been okay with that. It was just calcium, and not like anyone needed it any more; the idea of death as a sanctified thing seemed increasingly ridiculous. If the man in the volcano had said anything when Charlie came, he couldn't hear it over the growling of the earth, and in truth, his eyes streaming and skin burning from the yellow-black fumes, he hadn't wanted to stick around long to find out.

He still felt a bit guilty about that.

His job was all about sticking around and finding out. It was something he was learning to pride himself on. He felt, without being able to express why, that it was very, very important to his work.

Charlie looked up at a sky the colour of ash, and felt his constitution waver.

On the grey ocean, tall-sailed boats bobbed behind the concrete wharves where the fat orange commercial vessels offloaded their cargo of fresh vegetables, mobile phones and timber. A line of apartment blocks looked down to a beach of stone, and beneath the setting sun the brightly painted houses shimmered against the grey like threads of bright wool woven through a dirty jumper. The Harbinger of Death tried to find a grocery shop, but the only one open had sold out of all its fresh fruit except for a single, questionable-looking bag of apples. He ate alone in the hotel restaurant, ox burger with a side of chips. He ordered coffee, and the waiter brought him a cup that he proceeded to set on fire in an alcoholic explosion of blue-yellow light and curling acrid smoke. It didn't taste bad, all things considered.

In the evening, he watched football, two locals teams playing on a floodlit pitch. It wasn't the greatest game he'd ever seen, slow and quiet, and he bought the T-shirt from the losing side.

Afterwards, in his room, Charlie checked his online calendar.

Every day, appointments arrived and new journeys were arranged. Some appointments were years in the coming – the furthest ahead he had seen was for twenty-two years' time, when the Harbinger of Death (and there was no guarantee by this time that it would be him) would deliver a nickel button to a laboratory in southern France.

Other appointments were a few months in the future, but he didn't book the tickets, not yet. He never knew where he might be flying from, or how the situation might have changed. Initially he'd tried to be ahead of the curve, an economic, thrifty traveller with schemes laid well in advance. But his hotel had been bombed in Damascus three months before he was meant to stay in it, and the insurance company had dodged covering the cost; and the line down from Addis Ababa didn't run on time and he'd nearly missed the appointment, rushing shamefaced and terrified into the room, not sure what he could possibly say to make up for this rudeness, or how he would explain it to his employer if he didn't make it at all.

Charlie hadn't met Death yet. At least, not in his official capacity.

Milton Keynes never told him off, but were always quietly disappointed by every flight cancelled and hotel moved without the possibility of refund, and so quickly Charlie changed his travel habits. Reluctantly at first, and then with a growing sense of self-confidence, he had become an edge-of-the-seat traveller, a barterer for last-minute trains, a man who raced across town to find the last room in the last hotel before the chaos came, and only twice – once in Montreal during racing season, once in Bruges for reasons he had never understood – had he been caught short, and been forced to spend the night on a bench, barely sleeping, feeling maddeningly alive.

The Greenland appointment had come in with hardly any warning at all, which was unusual. More unusual – a first, in fact – was that his target, Professor Absalonoftsen, was not at the address he had been given. He had gone wandering, said his neighbour with a shrug. Sometimes he did that.

The Harbinger of Death had checked at the University of Greenland, which had only eleven full-time teaching staff and was bound to notice the sudden absence of 9.1 per cent of its educational faculty, but no, it was the summer holiday, the students were out and sometimes the Professor's work took him onto the ice.

"Don't worry about it!" said the cheerful secretary down the phone. "Professor Ule has been dodging polar bears since before you left nappies!"

These words, kindly meant, did not reassure.

The day before he hired passage on a cargo boat carrying

preserved meats and replacement parts to the villages on Baffin Bay, Charlie phoned Emmi, and couldn't get through.

Had a lovely time with you, he texted, wondering what time it was back in London, whether she'd be awake to receive this. *Hope to see you when I get back. Might not have reception for a while. Will text again when I do, if that's okay.*

He worried over how he should sign it – was a kiss inappropriate? – and having no answer, left it as it was, hit send, and immediately wondered if he sounded like a stalker.

He boarded the little boat as the sun rose across the eastern sky, barely more than a bathtub with a keel, and had lost signal on his mobile phone within a few miles of the shore and before receiving Emmi's reply, if she even got his message.

Chapter 12

In a treeless land . . .

. . . in a land where no trees grow . . .

Death sat cross-legged upon the ice and watched the polar bear hunting. She was old, wise to the ways of the land where the sun never set, never rose, balancing precariously upon a detached carpet of ice that was drifting ever further out to sea. She didn't mind hunting in such conditions, of course – not yet, she was a good swimmer – but her prey minded, and were being seen less and less upon these shores.

Death enjoyed watching the polar bear, if Death enjoyed anything much of anything in particular. She was a creature beautifully acclimatised to this place, where surely evolution should have given up long ago. Death also enjoyed watching sea lions trying to pull themselves along over the ice, before falling, relieved, into the frozen waters; he enjoyed swimming with the translucent, sometimes entirely transparent critters, snails and bugs that writhed along the bottom of the sea. He liked watching killer whales as they stalked a seal, tasted the hot blood of an animal caught napping, and clapped with delight whenever a diving bird nailed its prey, bang, a perfect drop from the sky, a perfect catch, another winter survived, another winter ended.

Now he watched the bear as it swam back to shore, and the bear after a while saw him, and recognised him for what he was, as all things do, and walked over slowly, bowing her head to press her great, puffing nose against his hair, and Death held her close, and felt her breathe, and waited.

Look! said the captain of the boat, and Charlie looked. Did you see its tail?

He looked and looked and saw nothing, and

the tail burst from the sea, wider than a double bed, smacking the surface of the turning ocean, slamming its own weight of water into the sky, which rained back down long after the creature had sunk into the depths, its skin peppered with barnacles, its eyes huge and ancient and tired of running, its flanks scored with the teeth of a hundred predators, its belly circled by shoals of tiny fish that fed off the krill that fed off the flaking skin of the beast.

Did you see? asked the captain. Did you see?

Yes, Charlie replied. I saw.

Beneath the ship, the whale turned, and for a moment Charlie thought that it was looking back at him, and that in its eye was written a prophecy he could not know.

Chapter 13

On the boat, sailing up the coast of Greenland, the Harbinger of Death concluded that he didn't understand cold.

"Look at you!" chuckled the captain, as the ship lurched and lunged and bounced and fell across the white-foamed water. "You are a pumpkin!"

Wrapped in shirt wrapped in jumper wrapped in coat; wrapped in trouser wrapped in trouser wrapped in sock wrapped in boot; wrapped in hat wrapped in scarf, Charlie said, clinging to the console of the little pilot's cabin lest his feet go out beneath him again, "What I don't understand is how you're only in boots and waterproofs."

"This is summer!" replied the sailor cheerfully, as another wave slammed sideways into the boat, swamping the deck with shimmying foam that ran away as soon as it had come. "You're wearing too much; look at you, you're almost spherical!"

"It's very cold."

"This? This isn't cold. Cold only happens when the salt water turns to ice. From November to May, I wouldn't even bother coming this way – wouldn't be able to get into port. Twenty miles of sea ice between you and the harbour – but this! This is summer, this is easy, balmy, look! You need to eat more meat, more meat, that's the way to go. Seriously – you're wearing too much. If you go on the ice, you need to be just a little bit cold, otherwise your sweat will freeze to your body and you'll die in minutes."

"That's reassuring."

"I'm just telling you what you need to know! Plenty of fools die a silly way! Hey, don't take it badly. I'm impressed you're not being sick more!"

"Thank you; I spend a lot of time travelling."

"Have you ever tasted ginger?"

"Yes, I have."

"I hear it's good for seasickness."

"You've never had ginger?"

"Me? No."

"What do you do for vegetables?"

The captain laughed. "We eat fish!" Even the smashing of the sea didn't drown out his laughter, as they sailed beneath the frozen sun.

*

35

And one night
    beneath a midnight sun
    Charlie stood on the deck of the fishing boat, while the other
men slept, save for the night pilot, and watched the sky fill with
purple and red, the sea reflecting gold, and couldn't quite see the
sun itself, but instead its scattered radiance in the heavens, a wet
explosion where the curve of the earth had burst against its rays.
Then he watched for a few minutes more, and the sun, which
had only set a few minutes ago, began to rise once again, and he
realised that he had signal on his mobile phone, he had no idea
why, and Emmi had replied.

    It was nice, she said. *Call me when you get back.*

    Charlie smiled, alone with the endless morning, and knew that
the world was beautiful beyond naming.

Chapter 14

Two days after boarding a fishing boat in Nuuk, Charlie got off
the same boat in the village of Oounavik, and nearly fell over.
His knees had no bones as he stood on the wooden quay; his
world rocked gently from side to side. He leant against a plastic
box filled with mussels, and waited for stability to come again.

    Oounavik – population 273 humans, 62 huskies and four
cats. It would have been five cats, but one got eaten by predator
unknown. The air was colder here, a few degrees above freezing. The snow had melted, but the steep climb of the black rock
above the village as it rose before dropping into the ice sheets
was still flecked with never-ending white where the sunlight
couldn't crawl.

    Charlie picked his way through a dockside of blue plastic sheets
covered in wide-eyed, open-mouthed dead fish, and asked the
first person he met who seemed to be a native – a woman with

sleeves rolled up, scraping scales from the side of the latest catch into a blood-flecked bucket – if she knew Professor Ule. He spoke Danish, not well, and with a heavy German accent.

She stared at him a moment, as if surprised to hear this language from a stranger, then replied, her voice perhaps more used to Kalaallisut, "Yes, of course. He came this way three days ago, stayed with Sven, then went north-east."

"North – more north?"

"Yes."

"How did he travel?"

"On foot."

"Into the glacier field? You didn't . . . " Charlie stopped himself, but the old woman smiled, feeling his intention.

"Stop him?" she chuckled, turning her attention back to the fish, the blade, its guts now coming out in a single neat slice and being splatted onto the bucket floor. "Of course not. He knows what he's doing."

"I need to find him."

"Do you? Has something happened? His family, his . . . ?" Her voice trailed off, for what else was there, except family?

"I need to give him something. My name's Charlie, I'm . . . "

She had already lost interest. "Talk to Ane and Sven. They handle people like you."

Though there were very few houses in Oounavik, there were no street signs either.

A pair of teenage boys on brightly painted skateboards pointed him the right way, and the second time he got lost, turned around by the higgledy manner in which the houses clung to the stone and the confusing way two had been painted red side by side, instead of the usual white-blue-yellow-red confetti of the buildings, a woman with an axe in one hand, a smartphone in the other, stopped what she was doing long enough to show him the way to the door.

"Not often we get visitors," she said in heavily accented Danish. "We should have a party."

The Harbinger of Death smiled wanly, and chose not to mention the purpose of his trip.

Ane and Sven lived on the edge of the village. Their dog team rose up at Charlie's approach, curious more than defensive, the younger, more naïve huskies bouncing behind the older, stalwart veterans to see the stranger come to their door. The dogs were more than an acknowledgement of an old way; they were a legal necessity.

"We hunt with dogs on the land, and in canoes at sea," explained Sven, six foot three, hair a black so bright it nearly shone, skin burnt wind-bitten red. "These are the only ways." He waited patiently in the cool corridor of his house as Charlie struggled out of his boots, shook out his coat, pulled off his under-coat, his winter trousers, stripping down at last to just the final few layers of cotton and fleece, then, seeing that his guest was finally happy, nodded once and barked, "In here."

Charlie followed him into a living room where a fire burned against one wall, fed by propane tanks outside the window. On the shelves were photos – photos of Sven holding a harpoon, Sven with his dogs, Sven and Ane on the steps of the tiny church that sat on the top of the hill above Oounavik, white flowers woven in her hair, a shawl draped over her dress against the cold. Ane being mobbed by the students of her school, all twenty of them, the youngest five, the oldest sixteen, dressed in sealskin coats. Sven and Ane repairing the sled, Sven and Ane on honeymoon in Rome, utterly out of place and bewildered by the burning light in their faces, squinting against it.

Beneath the rows of images, a flat-screen TV, set to a muted drama about plague and time travel. Opposite, a couch, covered over with quilt and wool. "You can sleep there," he explained. "We will give you breakfast."

"Thank you, but I—"

"You want to go onto the ice, yes?"

"Yes."

"It's a bad time for it. The summer has been too hot; the

38

glaciers are melting. The sea hunting is bad – you can get cast adrift while you sleep. There is flooding in the south, there's nothing here now."

Sven's English was clear, crisp, to the point, and Charlie suspected that his Danish or Kalaallisut would be just as blunt. "What did you want to see? The Northern Lights? The sun isn't down long enough at this time of year, you won't get a good sight; come back in winter. Whales? The seas are changing, the currents are all wrong. Polar bears? They're dying. You are sad to hear this? The government said don't worry, this is a time of opportunity, this is a time when the green things grow, but the narwhal are few and the birds change the routes they fly and all things ... " He stopped, shaking his head, turned away lest Charlie see even a flicker of emotion on his long, tight face.

Charlie said, into the silence, "I'm looking for Professor Ule. I was told he sometimes comes here, to Oounavik."

Sven turned back, fast, curious, and for a moment Charlie wondered if he'd said something wrong, given insult. Then Sven drew himself up a little straighter, proud, even. "Yes, he comes here. He came here four days ago."

"You saw him?"

"He visited."

"Did he stay here?"

"No. We have a difficult relationship."

"I don't understand."

"You don't know?"

"I neither know nor understand." Again, surprise, mingled with something else – was Charlie mocking him, was this stranger, come to his fire, playing the fool? Charlie shifted uneasily on the couch, then added, "I'm just doing my job. I've ... I have to give him this." He gestured at the tin of tea, gift-wrapped in bright red tissue paper, that he'd carried all this way.

Sven, no more enlightened, looked from the tin to Charlie, back to the tin, back to the man. "Why?"

"It's my job. I'm the Harbinger of Death."

A while Sven stood, and the fire burned, and the sun shimmied

39

around the horizon, barely setting, barely dipping its fingers beneath the edge of the boiled-black mountains that towered above the village. Then, without a word or a change to the expression on his face, he walked out of the room, leaving Charlie sitting on the couch, holding the tin of tea, staring into the fire.

Chapter 15

"It was a good hunt, a good kill, we use every part of the animal ..."

"No rabbits were harmed in the testing of this product."

"I think it's disgusting, what they do, just disgusting ..."

"Beagling is a time-honoured tradition ..."

"Werewolves!"

"They take the blood and they *smear it on their faces* ..."

"Let's be honest here, shall we, let's speak honestly? The real problem is that poor people are jealous of our way of life ..."

"I don't stand for no gun control laws 'cos I need my gun for hunting the deer."

"That counter just keeps on counting ..."

Menu, Polaris Restaurant, Nuuk, September 2015

Smoked mackerel with horseradish, mustard seed and milk.
Heart of musk ox, served with spelt, buckthorn and house mayonnaise.
Saddle of reindeer, reed cabbage, marrow and blackberry.
Suaasat — soup with seal, onion, potato and bay leaf.
Narwhal tartare served with crisps and crowberry compote.

All our dishes are made from the freshest, finest ingredients.
Bring your own fish!

Chapter 16

Ane taught at the school. Ane was the school. When she wasn't teaching, she had a sideline making jewellery and ornaments from bones, skin and stone. Some of her work had been exhibited in Nuuk – one of her pieces had been bought by an American for a celebrity client who was apparently involved in a campaign for the protection of indigenous peoples, but she never saw it again or heard what happened next, and besides, she was a half-blood and had never understood how people in LA were going to protect her, or against what, but hey, at least she got paid.

Now she stood in the kitchen of her little house at the place where salt water met white ice, and whispered low and long with her husband of fifteen years, while in the room next door where sometimes guests stayed on her mother's old couch, the Harbinger of Death tried and failed to get a signal for his mobile phone, and watched the fire, and waited.

He's not . . .

. . . but coming here . . .

. . . doesn't mean . . .

. . . the summer ice . . .

. . . Ule went without the dogs . . .

. . . always without the dogs . . .

Will we know Death, when he comes?

I don't know. I don't know.

At last, as the shadows stretched and the sky turned purple-grey for the long, light-soaked night, Ane and Sven went into the room where Charlie sat, and she said, "Ule went towards Vituvasskat four days ago. He went without dogs, without much water or food. Is he going to die?"

"I don't know," Charlie replied, then, quickly, "I'm the one who's sent before. I'm not . . . My presence is not the end. Sometimes I am sent as courtesy, sometimes as warning. I never know which."

"As warning?"

"A warning that may cause Death to pass you by."

"You know of that?" she asked sharply, a tiny woman, an oval in a woven coat, dwarfed vertically by her towering husband, pushing him almost into invisibility on the horizontal plane. "You know of warnings?"

"I'm just the messenger," he replied with a wan smile. "That's really all I do."

Husband looked at wife, wife at husband. Theirs was a quiet home. Theirs was a quiet town. Gossip was poisonous in such a small community, and so they never gossiped. The snow rarely melted from the hill to the east, and so they did not discuss the changing weather, or seas, or skies. During the dark months of November to April, when no boat dared make the crossing, and the helicopter only came for those who died, the grocer's stood empty, except for preserved meats and fermented birds, feathers and bone still stuck in the meat. On the ice, or on the sea, the wind carried the words of the hunters away, and the town's internet connection moved slower than the glaciers that dwarfed it – certainly too erratic and faint for their world to fill with digital news and stories. Ane spoke Kalaallisut to her friends, Danish to the fishermen and English to her elder students, who longed to go elsewhere and were terrified to leave, and having so many tongues in her head, didn't feel the need to flap about much when at rest. And so their marriage was conducted quietly, and in silence they communicated, reading every part of hand and eye to express all the thoughts that words were unused to.

And in this way, they spoke long and hard, the pair of them, standing in the doorway of the living room, until at last Sven turned to Charlie and said, "Tomorrow, we will go together and look for the old man."

That was the end of that.

Chapter 17

Pestilence sits in the economy-class cabin of the long-haul flight and says, "It's the sex. See him, over there? The film's just got to the sexy bit and he's playing cool, playing so cool, thrusting, pumping buttocks, breasts, it's all so much less without the sound of course, not arousing at all, not sexy, just – but look, she's checking that no one can see, angling the screen down, a little privacy, it's not private though, nothing private about this, getting turned on on a night flight down in cattle class, in scum class, in the place where the people are. This is how I love to fly, love flying where the people are ... "

Famine sits further up front, in premium economy. Not quite business class – not that; the NGOs and low-level government civil servants couldn't afford business class, but neither would they admit that budget travel was the only way to go, that times were so bad, the money so tight and so ...

"I'll have the chicken curry," she breathes, voice low enough that the stewardess has to bend down against the roar of the engines. "If you have any left, that is."

War flies first class. Champagne, champagne, arms dealers and champagne, squeezing the buttocks of the stewardesses, ogling the stewards with their slicked-back hair, and some

ogle back.

Once, War gave a golden card to a man at Heathrow airport who'd comforted a crying woman. She'd come to the airport to meet her son, but her son had never got off the plane. He'd been arrested on the Turkish side of the border for acts of terrorism, and she wept and wailed and said he was a good boy and the man in the airline uniform with shiny cufflinks at his wrists and a silky cravat at his throat held her and comforted her and said he was sure it was a big fuss over nothing, these things always worked out all right.

War watched this encounter, and afterwards gave the man a

golden card, sign of prestige within the airline, and whispered in his ear, "The boy beheaded three women and a teenage boy last week, but I like the way you roll, my son, I like the cut of your jib."

Death flies because it is the modern way of things, but doesn't particularly enjoy it, except for occasionally, when he rides up front with the pilot.

Chapter 18

Was this first light?

In this place, with the sea below and the sky above, Charlie felt the turning of the earth for the very first time, and believed that the sun stayed still while the earth revolved, and thought now he understood the mindset of the ancients who had looked on the dawn and seen God in it.

In a frozen land of endless sun . . .

He wanted to stay awake for ever, and drink in this sky. At first, he'd thought he'd take pictures of everywhere he went, but somehow had never dared, didn't think a photo could capture the feeling inside his chest as he watched the sun circle the horizon.

Besides, what would he say of his photos if they were ever shared online?

Here is the mountain above the endless coral seas, the sun rising over a forest filled with flowers, where I went to tell a woman that she would die. #work #anotherdayattheoffice

He didn't take pictures. Instead he stared until his face hurt, and tried to burn everything he saw into his heart.

This hour was, Sven assured him, the nearest equivalent to first light that his bewildered, blackout-blind-befuddled body would understand, not that the light really mattered at this time of year, so the two of them loaded heavy bags upon their backs, and shoved packets of dried ox meat into their coats, and set out, away from the sea.

No dogs, Sven explained. There isn't enough snow on the ground for the sleds, the world below is too exposed and uneven. We'll have to walk. Can you walk, Harbinger of Death?

I guess I can, he replied. I haven't done anything like this before.

Sven pursed his lips, but said nothing, and perhaps wondered what qualifications for his career Charlie had, and whether they were useful in the snow.

Walking without the passage of the sun to keep him company, Charlie drifted in a halfway state between sleeping, waking, moving, falling, and somehow without thinking, his legs moved, his eyes looked, he climbed, he thought, he did not think, and time passed without motion. Sometimes he remembered he had feet, and they hurt, and then he forgot, and there was only walking again.

The first part of the journey was easy, ground hard, stone underneath, what little snow there was undisturbed. Then they scrambled uphill, over black rocks bleached with millennia of bird shit from the migrating creatures that sometimes nested in the crags, and Charlie's chest had ached in the bitter air and his lungs had dragged and he'd had to ask that they stop at the top of the hill, and Sven had looked at him with something that might have been pity.

Charlie swore to himself that he wouldn't ask to rest again, and looked down and saw, on the other side of the ridge they'd been climbing, the ice. Not snow, not yet – it wasn't moist enough for much snow to have fallen in recent weeks – but the packed ice that filled the fjord, not a smooth rolling thing but rather a razored desert of dunes and towers, of juts and spikes pushed up and compressed and shattered and re-formed by the constant shifting of the glacier in the valley. He thought perhaps he stood on a valley wall, but couldn't tell – the shape of the land had been ground away, so that what lay hidden and underneath was lost to him. He listened, and heard the noise of thunder, and thought it might be a storm, and saw no clouds, and realised it was the glacier, moving, moving, destroying itself and being reborn.

He looked at Sven, mute, unsure, hoping for a walk that didn't take them into that pincushion of white and blue. Sven looked up at the sun, as if seeking a similar inspiration, then back at Charlie. "Well?" he said. "Do you know where to go?"

"I just have to find Professor Ule – I wasn't told how."

The tea tin, a ridiculous encumbrance strapped to his bag. Two pairs of gloves, the taste of dried meat in his mouth.

Sven nodded again, without surprise, then stared down at the fjord, almost glowering into its depths. "I think I know where to look."

White in the heavens, white on the earth. Perhaps they flew a little while; perhaps they were white seagulls, or no, white worms, wriggling through the snow. There was a kind of worm, Charlie vaguely recalled as his mind drifted through pale nothingness, that lived in the snow and dissolved in the sun, its body melting away with summer.

They skirted the edge of the fjord, walking a few feet away from that dividing line between ice and rock, staying on the rock side, the sounds now of grinding, cracking, tearing, shaking, thumping growing great enough to drown out any pretence at speaking, even if they'd had anything to say. Once, something cracked in the ice flow, a mountain falling, and Charlie jumped, thinking a bomb, a volcano – but as he looked out, he couldn't see the thing that had collapsed, and Sven seemed utterly unperturbed.

He had a watch on, somewhere beneath the layers of sleeve and glove that covered his skin, but the idea of looking at it seemed quaintly obscene. Once, he thought he was sweating, and was instantly afraid, imagining that the sweat would freeze on the back of his neck and that would be it, death in an instant, but he lived, and if it was sweat, it did not freeze. Another time, they stopped, to drink and eat dry meat and a couple of loose, tasteless

46

bars wrapped in foil, and he realised that he was cold, shivering, shuddering, and looked at Sven to see if this was all right, and it seemed to be, so he let his teeth chatter and they kept on walking until his teeth chattered no more.

When the sun was low – but not setting, not that – Sven declared, "We make camp here."

A mist was rising, turning into fog; it came fast, just a greyness above the ground that quickly spread upwards, blocking out the endless sun.

Charlie took his bag off, and nearly fell over.

Beneath the ice, vanishing fast into the grey, industries churned, slaves of crystal died and were turned to water, factories were built and cathedrals destroyed, shaking through the earth.

"Here," Sven said firmly. "Don't take your boots off. If you need to piss, leave your bag here, tie a rope to the bag. Don't wander; don't go onto the ice. A man died last year ten yards from his front door, because he couldn't find it in the fog."

Charlie did not take his boots off, and for the rest of the yellow-white night continually jerked awake, certain that he had not been asleep to wake at all.

Chapter 19

On the second day of walking, Charlie looked at his watch, and was astonished to see that it was only six a.m. The fog had burned away as he not-slept, and if he concentrated, he seemed to remember waking from his not-sleep to notice that it had gone, but perhaps that was a lie, perhaps he was only imagining that he'd woken to that experience, now that he was moving again, in the light of day.

They walked, an unchanging world, ice to the left, breaking, stone to the right. Charlie looked at his watch again, and was astounded to discover that it was half past nine – and then, hours later, it was only quarter to ten. After that, checking the time became an obsession. He was startled to discover that only six minutes had gone by since he last checked, since surely he had walked for an hour. Then he was surprised to find that three hours had passed, and he had slumbered while walking and not experienced it. He felt sure that there must be some great meaning in this, some strange way of expressing the concept of time, of answering the child's irritating question, "Mummy, what is time?" – perhaps by plonking said child out here, with just a woolly hat and a pair of gloves held together with long elastic, and saying, "Here is time, child, here it is, here where nothing changes and the ice down there was formed when Krakatoa blew and you can walk for ever and nothing passes except the white and the noise."

After a while Sven said, "Give me your fucking watch."

It was the first thing he'd said all day. Charlie opened his mouth to speak, to object, and looked into Sven's eyes and wordlessly gave him the watch, and nearly cried with relief to have it taken from him.

On the edge of the ice, as the world cracked and crumbled, Charlie looked up from studying nothing much with great care, from walking, walking, walking, and saw five people on the ridge above, walking the other way. They wore thick, heavy-duty snow boots, and belts with ice picks, crampons and flasks around their waists. They carried large khaki rucksacks, strapped tight across their shoulders and bellies. They wore gloves, and two of the five wore hats. Of the remaining three, two were blonde, one had deep, dark hair. They were wearing nothing else. They waved as they walked by. Charlie waved back, and looked at Sven to see if he too had seen this sight, or if he was indeed hallucinating. Sven raised one hand in greeting to the hikers on the ridge, but politely didn't stare.

*

Then they found a bag, discarded on the edge of the ice. It was a rucksack, much like the ones that Charlie and Sven carried. The wiser man squatted down, went through its contents, tutted and said, "This is Ule's."

"Why is it here?" Charlie asked.

"He must have dropped it. It has his food, drink, compass . . . "

Charlie said nothing. His feet felt flattened in his boots. When he took them off, he was confident that they would have no bones left in them, just beaten-out tissue and hard patches of skin. He looked forward to the grinding ice, and back over his shoulder, and as he looked back, he thought he beheld

a pale rider upon a white . . .

but he blinked and shook his head and clearly he hadn't, and that was that.

"Come on," barked Sven, and started walking again, faster, following the frozen fjord. Charlie hesitated, looking down at the abandoned rucksack. For some reason it felt like littering, or a kind of defeat to leave it, but as he went to pick it up—

"Leave it!" snapped Sven, so Charlie left it, and marched on after.

The Greenland man's pace, previously a confident walk through an empty land, now picked up, leaving Charlie's face flushing hot, lungs tight against the cold air as they scrambled along the side of the rolling glacier, scuttling through pale dirt and up rocks where sometimes thin white flowers bloomed, and the rest of the year everything died. Once Charlie thought he saw a hunting bird soar overhead, and wondered if it liked its meat fresh or if decayed human would do; once he imagined he saw a polar bear on the flow, and nearly cried out to Sven look, look – but it was just a curved piece of ice that collapsed even as he watched back down to dust.

He hit a physical wall, and knew that was what it was, had to move each foot deliberately, consciously, willing them to lift and fall. When at last walking became easier, his whole body flooded with light, and he felt as if he might run, laugh and skip round the sluggish Sven like a barking dog. For a moment he knew he was immortal, invincible, and at that same instant it occurred to him that he was in danger, and that too was wonderful. He might fall, he might freeze, starve, slip, become lost in the wild, and he was delighted at the thought, thrilled by it, for he was the Harbinger of Death, the one who went before, and he did not think, could not imagine, that Death would come for him yet, and surely, therefore, his was a charmed life.

Emboldened, he nearly laughed, stood up straighter, shifted his weight and almost immediately lost his footing, slipping and landing hard on his back, breath knocked out of him, neck creaking where it slapped back against his rucksack, and Sven turned and glared, so sheepishly Charlie crawled back to his feet, and walked humbly through the snow.

The sun skimmed the edge of the horizon – didn't that mean something here? – and began to rise again.

Strength, heat and thought ebbed away, and Charlie forgot that he was immortal, and remembered only that he was walking again. The quality of the ice was changing, fewer pyramids and spires, but rather tight little waves crystalled over with old snow, the fjord expanding, growing wider and deeper, until suddenly Sven stopped again, and knelt on the edge of the snow and said, "There!"

Charlie looked, legs shaking, arms shaking, shoulders beginning to wear thin where his backpack was digging through, and saw a footstep, only one, barely visible where the snow was just thick enough to retain its memory. "He's gone onto the ice," whispered Sven, horror blooming behind his thick mirrored glasses. "Damn him."

Charlie followed Sven's gaze across the frozen fjord. Here, in this place, it seemed that a gentle sea had frozen on the glacier's surface mid-ripple, and the ice was a deeper blue, not the hard grey-white of the shattered flows they'd seen before. But still beneath, the noise, the grinding, crunching roar – and all around the sharpened cracks and torn-down gulleys of ice, creating valleys and cliffs, tunnels and falls where the structure was breaking apart. Thin rivulets of water flowed over the smoother shapes on the surface, following a gradient he couldn't perceive, trickling in busy quiet against the industrial roar. The glacier was melting. The cold sun was hot on his skin, hot on the ground, and the world was melting.

Then Sven stepped onto the ice, and began to walk towards a horizon that Charlie couldn't begin to perceive, white on blue on white.

Charlie staggered, nearly fell, caught his balance badly, stood with his hands on his hips, drawing heavy breaths, and didn't move. His sense of invincibility tottered; the chemicals that had pleasurably filled his system faded.

Sven looked back at him, and for the first time, there was a flicker of sympathy in his voice. "You can go back," he said. "There is a GPS phone in my bag. You don't have to go on."

After all, it's only a job.

Only a job.

Charlie looked down, and saw that his footprint had obscured the other man's, the man whose foot had gone before. He moved his feet quickly to one side, feeling he'd somehow sullied something sacred, and looked up at Sven, and thought he saw

who the hell knew what it was he thought he saw?

And with a shudder, not of cold, he stepped onto the ice.

Some time later
in a place where there was no time
Charlie fell over, and didn't get back up.

He was aware that Sven pitched a tent, wrapped him in his sleeping bag, gave him tepid tea, made him eat, and, when the worst of the wind was off his face, crawled into the sleeping bag with him, and held him tight, until his shivering subsided.

Charlie probably slept, it was hard to tell, and when he woke, Sven was asleep in the bag with him, and the sun was still spinning through the sky.

*

51

Sven said, "Can you go on?"

Charlie said, "Yes," and meant it. In his dreams he had seen the end of the world, and knew when he woke that only he could prevent it. "Yes," he repeated, shaking off this madness of sleep. "I want to finish it."

They walked.

Chapter 20

On what might have been the third day, they descended a spire of ice, crampons and rope, axe and spike.

Charlie supposed that in another time, he might have been afraid, but he wasn't now, he was just passing through, a man passing through his own body, his own experience, and so he obeyed Sven's every command, and made it to the bottom of the spire to where a smoother line of ice ran, and Sven looked at him with an expression that might have been impressed, and was perhaps a little afraid, and murmured, "Charlie, are you okay?"

"I'm good," Charlie replied, and found that whoever had spoken these words was not lying. "Let's keep going."

They walked.

The horizon – is it a horizon?

Is that a place where the ice stops, the edge of the glacier, where ice meets earth, a frozen waterfall, a plummet down into nothing?

Or is it just a trick of the eye, perspective gone mad, nothing to measure the flatness by, nothing to say this is high and that is low, no near or far, no colour, just

whiteness.

Walking.

*

Once in the distance Charlie thought he saw . . .

. . . but of course he didn't.

Then again in the distance he looked and he thought he saw . . .

. . . and this time, like the walkers on the ridge or the pale figure he had absolutely not seen at the edge of the fjord, he looked to Sven to see if Sven had seen it too, and at that moment Sven did, because with a sudden shout he dropped his bag, gave a cry, and started to run towards it.

Not sure what to do in this circumstance, Charlie lumbered after, dragging Sven's bag along behind.

A man lay on the ice.

He lay like one sleeping, a peaceful child, his knees tucked in, his head resting on his hands, his eyes closed. He was, Charlie felt absolutely certain, dead. His skin was white, his lips were grey, there was no rising or falling in his chest. Sven was already kneeling at the man's side, gloves off, fumbling at his throat, his face, listening, feeling for any sign of life. Charlie stood by and watched, mute, in a dream. What was this man doing here? Why had the whiteness not taken him, as surely it had taken them? Had he also died looking for the Professor?

Then Sven snapped, "Don't just stand there – help me!"

And it turned out that the man wasn't dead after all.

They pitched a tent, Sven slamming the poles into the ice as if each were his enemy, while Charlie manhandled the frozen man into his sleeping bag, half expecting his knees to snap, his arms to tear away in his hands as he moved him, so stiff and heavy was every limb. The end of his nose was turning black; Charlie didn't speculate what might be happening to his fingers and toes. One side of his body had melted the ice with its heat, and then, as flesh cooled, the meltwater had begun to refreeze, so they had to pull him from his frozen jacket and top, stripping him down to bare, bloodless skin, before Sven pulled his own jacket free and clambered into the sleeping bag too.

Charlie sat on his rucksack and watched in silence as Sven held the man tight, warming him with his heat, sometimes feeling for a pulse, checking for breath, whispering, now in Danish, now in Kalaallisut, "Don't die you fucking idiot don't you fucking die ..."

Charlie realised that this was it, the end, that they had walked across the ice and they had found their target, and this man was it, this sack of frozen flesh, what a disappointment, just a man after all, not a figure waiting for them at the end of the world.

He realised that he was more tired than he had ever known, and that the world was dead to him, washed out with white, and that his blood had never been so hot and alive inside his skin, and that humanity was the most beautiful, precious thing in the universe, and that all life was insignificant and the destruction of it would not matter a jot, and that all these things were true, all at once.

He realised that he was crying, and only noticed because of the searing, skin-bursting salty heat of it on his face. He tried to wipe away the salt with his sleeve, but it just burned more, so he let the tears roll, without feeling really sad, and chewed on dry meat, and waited.

He wondered whether he should be sitting here at all, all things considered. Should he have helped put the man in the sleeping bag? He was, after all, the Harbinger of Death, the messenger who went before the ...

He drank water warmed by his body, and dismissed the thought. Jobs were a thing that happened in another place; the past had melted with the glacier, gone for ever.

The sun turned overhead, and Sven held the old man tight, and Charlie dozed.

Thunder, roaring, the end of the world come at last. Charlie started awake from where he had slumbered, still sitting on his rucksack, and saw the world collapsing. The horizon tore away, shrinking, crawling nearer, the earth shook, the ice cracked, he scrambled on his hands and knees to the tent and started tearing the sheets away, shouting over the roar, "Ice! The ice is collapsing! *The ice is collapsing!*"

Sven, waking groggy, crawled from the sleeping bag to see the glacier's edge, a few hundred metres away, coming closer, a solid waterfall plummeting into the depths below, clouds of crystals spiralling upwards from the impact, the ground shaking as in an earthquake, the world cracking, crazy snakes of meltwater bouncing, splitting, rippling along the ice.

"Help me!" Sven roared over the din, grabbing the sleeping bag in which the still-slumbering man lay and pulling it away, back from the edge, Charlie slung his sack across his back, grabbed the other corner and heaved too, falling over his own feet, dragging the man across the shuddering ice by the corners of the bag, bouncing, banging, surely the bag would tear, surely they would fall, running as the world fell behind them, the ground beneath their feet stabbing and bucking, pools of slush breaking to the surface in great bubbling bursts like frozen lava, the melting surface giving way so they fell and crawled on hands and knees, and then climbed to their feet again, then fell again, and finally both of them wriggling along the ground, dragging the man in the bag behind them until at last

with a distant creaking, like the bilges of a submarine before the metal cracks

like the settling of hot metal cooled too fast

the world grew still again.

Charlie looked back, and saw that the horizon, which had before been many hundreds of metres away, was now no fewer than twenty from his feet. Their tent, Sven's bag, all was gone, and a fog of snow and shattered crystals, of disturbed mist and icy damp, filled the void where they had slumbered. He looked at Sven, and saw the other man lying on his back, the sleeping bag with its unconscious cargo still held close, knuckles white, never letting go.

Charlie turned away, took his bag off, crawled to the very edge of the glacier, and looked down into a melted land.

A land where no trees grew.

Water rushing out from beneath the ice, the ice floating on water.

A land of stone, and beyond the stone, the sea, stretching far away, the sea ice gone, a distortion of grey-blues and green-blacks, shadowy darkness against the endless light of the top of the glacier, and he thought, seeing it, that it was a strange kind of ugly, and knew now that Death had no need at all to show his face to anyone, before the ending came.

Sven said, "The satellite phone was in my bag."

Charlie didn't answer. Sven sat on his haunches, no jacket, no hat, and didn't seem to mind. "We get him off the ice. It was foolish to stay here."

Charlie looked wearily back at the sheets of ice between them and the ridge from which they'd come, and couldn't see an end.

"You carry the bag. I'll carry him."

He nodded just once at the man in the sleeping bag, and Charlie helped lift him onto Sven's back.

Walking.

If Charlie had still been wearing his watch, he would have smashed it.

He walked one step at a time, because he knew that if he walked ten steps further, he would die. Instead, he put one foot in front of the other, and that was a victory, and hadn't been so hard really, so he then put another foot forward, and that was okay, and besides, it was clearly the first step he had ever taken, the first step of his life, and so the next one would be and so in this manner forward.

Charlie walked.

Twice Sven lost his footing, and fell, dropping the man in the sleeping bag, who groaned once, and didn't stir the other time.

Three times they had to stop, once for Charlie to catch his breath, twice for Sven to sit on the ice and shake. Charlie secretly gave him the last of the meat, pretended there was more. When they saw the edge of the ice, Sven seemed to have a sudden, second burst of energy, and nearly ran, until the straight line he took was stopped dead by a chasm in the ice, through which, far below, bubbling water ran. They walked another ten thousand steps before the chasm narrowed enough to cross. Charlie did not offer to carry the sleeping man; it would have been a futile gesture in this frozen world.

Rock far rock far
    still far
    near now?
    near yet far
    the ice roars the ice is breaking the ice is breaking beneath your feet walk and
    a thundering behind, the world growing short again, the collapse chasing them as they moved
    rivers of meltwater growing thicker now getting into Charlie's boots dangerous so dangerous feet cold
    feet cold
    fingers cold
    the wetness makes everything cold
    Sven shivering
    shivering now
    wet is the enemy
    the world coming apart

In a treeless land
    in the place where all things dissolve beneath the endless sun
    Charlie looked up and beheld a pale figure on the horizon, and the pale figure looked at Charlie and knew him for his own, and Charlie smiled, and looked away, and kept on walking.

Sleeping.
    How had he come to be sleeping?
    Lying on rock, the ice a few metres behind
    lying on stone
    Charlie lay sleeping on his back, the bag still on his back, beneath his back, arching his body, but his brain didn't care, he was sleeping

Sven on the ground, fallen nearby, the sleeping man by his side

Charlie thought that, if he wasn't so tired, he might be a bit resentful of this, the manner of his death in what were, frankly, by Greenland terms very mild conditions indeed

the wet being what would kill him of course, more than the cold

exhaustion

exhausted as the world fell apart

Then a voice, strange and new, brash, speaking English with a gentle southern accent, said, "Hold on, we'll get your boots off now . . . "

Charlie slept, and in his dreams he was warm.

Chapter 21

"First you create a mood board . . . "

"Oh look at him cooochy-cooochy-coo . . . "

"There's actually some very powerful things you can do with Excel now . . . "

"I just love saying oolong. Try it. Ooooolong . . . "

"This is the symbol of our club!"

"Have you been in an accident recently?"

"Reverse stitch at the beginning and the end to lock the seam and then . . . "

"Scared? Worried about knife crime? Get training now!"

"These two characters symbolise breath, which is also energy, and this is the four quarters of the world . . . "

"So they'd take an orange and inject it with water, then rub the surface down with formaldehyde . . . "

"Hello! Yes, ma'am, indeed yes, I am calling about your router; have you been having problems with your router, ma'am . . . ?"

"Except it could also mean rice. As in . . . rice breath. Or alternatively gas meter, depending how you look at it."

"I know you left it ambiguous, but for the movie we really need to know if it's happy or sad."

"You could be entitled to compensation!"

Chapter 22

A man sat on a rock outside a tent on the edge of a collapsing glacier, and checked his email.

How this man had signal on his admittedly chunky phone was a bit of a mystery to Charlie, as he blinked his way back to full consciousness. How, in fact, this man, dressed in bright high-tech blues and heavy walking boots, a hat upon his head and walking sticks resting by his side, had come to be here at all was something of a wonder.

Charlie crawled from the sleeping bag in which, somehow, he'd been laid, and looked around.

To his left, sleeping, Sven, huddled in a sleeping bag that presumably belonged to the man with the phone. Beyond him, still in Sven's sleeping bag, the man they'd pulled from the ice, his eyes open, awake, staring up at the sky, silent.

In this strange quartet, Charlie felt suddenly like the most ignorant man on earth. He looked at the man with the phone, equating this machine somehow with an almost mystic authority, and said at last, in English, "Hello," and immediately felt stupid for picking a stupid language.

The man looked up, smiled, and replied in the same language, tinged with something that might have been cricket, or maybe department stores, or maybe just a long time spent bickering with academics. "Hello. How are you feeling?"

Bewildered, it took Charlie a little while to process these

words, to process this language, in which time the man put his phone into a pocket, stood, brushed down the front of his trousers self-consciously and came to squat by Charlie's side.

He was in his early forties, or perhaps older and well-kept by exercise and doctors in that state in which he could be at once perceived as both youthfully energetic and mature and authoritative. His pale skin was reddened with the cold, but didn't yet have the circled patch of white around the eyes that prolonged walking beneath the northern sun gave, the light absorbed by glasses or goggles. His hair, where it stuck out beneath his hat, was dark brown, and almost perfectly straight. His eyes were grey-green, and if Charlie had to speculate, beneath the layers of coat and waterproof material was a well-kept body that perhaps enjoyed swimming, maybe lifted a few weights – nothing excessive, nothing less than what good form required.

He smiled at Charlie, and the Harbinger of Death felt again very small, and wondered if, when the glacier had finished collapsing into the sea, the land that was exposed beneath it would buckle, shift with the weight gone from it, sudden hills bursting up like sunflowers in spring.

"You're staring," said the man gently, into the silence of Charlie's spinning mind. "Are you feeling okay?"

"I . . ." His voice came ragged and alien, someone else's. He tried to find some spit in his mouth to swallow, found he didn't have any. Wordlessly, the man gave him a flask, and he drank gratefully, and then a little too much, gagging on the water and nearly choking it out again. The man waited until he had his breath under control, taking little sips, and then murmured:

"I've called an ambulance. They should be here in a couple of hours."

"I . . . Thank you. You're . . ."

"It's a helicopter. It needs to fly up from the south, but the weather's good and it should be able to make a clean landing."

"Thank you. How did you . . . I mean, why are you here?"

"I had a helicopter take me to the edge of the fjord. The climb was easier than I expected. Are you the Harbinger of

Death?" the man asked, as if it were the most obvious thing in the world.

Charlie sat up straight, head wheeling as blood readjusted to this dangerous change of position. He squeezed his eyes shut until the world was still, and for a moment couldn't distinguish between the blood in his ears and the roaring of the breaking glacier at his feet. "Yes," he mumbled at last. "Who are you?"

"My name's Patrick Fuller. I was invited to see the end of all things."

"I don't understand."

"Don't you? Didn't you invite me?"

"I don't know who you are. Why are you ... What do you mean, the end of all things?"

A little surprised, the man called Patrick leaned back, studying Charlie's face anew, and seeing nothing in it but bewilderment. He smiled again, patted him gently on the shoulder and said, "Don't worry. Everything's going to be fine."

Then he rose, and went back to his stone, pulled out his phone and resumed texting.

Chapter 23

The man they had dragged from the ice
    a man with a scraggly white beard, silver hair
    skin burned by the cold
    the ends of the fingers on his left hand, black, ready to be snapped off like twigs
    lay still as Patrick held his head and Charlie held the cup and he swallowed the painkillers down
    body little more than bones, too weak to move by himself at first, had to be raised to sit
    the man they had saved from the collapsing world

looked at the tin of tea that Charlie had somehow, miraculously, brought with him from the other side of the planet, and said, a little distant through the drugs now shooting through his system, "You can't get this stuff where I live. Go on then, let's have a cup."

Patrick set up a small burner and put a metal cup on it. Charlie added his cup, and the three of them sat in silence round the blue flame as water started to boil. Sven lay in his bag, eyes open, watching them, and didn't speak.

Patrick said, "I don't know your names . . . ?"

"Charlie."

"Ule. The quiet one is Sven."

"How do you feel, Mr Ule?"

"Professor Ule, and my actual name is . . . To hell with it, Ule is fine."

"You were in a bad way."

"Who says I'm not now?"

"Your fingers, your feet, I took your boots off and . . . "

He shrugged. "Amputation doesn't bother me."

"Are you in much pain? I have more painkillers, but I don't know if—"

"Why do you have the tea?" Professor Ule cut in, quick and hard, attention on Charlie, causing Patrick's eyes to flicker a little in disapproval at the unexpected interruption.

"Hm? Oh – it's my job."

"To bring tea to an old man on the ice?"

"Yes."

"What kind of job is this?"

"I'm the Harbinger of Death. I was given your name, told to find you, bring you some tea. It's never been this hard before. Perhaps it's meant to warm you up?"

Silence a while. The three sat as the water boiled, and out on the ice, the world grew shorter, caving away, the frozen world tumbling down to dust. At last Professor Ule grunted, just a single sound, "Ah."

They listened to the world fall apart.

Then, "Ah," he said again, and with a little shake of his head, "Well, here's a thing I didn't expect."

"I don't entirely understand," mused Patrick. "You're the Harbinger of Death, but as I understand it, you've just saved this man's life?"

"Yes," murmured Charlie, mostly to himself. "It looks that way, doesn't it?"

Ule reached forward and removed one bubbling cup from the burner. Patrick turned off the heat. "This isn't how you're supposed to do it, of course," muttered the Professor as tea was added and stirred around. "Water onto the tea, not tea into the water, wrong kind of cup, wrong kind of boil, wrong kind of water really, but ... " He blew a little cloud of steam off the top of the cup. "You make do, yes?"

So saying, he tried a sip, and his body seemed to sigh in relief as the heat sank down through him. Charlie and Patrick shared a mug. It didn't taste as bad as Charlie had feared. Patrick tried a little, wrinkled his nose, tried a little more, muttered he could probably get used to it, but really he was an Earl Grey kind of man.

Sven watched, and said nothing.

A few metres from their feet, the world cracked beneath the summer sun.

Ule said: "So. Harbinger of Death. Like the work?"

"Yes. I mean ... this was ... this trip is the first time that I ... but yes."

"Do you only visit the imminently deceased, or is it more ... " A vague gesture with a wrinkled, blackened, soon-to-be-lessened hand, taking in the world around.

"So far the work is varied," Charlie replied. "I went to Palmyra before the bombs were rigged to find a statue of Baal, had a fresco in a Byzantine church in Sicily removed before it was torn down to make way for an office block. In Scotland a man taught me how to fish with my hands; in Peru I talked with a woman whose language will never be heard again. My employer feels it is important to honour . . . a manner of life, as well as the living themselves. He says that to know what it is that is ending, first you must walk down the roads they themselves have taken, and breathe the air they have breathed. I like travel. I like meeting people. I think . . . It makes me feel . . . " His words trailed away.

"Even people about to die?" asked Patrick, and then, seeing Ule's eyes flicker to his face, added, "Oh, I mean, I don't think . . . "

"It is a good question to be asked in this place," the other replied with a placating hand. "In this place especially."

Charlie's face crinkled. "Sometimes . . . There was a child, and she . . . and her parents, they cried, but the girl was . . . Sometimes there is strength in reality. When I come, things that were terrifying ideas become tangible."

"And you bring tea."

"And sometimes I bring tea, yes."

"And who fears tea?" mused the Professor, rolling the mug between his blackened, bitter fingers.

They sat in silence. Across the ice, an internal chord played, a small island collapsed into the maelstrom, the drums rolled, the horizon grew a little nearer. Ule flexed his bloodless feet inside his boots, rolled his head from side to side, took another sip. Sven watched in silence.

Finally Patrick said, "I was sent an email. It asked me to come to this place, at this time. It was from an address in Milton Keynes, signed by a woman called Samantha on behalf of Death."

"There is a Samantha in the Milton Keynes office," Charlie murmured, not looking up from his contemplation of the falling ice sheet.

"Death has an office?" interrupted Ule, quick and curious.

"Travel arrangements, accommodation, bulletin reports, theatre tickets, gourmet dining – I once had to fly a fugu chef to the jungles of Colombia. Do you know how hard it is to find bamboo socks in Boko Haram-controlled Nigeria?"

"Death is picky?"

"Death can be unpredictable. Death . . . likes to behave in what he sees as a human way. Sometimes it is human to go walkabout with no shoes on. Sometimes it is human to take a bicycle along a dangerous highway, and sometimes . . . sometimes it's human to want a shisha pipe in Pyongyang." He glanced up at the silence of his companions, taking in the raised eyebrows on Patrick's face, the concentrated frown on Ule's. "I told you the job had its interesting moments," he muttered, looking away again. "Karaoke night with the Harbinger of Famine in a camper van on the Yalu river was one for the grandkids."

Again they lapsed into roaring, melting silence.

Then, "What did this email say?" asked Ule. "The one from Samantha in Milton Keynes?"

"Oh – various salutations and greetings, some praise for my work, a few predictions of things to come, an invitation to see the ending of the world."

"Was that the phrase?"

"Something like that. Ending, turning, changing, death – the language was a bit florid. At first I thought it was a joke, but a few others received them too, a couple of people I know, one or two very interesting characters. I did a little research and . . . well. Even if it was hokum, it seemed like a curious notion, so here I am."

"At the ending of the world," mused Ule.

"Not much to look at, is it? Do you suppose we're waiting for something? A meteor strike, perhaps?"

Ule laughed, a strange in-out chuckle through the nose. No one else did. Sven lay back on the ground, staring up at the bright white sky. Charlie looked down at his feet, and wondered what he'd find beneath the dry socks that Patrick had put on him while he slept. Would his toes be black, like the Professor's? Probably not. He doubted anything so dramatic would repay him for the exhaustion that had liquefied his bones.

Then Ule said, "There is no meteor," and his voice caught, and he took another slurp of tea, finishing it down to the dregs, and laid the hot cup down and tried again, breath puffing in the air. "There is no meteor," he repeated. "The clock that measures the death of humanity stands at three minutes to midnight. The debate is whether to move it forward, not back. I was asked to advise and I said it's too late, the night is over and the morning is here, but we won't live to see it. Carl Sagan published a paper in the 1980s – the nuclear winter, the winter that would fall when the bombs dropped – and was called a traitor by everyone for daring to speak of the end. In the US, the Senators and Congressmen who decide what one of the most powerful and polluting countries in the world will do about its emissions say that the evidence is unclear. Unclear! I went diving with some of the NASA team to see the places where the coral had blanched and I couldn't breathe, my mask worked fine and I couldn't breathe.

"In the Amazon, you may walk for days without seeing a tree; in Beijing, the air is the colour of a bruise. Three thousand miles of litter floats in the Atlantic Ocean, plastic bags and old nappies, bumping against the side of the ships. The rhino's horn was cut away from its still-living flesh as it died by the empty waterhole. Mud slipped down the treeless slope, crushing the village; children are born already poisoned by the water their mothers drink. I sat before a committee in Brussels and they said, 'What do you want us to do about it? If we change now, we'll destroy our own economies,' and I said, 'You have destroyed your own world' and was asked to leave for being too subjective in my testimony. I walked the ice; as a boy I came here and I walked the ice, me and your mother, and saw so much life, life clinging on where you would have thought it would die, life that begets life that begets life that sustains the planet, just . . . life."

Sven stared at the sky, said nothing at all.

"There is nothing complicated about understanding ecosystems," sighed Ule. "We are taught at school that the plant releases oxygen that sustains animals whose bodies, as they rot, release nutrients that sustain the plants. It is no greater a step to say that the wind that blows across the mountains of America will one day touch the lakes of Zimbabwe. We have always been

66

parochial. I understand what you mean about making a thing real." Charlie looked up, found Ule's gaze on him. "I understand," repeated the old man, softer. "Death is a thing we hide from, until we can't any more."

Silence, as the world fell apart.

At last Patrick said, "I think you're wrong, Professor. I think man is infinitely ingenious. I think you're wrong."

Sven glanced at Patrick, at Ule, looked for a moment like he might cry.

Charlie stared at his feet, and only half listened.

A beeping in Patrick's pocket; he checked his phone, then looked up.

The helicopter was already close before they heard it, the sounds of its rotors drowned out by the cracking of the ice. Patrick rose. Uncertainly, his shoelaces undone, Charlie tried to stand too, and his head swam, and he gave up on the idea. Sven lay where he was, body turned to one side now, propping himself up on his elbow, watching Ule, as the tiger watches another of its kin, caught hunting, unexpected, in the jungle. Ule stared back. Sven shook his head, slowly, an answer to a question that had not been asked.

Ule smiled at him, looked away.

Sven reached out to hold the old man's arm, but he was just out of his reach.

Patrick on the phone, talking to an unseen figure in the bright yellow helicopter, shouting now to be heard over the bursting of the engines, the wind pulling up jagged crystals of shattered ice from the glacier, tearing at skin and hair, the temperature plummeting with the movement. Charlie shielded his eyes against it, and was slow to notice Ule, swaying, uneven, climb to his feet.

"Charlie!" Sven cried out, voice sucked away even as he spoke, rolling, trying to extricate himself from the sleeping bag, tangled up in limb and fibre. Charlie looked round, saw Ule staggering like a drunkard, back down towards the ice.

"Wait! Stop!" Charlie crawled to his feet, teetered, caught his balance with his hands on the rock, tearing at glove and skin, stumbled up again, ran after the old man. Ule slipped as his feet hit the ice, but caught himself and ran on, arms flapping like wet flags at his sides. The glacier was not smooth, the meltwaters flowed across its surface, sores and scabs had burst within it, the packed ice snapping down and stabbing up under its own moving, internal pressure. Charlie scrambled onto the ice, fell at once, crawled back up, feet struggling to gain purchase, Sven now at his side, but the old man was already ahead, running wild. He shouted something at them as they followed, but the wind from the helicopter pulled it away.

"Stop!" Sven screamed through the engines and the thunder of the melt. "*Dad, stop!*"

Without stopping, Ule turned, smiled, raised one hand in a kind of greeting, and fell backwards.

Charlie didn't even see the open wound in the ice into which he stepped, didn't see if there was air or water below, couldn't judge how great the gap was. Perhaps Ule was lodged in there, just a few feet down, too wide for the opening? Sven gasped, a place where sound should have been and wasn't, and scrambling on all fours, no boots on his feet, galloped like an animal across the ice, slipping and sliding on his belly to the edge of the void, throwing himself down to peer into

an empty depth

a place where the light failed

a river beneath the flow, the walls melting fast, water running out to the wide, waiting sea.

Sven looked down, and wept.

But Charlie looked up, and beheld a figure standing on the edge of the glacier, his back turned to the scene, a hat on his head, gloves in his pockets; but still, for all that he appeared to be but a walker on the ice, he was what he was, unmistakable in the midnight sun, and he was Death, the destroyer of worlds.

The glacier shook, the world crumbled, and Death too was gone.

Chapter 24

Sometimes ... There was a child, and she ... and her parents, they cried, but the girl was ... Sometimes there is strength in reality and ...

I'm not telling it right. Let me start again.

(Charlie isn't very good at telling stories. Discretion is an important part of his remit.)

There was a child, thirteen years old, in a hospital in Mumbai. I'd known this one was coming, I knew it. Up to then it had almost been ... easy ... but the appointment came and I was ready for it, even though I wasn't. I took the plane, then a cab, and ... She'd been born so ill, she didn't have a right arm or a right leg, her face was all ... The doctors said she was going to die within six to nine months, but she lived. She lived until she was five, when she got pneumonia, and her parents prepared her for death, but still she lived, and demanded to go to school and made friends with the other children on the ward – she spent most of her time in the hospital – and all the doctors and nurses loved her because she was such a happy child, such a cheerful, outgoing, beautiful child, and then when she was thirteen, her white blood cell count began to plummet and they couldn't work out why and her name appeared on my calendar and I went to see her with a copy of a book that she'd loved as a small girl but that had gone out of print – it was hard to find, I tell you that now – and she said, "Why are you here?"

"I'm the Harbinger of Death," I replied.

"Oh. That makes sense. Can you stay, or do you have to go away now?"

I had imagined a hundred ways this conversation would go. A child, and I was not a warning. I had prepared a thousand things I could say, and then this – she wasn't angry or scared, she just wanted to know if I'd stay and talk, and I felt like such an idiot.

Like somehow I was making all of this about me. Unforgivable. It was just . . . So anyway, I said, "I can stay, a little while."

"Good. Tell me about Death. What's it like?"

I didn't have an answer, but I tried anyway, told her that it was nothing to be frightened of, that everyone died, and she said, "No, stupid, not dying – I've been doing that my whole life. What is Death?"

"I . . . I don't think I can answer that."

"Why? Don't you know?"

"I think everyone knows. And . . . and I think no one does. It's . . . I think it can be hard knowing that the answer is nothing."

She nodded at this, like a teacher whose students are finally learning an important lesson. "What's Death like? I mean, your boss?"

"I've only met him once."

"So he's a he?"

"No. I see him that way, but everyone sees their own form of Death, when he comes. Some see him as a figure all in black, others as a woman with a bone-white face. Some see their ancient gods, some a devil, others an angel. Some see the face of the vengeance they always knew was looking for them; some see a long-lost brother. It's always different, and every Death is always for you alone."

"And does everyone see Death?"

"In the end, yes."

"But you are human – you cannot visit every single person who's going to die."

"No. I am a courtesy, sent to places ahead of my employer for very special reasons. Sometimes I come to warn, and sometimes I come to honour."

"Which are you for me?" she asked.

"I think . . . I must be here to honour. I don't usually know, but . . . I think that is why."

She didn't cry, this girl in a hospital gown. The only time I saw her sad was when she thought about what her family would do now. I did meet the parents – I didn't want to, but they

70

were there as I left her room, and I didn't have the heart to tell them who I was, why I was there. Their names were not on my appointment book, I felt no obligation to be . . . I was just scared. I told myself that it would not have honoured them, not as my employer would have wished. To the girl my presence brought a truth, but to them that truth would have been . . . So I left, and didn't look back, but they must have sensed it somehow, because they were crying – only worse, they were trying not to cry, trying to put a brave face on it for their girl, and so they cried outside her room, and washed their eyes, and smiled when they went through the door. I . . . The way you do it is by never looking back. I am not Death. I visit the living, and when I leave, the living are still alive, and . . . and he follows after. Maybe I am a coward. When I took the job, I thought I was brave. I will do better, next time.

The girl's dead now, of course. I didn't see it happen, haven't thought about it until now, but here we are.

Here we are.

Chapter 25

"There is no consensus on climate change. No, listen to me, seriously, this is a bunch of left-wing lobbyists and foreign activists trying to cut down on American jobs, American industry, this is . . ."

"Human cause of carbon emissions but actually volcanos . . ."

"Last year we cooled!"

"Technology anyway, human ingenuity, the power of humanity to shape its destiny and the planet . . ."

" . . . a balmy island, vines, wine from the Midlands, wouldn't that be a wonderful thing?"

"Desertification . . ."

"Blanket the atmosphere with sulphur, which will create an effect equivalent to . . . "

"Is it the end of the world? No. The world will endure. Is it the end of humanity and all those species that live within the finely tempered balance of heat, gas, water and nutrition that is currently sustained by the global biosphere? That's a more interesting question."

"No. Frankly: no. Nothing you say will make me change my mind."

I should have been there for you.

Extract from a letter from Professor Ule to Sven Aglukkaq,
found posthumously amongst his papers

Chapter 26

After.
  On the ice
  in the place where the ice crumbled away to nothing
  water flowing to the sea
  water flowing of dead, black stone
  Patrick had said, "I've got a jet going from Nuuk to La Guardia. You'd be welcome on it."
  And Charlie answered, "Thank you. No." And found that he had nothing else to say.
  No one had tried to look for Ule's body beneath the crumbling world. One day, a medic from the helicopter ambulance whispered, someone will find it, perhaps, preserved just like it was, on the edge of the water. Or it will be carried out to sea, and vanish for ever, and perhaps that's for the best.
  Sven had walked, one man supporting him under each arm, to

the helicopter. They'd put him inside, and he'd said not a word, and seen nothing, and been surprised when they'd landed just outside Oounavik, the whole town gathering for his return. Ane had come with blankets to wrap him in, and reverently, gently, without speech or ceremony, they'd taken him home.

Charlie had stayed on the helicopter. It seemed disrespectful to walk amongst these quiet people again, and besides, his work was done.

There was a hospital in Qeqertarsuaq. There were two doctors on shift, and a nurse who also worked as a fisherman and was, he admitted, not really that well trained but he knew enough; the midwife was better at these things than he was, but she'd been called away to a village some seventy miles up the coast.

Charlie sat on the edge of one of the beds in a hushed ward of strangers, and let himself be prodded and poked. Light was shone in his eyes, feet examined, fingers examined, and finally he was told, "Just have a lie-down. Have a little sleep."

He slept for nearly twenty hours, and woke with the feeling that light would pass through him, and he wasn't there at all.

Inside the helicopter, flying south, there were words that Patrick had said, but Charlie had been too tired to hear them. Now, as he watched the endless low spinning of the sun across the ceiling of the hospital ward, he tried to piece them back together again, clutch them out of the roar of the helicopter engine, the fall of the glacier, the heaviness in his body.

I am a witness, the man had said. I am called to witness the ending of the world. Death called me, and I came. Was the old man it? Was I there to see an old man die? Who was he?

Charlie hadn't answered — at least, he couldn't remember speaking. He wondered if he would ever speak again.

Who was he? Patrick hollered over the helicopter blades. Why did he matter?

In the summer sun, the ice fell, and Charlie slept.

*

Another helicopter ride, then another, town-hopping south, back to Nuuk. In Nuuk, people smiled and were pleased to see him – how was it, how was your trip on the ice, did you see wonderful things, so beautiful, so beautiful out there!

And because they smiled, Charlie smiled back and said yes, yes, beautiful I suppose, but also strange, all of it so very strange . . .

The plane to Reykjavik, and in Reykjavik he found that Milton Keynes had booked a twenty-four hour stopover and a hotel with hot springs round the back, smelling of sulphur and eye-pinching minerals dissolved in the heat, and he sat in the pool and marvelled that this was what hot felt like, and imagined that frost was finally melting from the middle of his bones, and when at Heathrow the immigration man said, "Welcome home, sir," Charlie smiled and said, "Thank you," and thought the Piccadilly Line had never seemed so beautiful or the sky so bright.

The day after he got home, he phoned Emmi, asked if she was okay, if she wanted to . . . you know.

But she was in Newcastle for work, and then he received a new appointment in his diary, and the plane to Urumqi took off two hours before her train got back and for the very first time, Charlie was reluctant to go.

Part 3

CHAMPAGNE

Chapter 27

"Well of course she hasn't been doing as well in school as I'd like, and she's forgotten her times tables – forgotten them. I mean, she can do her five and her twos but that's it, and I use my times tables every day and so I was thinking of getting a private tutor, because at the school all they ever do are poster projects and that's the primary school syllabus, I know, but it's madness and she's so much better than that."

"Nipple hair is just the worst."

"How can you be a nurse and not believe in science? I asked her and she was just rude, rude I tell you, and I was like, did God put the drip in, did God fit the surgical drain, but she said that I didn't understand, that I was harassing her, questioning her deeply held beliefs, and she's lazy too, I'll tell you that, lazy. Maybe God does the paperwork."

"I think what you're talking about – women who get pregnant like that – well I think you're talking about a particular class of women. I think generally the women who get raped and beaten by their partners, well that's a particular part of society and actually is part of that society, not what you make it out to be at all."

"That's not new season, I've seen new season . . ."

"If you are self-employed then don't go crying to the taxpayer when you choose to have kids; your uterus is not our problem, thank you very much . . ."

"Men are not treated as equal to women. In the past women valued their looks, they were trained to be submissive, but now . . ."

"*Boom*! Lemme hear you say it!"

"He talks about social equality, about narrowing the pay gap, more hospitals, more schools, better transport, protecting the elderly, protecting the environment, about the rich not getting richer and the poor not getting poorer, but I want to know how is he going to pay for it? I don't want to pay more taxes; I just want this country to work."

Chapter 28

Some time after the ice . . .
　　. . . in a land of rolling hills . . .
　　. . . in a land of dark and Satanic mills . . .

It was raining when the Harbinger of Death took the 176 bus to the Longview Estate. It was raining when he got on the bus, pressed in amongst steaming bodies and crumpled shopping bags, and it was raining when he got off, scurrying from the bus shelter to the doorway of a second-hand mattress shop, umbrella flapping in the wind, struggling to work out which way to go now.

He knew the area around Elephant and Castle perfectly well – no one could live long in south London without at some point being swept up into the heaving roundabouts and belching one-way systems of the arterial junction, squatting in a pinch of land hemmed in to the north, east and west by the curve of the River Thames, spewing out bus routes and harried commuters to all corners of the city. Once, when he was new to London, he'd attended a very loud, very drunken birthday party at a music venue nearby. The lighting had been blackness sliced through with strobing green lasers; the floor had bounced as he walked on it; he was bullied to impress a girl, mixing drinks, and was profoundly and violently sick outside the venue door, and was denied readmittance and had to go home by himself. No one had really noticed his absence, and over the years he'd lost touch with that circle of friends.

Now he was back, a bright orange toolkit in a rugged plastic box held in one hand, complete with multi-head screwdriver, tape measure, claw hammer and adjustable spanner. Over his other shoulder he carried a satchel, and as he tried to balance these two objects with the umbrella clasped in his right hand, one slipped, the other bumped, and he cursed under his breath.

The sound of his muttering was swept away by the wail of a police siren, the swish of tyres through bursting puddles, the rattling of a drill on a new luxury penthouse estate development refurbishment village project zone of . . .

. . . a new building of some sort; he didn't bother to look too closely at the billboards.

Finally, by putting the toolbox on the ground, slinging the strap of his satchel across his whole body rather than just over one shoulder and negotiating the angle of his umbrella so that the flat top pressed into the wind, he was able to extract his mobile phone, check the map, and follow it into the muddle of streets that divided Southwark from Kennington.

Walking away from the traffic, quieter back roads, he felt a little calmer. These streets had always seemed to him like a proper part of London, more than the tourist walks of the West End, the crowds along the Thames, the queues at the Tower. Here, between the bus routes, white terraced almshouses with little gardens at front and back met fat Victorian homes, now converted into three flats apiece. Red-brick 1950s council estates squatted in between, built around eccentric courtyards during an era when everyone knew that rocket packs were only a generation away, and the great men of the time still remembered their excitement at the day they turned a tap on and hot water came out.

The Longview Estate was the collective name for five of these blocks, arranged by a hobgoblin around triangles of green, intersecting walkways designed to create the sense of a little world within its walls, a shelter for the kids, a community centre in the middle of it, now nothing more than a room with a broken kettle and bouncing floorboards.

Most of the estate was boarded up. Metal shutters along the ground floor; no-entry signs across the walkways. The first of the diggers were waiting round the side of one of the blocks; buddleia grew untrimmed from the roof. Charlie was turned around by a graffittied-over map by the entrance to the estate, running his finger along the sign, trying to find his way to one door, one building. He ended up looking at evens, not odds, and backtracked through a cracked car park, broken crates stacked in a corner, past a smashed CCTV camera and an empty stretch of grey wall where someone had written in block capitals:

NO WAY BACK

The paint had run, making the letters weep. A beer can bounced down the empty grey stairs; plane trees shifted in the cold breeze.

He climbed up, followed a walkway along, came to number 17, shifted his bag on his shoulder, his umbrella in his hand, and knocked three times.

Chapter 29

She had said, "I collect snow globes. You'll probably want to do something similar."

He'd replied instantly, knowing it was true, "I like music."

"Good! That's excellent. I see why she likes you so much."

"Tell me," Charlie mused, "you were the Harbinger of Death so long, and now this, here, retirement . . . What are you going to do?"

A question beneath the question – what is there that you possibly could do, having already done so much?

She considered a while, then ticked the points off her fingers. "Bake my own bread, read, go bouldering on a Saturday with the women's club, and learn to scuba dive. Also, it's really time that I gave my wardrobe a bit of an overhaul."

After Greenland, he'd written an email. He wanted to explain, thought she might understand.

I felt nothing. I felt the world was ending. I felt on fire. I felt frozen to the bone. I felt as if nothing had any meaning. I felt as if I were witnessing the most important act of man this world had ever seen.

She'd taken her time to reply, busy, perhaps, with her social activities, the power-walking group, the local book club, the hunt for the perfect ingredients for the perfect meal, now that she had time to do such things. Eventually she'd answered.

Sounds like you're settling in perfectly.

Chapter 30

September rain, and the Harbinger of Death stood outside a heavy wooden door covered over with a secure metal frame on a council estate in Kennington, and knocked three times.

Silence inside, silence on the estate.

He knocked again.

Nothing stirred.

He went to the window by the door, peered in through a metal grille, saw only chain curtain and the misty hint of cooker and fridge beyond.

Went back to the door, knocked three times.

A voice, female, loud, called from within, "Fuck off!"

Charlie hesitated. In the course of his career, this was not an entirely unexpected reply, but in this case he hadn't even begun the inciting conversation.

"Ms Young? Ms Agnes Young?"

"Fuck off!"

"Ms Young, my name is Charlie, I'm not from the council."

"Fuck! *Off!*"

"Ms Young, I'm the Harbinger of Death."

"Oh you just fuck right off out . . . " Her words vanished into quieter muttering, then re-emerged again. "*Fuck! Off!* Don't you get me?!"

Charlie swallowed, aware now that this was risking becoming a scene, and he never enjoyed such things. He glanced up and down the walkway, heard no one coming, saw no faces peeking out to examine him, so swallowed again and raised his voice a little. "Ms Young, I've been sent by Death to offer his respects and good wishes to you and your grandfather at this time. If you do not wish to see me, I entirely understand that view and will leave the toolkit outside the door so that . . . "

A chain was pulled off the door in front of him. A lock turned, followed by another. The wooden door was flung back, and there, five foot two of fury in pink tracksuit bottoms and a grey hoodie, fluffy vanilla slippers on her feet and a beehive on her head, was Agnes Young. Her skin was cocoa-bean brown, a pale line of acne across her forehead and down her chin. Her hands were small where they ground into her hips, her hips were wide as she filled the doorway, daring anyone to enter her kingdom. The smell of old cigarettes wafted out past her head, its shape lost beneath the explosion of jet-black lion-mane hair, slicked back from her forehead so tightly it shone and then permitted to erupt like a volcano at the top of her skull. She glowered at Charlie with huge brown eyes set above a small, flat nose, and snarled, "Are you taking the fucking piss?"

"No," he replied, resisting the urge to back away from the force of this girl's glare. "My name's Charlie, I'm the Harbinger of Death, I'm—"

"He's not fucking dying, he's not fucking dying, so you'd better be taking the fucking piss, otherwise you'll have a fucking problem, do you get me?"

Charlie hesitated, licking his lips, trying to find measured words. Rainwater flowed from a pipe above his head, splattering down onto the concrete near his feet, soaking the ankle of his left trouser leg and threatening to seep into his socks. "Ms Young," he said at last, "I am sent sometimes as a warning and sometimes as a courtesy, and my presence need not be about the death of an individual but rather—"

"You here for the estate? Too late – they're all fucking gone. It's fucking over but we're not moving, you hear? You go tell your boss, we're not fucking going anywhere."

The Harbinger of Death stood, heels together, back straight, and wondered if this was how the last-standing pillars of coastal chalk felt as the angry sea battered their bases. In the battle between the girl's anger and his professional cool, there seemed to be little doubt as to who would win.

Then an older voice, warm as flaky pastry from the oven, called out from behind her, and it said, "Agnes, let the man in, will you?"

In another land . . .

. . . before the razor-wire fence . . .

. . . the Harbinger of Famine stood before the loudspeaker that had been inexplicably shoved into her face and exclaimed at the panting, furious, fuming man who wielded it, "Yes, but surely genetic manipulation actually began with Mendel and the peas . . . ?"

On the edge of the sand . . .

. . . the Harbinger of War tugged thoughtfully on the end of her nose, disguising her surprise before murmuring, "How much again per barrel?"

Beneath the white lights of the laboratory . . .

. . . the Harbinger of Pestilence raised his hands defensively and exclaimed, "No thank you! I know it's sealed properly, but

I'm still not going to be the man who drops it, if it's all the same with you!"

In a council block in Kennington . . .

. . . the Harbinger of Death sat on a tatty brown sofa in a tatty brown room, the floor stepping-stoned with brown cardboard boxes full of ancient brown papers, while a man with short silver hair on a face almost ebony black, wearing a dark blue jumper and brown corduroy trousers, blew steam off the top of a mug of tea and said, "Have you had to come far today, son?"

"No, sir," replied Charlie, as Agnes pushed a Liverpool FC mug into his hands, the handle long since lost to the gods of the kitchen. He held it tight, letting the heat settle through his soggy fingers, while old Jeremiah Young examined the toolkit Charlie had left on the seat next to him. "I live in London."

"Ah – that's good. Does Death have Harbingers in every country, or do you travel a lot?"

"I travel."

"You enjoy it? You must spend a lot of time at airports. Unless you have a fiery steed, that is."

"No steed. I . . . Yes, I enjoy it. Travel is better when you meet people, see the way they are living, isn't it?"

"Even if their lives are ending?"

"Sometimes . . . sometimes yes. Sometimes it's for the best . . ." Charlie's voice trailed away; he gestured limply with one hand.

"You don't see the end, is that it? Just the beginning of the end?"

Jeremiah smiled weakly as Agnes perched on the edge of the couch next to him, the toolkit forcing her to sit away from the back, body angled so her knees pointed towards her grandfather, her shoulder turned hard against Charlie. She didn't look at the Harbinger, and he still felt the urge to look away, study the threadbare carpet beneath his feet, torn so thin in one corner that you could see the splintered floorboards below.

The old man went on, without malice, chuckling occasionally at the memories that rose, "I lived here for thirty-eight years. Were you born thirty-eight years ago, Charlie?"

"No, sir."

"Thirty-eight years; when Thatcher was in power, they had a right-to-buy scheme, and I bought, sure I did, and so did any others who could afford to. Didn't feel much anxiety then, thought I was doing the right thing for my kids, but Agnes here . . ."

"Fuck off, Grandad," she retorted, without malice.

". . . can't afford London rents. Where was that place you found in the end?"

"Harpenden."

"Harpenden – that's the nearest place she could afford, but what with the train tickets costing so much, it worked out much the same. And a flat like this, to buy – it'd take you how long to save up for it, on your salary?"

"Thirty-seven years."

"Thirty-seven years. Of course they're not just evicting us – they're gonna buy us out. I've been offered two hundred and fifteen thousand for this place. I said, two hundred and fifteen thousand, there's nothing in all of London you can buy that cheap, and they said that's the going market rate, but I had experts round, estate agents and surveyors . . ."

"Surveyors," agreed Agnes, distantly chiming in with a story she'd heard told many times, a tale now settled deep in her soul.

". . . and they said I was being robbed, and that when they tear this place down like they're gonna, they'll be building one-bedroom flats that'll sell for at least half a million. Five hundred thousand pounds, can you imagine it? For one bedroom – and that's the affordable housing; over there, on the other side, they're building another block, of luxury apartments, once they've taken the building down, but they'll be gated off from the affordable . . ."

"Affordable," snarled Agnes, face twitching into something tight as her fingers idly traced the shape of the hammer in the box.

". . . apartments so that the luxury apartment blocks don't have to feel threatened by all the people who can only get a half-million-pound mortgage for a one-bedroom place, and I said . . ."

"Fuck. Them."

"Agnes . . . I said, I've been here thirty-eight years and I know the place needs work, but we can do it, it was only built sixty years ago and there are buildings still standing that are centuries old, and they said . . ."

"They're being paid," Agnes snapped, head rising to glare at the wall to the right of the Harbinger's head. "The council sold the estate for forty-five million. Do you know how much money they've spent getting all of us out? Forty-nine million. That's their big money-saving scheme, sell the place and spend *our money*, our taxes, so that some rich fucker can build some rich fucking tower block for rich fucking . . ."

"Agnes . . ."

"They said we could be easily rehoused. They sent me a picture, isn't this fucking lovely? You know where it was? Bracknell. I don't even know where fucking Bracknell is, but I looked it up on the map, and it isn't even in the fucking city. You need like, a car to get there, just to drive around, and there's nothing, and I said look, I work in a shop on Tottenham Court Road, I can't live in fucking Bracknell, and they said there are trains every half-hour to Waterloo and I was just like . . . I was like . . ."

She was crying. Back straight, fingers locked on her lap, she was crying. Her grandfather held her hand, and she held his, and the two of them stared into visions only they could see, as tea cooled and the silence shrouded the world beyond their window. Then finally Jeremiah raised his head and looked into Charlie's eyes and said, "Does Death come for an idea? Does Death come for the soul of a thing?"

"Yes," Charlie replied, unable to tear his eyes away from the silent, glaring, weeping girl. "Yes, he does."

"Good. Let him come. I would like to talk with him, I think, about some past and future things."

*

An hour later, the tea drained from its stained mug, Charlie left them, the old man and the girl, and walked back out into the fading rain, head low, feet heavy. He wondered if it was the use of English that made this particular job weigh upon him – in other lands, speaking other tongues, there was something of a barrier raised between himself and his duties, a linguistic wall that made sadness, sorrow, regret, despair into concepts that were expressed phonetically rather than in any emotional way. Speaking his native tongue, in a city he had slowly grown to consider his own, these words had a meaning that needed no translation.

He walked back to Dulwich through the fading light, the streets black mirrors beneath his feet, the yellow lamps coming on all around, the commuters dragging their shopping bags and pouring, sticky-armed and red-faced, from the hollow mouth of the Underground as he walked by.

In the evening, candles burning between them – not because it was special, just because it was nice – Emmi said, "Do you feel English?"

"No. I don't think so. What does English feel like?"

"If you have to go to visit someone in England, see something who's dying ..."

"Death is Death."

"You say that a lot."

"Sorry, I didn't mean ... It's ... Everyone lives and everyone dies. The world changes, and it's the world, and I will live and I will die and ... Do you want to talk about something else?"

"Death doesn't care what nationality you are?"

"No."

"So you don't feel English."

"I feel ... alive. Sometimes being alive means you remember what it feels like for everyone else to be alive too, I guess."

"More fish?"

"Yes please."

"More peas?"

"Definitely."

"There's custard tarts for later."

"You might have to carry me to bed."

And the next morning, he got an email from Maureen in the Milton Keynes office, who said he should probably turn the radio on, and he did, and he heard Agnes's voice ringing out across the airwaves of the local station as she explained, "We'll never stop fighting, never. We'll never give in. It's not about the money, it's not about the council or the building – it's about justice. It's about injustice. It's about us standing up for our homes and our lives. Yesterday the Harbinger of Death came to see my grandad, and he told him to his face, go back to your master, tell him that if he wants to find me, he'll have to come to the Longview himself."

Five minutes later, Charlie received an email from an old drinking friend, whose friendship had grown awkward down the years, with a link to Twitter. There, shared several thousand times and rising, was a picture of the side of his face, taken from the balcony above as he shuffled away into the night.

Chapter 31

"Maureen ... ?"

"It's Dolly, actually, dear."

"I'm so sorry, it's a terrible line."

"What can we do for you, Charlie?"

"I heard the radio, saw the picture ... "

"Ah, yes! I wouldn't worry about it, love. You know, the last Harbinger once found herself shoved onto a catwalk in Tokyo in the middle of a show. Did very well with it – strutted to the end, then back the other way, waved a little, everyone was very proud. Not sure what the promoters got from it, but then you never know how these people ... "

"So I shouldn't worry about it?"

"Not at all! Won't be the first time people have got in a twist about the Harbinger of Death knocking on their door, doubt it'll be the last. You know there was this one time, just before the Berlin Wall fell, and I mean we looked everywhere, we thought maybe the Stasi, maybe the Lubyanka ... "

"Thank you, Dolly, you've been very helpful."

"Any time, love, any time! How's the weather in London? It's been pissing like an elephant with cystitis up here in Milton Keynes!"

Voices.

As a student, Charlie had loved eavesdropping on other people's conversations. In the library, on the train, waiting outside an office, he found the lives of others enthralling, fascinating. As Harbinger of Death, he still enjoyed listening, found that the words washed over him, soothed any doubts and fears after a difficult job, burned away ...

... a child in a hospital in India, born without an arm and a leg ...

... the cracking of the ice ...

... bone feet on stone.

When you were listening to voices, you swam in a living sea, and the turning of the world cleansed all things.

Most of the time.

Maybe not this morning.

"I mean, who the fuck does he think he is, Death, getting involved in a political issue like this? Sure, we all know him, we all respect him, primal force of the universe and that, but really, if he wants to stick his nose into public affairs, then there are more appropriate channels ... "

"If the Pope wants to come to the US, then he's gotta understand the folks he's dealing with here. You can't say that trickle-down economics has failed, that's just Marxist talk, that's the Pope being the mouthpiece of left-wing liberals jealous of what we've achieved. Now I'm not saying he's a bad man, but clearly he's been got at by the environmentalist lobby, by gays and Zionists, by the communist conspiracy, and you know what,

God may have made him infallible in religious matters, but when it comes to politics, he's just a guy in a funny hat."

" . . . yeah, I get it, I get where she's coming from, but like, talking to Hezbollah? I was like, whoa, I mean, bombing isn't working, but *talking* . . . ?"

"I don't feel the need to dignify that with an answer."

" . . . a pig's head! A pig's head and he shoved his penis right into its . . ."

"God said thou shalt not kill. Shall you kill your unborn child in your womb?"

"Is this your girlfriend? Oh my God, she's beautiful – you've done so well! She looks just like that actress – you look just like that actress – oh you must be pleased."

"Yeah. She's also really clever."

"And are you two . . . you know . . . thinking of a day?"

"No."

In his bedroom, carved into the slope of the roof in a small flat in south London, Charlie lay on his back as the rain tap-tapped on the skylight, and listened to music instead.

His newest CD was a compilation sold for approximately £3 a disc by the woman who ran his hotel in Nuuk. She'd put it together herself – with the consent of the artists, she swore – and with Greenland being the size it was, Charlie found it easy to imagine that everyone he heard was at the very least a distant cousin of hers, if not a close personal friend. The first two tracks were pop songs from the 1970s, sung in Danish in a style that was best described as Abba without joy. Then electric guitars started growing distorted, Auto-Tune arrived on the mixing desk, boy bands joined in some rough semblance of harmony and the songs became a mixture of Kalaallisut and broken English, ballads sung to forsaken love and low job prospects, electric zooms and swishes at the beginning and end of every phrase.

Charlie listened, and tried not to feel disappointment. The rain fell and his next appointment wasn't for nine days. Sometimes it was like that – sometimes he'd fly twelve thousand miles in a couple of days, zipping across the continents without sleep to deliver this or that to Death's awaiting appointees; sometimes nothing would happen, and no news would come, though surely Death continued to wander the globe, and children were born and old men died, while Charlie stayed at home.

He rolled onto his stomach, pulled out his mobile phone, flicked through his calendar. His next appointment was in northern Italy, a police chief suspected of being incorruptible, who'd retired early before his disease of moral correctness could infect the rest of the department. Charlie stared into the clean-shaven face of the man on his screen, and wondered what his fate would be. In another life, twenty years ago, he could have been a model with a jaw like that, but too much time as a copper had set his features into a frown, and now the only brands that would hire him would be men's outdoor clothes, trying to tap into a macho market of account managers and insurance salesmen who knew that in another life they could have hunted bears with sharpened sticks, oh yes they could . . .

Now he was on Charlie's visit list, and maybe he had a dodgy heart, maybe something genetic, maybe he'd said something a little unwise about some crime lord, or some gangster's pet politician, maybe . . .

Charlie turned his phone off, rolled onto his back. Nine days. He could take the train to Italy; so long as he found an equivalent flight, claimed expenses only up to the same amount, paid for the rest of the journey from his own pocket, it could work. Eurostar to Paris, coffee in a bistro, sleeper train down to Venice, or maybe even the daytime service, the scenic route past Geneva, through the Swiss Alps, make it a proper trip, see if Emmi could come, when was half-term? Get away from it all for a while, get away from . . .

. . . home.

And other foreign countries.

The music changed. No more drums, no more electronics. An old man's voice, speaking a language Charlie didn't understand. A song he didn't know, a tune he couldn't replicate, hard to say if it had a key or obeyed any classical music rules. It came from somewhere far behind the singer's nose, a strange, rattling sound that might perhaps mimic the song of the wind through narrow corridors of ice. Not a human sound, but an animal perhaps, a singing wild animal somewhere in the dark, a creature that stood upon a breaking glacier, that lamented its dying world, the falling white, the way the Professor ran towards the . . .

Charlie sat up fast, turned the music off. Went into the living room, turned the computer on, stared furiously at train times London–Paris, checked his bank account, put on easy Europop, valiant love triumphant at great odds, beautiful girls and hunky men, you are my sunshine, my moonlight, my fire, my ocean, my summer's sky, my ice queen, my goddess, my warrior, my joy, my sorrow, my raspberry jam on toasted brown bread with the crusts cut off, my . . .

He chose his seats for the Paris train, moved over to the checkout, ready to buy.

The phone rang.

He answered, without really paying any attention.

"Charlie?" said a voice, familiar and far away. "Charlie, it's Patrick."

Chapter 32

They met in an office off Piccadilly. A long desk in the lobby was staffed by three people, none of whom seemed interested in dealing with Charlie until he'd stood at least five minutes before them, hoping for attention. When they finally decided to notice him, they took his name, his postcode, his photo, and a contact email address. Then they asked him to wait while they phoned up.

He waited on a sofa. To his right, a long bank of TV screens displayed the news, current stocks and shares, and the inspirational message of the moment.

Excellence is a never-ending journey.

Magazines were artfully fanned on the table, untouched. Barriers opened and closed quietly between him and the lift banks. When someone came down to find him, she was young, dark hair tied in a high bun, sharp heels clacking on the polished floor, ankles slightly unstable as she walked. There were two consoles controlling four lifts, and no buttons inside. Instead, you selected where you wanted to go in advance, and the console pointed you towards the lift you required. Inside the elevator, screens gave more helpful advice.

We take pride in service.

Customer satisfaction is our no.1 priority.

Ours is a loving corporate family.

"This is . . . nice . . . " he murmured into the awkward silence of the lift.

The woman smiled. "There's two toilets for four hundred people."

On the seventh floor, the elevator stopped, and Charlie followed the wobbling woman through two more sealed doors, which she opened with a badge hung around her neck on elastic. An open-plan office was revealed, the workers in straight rows, some wearing headphones, most silent, a computerised hush over all that could only be created from a lack of privacy leading to a lack of conversation. The same lamp sat above the same screens; the same stationery was in the same white pots on the same desks. Very few had bothered to personalise their areas; only one or two rebels in the furthest corners had thrown up calendar cut-outs of favourite actors, photos of smiling friends, a burbling child.

Numbers rolled across screens, and eyebrows drew together at their mysteries. No one looked up as the Harbinger of Death passed by, and he found himself feeling unclean in this pristine place.

A little bank of rooms, segregated by soundproof glass, lined a window looking out across the street towards more offices of more busy numbers. Inside a few of the largest, men and women sat round tables covered with notes, and flipcharts showed crude diagrams of numbers going up, numbers going down, numbers wobbling unconvincingly. In one room, a single A2 piece of paper pinned to the wall simply said: EXPLORATION.

At the end of this row, another glass room, like any other, with a white desk, white pencil pot, white pencils, and sitting behind this looking at a white computer screen, a man in grey and blue, no tie, a flash of titanium-white at his wrist.

Charlie didn't recognise him at first, his hair combed, his shirt ironed, his shoes polished and bright. But look again, and there was the face he'd met on the ice, frowning at something Charlie couldn't see. Patrick Fuller, busy man in a busy world, glancing up as Charlie opened the door, his face splitting at once into a friendly smile. Getting to his feet, firm handshake, Charlie, he said, so good of you to come.

"Mr Fuller," he murmured, sitting stiff on the edge of the seat opposite the corporate man's.

"Patrick – surely you must call me Patrick."

"Patrick. I didn't expect your call."

"Heard about you on the news. I was in town, and as you see ... " A gesture, taking in the office, the computer, the empty walls, the bare floors. Charlie frowned, wondering what it was he was meant to perceive in this vacuum. "How have you been?" he added, riding quickly through Charlie's confusion.

"Fine. Good. Fine. You?"

"Excellent, of course, keeping busy, you know how it is, but ... excellent, yes, as always. You made it back from Greenland in one piece, then?"

"Yes."

"Good! You should have let me give you a lift, but I understand how these things ... "

"Milton Keynes covers all my travel expenses, but thank you. And on the glacier ... thank you for that, too. For ... I appreciate it."

"Not at all. It's not every day you are invited to see the end of the world by Death himself."

"And did you see it?"

Patrick puffed his cheeks, an oversized expression for the question. "Hard to say." He leant back in his chair, which pivoted back gently with him, huffed out his breath, gave a little laugh, as if relieved this tricky introduction had been handled, and then, in the brisk manner of a man sharing a familiar joke, said, "So – the Longview Estate, yes?"

Charlie, sitting barely on his chair, feet flat on the floor, heels together, toes pointing straight to the front. Patrick Fuller, lounging back in his executive throne. Two men in the same room, worlds apart.

"Yes?" he said at last, not sure what else was expected from him.

"You've been paying a visit – business, I assume?"

"Business. Yes."

"Hope they didn't take it too badly. There's been a lot of problems down there, of course, you'll have heard the stories."

"They were ... Are you here to witness again?" Charlie blurted. "On the ice you said you were to witness."

"Yes," mused Patrick, gently rocking the chair from side to side at the contemplation. "Yes, I was. But no!" The chair stopped, he leant forward quickly, steepling his fingers and smiling over the tips of them. "Not this time. Consultancy, mostly, the usual thing."

"Consultancy?"

"For the developer. Investment, that's what we do. Usually we do large-scale infrastructure – electricity, water, telecommunications – but sometimes housing, corporate, you know the kind of thing. I was in town, and I heard about your visit to the estate and I thought ... well. There's someone I know. And your boss, of course, never far behind. Like a garbage truck at a picnic, yes?"

"That's not how most people describe him."

Patrick's lips smiled, and his eyes did not. Then again, leaning back, every motion he made, every twist and lean and turn of his body, a punctuation mark, a line break, a new idea about to be fulfilled. "I've thought a lot about what happened on the ice," he said briskly. "At the time I didn't understand it. The old man . . . it was very sad, but I thought . . . The message said the end of the world. Death invites you to witness the end of the world – no, the end of *a* world, I think that was it, very important distinction of course, very important; there I think hangs the rub. I thought, what the hell is he playing at, dragging me out here to see – with all due respect – a man die like that, I mean, what the hell? But I talked to my wife about it –"

"You're married?"

"Yes."

"I didn't know."

"She's in the States, that's where I'm based, of course, most of the time, but work is – you know how it is. Anyway, I talked to my wife, told her about the old man and the glacier, and do you know what she said?"

"No."

"She said, 'Of course you saw the end of the world. A man died, and his world is over and will never live again.' Do you think that's what Death intended? Do you think it was a lesson?"

"I couldn't say."

"Come, come, you're the Harbinger, the one who goes before, you must have views!"

"I am . . . I am the bridge. I am . . . I hadn't ever seen someone die. I mean, I've seen . . . When I was younger, my father died, but it was slow. I was there at the end, and I saw . . . As Harbinger, you arrive, and you go before, and then you leave, but on the ice, for the first time, I saw Ule die and Death was there."

"By which you mean . . . "

"Death was there. He stood on the ice. You didn't see?"

"No, I was rather preoccupied. Death himself, the actual . . . ?"

"On the edge of the glacier. He vanished when the ice cracked. He's . . . unmistakable."

"I imagine. Maybe I can't, maybe that's a lie, maybe I . . . but maybe I can, at that. And now Death sends you to a housing estate in Kennington."

"Yes."

"For the old man?"

Charlie flinched, wasn't sure why. "I don't know."

"You gave him a gift, didn't you – that's something you do?"

"I did."

"May I ask ... "

"No." His answer, harder than he'd intended, surprising himself.

Patrick smiled again, a default expression that should have been something else, and which time had trained into a neutral smile, and made meaningless in the process. Seeing it, Charlie felt again the cold of the ice, a weight dead in his bones, and wondered what Death felt when he walked upon the earth, and what Patrick would see when he beheld him at last.

Then Patrick said, "Charlie. I was asked to talk to you. By some of my partners. This business with the estate, the girl, the old man ... it was all in hand and then the Harbinger of Death comes and ... Whoever said that business and pleasure can't be mixed clearly was in the wrong business. It's good to see you again."

"You too."

"Dinner. I'm having drinks with some people who I'd love you to meet."

"I don't ... "

"Charlie, we were both on the ice. Please. When you tell people that you are the Harbinger of Death, how do they react?"

"Depends."

"For the most part?"

"The young are more frightened than the old."

"Do you have many friends – forgive me, impertinent question, but I thought ... "

"I have ... " Charlie stopped, smiled, looked away. "I never had many friends. That's me, I think, though. It's just ... me."

"But the job ... "

"Perhaps making new friends is a bit harder, yes."

"I can't imagine people refuse to talk to you."

97

"They answer the phone, if I call."

"But don't call back."

"Not very much, no."

"You must have known that would happen, when you took the job?"

"I . . . It wasn't a price I minded paying."

Patrick nodded, stood quickly, pulled his jacket off the back of his chair and pushed his arms into the sleeves, tutting briskly to himself. "Charlie," he exclaimed. "I am not frightened of you, or your work. Death called me to witness, and I came. Your work brings you to London; London has some fantastic restaurants. Now – let's get drunk."

Chapter 33

A bar, squirrel bulbs above polished wooden surfaces, dull-growing yellow filaments, waiters in white clerk's sleeves, black waistcoats, pristine white tea towels tucked into their belts, never to be used.

A drinks menu, cocktails that sizzled, cocktails that smoked, wine from before the digital age, wine from the mountains, wine from the hot valley floors. Beer brewed by three men in a tiny factory in Hoxton; beer brewed from berries hand-picked by women in Sweden. Charlie looked at the menu and prayed that Patrick was paying, and was unsurprised and relieved when the other man put his card behind the bar.

There wasn't any music – didn't need to be. A queue at the door that Patrick bypassed with a smile, crowds pressed in close inside, the chink of glasses, the delight of friends long-parted, their friendship ready to be re-baptised in alcohol. Flirting couples, your eyes are full of colour, there is a golden band around the rim . . .

"Why are there two pink pompoms on your phone?" asked the woman, all leg and hair, a travelling ozone disaster around every perfectly permed yellow lock.

"Touch them . . . " said the man, hips forward, shoulders back, his body bowed in expectation.

She touched them.

"You just touched my balls!" he exclaimed, whooping at his own cunning, and she laughed, a high-shrill titter, as if a mad scientist had combined a piccolo with a Gatling gun, each bullet a polished white tooth, a weapon to be fired only when smiling.

Charlie looked away, wondered if it would be rude to leave already, to catch the bus back to Dulwich, the train to Paris, hire a car, get away to somewhere else, go talk to a woman in the mountains or a man by the sea . . .

Then Patrick saw three of his friends come through the door, and he waved cheerfully and called them over, and they waved back and smiled the same alien, baseline smile that was always on Patrick's face, and said, "Oh my God, this is the *actual* Harbinger of Death, it's just, well I thought you'd be dressed all in black!" and everyone laughed, and Charlie decided that the time had come to get very drunk indeed.

Chapter 34

No, but yeah, but listen to me . . .

Ms Young, you can ask your questions at the end of this meeting.

I've been asking questions! I've written to my MP, to my councillors, I went to the housing office, I went to the fucking library to look at the fucking planning permission . . .

Ms Young . . .

LISTEN TO ME! Please, please just listen to me. You're

gonna tear down our homes, the place where we live, and I get it, you're skint, you're skint, you need more cash, basic services and that, but like, there's nearly two thousand of us, mums and dads and kids and grandparents, and we're all living there fine, just fine, and like, most of us work nearby or go to school round the corner, and our lives, we built our lives, not just work but like, everything we do, and you're gonna sell it and I looked and they're gonna build new homes . . .

There are obligations to build affordable housing . . .

Yeah, but Section 106, which is like, what you're talking about – that was changed so that developers don't have to and now like, affordable in London is nearly half a million quid, and that's not affordable, I mean, maybe it is for you, but it's not for me, I don't think it's affordable for any of the flunkies you've brought with you . . .

Ms Young, if you will not behave in a decorous manner . . .

You're killing us. You're fucking killing us. You're destroying our lives. And when you're done, you're gonna have spent more money on doing it than you made on the sale, and there'll be less housing for fewer people, and our lives will be done. I don't know what we're meant to do. Every time I speak I just get told to talk to another department, and it never ends. No one takes responsibility; no one has a final say. What are we meant to do? What the fuck are we meant to do?

Chapter 35

Voices.

Usually they cleanse, usually they wipe away the weight of the soul, but tonight . . .

. . . so look, I'm a woman, yes, I'm a woman and I run a business. I admit, when a woman comes to me, applying for a senior role, I hesitate. I do, I really do, of course, because she might get pregnant, she might meet someone, decide to have a baby, and then that's maternity leave I'm paying, that's maternity leave and no guarantee she'll come back, so now I've hired someone to cover her work and just as they're learning the skills, just as they're getting useful, she returns but I still have to pay the cost of the cover's insurance, of their redundancy. I mean if you're going to pursue work pursue work, but even a woman who says she's not going to, I look at her and I just think – darling, one day you'll have a baby, and then you won't care about my needs, so what use are you to me?

I'm not sure that's how maternity cover works . . .

I'm just telling you as someone who runs a business how I feel about this. I'm a job creator, I create jobs . . .

The problem with asylum seekers – no, hear me out – the problem is that they come over here, and they expect to be looked after. They're not interested in working, they don't care about the strain they put on the system, they feel entitled – that's the word, isn't it, *entitled* – to everything the country has to give them, and why? Because they've suffered. Well, we've all suffered, people in this country are suffering, and they're more entitled than you are, I hate to say it . . .

(Charlie.)

That's bullshit, that's bullshit, I'm sorry, I have to call bullshit because they're people, aren't they, they're all just people, and as for women, well, by what right do we judge women, I mean all women, and there it is, isn't it, there it is, all women judged, everyone put into the basket of "you're going to have a baby so I can't hire you". I mean, Jesus, men have penises and they put them in some fucking stupid places

(Charlie.)

and they go off their fucking heads and I'm not like "you're a man you might be an arsehole so I can't hire you", because "you're a woman so you might have a baby". I mean what the fuck? What the fuck are we saying to our children, to our daughters, my daughter is never going to get equality because . . .

101

(Charlie!)

Charlie jerked, nearly spilling his drink, blinked some semblance of awareness back into his face, saw Patrick, smiling at him wearily over the bar, while around him, Patrick's friends and acquaintances — somehow grown to seven in number — argued and bickered from atop their stools, hands flying in tight circles as they strove to both express their indignation and avoid hitting each other with their polished fingernails.

Patrick waited as Charlie forced himself back into the room, pulling his mind out of ...

... some other place, where rumbled the sound of thunder.

"Are you all right?" Patrick murmured. "You seemed a little lost."

"No. Sorry — I was ... sorry."

The nearest woman turned to Charlie, a gold choker at her neck, gold rings on her fingers, and said, "What do you think?"

"About ...?"

"Migrants."

"I don't know if I ... What kind of thing do you mean?"

"Do you think we should let them in? I mean, I understand war, of course, I understand how difficult it must be, but ... "

(On the border of Iraqi Kurdistan, the Harbinger of War took another selfie of herself with the tribal leader, before turning to him and his men and saying, "I'm sorry — whose side are you on again?" The soldier waited for her words to be translated, then started back in surprise before at last, pointing with his index finger into her bewildered face, he exclaimed, "Very funny!" and told his men the joke, and they laughed and laughed and laughed.)

"I don't think it's simple, I don't think it's ... "

"Someone has to make decisions, don't they? Someone has to make a clear, executable choice ... "

(In the footsteps of the Harbinger of War comes her master. Today he comes by Honda, that being the only car available for hire at the local airport, and Death sits in the passenger seat and tries to find north on the map, and the world burns where their shadows fall.)

102

"Leadership should be clear. Leadership doesn't need complexity."

(Charlie? Charlie . . .)

Charlie stood in the men's toilets, pressed his head against the wall as the Tornado 3000 ("The world's most powerful and hygienic hand dryer!") rippled the skin across the back of his hand, pulling and tugging at flesh like waves across the sea. There was ice in the urinals, for reasons he didn't understand, and hand-moisturising lotion by the sink, and the mirrors in which his tired grey face reflected back at him were tinted bronze, as if attempting to offer an instant tan to its clients. Dried flowers were carefully arranged in white clay pots, a strange, dead mockery of Japanese flower arranging, tied up with silver wire.

Two men came through the door.

. . . if he can't do the job then I'm sorry, he's got to . . .

. . . yes, but disabilities, the disability means . . .

. . . I've got a business to run, I've got money to make, I've got . . .

Charlie nearly ran from the toilet, head pounding.

Standing in the street, breathing cold air. The grumbling traffic of Haymarket to the left, waiting to get through the tangle of street lights around Piccadilly Circus. The imperial luxury of St James's below, palaces and old nobility, offices owned by Lord Such and Such, son of Lord and Lady Such and Such, men and women who grumbled it was such a burden being aristocracy these days, such a lot of hard work. Hairdressers to the movie stars, tailored suits and polished brass buttons, regalia, private drivers in black caps and white gloves, trouser legs creased down the middle . . .

Charlie couldn't breathe. He turned to press his hands against the glass front of the bar, stretching out like a runner, and exhaled slowly through his nose, counting backwards from ten. Then, again, and one more time, when a voice said,

"Charlie?"

He looked up.

A woman – one of Patrick's friends, he couldn't remember

103

which – a vanilla-cream trouser suit, jacket slung over one arm, cigarette drooping out of the corner of her mouth, high heels that made her even taller than she already was, hair dyed to hide the onset of grey, mouth pulled back wide into the same habitual, welcoming smile he always saw on Patrick's face. Only no, more than that – the smile had nuance, it greeted strangers, it appreciated a wry joke, it marvelled at its own foolishness, it flickered in anger, it expressed a whole range of sentiment except, perhaps, pleasure. It was the smile of the consummate businessman, and in that moment, Charlie knew he'd never be able to smile that way.

He straightened, self-conscious, cheeks burning, and tried to force something to match it onto his face, and failed. "I'm sorry, I was just ... getting some air."

"Are you all right – ah, cigarette?" A question, immediately forestalled in case Charlie might want to answer. She held out a cigarette case of embossed gold, two initials – KL – blazoned on the front. Charlie hesitated, for a moment tempted, then shook his head. He'd tried smoking back at college, and it had always made him cough and feel sick, though he'd pretended that, like all Strong Men, he enjoyed it and felt fine. No one had believed him, and out of sympathy his friends had stopped offering.

"I'm ... fine, thank you. I'd ... I'll go back inside, maybe say goodbye to Patrick. It's been a long day, and I've got a train ... "

He moved to go, but as he did the woman said, "Charlie? I may call you Charlie, mayn't I?"

He hesitated, turned back, realised that in her heels, she was a few inches taller than he was, and the height of her shoes created strange curves in her body so that her hips came forward, her shoulders tilted back, her chin stuck down again to counteract the overall effect, and like a rippling sine-wave, there was no part of her that wasn't in some way contorted. It wasn't an unpleasing effect, but he couldn't imagine it was a comfortable one to maintain.

"You don't know me," she smiled, one hand resting on the top of his shoulder, holding him in place. "But Patrick told me all about you. How long have you been the Harbinger of Death?"

"Bit over a year."

"That's not so long. Do you like it?"

"It's all right."

"Do you meet the big man much?"

"No."

"You're just . . . how did Patrick put it . . . the one who goes before?"

"That's right."

"Interesting."

She took another long inhale of cigarette, her hand still latched onto Charlie's shoulder. Exhaled out of the corner of her mouth, blowing the smoke away from his face, smiled again, crocodile bright. "I've got a friend who says she met Death, saw him hold the hand of a cyclist who got hit by a bus. Said he was fearsome and wonderful and terrible and kind and . . . She's getting married to some guy in a few weeks' time, usually I'd say she went for the wrong type, but this one, he's almost too good for her. He teaches kickboxing and manufactures valves for plastic pipes. I like him. I think they'll be . . . very happy together."

Is this a good thing? Is this a bad? By her voice, it's hard to tell.

Another exhale, a puff of smoke, stubbing out the remains, is he sure – yes, he's sure, thanks, he'll just be off . . . "And did your boss ask you to stick your nose into the Longview job?"

Her hand, on his shoulder, tighter now. Charlie found it hard to meet her eyes, looked away, hated himself for looking away, looked back, anger coming from somewhere, he wasn't sure where, something deep inside. "Yes," he replied, voice hard and flat as slabs beneath his feet. "He did."

Another pull, another puff, taking her time. "Why do you think he did that?"

"Presumably because something, someone, is dying."

"The old man?"

"Mr Young," he corrected, sharper than he'd meant. "Maybe."

Again, the smile, now the last pull of the cigarette, drop the stub, stamp it out beneath her shoe, still holding his shoulder, the smile wider. "Bullshit," she said. "It's bullshit. I talk the way I find it, it's how I get by, my time is precious, I don't have time to waste on meaningless words. Patrick wants to take things softly, he's always put value on these things, but not me. People call me blunt, and that's good, I'll take it, thank you very much. The old man is going to die, and Death gives a fuck – well bullshit to that. Do you know why it's bullshit? *Because all he has to fucking do is move house.* Jesus, it's not like where he lives is fucking Marble Arch anyway – it's a shitty little flat in a shitty little estate, he should just take the money and go somewhere decent, old folk's home, maybe, spend the cash on a bit of residential care, and when it runs out, he can sponge off the state like everyone else he's ever fucking known."

These words, said without malice, the smile still in place, her hand still on his shoulder, fingers digging into bone. "And that kid of his? What the fuck does she even think she's doing, living with her grandad? Fuck me, how old is she, get a life, get a fucking mortgage, just get on with it! When I was her age, I was already two promotions up the ladder and accelerating, and I didn't come from much, I didn't have the cash, the family home, but I worked for it, I just worked to make it happen."

Charlie tried to move away, and she held him tight, weight-lifter arms beneath her silk blouse, turning her body to plant it between him and the door. "Capitalism," she explained softly, "requires that there is a difference in wealth. That's just how it works. And I don't say it's fair, and I don't say it's nice, but it's the best system we've got and the wealth that these people have, the money the council is giving them – that's more wealth than most people could ever fucking dream of, and they're giving us shit?"

"Us?" stammered Charlie, neck bending to stare up into the woman's face.

"I run the project," she replied, casual as a butterfly in spring, a flick of her fingers at the empty air to encapsulate the money, the people, the tools at her command, a little thing, such a little thing. "The estate is mine, I bought it from a council willing to sell, and I'll sell it to the people, to the grateful people looking to buy. And they will be grateful – there's a housing crisis in this country, haven't you heard? At every stage, at every step of the way there will be people getting down on their knees and thanking me for having the vision to make something better; the people I employ, the people who buy the homes, the businesses who come to cater to them, the council for raising the quality of the area, I am ... " She hesitated, licking her lips, searching for the words. "I am a developer, and proud of that word. To develop – I make something better from something old. The Longview was a shitty mcshitty bit of old; it was old bricks for old ideas. We're making something better, and I do genuinely believe that, and if your boss, if *Death* thinks there's something worth shoving his nose into, then you tell him to come talk to me in person, *in person*. I'm not afraid. Fear is the only thing that has ever held humanity back from progress, and I ... am a humane person. Do you understand, Charlie, Harbinger of Death? Do you understand what I'm saying?"

He nodded, slow, no words coming to take their place.

Her smile, which had never faltered, brightened now into a thing that was almost real. She let go of his shoulder, reached down for her cigarette case, drew another from its shell, popped it between her lips, smiled again, causing the end to bob up and down, and talking with her lips barely moving as she clasped the tube added, "Patrick can get romantic about these things. He thinks we should respect the forces of history and the forces of nature. I have no such fucking stupid ideas."

A silver cigarette lighter, the glow of embers as she inhaled.

Charlie stared at her dumbly for a moment, then blurted, "What if Agnes and Jeremiah refuse to go?"

Her eyes flickered sideways, incredulity on her face. "Then we fucking tear the building down around them, are you kidding me?" She spun quickly on the spot, an idea now lodged and taking root, snatched the cigarette from her lips and with the burning end stabbed it through the air towards Charlie's face, emphasising every idea as it formed. "Did you see the campaign they tried to run? Not just them – the entire estate. They got fifty-three thousand signatures on a petition to save the place, presented it to the council, tried to get it debated in Parliament, took it to the local newspapers, got eighty thousand Twitter followers and a Facebook campaign, and do you know what it counted for? Do you know what it meant at the end of the day? It meant shit. It meant fucking shit. And why? Because the deal was done and could not be undone; the papers were signed, the money was paid. That's law. That's the way the world works, and no amount of whining changes it. And you know what else? All the bad publicity they brought down on us, yes, it came, and yes, it hurt us – for a day. That's how long the dirt clung, maybe a bit less. Twitter, Facebook, TV and internet news – you know how long a story stays up on a news website these days, unless it's about some celebrity scandal? Guess. Go on – guess. Three hours. That's how much we hurt. And then the world turned, and someone tweeted something new, and everyone retweeted it and moved on, and nothing fucking changes. That's the world. That's people power. That's all it fucking means."

And the Harbinger of Death stood silent in the street, before a twenty-thousand-pound face and a ten-thousand pound suit, his toes bumping against seven-hundred-pound shoes, and for a moment he thought he saw a figure behind this woman, this snarling woman whose smile now had vanished completely, lips curled and teeth bared – he thought he saw a figure, watching far off, who shook his head and walked away.

And Charlie looked into the woman's eyes, and realised he had nothing to say.

(And in the great shopping mall, Famine stands outside the health food shop, and stares at the giant vats of protein shake, and watches the videos of workouts on the wall, and looks down again at the detox dietary supplements, and finds herself in the awkward position, for a rider of the Apocalypse, of not really knowing what to think . . .)

(On the coast of the Black Sea, War holds out his glass with a cry of, "*Zdorovye!*" and chuckles as the captain of the war-ship chinks back and smiles uneasily, pennants fluttering in the breeze.)

(In a clinic in southern California, Pestilence nods emphatically, her chin cupped in the palm of her hand, and says, "Oh I know! I *know*. I know! Vaccines are just about making money, at the end of the day ... ")

And at the foot of Nelson's Column, Death sits on his haunches by the beggar man, and drops some pennies into his cup and muses, "Tell me — would you say that the rise of contactless credit cards has changed the nature of your work?" and the man shudders, and makes no reply, for the rain has soaked through his coat, and the cold is settling on his bones, and no one has spoken to him for a very, very long time.

And that night Death rode a pale horse across the surface of the earth, and walked to the waiting boat with the barefoot migrants, and knocked on the bars of the prison door, and held up the chemicals to the light and said, "These look a little cloudy to me ... " and snipped the umbilical cord of the newborn child and whispered, "I'll see you some other day," and held the hand of the widow as she lay alone, and laughed and laughed and laughed as the city burned and

Charlie said, "I should go home now."

The woman — he hadn't learned her name — smiled again, always, smiling, as if she had never done anything else with her lips in all her days, and took another puff of cigarette. "Tatty bye-byes," she said, staring out to some other place. "Tra-la and all that."

Charlie hesitated, thought of defiance, of rage, of spitting in her face, and instead hung his head, and walked away.

Chapter 36

Well I used to live in Mumbai, but actually, Mumbai, there's such a disconnect between ...

Paris. Proud of Paris, love Paris, and for my work it's very . . .

Canberra. You've never been to Canberra? No. Neither has anyone else.

Birmingham, the Harbinger of Death explained. But I live in London now.

The others laughed, the Harbinger of Famine rattling her chopsticks against the side of her plate. They didn't often get together, not like this, not the four of them, but sometimes for an earthquake, sometimes a tsunami, sometimes a rebellion or a bombing or . . .

"Sorry, sorry," said the Harbinger of War. "I know I never get to come to your natural-disasters club, miss out on all the floods and the avalanches – Mosul! I spend just so much time in Mosul . . . "

"The taxi fares in that part of the world have become exorbitant . . . "

"My favourite hotel, such a beautiful place, but these days . . . "

"Trying to get Airbnb in Mogadishu. I said, no, you stay with the family, but you pay . . . "

"I thought maybe I should have a base, a house," mused the Harbinger of Death, "somewhere to make mine. Maybe settle down one day, put down roots, a community, a choir, a place with little shops, people who'd know my name . . . "

Again, uproarious laughter, Charlie, you're so funny, too funny!

"This one time, in Beijing, the smog got so bad that I . . . "

" . . . camels, camels are the most amazing creatures, it's just . . . "

"Problem is, there's oil underneath, isn't there? Whenever the geologists turn up, that's when I know we're in for . . . "

"I saw a football game in Sri Lanka," mused Charlie. "And there was this boy there with the most amazing left foot you'll ever see."

Afterwards, once the four of them waved off the UN convoy, and the Harbinger of War had gone to take a piss with a man from the Russian Embassy, the Harbinger of Famine turned to

Charlie, put a hand on his arm and said, "You must choose the life you live at the time you live it, Charlie."

He, confused, his face swept by the headlamps of the departing lorries, sodium at his back and wire fencing all around, stared into the older woman's face. "Once upon a time, in India, the young men were all told to work hard, make money, build a house, be a soldier, be a man. Then they grew older, and married, and were soldiers no more, and ploughed the field and picked fruit with the children and taught them how to hunt. Only when they had done these earthly things did they retreat into the ashram or sacred grove, to think on life's mysteries. They were always going to do this deed, they were always going to come to the sacred place, and always had the holy man within them. But before they were holy men, they were sons and fathers, until the time was right. You still have time, Charlie. You can still choose."

Charlie tried to find something to say, but the Harbinger of Famine had spotted a medic from an NGO she knew, and to whom she had so much more she needed to say.

"Emmi? Emmi, hi, I'm sorry, I . . . "

"What time is it?"

"I'm sorry, I was just . . . "

"Jesus."

"I'm sorry. I didn't . . . I'll go away."

"You've woken me up now. What the hell is wrong, Charlie?"

"I . . . I don't know. I went to a housing estate and then a man called and there were drinks and there were people and . . . and one spoke to me, she said that . . . I'm very tired. I might be a little drunk."

"You think?"

"I'm sorry. I didn't mean to . . . Sorry."

"Are you okay?"

"I'll be fine."

"Bullshit, that is."

"I'll be fine, honest I will."

"Work getting you down?"

111

"I thought . . . You wouldn't think that this bit . . . but . . . I'll call in the morning. I'm sorry. I didn't mean to wake you. I'll . . . I'll make up for it, I . . . "

"Charlie, listen it's . . . "

The empty sound of the broken line.

Alone, awake in his flat in London

– his flat in London, fucking hell, what's he ever done to make it his? Music collection around the floor, not enough shelf space, a chest of drawers shoved full of T-shirts from obscure football clubs, but anything else? Pictures, paintings, scratches on the walls, stains on the carpet, the wear and tear of a house well lived in – fuck that, not him, not here, not the Harbinger of Death . . .

Alone.

Awake.

In his flat in London.

The Harbinger of Death stared up at the slanted ceiling, and felt cold, even though after the ice, he'd thought he'd never feel cold again.

Chapter 37

"I'm not an actor, I'm a performance artist. Conventional theatre has given in to money, corporatism and money. Look at the West End – it's all the same old stuff designed to please, to make people happy. Theatre should be powerful, it should be a tool for social change, it should make you question everything about yourself and the world you live in! I don't think traditional plays do that. They're just words written by middle-class white people about middle-class white problems. Look, I know *I'm* middle class and white, but I actually have things to say, stories to tell that matter. No, I can't afford to pay you for your time. No, there isn't any

112

budget. You'll have to make do. This kind of work – well, you do it for love."

" . . . that's not really what I had in mind . . . "

"If I had to choose between funding a theatre or building another hospital, it's not even a choice, is it?"

"My voice is my tool!"

"Maybe you just don't know how to be what I want you to be."

"Are you the lighting girl? No, I don't know anything about lighting. Of course, I'm sure you'll do a great job, and I trust your artistic judgement and value your opinion. So I've written down exactly what we want, and my cousin is going to tell you how to..."

"Red lorry yellow lorry red lorry yellow lorry red lorry . . . "

"Personally I play as a thief-wizard fusion, usually with a weapon specialisation of short sword and maxed-out points in the elemental school. It's great, just so much fun and really beautiful to look at, but is it *art*?"

Chapter 38

The day before they started demolishing the Longview Estate, the bailiffs came. They pulled out the furniture and left it in a pile outside the door, except for the bed, which was too big to fit in the raised walkway, so they dropped it down onto the concrete below. They smashed a picture – not on purpose, just because they didn't really care about the handling – and broke some plates, and all the paper fell out of Agnes's schoolwork files when the ring binder gave way, and fluttered up into the sky like feathers from a dove. Jeremiah sat mute on his old sofa outside the kitchen window. Agnes screamed and cried, and in the end the bailiffs called the police. In fairness to the cops, they were shocked – genuinely shocked by what they were seeing – but they couldn't stop it, not now, the law was the law. A WPC sat by Agnes, once she had no more fight to give, and said, "Look, love, let's get a van and let's find a place to store this stuff, and we'll find you a hotel and . . . "

Agnes Young looked up into the face of the pig, the filth, the fuzz, PC Plod, the law, and for a moment almost managed to see a human being looking back at her, but then the uniform got in the way and she looked down and didn't speak, so the copper went to her grandfather, and eventually the pair of them hired a man with a van (exorbitant, demanded an extra £50 after he had a hard time parking), and found a storage centre with room to spare (not as badly priced as it could have been) and a hotel room for the night, and Jeremiah shook his head as he tallied up the cost of this day on a piece of paper and said, "I only get seventy-two pounds a week to cover everything . . . Will that stop, now I've got money for my flat?"

And the copper wasn't sure, but wondered if maybe it would, if perhaps now that Jeremiah had savings and no roof above his head, the government didn't regard his welfare as its concern.

And the world turns.

In a club near Whitehall, Famine chinked glass on glass, pale champagne sloshing against the rim, and said, "Ultimately, what is government for? It's not about looking after people, we're not the nanny state, that's such an old-fashioned way to look at things . . . "

And in the empty car warehouse beyond the Thames Barrier, where river gave way to swamp, Pestilence drew doodles in the soft mud and whistled as the matches failed to strike in the empty oil drum, and the grey faces huddled tighter together against the cold.

Looking out of a newly opened fast-food joint two streets down from the Kremlin, Russian-style cooking only, none of this Western shit, War folded his blini tighter round its mushroom heart and chuckled to himself, singing under his breath, " . . . goes around, comes around . . . "

114

And in the Houses of Parliament, Death sat in the viewing gallery as the junior minister cleared his throat and began. "We have already done much in this Parliament to reclaim wasteful spending. Twelve billion pounds of working-age benefits; twelve billion pounds, that is what we must recoup to save other, vital services. The young must find work; we must cut back on this culture of supporting so-called disability claimants and housing allowances where the case is not justified; the new generations must learn to give, not to take, and I say to it, to it . . . "

And Death nodded quietly to himself, and remembered another time, a long time ago, when he had sat in the viewing gallery, albeit in a different building that stood upon this site, and heard . . .

"So much misery condensed in so little room is more than the human imagination had ever before conceived . . . however, not to trust too much to any sort of description, I will call the attention of the House to one species of evidence which is absolutely infallible. Death, at least, is a sure ground of evidence . . . here is a mortality of about fifty per cent, and this among negroes who are not bought unless (as the phrase is with cattle) they are sound in mind and limb . . . A trade founded in iniquity, and carried on as this was, must be abolished. Let the policy be what it might, let the consequences be what they would, I from this time determined that I would never rest till I had effected its abolition."

Death had come then too, to listen to William Wilberforce speak, and the day slavery was abolished in the British Empire, the old man had cried, and the men had cheered, and Death had been pleased to perform his office that day, which was given in service to an idea, and the turning of the world, and the abolitionist had perhaps looked up and beheld him in the gallery above, and had smiled, and not been afraid.

War, a little tipsy, sings as he shuffles through the night-time streets of Tripoli, raising his empty glass to the sky:

"What goes around . . . comes around . . . what goes around . . . comes around . . . "

*

115

In London, Agnes and Jeremiah Young stood outside the flat that had been their home, as the last of their furniture was loaded into the back of the truck, and stared at nothing and did not meet each other's eyes, and the bailiffs waited until the lock had been changed, then nodded once in polite farewell to the pair, and walked away.

No one came, no one was left.

Agnes had no more tears to cry; Jeremiah had few – so very few – heartbeats left to give. They rode in silence in the van to the storage place, and the driver refused to help them take their belongings inside, but a girl, a few months into the job, doing it to pay tuition fees, saw the two of them and heard their story, and she got her mate down from the office who fancied her and couldn't wait for her boyfriend to finally leave her, and together they helped carry the Youngs' worldly goods into a secure locker at the back of a building that had once been a car park, and when they were done, they gave Agnes the key to the padlock on the door and pretended to forget to charge her for this extra service, and went to close down the storage for the night.

Agnes and Jeremiah stood alone in the middle of the rushing street as the sun went down, a small bag held in Agnes's right hand with a change of pants, her mobile phone, toothbrush and her grandfather's razor and shaving cream, and they had nowhere to go.

"Excuse me?"

The Harbinger of Death stood on the corner of the street, a bus grumbling behind him at the traffic lights, a one-legged pigeon hopping busily out of his way. He held an umbrella under one arm against the return of rain, and stood, heels together, back straight. The two turned to stare at him, no words left, silent in the sodium-soaked dark.

Why is he here?

He's not sure he knows the answer himself.

"I went to the estate, but you were already ... but I met a policewoman and asked if she knew what had happened, and she said you were ... and so I came to see if I ... " He stopped, looked

116

down, then looked up and tried again. "I'm not here on business. This isn't . . . I met a woman who said that . . . Look, I'm on a train out of the country tomorrow, and I won't be back for at least three weeks. I have a flat, it's . . . it's not much, it's . . . Whenever I come home it's always very cold, at least it seems that way, it's not . . . I think I'm trying to say, if you need a place to stay . . . "

His voice trailed off. He studied his feet, as the girl and her grandfather studied him.

Then he looked up, and for the first time there seemed something in his eye that was made of stone, and there was fire in his voice as he said, "Something human. Something good. If you want it, my home is yours."

Agnes looked at Jeremiah, Jeremiah looked at Agnes.

There was a moment when Agnes thought of the words that should have come, the fuck you, the we don't want your pity, the fuck you world fuck you world fuck fuck fuck fuck FUCK

but her grandfather, who had loved her and raised her after Mum died, who had fought even though his strength was failing, and he was so old now, older this last week than she'd ever thought he could be – her grandfather was cold, and frail in the middle of the road, and she looked at the Harbinger of Death and thought that perhaps he too was frightened, and didn't really know what he was doing or what he was saying, but that it mattered to him more than anything that he said it, and so she nodded just once and said, "Yeah. Okay. Thanks."

Charlie nodded in reply, and the three walked in silence through the night.

Chapter 39

"Charlie . . . "
    "Saga . . . "

"It's completely ... "

"I just wanted your advice."

"Did you think that ... "

"Because I don't want to overstep, but this didn't feel like ... "

"You're a free man!"

"Within the constraints of the ... "

"A job is just a job. You know that. The job is just the job."

"As Harbinger of Death, did you ... When you had my job, did you ever ... "

"Of course I did. Of course. She didn't mind. You're only human. Charlie? What have you done?"

"There was this old man and his granddaughter."

"Ah – a classic. Clichéd, even! The young, the old, your heart bled a little to see ... "

"No. No, not that. Just ... Well, maybe that. In Greenland the ice broke and a man died and I felt so tiny. What can one man do? And here ... In Germany they took in a million refugees, welcomed them with flowers, food, old women gave up their homes, strangers invited other strangers to sleep on their sofas, without another thought, and then in Cologne on New Year's Day ... "

"You're concerned."

"No. It's not ... "

"The job?"

"Silly to worry about work."

"Silly, yes, silly. But then again, Charlie, the work is life."

"Is ... "

"Life, yes, as I said. When you are Harbinger of Death, you go before, and before there is death, there is life. You go to greet and to honour the living. It would be ridiculous, obscene even, if you didn't honour life. What music have you been listening to?"

"What? There was ... there's a choir at SOAS, international music, also a secular choir, at Christmas they ... "

"Charlie. You are a bridge. You stand between life and death, sometimes in a very literal sense. It is very important – most important – that you are human. That you see humanity in everything you do. Otherwise you do not accord to the living the honour that they are due from Death herself. Charlie? It is human to care."

"So I shouldn't ...?"

"No."

"And it's okay to ..."

"Absolutely."

"But why this one? I haven't been in this job long, but Mama Sakinai died and it was ... I didn't feel like I should try to save her – ridiculous word, 'save'. I'm sorry, you must think I'm ..."

"It was her time, and she was not afraid."

"No. I suppose she wasn't."

"And the ones you've helped today?"

"It is not their time. It is ... it is not their time."

"Injustice – you will meet that too, you know. Sometimes the bus that slips off the motorway is full of children. You will have to be there for them too, and you cannot stop the ice when it is time for it to melt."

"I ... I know. But this once ... just for a while ... I thought maybe I could help."

"That's good. You may think it doesn't make a difference; it does. One person at a time, it makes a difference."

"Thank you. I thought perhaps ... but thank you."

"Any time, Charlie. Any time."

Three people sit in a flat in Dulwich and watch the TV.

The words they hear; though they watch the same things, they hear differently, and Jeremiah Young, already half asleep, head on one side, breathing loud through his nose, hears ...

" ... the sea turtle as it lays its eggs knows that only some of its children will make it to the ocean's safety. Her brood safely buried, she crawls back the way she came, slipping down into the safety of the darkness before the tide can turn ..."

Agnes Young, who's got work tomorrow morning and is scared she'll lose her job, because she's been distracted, short-tempered, moody and sometimes late to the shop – but hasn't said anything, didn't want to make a big deal of it, it's just ... it's

119

her problem, her shit, that's all – Agnes Young watches the TV and hears . . .

"Will they find true love on the paradise holiday, or will those grapes turn sour? And also, after the break, our magical couples go jet-skiing: 'I was like, I thought I was going to die' . . . and climb a mountain for the perfect romantic photo opportunity: 'Oh my *God*! It's just . . . it's like . . . wow, oh my God, it's just so *amazing*!' . . . and we reveal Hunky Josh's big secret! All this, after the break . . ."

And the Harbinger of Death sits beside this strange pair on his too-small sofa, and watches the TV, and for tonight hears only voices, lifted in celebration, and smiles, and is content.

Part 4

RATS

Chapter 40

"If we were to go to have a coffee together – no, that wouldn't be acceptable. I'm a married woman, and being alone with a man who's not my husband, who knows where it might lead? I mean, I don't think with you it would lead anywhere, but you never know, so I just avoid the risk. It's an important part of what this is about – avoid the risk, that's all."

"Why would you do that to your body? Why would you stain your body for ever? I just don't understand it, I think it's wrong, frankly, just wrong . . ."

"So it's sixty pounds for the membership, and then another twenty a week for personal trainer sessions, and like maybe thirty-five pounds a week for you know, the supplements and that, and then fifty pounds every two weeks for hair and nails, so what's that . . . Yeah, I know, but like, this is how I feel good, like, this is how I'm someone, someone who actually matters."

" . . . and then he was like, 'I'll put the pictures online' and I was like, 'I don't fucking care if you put the pictures online, you look like a douche too' and he was like, 'Give me cash' and I just laughed at him, fuck that, I mean, it's my body, it's just my body . . ."

"When I go to the men's section I sit behind a screen, but sometimes if a man comes over to the women's area then he has to sit behind a screen too. I mean, the protection, it works both ways . . ."

"So. These photos. Obviously it's sending a bad message to our clients."

"It's four and a half thousand dollars for the donor, plus passport costs, then we sell on to the broker in Saudi, who takes his cut, and he arranges transportation to the recipient, who's usually paying about seventy-two thousand dollars for a good kidney match ... "

"To quote a dead white man: 'Society does not consist of individuals but expresses the sum of interrelations, the relations within which these individuals stand.' I'll tell you who said it later ... "

"Actually, I think money isn't a bad metric at all for assessing a person's value to society. Seriously, what else are you going to use?"

Chapter 41

The Harbinger of Death and the Harbinger of War met at Esenboga international airport.

"Charlie! Oh *Charlie!*" sang out the Harbinger of War, as Charlie wandered through the international departures lounge in search of a water fountain or a cup of tea.

"Marion – what are you ...?" A limp gesture round the hall. Esenboga was like every international airport in the world, a terminal opened to serve the growing Ankara traffic, glass ceilings, white floors, escalators, orange letters on the electric departure boards, the same shops selling the same clothes, the same coffee, the same inflatable neck pillows and the same travel padlocks, broken with a single tap of the hammer. Arrival, departure, arrival, departure – sometimes it felt like Charlie's life was one sort of waiting room or another.

"Catching the 1714 to Warsaw – another terrible tour of Ukraine, Belarus, the Baltic Sea, you know how it is." She paused to kiss Charlie once on either cheek, her fading brown-grey hair piled on top of her skull, her beige linen trousers ruffled from travel. "Had to stop off in Ankara to visit a peace march, the Kurds, the Turks, the Turks, the Kurds, it never ends; came through Gaza, Egypt, Libya, the usual spots. The service in some of my usual hotels has gone absolutely downhill – it's the death of the tourist industry, I can tell you that. Where are you heading? Not Sudan again?"

"No – Syria, maybe Iraq."

"Ghastly! Used to be so wonderful, so wonderful, and now – did you ever see Palmyra?"

"Yes, I did."

"And now the state of things! Well don't let me hold you up, busy busy busy, give my love to the old place!"

So saying, she headed in the opposite direction, and Charlie continued his search for a lovely cup of tea.

Chapter 42

The first time Charlie met Qasim Jahani, the war in Syria was only a few months old, and Charlie was very new to the job. He had travelled almost directly from Mama Sakinai to Turkey, and his heart filled with busy, bustling excitement as he queued at passport control, looking at the faces around him and wondering if anyone knew, if anyone could sense the importance of his office, the scale of the duty he had to perform.

Children cried, travellers grumbled, no one met anyone else's eye, and it seemed that, despite the magnitude of the responsibility upon him, only he knew of its might.

When Charlie had signed up for the job, he'd had a feeling he would be sent into war zones, of course, and the thought hadn't bothered him. If anything, it had been an attraction, an opportunity to finally see all the images that lay just outside the frame of the news camera, to hear voices that weren't edited to a few words meant to encapsulate the conflict for viewers with limited patience for complexity, and yes, to one day return and be able to look his friends – already a fading, distant brood – in the eye and say, I was there, I saw this, it has changed me, but I endure, picture it if you can.

The thought that he might be harmed hadn't really occurred to him. Why would Death send his Harbinger, if his Harbinger was going to die in the attempt? Only afterwards – after the ice – would the possibility grow in his mind.

At that time, as he crossed the still-open border to Syria, the war was largely a civil war, though the quality of it was rapidly evolving into something else, something that didn't have a name. The cluster bombs were beginning to fall on civilians, and suicide bombers had killed themselves outside police stations, and men with guns had hidden amongst schoolchildren, and tanks had shelled still-sleeping apartments, and somehow, as the rubble fell and the smoke billowed into the streets, it was becoming harder and harder to tell what anything was any more, and who was killing who, let alone why.

Civilian populace was an interesting turn of phrase, Charlie mused, as he rode through the towns of northern Syria in search of his quarry. Two words that somehow didn't seem to cover the old women queuing for eggs, the smell of cumin from the kitchens, the children trying to out-stare the skittish stray cats, the schoolrooms where history was taught in the morning, emergency bomb drills in the afternoon. Civilian populace, in Charlie's mind, implied a country where all things were frozen, as if every single person had, at the outbreak of war, become rooted to the spot, waiting for their turn to come.

Civilian populace was not a term that covered . . .

"You like football? I love football! I love Arsenal. Arsenal are the best. But they always let themselves down in the Champions League. They're just like the English – one or two good players, a lot of hard workers and terrible at penalties!"

Was this war? Charlie wondered as he bought a football shirt from a beaming man who ran a five-a-side team on the outskirts of Aleppo. Was this what civilian populace meant?

"We haven't been hit too badly by the fighting, I suppose, but my children – they haven't been outside for nine months. They live in their bedroom, the kitchen and the bathroom. I have to let them watch more TV, when the power's on. It's the only way, but I don't like it."

Back then, back before the ice and the London rain, back when the aid agencies were still daring to operate across the Syria–Turkey and Lebanon–Syria borders, Charlie had snuck in with a convoy at the Akçakale–Tell Abiad crossing, where the proud face of Syria's illustrious ruler still stared mightily into the middle distance in one direction, and trucks waited behind high yellow walls covered with razor wire to be inspected by the teams of men with dogs and guns on the other side. Just this once, when the border official asked him his job, Charlie replied that he was a nurse, and showed a fake letter that made him feel guilty whenever he unfolded it, remorse at abusing the name of an honourable charity to sneak in with his fake passport, his fake name, his weak Syrian Arabic.

He hadn't imagined that he'd ever not travel as the Harbinger of Death, hadn't imagined he'd need to lie. But as Milton Keynes put it . . .

"Certain places just aren't pleased to see you. They don't really understand the needfulness of the office, love."

He'd half expected to be arrested there and then, but the soldiers looked at his letter, his passport, noted a few words from both down on a piece of tatty paper, and waved him through. He'd climbed back into the high front of the truck he was riding with, with its cargo of baby formula, and his driver had nodded once with his chin and said in inflected English, "Now you go see Syria, yes?"

Charlie nodded in answer, hardly daring to speak until the engine had growled back up to full and the truck was pulling away from the dusty compound, skirting the edge of the scraggy border in search of the open road.

Again, as the world rolled by in a cloud of sepia dust, divided occasionally into a rectangular field where hardy green-grey plants grew, crawling unevenly towards the sun, Charlie could not believe that this was a land at war. When the road joined the tip of a river valley, trees began to sprout proud and wide, towns offering Coca-Cola and petrol stations, rising and falling amid the fields and scattered, water-hugging orchards. Charlie half closed his eyes against the reflected pink brilliance of the sun, and smelt the exhaust from the motorway and the smoke from burning wood, and thought that perhaps he could drive for ever down this endless road to the south.

Then the checkpoints began, and the traffic grew thin. Sometimes the checkpoints were police, bearded men with Kalashnikovs slung across their bellies, who ranged from uninterested to infuriated as they studied Charlie's passport, his letters. At one checkpoint, a man stood Charlie up against the side of the van and shouted at him, just shouted and kept on shouting, and Charlie looked nervously to the driver to see if any of the words being screamed at him, which were for the best part beyond his comprehension, should have him more than particularly worried.

Then the man spat at Charlie's feet, and sent him on his way. At another checkpoint, a different man, a soldier, saw his passport and exclaimed in perfect, fluent French, "Ah, you are from Paris!"

"Yes," Charlie lied in the same language, hoping his English accent didn't show too heavily. "That's right."

"I love Paris, I studied at the Sorbonne, ah, such times, such good times, the river, the people, the language, the language it is still a pleasure to speak it ... "

He shook Charlie's hand: if you have any trouble, any at all, just mention my name ...

... waved them on.

A few miles further down the dusty, near-empty road, Charlie turned to his companion and said, "What was his name?"

The driver shrugged; he hadn't been paying attention.

*

The first rebel checkpoint they met wasn't really in service of a rebellion at all, but was a barrier laid across the street by the militia of a town a few miles off the main road, grubby men with ragged beards, a mishmash of weapons – hunting rifles, pistols, even the odd axe or two – assembled casually around the blockade.

Down, down, they gestured, and they climbed out of the truck, the sun now setting, the heat of the day burning away in an insect buzz. Charlie presented his passport, told his story, and the man in charge, grey-haired and silk-skinned, sniffed and said, "No. You are a liar. Go home."

Charlie hesitated, then tried again, a medic, a mission, trying to get . . .

"We don't need your medicine here, go home!"

He hesitated, looked to the driver, who still didn't seem to care, looked back to the soldier and said, "I am the Harbinger of Death."

This took some translating, with the driver finally stepping in, rattling off words that caused consternation, men now fingering their weapons a little closer as they re-examined Charlie by the fading light of day. Finally the captain said, "Come, come come come!" and limply Charlie followed him into what had to be militia headquarters, and which perhaps had been in another life a small bar or coffee house, where the TV on the wall still showed a grainy, bad signal beamed from the Turkish side of the border, football matches and soap operas about intrigue in the Ottoman court.

"*You never loved me!*" exclaimed a figure on the screen, her face obscured by the zigzag of interference, colours faded. "*You only ever wanted the Vizierate for yourself!*"

"Sit sit sit sit!"

Charlie sat, hands in his lap, back stiff and straight. Men came, men went.

"*You harlot! You she-wolf! He will never be with you, never!*"

After a while, the driver of the truck came in and with a shrug put Charlie's meagre travel bag at his feet. "Good luck," he said, holding out a meaty, mottled hand. Charlie shook it, mumbled something back, sat back down, waited.

"The Austrian king is weak, and his advisers are all cowards . . . "

The darkness grew thick; the power went out and the men milling around the room didn't even sigh. Candles were struck, torches turned on, one man's face glowed white as he continued working on a laptop. After a while, the commander came in, saw Charlie and seemed almost surprised that he was still there.

"Death?" he asked. "Come come come! Come follow."

Charlie followed.

A night-time street, no lights behind the windows, the stars brilliant overhead. Charlie turned and felt cool air fresh from the mountains, heard the barking of dogs somewhere in the night, looked down and saw a few headlights moving along the road in the valley below.

The commander pulled on Charlie's sleeve, annoyed at his slowness, and led him to a house. Here a woman, headscarf tied beneath her chin, five teeth left in her gummy mouth, grinned brightly at Charlie and gestured him inside. Up a creaking flight of stairs to a room that smelt of deodorant, a desk in one corner, clothes across the floor, an empty bed visible in the candlelight. The sheets were ruffled, disturbed, the room smelt of human habitation; but there were pillows, and the hour was late, so with a grateful smile Charlie curled up, still fully dressed, beneath the blanket. Three hours later, the teenage boy whose room it was came home, found Charlie sound asleep, cursed under his breath and crawled in next to the Harbinger of Death, who rolled over at the disturbance, but did not wake.

In the star-soaked night, War does not sleep.

War perches casually on a stool in an office in Damascus, picking seeds from a pomegranate as soldiers in fine brocade argue, argue into the night, and War smiles and says nothing except occasionally, perhaps, "Do carry on, gentlemen."

And in the high mountains where the Kurds wait, are waiting, have always been waiting for a chance to make laws in their own language, War watches the moon rise with a boy who at last, today, was given a chance to handle a gun, and pats the lad on the head and says, "Tomorrow will be different for ever."

In Lebanon, War whispers to the old fighters of Hezbollah, the grave men who once resisted Israel, and they listen in silence, knowing already the words the stranger speaks

for they are the same words, give or take a couple of names, that War speaks to the quiet, biro-twiddling Mossad men of Tel Aviv, a map spread out between them, a nervous city slumbering against the sea.

In the mountains north of Tehran, in the valleys where usually only the goats climb, War scrambles through the dark with the men in masks and night goggles, stops when they stop, raises his fist in command, spreads his fingers to give a direction, and scurries on, silent in the night.

War smokes a cigarette outside the West Wing in Washington, and inside their offices the staffers smell the fumes and wonder who'd dare, and a few nicotine cravers itch for their fix, and bow their heads back to the computer screens.

War takes the hammer off the man who has just nailed down the lid on the crate of Buk missiles and says, "How long does one of these take to get to thirty-five thousand feet?" and the man is ashamed, and doesn't answer.

War rides with the tribesmen on the back of their pickup trucks, shooting bullets triumphantly into the sky

War murmurs softly in the dreams of the President as he sleeps, belly full, between silk sheets

War keeps watch on the borders of Kashmir, breath steaming in the cold

War squats on the edge of the jungle path and asks if this was the way the refugees ran

War cries freedom.

War sobs terror.

War has been summoned by so many people, so many men,

strong men, men who were raised to be strong, so many have put on his armour and drawn his bloody sword, so many men have knelt down in the stained ground to whisper their imprecations to this ever-lasting deity, and of course, War is a sociable creature, he came when they called, but being summoned, it is very unlikely indeed that he will ever obey.

Famine and Pestilence are getting impatient now; they want a piece of the action.

Come join me, War replies. There's plenty of room.

We're gonna have a whale of a time.

Chapter 43

Charlie woke because the teenager he was sharing the bed with had somehow managed to take all the blanket.

For a moment, lying there, he didn't know where he was. By the light of day the room was an alien, unfamiliar little coffin, strewn with a stranger's clothes. By the light of day, he was in an unknown land with an unknown body pressed against his, and he jerked away suddenly, bewildered, and stared down at the slumbering boy next to him, and didn't entirely understand.

Outside the bedroom window, a chicken clucked, an engine revved, a truck pulled up and passed by. The Harbinger of Death shuffled slowly to the furthest edge of the bed, careful not to disturb the sleeper left behind, picked up his bag and slipped out of the door.

The house was full of sleeping people. The sometime living room was spread with pallets and sleeping bags; even the kitchen floor had been given over to two teenage boys, lying together like lovers. Some slept with guns hugged close like teddy bears, others had sprawled out like pointed stars, toes upwards, arms wide, lips trembling as great snores rocked their bodies. Charlie crept to the door, found his shoes amongst a mass of muddy boots and hard sandals, pulled them on, stepped outside.

A man with a gun between his knees sat on an upturned wooden box, saw Charlie, nodded with his chin, and did not smile.

The morning sun burnt down from a near-white sky, flecked with brown on the edge of the horizon, and Charlie had nowhere really to go.

Breakfast: flat bread and instant coffee.

Men woke, men stirred, men went about their business. Some went about their business with great purpose. Others milled, and wondered perhaps what their business was. To protect this settlement, certainly, but from whom? Other militia men? The government? The rebels?

"We are on the side of reliable electricity and fresh running water," explained one man, who had in a previous life been a roofer and who now, to his surprise, commanded twenty men. "We are on the side of good schools and proper healthcare."

"And who is going to give that to you?" Charlie asked.

He shrugged. "We have to protect what we've got."

A little later, he met the man who sold him a T-shirt for a football team no one had ever heard of from Aleppo.

A while after that, a girl, her face hidden by the veil, maybe twelve or thirteen years old, came over with her nine-year-old brother and asked if she could practise her English. She wanted to be a diplomat when she grew up, and travel the world. Her brother wanted to be an actor, and every time he said so, she hit him on the arm and hissed, "Don't say such things!"

Her English was good, and they chatted until her mother caught them talking and, shouting, chased the girl away, glaring daggers at Charlie as he sat on a breeze block on the side of the street, waiting.

*

133

At midday, a car came barrelling down the middle of the road, spraying yellow dust. The windscreen was a half-circle where dirt had been scrubbed away, the engine ticked high in the heat. A man leapt out, a woman in owl sunglasses remaining in the passenger seat.

"You!" he exclaimed, in bright, merry English. "You are the Harbinger of Death?"

"That's right."

"My name is Qasim Jahani! I am the one you are looking for!" He raised his hands to shoulder height, and wobbled them back and forth in a straight line, like a man testing the strength of an imaginary piece of string. "Yaaaayy!"

They sat cross-legged in the shade of a pomegranate tree. Qasim, overgrown straight black hair, wide mouth, little bright eyes squished tight against a magnificent eagle-beak nose, dusty striped shirt and faded blue jeans, talked at runaway train speed.

" . . . and then I heard the Harbinger of Death, to see me, what have I done, I thought, I mean, I don't think I'm ill – my wife is a doctor – she said you're not ill but it's the Harbinger of Death and maybe it's a lie, maybe it's a trick, someone playing a practical joke hahahaha, but it's not, is it, you're actually here to see me and so if I'm going to die – and I pray I am not – but if I am going to die I have to ask, do you think it is in a good cause?"

Charlie opened his mouth to answer, not sure, not really his field, but before he could speak, Qasim was off again.

"And then I thought maybe it doesn't matter if it's in a good cause or not, maybe this is just ego, ego ego ego, but why would the Harbinger come for me? Death comes for everyone but the Harbinger, does that make me special? I'm not sure I want that kind of special, not special in that sense, but here you are and you're real, you're strange but you're definitely real and . . . "

He stopped again, as suddenly as he had begun, put his head on one side and said, "Will I be a martyr?"

Charlie waited to see if the question was real, and when Qasim still seemed to expect an answer, he laid his palms face-up across his folded legs, took a deep breath and said, "Sometimes I am sent as a courtesy, sometimes as a warning . . . "

"We're at war with our own government," he chuckled. "Consider us warned!"

" . . . and sometimes I am sent for . . . for an idea, as well as for an individual."

"An idea? What idea?"

"Well . . . I met a woman who was the last who spoke her language . . . "

"Ah! These things are precious!"

"And before that I was in the West Bank . . . "

"Terrible thing, the Israelis . . . "

" . . . with the previous Harbinger, shadowing her, her last job, and there was an Israeli orchestra playing with a Palestinian."

"Ah. I see! Well, there are good Jews, people are people, it's easy to forget that sometimes."

"The orchestra was run by a conductor from Haifa. Once every week, the Jewish musicians would cross through the checkpoints to go to Ramallah. It was easier for the Israelis to cross than the Palestinians, security being what it is. They would meet in an old school hall, and sometimes the Israelis would bring new strings for a broken violin, or resin for the bows, but usually the Palestinian players were fine, they used the instruments of their fathers and their grandfathers, preserved against the years, and together they put on these concerts, for everyone of every faith, music for peace, music for . . .

"We were only meant to visit for a day, to give a copy of *The Gulag Archipelago* to the conductor. He was surprised, said he'd always meant to read it, but had never had time. He thanked us, me and Saga, asked if we enjoyed the work. Saga said yes, she did, but that sometimes there was a time to do something else, and that these things had to end, and that I was new, and loved music, and she was sure I'd do very well. 'Ah, you love music!' he said. 'You must stay and listen to the concert!' I wasn't sure I was allowed, it was . . . but Saga said stay, stay, I chose you because you love music, that was the only thing that got you through the

135

interview really, you should stay, listen. So I did. I felt like a child, being left alone by my mother, ridiculous really, but then . . .

" . . . I watched them rehearse, Sibelius, and – this will sound clichéd, I'm sorry, but I was – I was about to become the Harbinger of Death, I think maybe I heard something in it that was all about me, really, I mean, that's what music is anyway, you hear yourself, but . . . it was music like nothing I had ever heard, from the first note to the last I felt it, in every part of me I felt it, and I should have left, Saga was back at the hotel already on the other side of the border, but I wanted to hear the concert. So I did. The school hall was packed, parents holding children on their heads, teenagers climbing up the walls to sit on window ledges. They began to play, and the room didn't breathe, I don't think I breathed, only the sound sustained us, that sound, and the first note where the orchestra all came in together, every section, every piece of it, I thought my body would tear in two, and there were people just crying, smiling fit to burst and crying, for what it was, for what it wasn't – not Jew and Palestinian, just music and people. Words are made by history, we build them and they change meaning through time, but the music they played . . .

"Then a crowd of boys came to the door, maybe twenty of them, and they had beards and white robes and they started shouting through the door, haram, haram, this is haram, and they were shouting and screaming and the orchestra mostly drowned them out, but then they started to throw things, pushing and shoving – they were especially interested in the women, cursed them as whores – and the orchestra made it through the second movement and then it had to stop, because by now the whole back of the hall was moving, people pushing and shoving and shouting, just because of these kids, these stupid fucking kids who'd come.

"The musicians all talked together while some of the ushers, the men and women who'd organised the event, tried to get it under control, but someone fell, and their leg was broken, and a bigger crowd was gathering and the musicians realised that it probably wasn't safe to stay, so the Jewish musicians snuck out the back and headed towards the border, leaving behind the Palestinian musicians, who of course didn't have anywhere else to go. I watched it. I saw it all. There wasn't order to the riot, there wasn't any meaning, there was just shoving and pushing and shouting and running, people hitting other people for old grievances that had nothing to do with music, and eventually three or four of the angry boys made it round the back and found some of the Palestinian musicians, and they smashed their instruments, and kicked them on the ground, and then the police came, and they ran away.

"I hid, frightened that if they found me they'd hurt me – I hid at the back of the upstairs viewing gallery, behind a curtain, can you believe? Actually hiding behind a curtain with two other people who had the same idea, but I watched through the gap in the middle and no one died – miraculous, no one died – but as the crowd was finally dispersed, as the police finally managed to bring back some sort of order, I stepped out of hiding and I saw Death. He was sat at the front of the gallery, feet up on the balcony's edge, just watching it all, fingers folded, twiddling his thumbs. I saw Death, and Death looked round and saw me, and knew me, and looked away.

"The orchestra hasn't played since. The Israelis advised the conductor that his life was in danger from ultra-Orthodox Jewish radicals who believed that he was conspiring with terrorists, and that soon there would be military operations conducted against Palestinian extremists and they wouldn't be able to guarantee his safety. Some of the Israeli musicians tried to go back, but the Palestinians were told it wasn't safe to be seen conspiring with their enemies. The conductor is retired now. He has plenty of time for reading."

(In a flat in Tel Aviv, a man with greying hair turns the page of his book, and reads by the light of a desktop lamp. "The Universe has as many different centres as there are living beings in it. Each of us is the centre of the Universe, and that Universe is shattered when they hiss at you, 'You are under arrest.'")

Charlie stopped talking, and for a while, the two of them sat in silence, the Harbinger of Death and the small, bubbling man from Syria. Then Qasim said, "What did your boss say? I mean – this Saga, not Death. What did she say?"

"Nothing. She was waiting up for me in the hotel bar. She looked at me, saw my face, and ordered vodka. We drank together, and then we went up to our rooms and slept."

"That was it?"

"Yes."

"She didn't say . . . "

"I think she knew what had happened. Not the concert, exactly, but . . . what I had seen. Who I had seen. I think perhaps she took me there because she knew I would stay for the music, and she knew that Death would come. Maybe it was a way of meeting the boss, without . . . I don't know, really. I'm still very new to this. I don't know. We didn't talk about it after."

Qasim nodded, then, quietly, "I think I would rather that I died than my words."

Charlie hesitated, began an apology, sorry, I'm still very bad at this, I come here, talk about my troubles . . .

"No, no, not at all! I am interested in learning about Death! Death is all around us here, we all sense him coming nearer with every day, faster, nearer, it is good to speak of these things without fear!"

. . . yes, I suppose it is . . .

"Good that you are here, in fact! A Harbinger of Death, just a job, someone to talk to about these things, death, terror, the end. Have I told you about my ideas?"

Again Charlie paused. Technically, his duty was done. He had travelled into Syria; he had given Qasim his gift – a box of mousetraps, to which Qasim had exclaimed, "But there aren't any mice!" – and now he could leave this strange, quiet place, where apparently war raged but no one seemed to know where, how or for whom, and go home.

This was the sensible course of action, but this was his first foray into chaos and he had come to honour the stories of those who lived within the maelstrom, so instead he blurted, "What are your ideas?"

Qasim, whose face had fallen during Charlie's story, now brightened, sat a little straighter, exclaimed, "I am a poet!"

"I see."

"For fourteen years I have been campaigning for freedom! Freedom, equality, justice, brotherhood. I also had to work as a cleaner to supplement my income, of course, but my heart has always been in the freedom of the people. You are from the West, yes, you take these things for granted? You are not frightened when someone makes a joke, you are not afraid that you have been overheard when someone speaks the truth. When something doesn't work, you can complain about it, you can say 'it is not good' and you do not have to fear imprisonment or death, you have merely seen and expressed fact. Do you know how tiring it is, to live constantly in a lie? To lie to others as you say 'yes, this is wonderful' and to know that others lie to you? To live your entire existence knowing that if white is black, and sky is earth, well then this must be your truth, your new truth. It is like men are eagles and at birth we are told that eagles were destined to swim, and so we swim, gasping, drowning, desperate to fly but not seeing the sky. We will find a new path. We will make a better future."

(A voice yet to come, a voice already heard: *We will build Jerusalem.*)

(A conductor in Palestine: *Humans hear music. All humans. Everywhere.*)

(A girl, who Charlie does not yet know, sobbing in her local town hall: *Please, please just listen to me.*)

Qasim must have seen something resembling doubt in the Harbinger's eyes, because he drew back a little, haughty, arms straight, and added, "Until you have not been free, you cannot understand what freedom means."

Charlie was silent.

In the valley, far, far below, War prodded the tracked surface of the road with his toe, sucked his teeth in a little, then exhaled and declared, "I think it'll do ... it'll do ..." and all the soldiers cheered.

Famine walked by the old woman, her life's goods on her back, the village burning behind her, and said, "Chin up, missus, things can't get any worse ... "

Pestilence held a finger up to the wind, and mused, "The problem about building latrines in these sorts of conditions ... "

Charlie sat in silence with a man called Qasim, who was suddenly quiet, and for the very first time, afraid. Not of Death, perhaps, not of his own physical demise, but of the words he spoke and the ideals he upheld, and of the gift of mousetraps sitting in his lap.

Two years later, twelve weeks after the Longview Estate began to fall in south London, and four weeks after the first prospective apartment in the new development was sold for £575,000 to a buy-to-rent landlord from Horsham, the Harbinger of Death sat once more in Esenboga international airport, looking for Qasim again.

Chapter 44

"I want to go to Germany to become educated. Of course – they have money, they have schools, they have hospitals, of course they should help me, I have nothing. I think it is only fair to expect that from them, since they are so wealthy."

"They killed my mother, my father, my uncles, my sister, my brothers, my neighbours, my friends ... "

"*Wir sind das Volk!*"

"She's having a hard time at school, understandable, but we don't really have the resources to counsel someone who's been through what she ... "

"The schools can't cope, the hospitals can't cope ..."

"What do you mean, there's no tomato ketchup?"

"I don't believe you're sixteen. I don't believe your story. I am sorry but your application is going to be ..."

"Wir sind das Volk! Wir sind das Volk!"

"They drive the wages down, undercutting the natives here, and fundamentally if that's what's happening, if they're working longer hours for less, and I know that it's us who hire them because we like things cheap, but even so, being given that option ..."

"Fourteen different types of condensed milk! Fourteen! And that's a fundamental part of their cuisine. I mean, what do you even do with ..."

"The nurse was Polish and actually, given where she put it, I thought she handled it very well, I hardly felt a thing ..."

"Last year Japan accepted eleven asylum-seeker applications from five thousand; the USA takes about forty-eight thousand; Sweden with a population of nine and a half million took nine thousand four hundred and thirty-three; this year Germany is expected to process four hundred thousand asylum applications, and what I want to know, what the burning question is ..."

"I don't want to generalise, but Mexicans *are* criminals."

"Brexit promised three hundred and fifty million a week for the NHS, they promised controls on immigration, they promised an end to the housing crisis, to the education crisis, to the economic crisis, to the ..."

Human human human human human rat ...

"Luegenpresse, luegenpresse! Wir sind das Volk!"

"What I don't understand is that when the British public voted to name a research vessel *Boaty McBoatface*, the government said no. But when we voted to commit cultural and economic seppuku, the powers-that-be didn't seem to have a fucking clue ..."

"But you see, some of my best friends are black."

Chapter 45

A nightmare journey. This was not how it was supposed to work, not repeat appointments, he'd never heard of such a thing, and the way it had been organised, Charlie's calendar had updated with less than forty-eight hours before he had to fly out; very odd. He wondered if Saga had ever heard of such a thing, not that it was a problem, he was growing confident now, just all very strange, and here he was again . . .

. . . a few miles north of the Syria–Turkey border, lying on the hard, biting mattress of the hotel, staring at a line of insects marching in a perfect straight line across the ceiling, wide awake. Heading back to Syria, looking again for Qasim Jahani, unheard of, Death tended not to visit twice . . .

(A frail deduction made in the middle of the night. True: the Harbinger of Death tended not to visit twice, whereas Death was a constant recurring companion in so many lives . . .)

Not that this is frightening. Charlie is now an old hand at dubious border crossings – remember the three nights spent on a donkey in Honduras? Those were the days . . .

No. What is causing him to lie sleepless and confused in the middle of the night is this: he has been told how he'll get into Syria, but not how he'll get out. And while he has a huge amount of faith in the Milton Keynes office and their ability to organise things, up to and including a tapas tasting menu in Peshawar and a string quartet at Fukushima, this is not the first time he has been to Syria in recent years and the thought is . . .

. . . disquieting, all things considered.

Not that he believes everything he sees on the TV. Hardly believes any of it at all, not any more, not really. Travel has blurred the edge of certain commonly perceived truths.

Charlie lies awake, and watches the insects, and must sleep, because at some point he is shaken awake to see two men, their faces lit by torches, leaning over him.

"You Harbinger? You come!"

Their arrival, while heart-jumping, is not entirely unexpected. "I come," he grunted, reaching for the light switch.

"No! No light! You come."

"No light, I come," he repeated, rolling groggy out of bed. By the glow of the street lamps outside he collected his small travel bag, pulled his trousers over his pyjama shorts and a shirt over his pyjama top, and coat barrelled round him like a hypothermic sea lion, he shuffled out through the darkened kitchen of the hotel and into the night.

The two men didn't give themselves names, didn't say who they worked for. Milton Keynes had told Charlie to wait at a hotel, and he had waited, and they had come, and that was pretty much the full extent of what he knew. He remembered Qasim Jahani's name, with fondness even, a smiling, bubbling poet with dreams of freedom, and this gave him some comfort as the two men opened up the boot of an ancient Fiat and said, "Inside!"

He stared into the darkened back of the car, mumbled a mute enquiry.

"Inside inside!" they snapped, eyes glancing fitfully around the street. Charlie hesitated, then shrugged, and crawled inside.

In many ways, the inside of the boot was surprisingly peaceful. Sleep deprived, warmly wrapped in his coat, once he grew used to the relentless bouncing, it was possible to curl into a foetal huddle, head tucked into the nook of his arm. Sometimes the car ran smooth and fast, sometimes it bumped and shook, gravel pattering up loud against the undercarriage, so close Charlie half wondered if he wasn't going to wake with a pebble in his ear.

Once, the car stopped for nearly half an hour, and Charlie thought about hammering on the walls, but at almost the same moment he decided to do so, the engine revved again, and it sped off on its way. The second time it stopped, the two men came to get him, opening the trunk and barking, "Yallah, yallah!"

Charlie rolled onto the ground, stiff, feet tingling as blood began to flow, and zombie-like dragged one leg behind him as he hobbled across the rough ground. The car was parked on what once had perhaps been a scenic overlook, a dusty hill where a dirt road had been extended round one of the perilous switchback curves to create a parking and picnic area, allowing views down to a valley of straight-sided fields of machine-ploughed earth and the occasional stubby smoky chimney above a metal-roofed town.

Waiting a few metres from the first car was a second, a boxy, polished four-wheel drive, black sides, black-tinted windows, the passenger door standing open at the back, two men in grey combat fatigues, great keffiyehs of red and black woven round their necks and heads, pistols in holsters at their sides.

He was waved towards the vehicle, climbed in. The seats were synthetic cream leather, the air smelt of pine freshener. There were some old magazines in the seat pockets in front of him – a copy of *Time*, a copy of the *Washington Post*, the pages yellow and curled; a Syrian road atlas from 1994. The men sat up front, their keffiyehs hiding their faces. One leant back and said in heavy English, "Drink?" and waggled a bottle of mineral water in front of Charlie's nose.

He took it gratefully, thanked them. The water was cold, clear. He didn't know where to put the empty bottle, so put it in his bag, in case it was useful later. Something bumped against his foot. He picked it up. A single 45 mm shell casing, cold, a tiny incision on the back where the bolt had struck. He stuck it in the curve of the seat besides him, and watched the darkness roll by.

In the distance, fire, which at first he thought was dawn. A pinkish glow on the east, which only when it failed to spread, failed to lighten, did he understand for what it was.

Once they pulled over, hard and fast, and shouted, "Move, move!" Charlie ran, because they ran, a blind, mad pelt, throwing himself down into a muddy, dried-up ditch some fifty yards from the dirt road, the car engine still running, the doors open, a beacon in the dark.

A plane rushed overhead, then another, flying low, the engines pushing hard against the sky.

They waited, five minutes, ten, and no more planes came, so gently they nudged Charlie back into the car, and drove on.

Dawn began to break – real dawn, spreading fast and grey against a land the colour of ash. Charlie didn't know where they were, where they were heading. He'd been told to wait at the hotel, and he had waited, and for all he knew he was in Iraq, or halfway to Jordan. The old signs had lost their meanings; no longer Syria, but government-controlled Syria, rebel-controlled Syria, al-Nusra-controlled territories that recognised no borders save those laid down by God.

In the rising light of the dawn, he saw a town with no roofs left, except for two or three houses bang smack in the middle that had somehow escaped the shelling.

In a field in a nowhere place, where nothing lived and no one could possibly have any reason for fighting, mortar holes like meteor strikes had filled with grimy water from the shattered irrigation ditches, and now long-legged birds waded between the scattered fingertips and torn clothing of the men who'd been blasted in its making.

On the side of a water tower, a banner hung, which Charlie slowly translated in his dubious Arabic. *When the horn is blown once, the earth and the mountains will be carried off and crushed; utterly crushed. That is the day when the inevitable event will come to pass.*

He wondered where the checkpoints were, and once they passed a barrier, swung to the side of the road, where a check-point had been, and once they passed a burnt-out shed near a shattered bridge, the face of the President charred all away except for the tip of his chin.

And once they passed a convoy of trucks, heading in the other direction, and Charlie thought they were fine until the last truck swerved to a halt and men jumped down, grenade launcher, assault rifle, pistol, axe, screaming at them to stop.

The driver stopped the car, casual, controlled, opened the doors with a sigh and gestured at Charlie to follow. He did, swathed in his coat, awkwardly bulging around his pyjamas. A conversation ensued, guns pointing, men shouting, the drivers replying calmly, calmly. Charlie struggled to follow it, but at one point the driver of the car took him by his shoulders and presented him to the shouting men, and they looked fearfully amongst each other. At another point, the man who rode in the passenger seat went to whisper to a man with a great beard and an AK-47 across his shoulder, and they talked earnestly with their backs to the rest of the road, and when they were done, the men with weapons climbed back into the truck to go about their merry way, and the driver turned to Charlie and said, "If you want piss, now is good time."

"I'm fine, thank you," Charlie mumbled, and with a shrug, the driver waved him into the car, while the other man went to have a piss on the side of the road.

They drove, as the midday sun grew hot and high.

Once they stopped, and barrels of petrol were pulled from the boot of the car and tipped into the tank.

And again, they stopped on the edge of a small town where only the dogs roamed, and if anyone else lived, they were hiding, somewhere beneath the rubble of their shattered lives. The buildings reminded Charlie of ancient, abandoned beehives, walls the colour of dust, peppered with bullet holes, strange geometric forms caving in on themselves, a criss-cross of cables overhead where electricity had flowed, now collapsed down to a giddy prism of unravelling coils. Some living being once smothered this street, and died, and now only a chitinous corpse remained.

They sat in silence, ate bread and olives and spat the pips into the empty street. Charlie grew hot under his coat, asked if he could walk away a little, change his clothes – they didn't mind. He shambled through the sun-pierced shadows of the streets, saw the sign hanging from the pharmacist's, blasted to nothing, and the broken-up cabin that had been the mobile repair shop, and at last stood, awkward and strange, in the shade of a fallen piece of ceiling, balanced over the street, to pull off his coat, his shirt, his trousers, and finally, his grimy pyjamas. Standing naked, he looked around, wondered what a watcher would make of this, and tangled his feet in his trousers in his haste to pull fresh clothes on, expecting any second to hear someone laugh at his bare backside.

Fresh clothes on, old clothes in bag. His stomach growled, his lips were dry. He walked back in the direction of the car, and as he walked, he felt someone watching, and thought he heard the click of a gun.

Silence in the street.

Silence in the shade.

Charlie turned, slowly, and saw no one. Turned again, and thought perhaps he saw a distortion in the darkness, a tiny motion blinking from between the tumbled-down remnants of an old wall. He watched the dark, the dark watched him; for an eternity time lingered, locked in contemplation.

Then the driver of the car called out, "Harbinger! Harbinger! Yallah!"

Charlie walked away, and no one followed.

Glimpses of a strange world, of a world turned mad.

A village, pictures hanging of heroes who Charlie couldn't name or recognise. Children in the streets, old women kneading bread, a man berating another for breaking eggs. Is there war, in this place? Perhaps not, until they pass the wall where the photos of the fallen lie, men smiling proudly to camera, all dead now, all dead.

A group of men, sunbathing on the side of the road. They wave at the car as it goes by, and continue lounging, reading books, picking at sweet fruits with their fingertips.

A hill, half blasted to nothing. There was something military there, mumbled the driver, and it went away. God took bites out of the mountainside, left jagged marks where his teeth had been.

A family of five, Pappa, Momma, Grandma, the two kids, walking north. They have a cart pulled by Pappa and the kids. Momma walks behind; Grandma sits on the top of a hill of family furniture. Charlie wants to ask where they're going, but there isn't time.

Four children, in dusty vests and flip-flops, run by the vehicle laughing as it navigates a particularly slow, grubby bit of road.

A town where the electricity still burns, the roar of generators. An old woman in a black veil keeps the library open, though the windows are boarded up. It's important, she whispers, as the car stops to buy water, it's important that we keep these things going.

A funeral procession. The women scream until they fall down in a faint, the men hold them up, the boys cry silently and swear to take up arms in their father's name. It is the same funeral procession that their fathers saw, their fathers before them, and their grandfathers unto generations unknown, where the same vow was taken.

A hot air balloon, bright stripes on its side. A group of happy tourists look down from its height, enjoying the day, enjoying the view. Where have they come from? Why are they here?

(They come from Latakia, where War has not yet visited, and the sea shimmers with a suntan oil slick. But the Harbinger of War was seen there a few weeks ago, buying a honeycomb ice cream, and the Harbinger of Famine booked a room with a view across the water only yesterday . . .)

Out of nowhere, the earth shaking, the world coming apart, the driver screams, out, out, and they run, plunging into dust and scrubby, biting tufts of grass. Charlie ran as the world exploded around him, grit in his eyes, thunder in his ears, the world jerking out beneath his feet. Something hard hit him in the side and pushed him down, he struck the ground and curled into a ball, hands covering his head, and still the sky fell and around him the earth burst open, scars popping out of the dirt and a falling rain of mud.

When at last it stopped, he opened his eyes slowly, his whole body wobbling like blancmange. The sound of the ground falling back down made a gentle pattering, like cake crumbs thrown onto clay. The dust was a swirling fog, the car lost somewhere in the grey. He climbed onto his hands and knees, saw the driver already on his feet, calling out a name, calling for his friend.

His friend didn't answer.

For nearly an hour they walked together up and down the ruined landscape, looking for the man in the passenger seat. The flat earth was now an undulating hillside. The car stood, untouched and dirty, in the middle of the storm. Charlie couldn't see where the shells had been fired from, asked, "Were they trying to hit us?"

The driver shook his head, spreading his arms wide, no words left on his white-dust lips, his bright-red eyes. There was nothing here, not a living thing worth killing, not a crop to uproot, not a hut to demolish, only dust and the smell of hot metal. Somewhere, someone who couldn't see his target had opened fire on nothingness, and where there had been nothing before, now even less of nothing remained. The mathematical incongruity of it kept rattling round Charlie's head; as he staggered dumb over craters and along the edge of the road, he found it almost impossible to think of anything else.

Eventually, they found the other man's right leg. The driver of the car saw it, turned, and puked. Charlie just stood and stared, not sure if this was a real thing. Perhaps some trickster had left it here, as a cruel and well-prepared joke, and if prodded, it would turn out to be plastic with a bit of paint. He found he couldn't think, that he had to deliberately force himself to remember the words that would surely be most apt – words such as grief, horror, shock, trauma, despair, fear, danger – but as every sound took such a phenomenal effort to hold in his mind, he let it go, and his mind drifted back to the mathematics of nothingness, and how much his left foot itched.

He sat for a while on the side of the road as the driver finished coughing and puking and shaking, eyes too dry for tears. Then, when he was a little more composed, the driver stood up and said, voice breaking on the sound, "My name is Murad. You ride in front," and that was all there was to it.

Charlie rode in the front, and onwards they drove.

*

By sunset, the petrol tank was nearly empty. At fifteen miles an hour, they crawled into a town whose name had been painted over so many times, Charlie couldn't begin to guess at it. The roar of generators from the town square was one of the only sounds. A few figures scurried indoors as they approached, driving up what might have been the central street past the low-domed mosque to where a large beige building was still glowing with light. An arcade of high arches ran along its base, and two wings stretched out either side of a pointed front hall, behind which a cupola sat. Great bands of black and white tile ran up the front and sides, and glass lanterns hung down behind every arch, filling the building and the square in front of it, where a fountain still trickled, with light. A flag flew high overhead, the script on it lost to sight. A woman, her face entirely covered, black gloves on her hands, rushed out of the main door as the car pulled to a stop, rattling off words too fast for Charlie to hear. Murad nodded, tired, and with a jerk of his head towards the waiting escort said, "Go. Follow her."

Charlie hesitated, suddenly loath to leave his near-silent companion. Should men who had been shelled together not have a few more parting words? But Murad's eyes had already turned away to some other place, contemplating some other thing, so Charlie slipped from the passenger seat, and followed the woman inside.

A military headquarters.

Men in camouflage gear, black strips of cloth tied around their right sleeves. As Charlie approached, some covered their faces – sunglasses, goggles, keffiyehs, balaclavas, a medley of goods from a hundred different sources. There was little resemblance between the camouflage clothes they wore, some yellow, some grey, some flecked with blue. Nor was there any uniformity in their weapons, but rather a mess of guns of every sort had been thrown together, and of the men Charlie saw, too many still had their fingers on the trigger, even here, and their heads jerked sharply as he passed, eyes flashing like startled cats. Voices, some

150

female, most male, drifted through the high corridors, the ceilings and floor mosaicked with great geometric lines and zigzags, now cracked and crumbling from the pressures of time and too many boots. Empty mirror frames, the glass long broken and swept away; empty picture frames, the canvas carefully removed by an unknown curator.

Up a flight of stairs beneath a crystal chandelier, along a corridor where once, perhaps, colonial administrators, fresh from Paris, had drunk good champagne and smoked small cigarettes and debated the best tax to impose upon this territory, and where now men who served . . .

. . . Charlie wasn't sure what . . .

. . . slept in hastily arranged bunk beds against the walls.

A door stood open at one end, the green paint scoured from the wood. Charlie was hustled in, the woman bobbing silently as she pulled the door shut behind her, and in the half-light of the single burning lamp on the heavy oak desk, he saw Qasim.

It took him a moment to recognise the little poet. He was thinner now, a trace of grey in his hair. Two fingers were missing from his left hand, and as he glanced up from the papers on which he toiled, he did not smile. He too wore combat fatigues; a pistol lay on top of the papers on which he worked.

His pen moved, his head stayed down, and in his elegant, flawless English he said, "Do you know the city of Deir ez-Zor, Harbinger of Death?"

"No." Charlie's voice, a tiny thing in this sprawling room.

"It is one of the last holdouts of the government regime in the east. As a result, it has been under siege for many months. A few weeks ago, the government closed the last of the bakeries to the civilian population, saying that the soldiers needed the bread. They are charging fifty thousand Syrian pounds for every man, woman and child who wishes to leave. It is criminal, you see, to run away from war; it is treachery. If the people run, do you know what they meet then?"

"No."

"They meet the extremists. They meet the boys whose fathers

151

died before they could teach them about humanity. They meet the angry men, the kids who never worked out who they were until God told them in a bloody dream. They meet the lucky survivors, the ones who escaped the bombs, and who, seeing their friends dead, knew it was only heaven that saved them. They meet the soldiers who did not want to fight, whose families will die if they do not. They meet the men who fight for a cause, and have chosen the cause over life. They meet the beheaders, who are happy to saw through the spines of teachers, doctors, nurses, journalists and children. They meet the men who stone women to death, and set fire to prisoners inside metal cages. Tell me, do you know the Harbinger of Famine?"

"A little, yes."

"She went to Deir ez-Zor a few weeks ago, to talk to the mayor. I was surprised that you didn't go with her."

"My work sent me elsewhere."

"Your work brings you back to me?"

"Yes."

Qasim's lips twitched, a tiny *hm*, a little nod of his head, kept on writing. Charlie stood almost to attention, clutching his travel bag in front of him, and waited.

Finally the poet finished his words, snapped the lid on his pen, leant back in his chair, hands folded behind his head to cushion it, one leg over the other, and seemed for the very first time to see Charlie, and looked unimpressed.

"So. Here you are. You gave me mousetraps and I lived, and others died, and now you've come back again."

"I guess so."

"And what do you bring me this time? That's what you do, isn't it? Death sends you before, and you bring ... ?" A flicker of his eyebrows, commanding, expecting obedience.

Charlie rummaged in his bag, pulled out the box that lay within, put it gingerly on the table. Qasim studied it for a long moment, then in a single motion unfolded himself, scooped it up, opened it. The box was some fifteen centimetres long, four centimetres wide. The fountain pen inside was stained with black ink long since run dry, the lid was cracked. A long while Qasim looked at it, and then he laughed. He threw back his head and laughed until the tears rolled down his face, and Charlie's shoulders jerked a little to be in the presence of laughter, though he couldn't find anything funny in it.

"First mousetraps, now a pen!" howled the little man through his merriment. "Death has a sense of the thing!" He leapt to his feet with sudden energy, nearly sprinted round the desk, slapped Charlie on the shoulder and exclaimed, "It is good to see you, my friend, it is very good indeed! Come with me – we must eat at once!"

Chapter 46

Charlie . . .

. . . he's not quite sure how this happened, but here he is . . .

. . . sits on cushions in the middle of a ballroom in a place with no name, as women in veils serve him dates and fresh fruit and hot bread and chickpea and mutton stew, and Qasim talks brightly about campaigns and planned victories and the perfidious Russians and the danger of aerial bombardment and the new aquifer he's going to have built and . . .

Charlie sits in a daze, and eats, and listens, and wonders what the hell he's doing here.

Death knows Deir ez-Zor.

She has been here many times.

Once, she marched with the Armenians, back in the time of the First World War. She had been busy in that time, huddled in the trenches in northern France, holding the hand of the man covered in mud, his screams unanswered in no-man's-land. Sometimes Death beheld her sisters – Pestilence, her face hidden

153

by the lice that roamed in a living grey skin across her face; War moving through the yellow-green clouds of gas, his bare hands blistering, rupturing, dripping pus. When it was over, Pestilence had said it was a shame, it had been such an exciting time, but wasn't flu interesting?

And Death had marched with the Armenians, across the desert of bones to Deir ez-Zor, and Famine had walked too, holding the hands of the old and the children, and when there were no more children to walk, Famine had walked with the mothers and the fathers, until at last they came to this city in the east, and Famine had conceded her work was done, and only Death remained.

Later – much later – the city had built a church and a memorial to those days, raised up words in honour of the dead, held prayers to the nameless lost, their bodies given to sand. Death liked that. Death always paid the proper price for the votive candles she lit.

For a little while, the church had stood, and then the war had come, and angry men who knew no peace had declared that it was obscene and heathen, and had blown it to dust, and in that dust Death stood, and felt briefly irritated that the ones she had taken were not being treated with proper respect, and resolved that before the day was done, many men would know her indignation. For Death, like all the riders of the Apocalypse, may be summoned, but once summoned, may not obey the will of man.

Behind Death, Famine stood, though in truth, she has too much going on right now to give the past much in the way of thought.

Busy busy busy busy . . .

There was music.

And there was dancing.

And there was knock-off Pepsi that made Charlie's mouth burn.

And there was more food.

And there was more dancing.

And when it was done, Charlie and Qasim staggered through

the tumbledown remnants of this had-been imperial palace, and Charlie said, "You're so kind, you're . . . so very kind . . . "

And Qasim, whose face was flushed a brilliant red from drinking something a little bit stronger than fizzy drinks, mumbled back, "For the Harbinger of Death, what man would refuse?" and laughed at some very funny joke, and showed Charlie to his room, which had an actual four-poster in it, and a copy of the Quran on a bedside table of beautifully carved wood, and a Tom Clancy novel in French on the table on the other side of the luxuriously puffed mattress, and Charlie mumbled thank you, thank you, thank you, and Qasim laughed some more and said, "No problem!" and went his own way to bed.

And five minutes later, Charlie's face wet from the bowl of water left by the heat-bent mirror on one wall, there was a knock on his door, and before he could answer, a woman came in wearing a silk dressing gown and very little else, and mumbled, "I was sent for you?"

"Uh . . . no?"

"You are the Harbinger of Death?"

"Yes, but you weren't sent."

"I was sent," she replied firmly, reaching to undo the gown. "I was sent."

Charlie flapped his hands like the wings of a frightened chicken, and made it to her just in time to stop her undoing the knot. "No," he mumbled in his feeble Arabic. "No I'm not . . . you're not . . ." He stopped, trying to find a way to explain, to unravel this mystery, and saw her flinch and realised he was holding her wrists tight, and the skin beneath his hands was bruised black and purple, old markings not given a chance to heal.

Abashed, he stumbled back, and the girl stared enquiring into his face. She was barely more than a teenager, her hair sometime recently cut brutally short, and only now beginning to grow back. "I'm married," he blurted. "I have a wife."

Her face fell, she stared down at the floor, pulled the robe tighter around her skinny shoulders. Guilt, fear, anxiety – he wasn't sure which emotion to name – welled up fast, hard enough

155

to make his head spin. "You can stay," he added, softer. "I'll sleep over there ..." a gesture at a low wooden couch, layered with pillows. "You sleep in the bed."

"I stay?"

"You stay. You sleep there, I sleep here."

She hesitated, seeming not to understand, so Charlie pushed his bag under the couch, rolled onto it, tucking his knees to his chest, and closed his eyes, making a great show of sleeping.

For a while she stood, staring at this bizarre man, before at last, seeing that he wasn't about to stir, and wondering if maybe his pretence had become real, she walked towards the great padded bed, crawled under the sheets, and stared up at the ceiling.

If either of them slept a wink, neither knew it, and she ran away at the first light of dawn.

Chapter 47

In the morning Charlie said: "I've given you the pen, I should be going ..." and Qasim exclaimed, of course, no problem, we'll get you a car, just wait here ...

And in the afternoon Charlie said, "I was told a car was coming, is Qasim ..." and the colonel said, I'm sure it's being handled, don't worry, I'll look into it.

And in the evening Charlie said, "Thank you for your hospitality, but there's places I have to get to, and it's not here, I've got ..." and the major replied, no cars, not tonight, not tomorrow, but you just wait, we'll get you out of here, you'll see.

And at night, there was a yellow glow on the horizon, and five jets skimmed overhead and someone muttered, "Damn Russians!" and someone else, on the other side of the courtyard muttered, "Damn Americans!" and no one was quite sure who was right, but what did it matter? As to those above, those below ...

And Charlie sat on the porch of the old palace, his hands between his knees, and asked if anyone had seen Qasim, and the poet was everywhere and nowhere. He was on the front lines, fighting with the men; he was in the city, defending the women. He was taking a piss, he was having a cigarette, he was seeing his mother, he was helping protect the granary, he was negotiating with a warlord from the east, a man who had no allegiance to anyone or anything. He was writing poetry to the moon, to the thin slivers of light that still shone over this dark land. He was skyping a girl he knew in South Korea. He was looking after the kids. He was immortal. He was preparing to die. He was a monster, walking over the graves of the dead. He was a hero, in every place at once, and nowhere his enemies, or Death himself, might find him.

Afterwards, when the generators finally powered down and the quiet men and women of the palace padded around with candles shrouded behind cupped hands, Charlie lay on his back, fully dressed, in his grand, ridiculous room, and stared at a ceiling where the frescoed image of a cloudy sky laced with moist sunset had chipped away to bare plaster, and thought he heard a man screaming in the darkness, before that scream was cut off, and realised he wasn't sure how he was meant to get home.

Chapter 48

Click click click click.

Hi, it's Charlie, is that Samantha?

No, dear, it's Maureen.

Maureen, I'm sorry, I should have . . . the line is very bad.

How are you, dear?

Thing is, Maureen, I'm stuck in a place in Syria and I don't know where I am. I've got a satellite phone but I don't . . . I don't want anyone to find me with it. I can't really say why it's ... I've got appointments next week, I'm in a war zone, is there a plan? The office said to wait at a hotel and I did and now ...

Syria, you say? Ah yes, I can see on the calendar – meeting a general, yes?

A poet, but yes, I suppose, a general.

Good good!

And now I'm stuck here.

No, not at all, you have meetings next week.

And no way to get to them. I have a plane ticket out of Ankara next Tuesday, but how am I meant to get to Ankara?

It's all been arranged.

Has it? I don't have those details, could you tell me ...?

I'll send you an email.

I don't have reliable internet access right now.

Just check your inbox first thing!

No, but I'd ...

Byeeee!

Click click click.

Chapter 49

Voices.

Listen to the voices, and find that calm that comes from lives, living, always living.

" ... for the six a.m. muster and then we move out to collect the water from the local ... "

" ... she said, but I said that is the most ridiculous thing I've ever heard, that is just – what planet are you even living on?"

"I like the dates they get from the west, there's something in it, not too syrupy but just the right sort of texture when you ... "

"That's disgusting."

158

"So the gun went from Belgium to France to Libya to the rebels to the Palestinians to Hezbollah to the soldiers to the ..."

"Problem is they're still weak in defence. Now if they changed formation, put three at the back and two up front I think they'd be scoring two, maybe three more every match ..."

"My brother was a finalist in the regional poetry championship. Listen, it goes like ..."

"Doctor! For God's sake someone get me a doctor ... I'm ... I can't ... I ..."

"He did? No. When? How'd it happen? No, I didn't know. Does his wife know? Of course he has a wife, didn't any of you tell her? Of course she needs to know, how can you be so ..."

On his third day in a place that might have been Syria, might have been Iraq – these things were hard to measure now, the border had been swept away by the fire – Charlie went to look in his bag for the satellite phone, and it wasn't there. He rummaged with a sudden fury, face flushing hot, and then tore his room apart looking for it, which was as futile an act as any he had performed because he knew, of course he knew, where he'd put it, the same place he'd put it every night as he reached out for rescue, to Maureen or Samantha or Lucy in the Milton Keynes office (they all sounded the same), who all replied with "Don't worry, dear, all in hand!" and never told him what it was, or how it was being handled.

Now his phone was gone, and with it, that lifeline to the outside world.

Charlie sat on the end of the bed and for a moment felt utterly alone, and hugely sorry for himself. A strange, childlike inclination to cry surfaced briefly – not in fear, but in a petulant frustration and impotence – and he stood up and paced from one end of the room to the other before it could overwhelm him, and so it passed.

Two hours later, a convoy of trucks pulled up outside the palace, and Qasim, dark sunglasses and a jaunty beret, leapt down from the front and bounded inside, and Charlie nearly took the stairs two at a time to meet him, catching him as he neared his office.

"Qasim! Qasim, I need to . . ."

The poet/general swept straight by him, as if he wasn't there, sparing him not a glance. Caught in a wake of lesser ranks, Charlie was buffeted and turned by the surge, reaching out, trying to grab the attention of the passing man, but Qasim was gone, the door slammed in his face.

In the afternoon, Charlie stood on the edge of the largest hall in the building, and watched men turn towards Mecca to pray. Afterwards he met a woman, come from the service in the room next door, and her eyes reminded him of the eyes of the woman who'd come to his bedroom on the first night he'd stayed, but her face was shrouded, and she quickly looked away.

Charlie drifted like a ghost through the bowels of Qasim's army, and had nowhere to go, and nothing to do, but like a fond puppy was fed and watered and kept warm at night, and generally ignored while the business of the day unfolded.

On the fourth night, the sound of jet planes was much closer. When they dropped the bombs, Charlie was surprised that the shaking was greater than the noise. The shock of it blasted the glass from his windows, bounced him out of bed. He crawled under the still-rocking bed as dust trickled from the ceiling, as the outside world went *thump thump thump*. When it stopped, he crawled to his feet and looked out to see that the building opposite the palace was gone. There was no remnant of wall or hint of crooked ceiling; there was no still-standing door or piece of furniture left behind. There was simply an absence, a great pall of dust, and here or there the odd brick raining down from the sky, pitter-patter, into the near-perfect circle punched into the ground, as if the earth had acne.

Men and women started to scramble out into the dark, torch beams clearly visible through the still-swirling fog. Charlie felt a cold breeze on his face through the broken glass, by candlelight

160

observed that the bed in which he'd lain was now ticktacked with shards, the headboard spined with embers. He wondered if he should tell anyone, but given the rising commotion outside, it didn't seem so important. He stood in the window and looked down, and beheld the rider of the Apocalypse on the edge of the crater below, his face swept by the moving points of light, dust on his skin, fire at his back, one hand in his pocket, the other caressing a cigarette.

Charlie looked at War, and War, sensing the gaze, looked up at Charlie, and smiled, and flicked ash to one side, and turned, and walked away.

Three other people beheld War that night, and each saw their own version of the same thing.

Nabil, a geology student who'd been studying at the University of Aleppo, right up to the day it was bombed, and who had escaped death by being late for his exam, looked up from his desperate, futile scramble in the dirt, a quest to find any living being that might yet be breathing beneath the flattened oval of the bomb's impact, and beheld . . .

War, clad in armour of ash, his eyes blazing red through the gas mask, a bloodied sword at his side, an AK–47 across his waist, an electric whip in his hand. The skin of his neck and wrist was visible, swollen, bursting with thick white goo from the effect of the poison gas that young Nabil had seen pictures of once, when it was used on the Kurds in the north, and which he had never forgotten. Though he was far off, as he walked, his footsteps crunched, cracked the earth, and he moved at a mighty, cumbersome pace, unstoppable as an avalanche, as inevitable as night itself.

And Amira, whose town this had once been and who had clung on, clung on, because her mother was too old to leave and her sister was too young, because there was nowhere to go and because she had to believe, had to believe in hope and the goodness of men, ran through the dust to help search for survivors, and beheld War and saw . . .

161

A man with a bandanna across his head, and dirt on his face, with ankle boots and camouflage trousers, with curly dark hair and a scar all the way round his neck, and she realised with a start that his face was the face of her brother, but not her brother, for he was dead, he had run away to fight and never come home and they said he had done some terrible things

but this was not he

but War himself, passing by.

And the Harbinger of Death looked down, and saw War, and knew he was War by the quality of his suit, perfectly tailored, cut to his slim, gym-built figure. And he knew he was War by the smartphone clipped to his belt, and by the cufflinks on his sleeves, and by the way he looked upon destruction and smiled, like a man sensing opportunity.

Qasim also saw War that night, but couldn't recognise the face he wore, having ordered all the mirrors in the palace smashed many, many months ago, for staring at him too reprovingly.

Chapter 50

A jump, a start, wake up!

Hands shaking him roughly. "You, you, wake up!"

Charlie woke, groggy, lying on the couch away from the window, his bed still full of glass, a blanket wrapped round his shoulders, fully dressed – somehow he'd got in the habit of sleeping with his clothes on. Two soldiers stood there; one held a flashlight, the other shook him even though he was awake. "You! Up up up now up!"

Charlie rolled to his feet, one soldier pulling him by the elbow, dragging him down the grey pre-dawn corridors, half-light slithering in, the grumble of a generator out back, chugging down petrol. He tried to pull free, mutter, okay, okay, I'm coming, but the soldier just held on, bizarre, almost pinching his elbow between his fingers, not exactly restraining but refusing to release. Charlie had seen a taxi driver do the same once to a man who couldn't pay his fare, hold him like a child as they walked across the street, in case he ran, stand by him with one hand on his shoulder at the ATM. He hadn't known at first if what he was seeing was two lovers out for the night, or a kidnap in progress.

The door to Qasim's office, opened quickly by a woman dressed all in black, a necklace of bullets slung across her chest, Charlie pushed through, the door closed behind him.

Blinking, the shutters open on the windows, Qasim framed by the rising sun, head bowed, writing, always writing, paper on the desk, paper on the floor, crossings-out and scrawls on both sides, different inks running over each other as thoughts came and went. Charlie hadn't seen him for days, every effort rebuffed, and now here he was, here they were, another day.

Qasim, wordless, tilted the tip of his pen towards an object on the end of his desk. Charlie followed the motion with his eyes. His satellite phone, bits of circuitry dangling by pale wires, the keypad caved in from where the butt of a rifle had struck it. Charlie stared at it, then at Qasim, and the adrenaline surge that had carried him out of bed faded, and there was nothing now but quiet, a silence where he felt sure some sort of feeling should have been, and the scratching of Qasim's pen.

Words across the page . . .

. . . *and we shall build a new world, the old world perishes and now only there is left the cleansing of the* . . .

. . . *of these ideas that old men speak of, we say to them now* . . .

. . . *Salafist, Wahhabist, republican, atheist, Catholic, Copt, Sunni, Shia, Sufi, Armenian, Orthodox, communist, fascist, capitalist, Daesh, Jewish, Azeri, Druze, Kurd* . . .

Charlie watched him write, found the movement strangely hypnotic, realised he was swaying where he stood, looked around for something to sit on, but the chairs were all gone from the room, taken away, everyone stands in the presence of the general.

What is the purpose of history? It seeds only hate. All the history books should be burnt, so that we are no longer the peoples of our lands, but merely peoples . . .

The sun rose higher, the shadows stretching out across the floor, the greyness giving way to yellow-white. What darkness was left in the room seemed deeper by comparison, and still Qasim wrote.

There once was a man who walked to Medina and in that place all the tribes gathered and in that gathering they spoke of peace and of

He stopped, the pen poised to find a word that never came.

For a moment, the world hung there, waiting: Word, pen, poet, and the Harbinger of Death.

Then, laying the pen down, the words still unfinished, Qasim sprung to his feet, marched past the Harbinger of Death without meeting his eye, threw back the doors and exclaimed, "Follow me!"

Charlie guessed that this command was meant for him, there being no one else handy, so he followed.

They drove in a convoy of five trucks. In the middle of it was Qasim's car, black and air-conditioned, a minibar in the front, speakers in the back pumping out the latest pop song from the UAE. Charlie sat next to the poet, aware suddenly in this pristine, clean vehicle of how badly he smelt, of his unshaven face and crumpled clothes, of his tired eyes and empty mouth.

If Qasim cared, he didn't show it, and they drove in silence, an hour, an hour and a half, music blaring, the car too cold inside to be comfortable, Qasim staring out of the window. Charlie also watched the land run by, but saw only yellow emptiness, obscured by the tint of the window. Empty fields and empty homes, bumpy roads and the occasional crust of a place where life had been lived, of schools and hospitals and things worth fighting for, all burnt.

When they stopped, it was on the edge of a village that could have been anywhere in the world. Little white houses with bright red roofs; a petrol station next to a convenience store, a few packets of crisps still in the window. A central street lined with lovingly cared-for palm trees. At the top of one, a nest of wasps had made their home amongst sprouting fronds, and the fat-bellied creatures hummed and clung to windows nearby.

Qasim hopped out of the car, busy busy busy, and gestured for Charlie to follow. He did, without complaint, but one of the soldiers clearly felt that more was required, and pushed him by the shoulder, causing him to stumble. He glared, but said nothing, and followed the poet into the belly of the town.

A playground.

A school.

A little dried-up bed where a stream had run.

A mosque, a hole carved in its white dome.

A vet's clinic, the glass torn out, the benches bare.

A field where once they grew ... Charlie didn't know, only stalks and dusty earth remained.

A ditch, recently carved in the earth.

The sound of flies, the smell, the smell that made your clothes rot from your body, the smell that made your eyes pop from your skull, the smell that you tasted in your throat, the smell that told the story to your very stomach, of flesh become liquid, liquid running into the earth, of blood drunk by wolves, of toes munched on by rats, of maggots popping from muscle, of

Charlie vomited before they reached the pit. Qasim stopped, already at its edge, and waited, impatient, hands on hips. When the puke was out, the soldier who'd pushed him picked him up, pulled him by the scruff of the neck to the edge of the earth, grabbed hair at the back of his head and forced him to look down.

A face stared back, a woman, her eyes open but their colour gone, her teeth broken, her dress torn. The child she had died protecting lay beneath her, one bare foot sticking out from beneath her back. Others had fallen face-down; some had their hands tied. The men were, in a way, easier to look at than the women, since they had had their heads chopped off first, along with their hands and their feet. Some of the boys had died from the machete too. At first Charlie thought that snakes were living on them, until he realised that the writhing masses he saw were the creatures still happily feeding on burst intestines, their half-digested matter spilt and black around the burst sacs of the bodies that had held them.

Someone had shot the baby through the roof of its mouth to quiet its screaming; another woman had perhaps fought back, and been shot no fewer than ten times, the holes strangely neat across her tangled, fallen body. Some of the corpses were naked; some were old, a man and a woman with hands reaching out for each other in death.

The flies buzzed, and the town was silent.

Tears ran down Charlie's face, triggered first by the smell, which his body seemed to want to wash away, but which clung to him the more he sweated. He whispered, "I'm going to be sick," and the soldier pushed him to one side. He fell onto his knees and heaved, but had nothing to throw up, and being on his knees he stayed there and wept, wept and wept, shook and heaved and shed salt onto the earth, and wept.

Qasim stood by, staring into the graves, and waited until there was no breath, no sound left in the Harbinger of Death. Then he pulled two objects from the pocket of his jacket.

One was a mousetrap, still in its packet.

The other was a pen.

He said, "We are fighting for a better land, we are fighting for freedom. We wish only to have hope again in our lives, to have a safe place for our mothers, our children. We wish for justice. We wish for holidays. We wish to go walking in the sea and eat ice cream. We wish for antibiotics when our brothers are sick. We wish for a job that finishes at six o'clock in the afternoon. We wish to pay rent, to cook food with our own hands, good food, to taste cinnamon again. We wish to decorate our homes, and smell fresh paint, and be proud of the lives we have built. We wish to practise our beliefs, piously and in peace. We wish to know our neighbours, and play simple games, and read books, and watch the TV. Is this so much? Is this more than any man desires? Do you understand?"

Charlie understood, and made no sound. "You said to me once that you were sometimes sent as a courtesy, sometimes as a warning. I thought then you had come to tell me that I would die. But how? Were you a self-fulfilling prophecy; would I hear your words and change my ways, and in doing so go to my death? Then I knew I would stay and fight, for my family, for my friends, for my beliefs, and I thought perhaps you were a warning that this fight would kill me, and I should flee, take the road to Europe, where your governments say that we are not people as you are, and you build walls to stop us coming. Swarms, rats, rats of people, fleeing the sinking ship, we are rats and then . . ."

He held the mousetrap up thoughtfully, then tossed it into the pit.

"Then I thought, this is what war makes of us, is it not? This is the meaning of your gift. These extremists, the ones ruled by fear and the gun, they rejoice at every massacre because those who do not believe what they believe are not human. They are animals. They are the lowest carrion that scuttle upon the earth. They are rats, scrabbling for a tiny scrap of meat, feasting upon the lowest gutter. Had I fled, I would have been a scrabbling rat. In staying, I have killed my fair share of vermin. Either way, Death comes. He comes."

So saying, he raised the pen. "Of course, I did not die. You came, and you gave me your gift — it is very funny, I see that now, ha ha — and I lived. And I thought, well done me, I have made the right choice. Had I fled, Death would have come for me, and now I have stayed, and so you were only a warning, not a courtesy, and Death, as they say, passed me by. Death passed me by, what a narrow view. Death has been my bosom brother for many years. I know him, I know his voice, his touch, his caress, more intimately and with more sanctification than you ever will, Harbinger of Death. He has spoken to me for so long, and I have spoken back, in his language, the secret language of lovers, and I have done . . . such things. And now you come again, speaking your crude, human speech, as if words that may be uttered have meaning any more, and you bring me a pen, a pen that was once my pen, the ink run dry. I lost it years ago but now here it is, returned to me, and Death laughs at me and says . . . I hate having to use words to translate it, but I will try . . . Death says 'told you so', and here we are. A world has ended, and only tomorrow remains."

He threw the pen into the pit, watched it fall, waited for it to stop, then turned to Charlie, examined him, curious, squatted down in front of him, brushed his face, felt the texture of tears on his skin, almost smiled, at a thing he half remembered but had long ago forgotten.

"The people I fight are not human," he breathed. "The men who burn other men alive. The men who beat their enemies with electric cables. The rapists. The mutilators. The ones who stone children to death. The government men with their prisons and their gas; the Russians and the Americans who kill us from overhead like we are pixels on a map; they have become animals. Do you understand? They were human, and war has made them something else. The world is better off without them. When my men killed this place, they laughed as they did it, because they were not killing people, only taking out the trash. That's all this was. That's all this is. The world is ending. We are come to a time of cleansing, and when all the world is cleansed, then we shall be free."

He stood up, brushed dust off his knees, nodded at one of his men. "Go home, Harbinger of Death," he said. "Go tell your master that I serve him well."

He turned away.

A soldier picked Charlie up by the arm, and the Harbinger staggered in his grip, knees buckling, the tears pricking his eyes again. Another soldier came to help, and the two of them helped him away from the edge of the pit, back towards the car.

And as they did, Charlie looked up through a veil of tears, and at the far end of the field he beheld a pale figure leaning against a blasted tree, and it seemed to him that the land withered beneath his feet, and the sky blackened above his head, and his name was Death, and hell followed him.

Chapter 51

How deep is the sea that separates us now?
My beloved, do not cease your singing
The water carries your voice upwards
I dive
I am coming
I wear this skin of weeds
I do not fear the monsters with eyes like the broken
    moon
The ink that fills my veins gives me breath
Your lips guide me
We go down to the deep together.

Unpublished poem by Qasim Jahani, 2012

Everyone meets Death. The tired welcome her; the just rage against her coming. The young do not understand her; the great do not realise that she cannot be bought. But of all those for whom she comes, it is always the lovers who are the most afraid.

Extract from an email, Saga Kekkonen,
"Advice for a new Harbinger".

Chapter 52

A car drove him to a place.
  In that place, another car collected him.
  Drove him to another place.

He slept one night in the back of the vehicle, in a barn of corrugated iron.

Then they drove.

And when they stopped, a man in a suit and a woman in a white dress met him, and said in English, heavily accented with French, "Good morning, Mr Harbinger. We have been sent by Milton Keynes to take you home."

They gave him fresh clothes, and he saw that the sign on the side of the road was in Turkish, and pointed the way to Ankara.

"Wait," he said, and they waited, and on the edge of the road he stripped naked, and tipped a bottle of water over his head, and let the heat dry him, and changed into the clothes they'd brought, and burnt everything that was left behind.

Chapter 53

" ... and everyone's complaining, but when it comes to defending democracy, who you gonna call?"

"The Chinese record on human rights ... "

"Save the Sikhs! The government of India is committing genocide against our brothers and sisters, the great temple once again is soaked in blood, and the people ... "

"I'm just like, fuck, if you guys want to kill each other, that's fine by me."

" ... secular activist was hacked to death as he left his apartment today ... "

Tick. Tick. Tick.

"Poor kids would do so much better with National Service."

"*Ghostbusters!*"

"On behalf of His Majesty and the people of Saudi Arabia, I demand an apology for the outrageous suggestion ... "

"Free Raif Badawi, free the journalists vanished in Eritrea, free the citizens on death row in Malaysia, free the bloggers imprisoned in Belarus, free the . . . "

"Are my kids safe? Is my family safe? Are we going to get through the winter? That's what I care about, and the rest, frankly, the rest you can just shove right up your . . . "

"Investment investment investment."

"Aung San Suu Kyi spoke for all the peoples of Myanmar, even when she was silent, locked behind doors, but now we are dying, the Rohingya, the Kachin, the Karen, and where is she, where are those words now?"

"There is an Armageddon clock that assesses how close humanity is to self-destruction based on a number of factors compiled by a committee in . . . "

"*Oh say can you see by the dawn's early light!*"

Tick. Tick. Tick.

"This is a global age, a global society; if you ignore issues like this then take it from me, it'll come and bite you, and I mean *hard*."

"Human human human rat human human rat rat human human human rat rat rat human . . . "

"A panel of retired judges will decide whether the government can see your stored web browsing history, providing safeguards against . . . "

"The time now is three minutes to midnight."

Tick.

Tick.

Tick.

Tick.

171

Part 5

CLOTTED CREAM

Chapter 54

On the shores of the sea . . .

. . . in a land where all things grow . . .

. . . the Harbinger of Death walked side by side with a woman.

Her name was Emmi. She was a deputy headmistress at a secondary school in Barnet. She wore blue jeans, bright cyan and grey trainers, a waterproof coat and a light white scarf, which had been given to her by students at her last school, who were so surprised to discover that they'd got a range of A–Cs in their GCSE Chemistry that they'd banded together to get her something to show their appreciation. The scarf was beautiful; the book about cocktail making was perhaps inappropriate.

"We just thought you needed to get drunk more, miss!" explained the boldest of the pupils, and in her way, she had correctly sensed a void in Emmi's life that she had always struggled to fill.

Emmi was black, of that deepest, richest dark that came from the west coast of Africa, her heritage steeped, so her mother had always said, in the noble kings of ancient Liberia. Her ancestors had commanded armies, conducted ancient rites, sat in judgement over life and death, and Emmi had been born in Denmark Hill and grown up in a two-bedroom flat in Clapham before Clapham got pricey, and had been to Liberia twice, and secretly not enjoyed it as much as she had wanted to.

No one could call her slim, but no one could call her fat either. Her body was all curves, and while as a teenage girl she had looked in the mirror and despised herself, now that she was a little older, and her work had taught her a duty of care for the self-image of the girls in her flock, she had come to love her body, and had only been mildly troubled that there wasn't someone else out there who seemed to love it too.

The Harbinger of Death loved Emmi's body.

The realisation had come slowly to Emmi, fast to the Harbinger. It wasn't merely that he was falling head-over-heels for her as a human being that surprised her; it was that he seemed to see in every contour of her face, in every flick of her wrist and stamp of her foot, another part of her, a new piece of her soul manifesting physically, and every part he saw, he loved.

He didn't say so very often, of course. The Harbinger of Death was not renowned for being talkative. But one night, she had gone to his flat, not at all confident of what this relationship was or if she was even that interested in a man who worked for Death, let alone someone who spent a lot of time out of the country, and found an old man and his granddaughter in the living room, and Charlie had muttered something about how they were staying for a little while, hope she didn't mind. (She did not.)

And the months had rolled by, and she still wasn't certain, he wasn't around enough for her to be sure, and then last week they had gone out together for a Vietnamese meal, and Charlie had been quiet, and his eyes had wandered, and his mind had floated to some other place, and Emmi had told herself well, this isn't going anywhere, is it?

Charlie? Charlie?

And the clock on the wall went tick, tick, tick.

And she'd blurted, "Charlie, are you listening to me?"

Tick tick tick.

And he'd looked down, food barely touched, and she thought perhaps he was going to cry, and then he'd told her everything.

Told her about the graves. About the bombings, the journey through a broken land. Told her about War, smiling as the dust settled, about Death, standing on the edge of the field, the edge of the ice. And Emmi had said to herself, *Well, this is all very good, isn't it, but just because he's in a state doesn't mean you have to get*

176

involved. But he had talked, and she had listened, and afterwards they had walked back to his flat together, and she had thought, *Ah, fuck it, I'll walk away when I want to . . .*

And that night he had declared, simply and without needing anything from her in return, that he loved her, and that she was the most beautiful woman he had ever known, and that her beauty was in her skin, and in her eyes, and in her smile, and in her laughter, and in her frown, and in her talking, and in her silence, and in all the things good and bad that were her, because she was all beautiful, every part of her.

And Emmi had stood in the bathroom, the morning after, and looked at herself long and hard in the mirror and said, "Emmi, my girl, this is not a relationship you want or need," and had realised, even as she said it, that she was probably wrong.

She'd dump him, of course, as soon as he cocked up, or if she decided that long-term, this relationship was a drain, not a bolster to her life.

But for now

one day at a time

in full knowledge of the good and the bad of what she might be getting into

she was willing to give it a go.

On the shores of the sea . . .

. . . in a land where all things grow . . .

Emmi walked side by side with the Harbinger of Death along the top of a slate cliff, as the stiff-spined flowers rattled in the wind and the sun glistened off the ocean beneath their feet. And as they walked, they talked – of difficult students and annoying teachers, of heads of department who just had to mouth off in staff meetings, of the latest cuts and government objectives, of how she'd always wanted to learn a bit more about woodwork and was hoping to sneak into the workshop after the pupils had gone home to get some tuition from Mrs Daws; of how the parents blamed the school, the school blamed the parents, and the kids were the only ones who ever blamed themselves. And he'd talked of long stopovers at Dubai and Frankfurt, arrivals, departures, arrivals, departures; of sitting by the beds of dying men and women; of bringing flowers to a school where in a few days' time a gunman would attack, killing fifteen. Of seeing the parents of those children and whispering, sometimes I am a courtesy, sometimes a warning . . .

Of knowing that of the twenty-three children who'd died one day in a shooting up in Iowa, it could have been twenty-four, but a mother who had talked with the Harbinger in the hall had decided, when her daughter said she had a cold, to believe her, even though she knew it was probably a lie.

"There is a battle," he mused, as the sun rolled overhead, "between what people sense to be true, and what they reason. A man comes up to you in the street, and you instinctively feel that something is off, you just know it, you know that he's . . . but he's smartly dressed, and this is a civilised land, and so you shake it off and tell yourself don't be stupid, don't be daft, you're being afraid of nothing. Then he follows you into your home, and you realise now that you didn't ask him to approach you. You didn't ask him to pick up the shopping. You didn't ask him to walk you to the front door. The man who you fired, and who laughed and said you'd be seeing him again, and you shook it off, heat of the moment, and you were also so afraid, and again he comes, he comes and there is . . . "

Emmi put her hand in Charlie's, and they walked in silence, the smell of salt, a family of fossil collectors scrambling amongst the black stones on the beaches below.

"Could you have done anything?" she asked, at last. "Could you have saved children at that school?"

"I don't know. I don't know the name of the attacker, I don't know what I'm there for. Once I went to a school in Pakistan, and I thought, oh God, kids, I'm seeing kids, Death is coming and . . . but then they opened their gates and the girls went to school along with the boys, and they learned the Quran and also they learned the history of the Bible and the Torah, and the teacher said, 'We are all of us simply people, doing our best,' and

Death was there for that too, and I went before to honour another way, and then in Iowa ... I was going to say you never know, but I went to that school, and I think I knew. Sometimes Death comes of his own accord, bringing fire and flood, earthquake and tornado. Sometimes Death comes because people summon him. I go before, and everywhere I go, you know the thing that amazes me?"

"No."

"Most of the time, no one is surprised to see me. At that school – no one was surprised to see me at all. And nothing changed, until it did."

They walked together, by the sea.

Chapter 55

Settle down, all right, settle down! Yes, that includes you, Ms Woods, phone away – phone away! We're going to be picking up from where we left off last class with human reproduction. We've already discussed the formation of eggs and sperm by cellular meiosis. Today we're going to talk about what happens during sex, fertilisation and the development of the foetus, *thank you*, you can laugh, of course you can, but I would argue that this is the single most important topic we are going to cover in this class all year. Nothing else you will learn will have such a profound impact on your lives, and for this purpose, we are also going to talk about contraception. Now, to address something that I've heard from a few people, and you know who you are, let's clear one thing up. Having sex standing up does *not*, I repeat *not*, protect against pregnancy or sexually transmitted disease ...

Chapter 56

"Charlie?"

"Um?"

"If tomorrow you got an appointment in your calendar, if you had to pick up and go ... If it was me, if the appointment was me, what would you do?"

"I don't think ... "

"Come on. This is serious."

A creaking in the bed. A rolling over white sheets. The sound of water through the window, the smell of salt. Curtains billowing in a westerly breeze, catching the sun, light reflecting off white and blue, the ocean a mirror to the sky.

At last: "If I had to visit you. As Harbinger."

"Yes. What would you do?"

"I'd tell you."

"Seriously?"

"Seriously."

"You'd tell me that I was going to die?"

"It's not always ... "

"Screw that, I know it's not always, but you'd be okay with it? You'd be fine doing that?"

"Yes."

"After Syria, after seeing that, you'd be ... "

"Sometimes people don't want to know. It's better not to. Your lover is hit by a car in the street, the pain of that, the sudden shock, a life in pieces, you don't want to fear, you don't want to think, knowing would be ... but if I saw your name, I'd know. And maybe there would be nothing to be done, maybe it would be ... and telling you would be the cruellest thing in the world, it would be unforgivable, it would be ... but sometimes I am a warning. And I would move the sky to protect you. I would risk everything. If knowing is the price of living, then I will pay that price a thousand times. We all die. We don't have to live our lives fearing it."

And after:

"Long-term, your job is gonna be a problem."

"I know."

"When you started ... "

"I did it for a lot of reasons, some good, many bad. I thought it would be an adventure, meet people, see the world, learn something ... important. I thought I would be important. I'm not an important person, you see."

"And now?"

"Now I still think the job is important, even if I'm not."

"Why? Why is it important that you go before?" He opened his mouth to answer, but she stopped him. "For the living, I know. You go for the living. I get how that matters. But I'm telling you, five years, maybe, maybe that could be a thing, but after ... "

"I know. We'll see. We'll find something together."

Chapter 57

A few days later, far from the shores of the sea, Agnes Young cleared her throat.

"So yeah, I didn't think like, I'd ever be doing anything like this or nothing, but I guess like, things don't turn out the way you planned. My grandad, he was – well, you're all here, so I guess you know what he was. He was good. There's lots of big words you can use as well, like as how he was funny and generous and patient, always patient, even when you just wanted him to start shouting at you 'cos of how that'd be easier, like, easier to be angry with him if he's angry and you're just even more pissed that he ain't – but look, those words, they're ... they're just like the icing, you know? They're the words that come from the word that means everything for him. He was good. He was a good man. And there's lots of people in this world who think they're good, and I don't think he was one of them. He was a man who just thought that it was what you did, helping people, caring about people, seeing strangers and giving a damn, and a lot of people say they think about that and don't really, and that doesn't make them bad, but he never said it, and always did it, and so he was good.

"He died in the nursing home. He didn't really want to be there, I think, never wanted to leave his home, but that wasn't a choice he got to make. He didn't leave much, but what he left matters more than anything that gets written in no will. He left memories; he left an idea of a way of doing things. He left us all changed. I ain't who I thought I'd be, and 'cos of him, I think I'm better. He never liked to make a fuss, but he never turned away from the battles that needed to be fought, not 'cos he was angry or scared of losing what he had, but because the fight was good and the cause was right, and because sometimes you gotta fight for the quiet man, the best of ways. A world is ending, and there is no bringing it back, and we carry on. He taught me that, and as I live, and as you remember, he lives too, always, with us."

And in the congregation ...

The Harbinger of Death sits quietly and nods at the words that come, and holds Emmi's hand, and cries with the rest of the room, not in raging grief that shouts and screams, but at the size of the hollow left behind, which no one now can fill.

And outside the church ...

Death waits, but does not enter. Her work is done, for today, and funerals she feels are a ceremony for the living, not the dead. She has no interest in corpses.

Chapter 58

"It's so good to meet you, so good, we heard that Emmi had a man but she hasn't really told us much about you, it's lovely . . . "

"Thank you for having me over. I know you've known Emmi a very long time . . . "

"All the way back to college! How long have you two been together now?"

"Over a year now, it's been so . . . "

"And you just got back from – did she say Japan?"

"Yes."

"Incredible, I've always wanted to go there, it just seems so . . . *different*."

"There's some social and cultural things that may seem strange, but I find that people are people wherever you go."

"Very true, very true! And what do you do?"

"Emmi didn't say?"

"No, just said you travelled a lot."

"Are you a teacher?"

"Me? No – quit years ago, couldn't do it. Lousy pay, long hours, no support, the government constantly moving the goalposts. I should have stuck with it, I know, I felt huge guilt, but now I get to see my family, my actual kids, *my* kids, and I'm just so much happier. But you didn't say . . . "

"I'm the Harbinger of Death."

"Oh. I see. And you . . . like the work?"

"It has its ups and downs."

"May I ask, how did you . . . ?"

"I think . . . I used to feel that it . . . When I started, it was a job and I didn't have a job, graduating into a recession and that, and I was flattered to be asked, I mean, to be trusted with something this big . . . I read this interview with Alfred Pierrepont, you know who he – the last British executioner."

"You see yourself as an executioner?"

"No! No, not at all, that's not … I read this interview and he was asked does he feel regret and he said no, because they had to die and he was always sure to treat everyone with kindness and dignity, to meet the eye of everyone he hanged and be sure to see something human, and I thought … I'm not an executioner, I go sometimes as a warning, sometimes as a courtesy, and I meet … I met people and some were dying, obviously, some were dying alone and Death was coming and I was sent before and I thought … there is something in this that is good. Something that is decent. So long as I am. My employer believes in … courtesy. Courtesy and respect above all else. Everyone who dies was once a child; every child once had a dream of something else; every child must die. It is important to remember the human behind the story, and I find it … good."

"I see. Less of an executioner, more of a … historian?"

"I don't record the stories."

"No, that wouldn't be … "

"Discretion is important."

"A confessor, perhaps?"

"Perhaps. No matter what you've done, no matter who you are … it is important that someone listens. At the end. And important that … that sometimes you know. Sometimes you simply know."

"Christ, I wouldn't want to know when I die."

"Maybe not, but if that knowledge changed the way you live …?"

"You're implying pre-destiny here, you're suggesting … fate?"

"Not at all. Death comes when he is called. Sometimes he is summoned by men and the things people do, and sometimes he passes people by."

"You sound almost … fond."

"I do not fear Death. I don't. I fear … something else. The bits in the middle. When I was young, my dad died, slowly; it was horrid. He had ALS – this was before the ice bucket thing, before people really knew or talked about it. The nerves die in your muscles and they atrophy from the outside in until you can't

184

even breathe without support, just lie there on a respirator, can't swallow, can't chew, still alive only 'cos medicine keeps you alive, and I was there, of course. I was there and Mum was there but she couldn't take it and I couldn't take it so we'd go in shifts, I'd do a few days, she'd do a few days, to give the other one a break, and so it was me, with Dad, in the hospital room as he died. Took nearly two years from the first time he lost his balance to the moment we pulled the ventilator and . . .

" . . . and Death sat with me. Only for a little while, only at the end. The night my Dad died, it was just him and me in the hospital. We'd turned off the ventilator, but he still didn't die, just lay there, gasping, for hours. Mum went to the toilet and just stayed there, half an hour, forty minutes, she didn't want me to see her cry. I didn't cry – I hadn't cried for a long time, by then. And the door opened, and it wasn't Mum, it was Death. I knew it was Death, as you always know, even though he looked like a doctor, white coat, the whole business, but I knew. You always recognise Death, when he comes, and you always see him in your own way.

"Anyway, I'm there, and I'm fifteen years old, and Death comes and pulls up a chair and sits by me, and doesn't say a word. We just sit there, watching, waiting, and after a little while Dad opened his eyes, and I think he saw Death, and he . . . he smiled. And Death smiled back, and held my Dad's hand, and Dad died. He died, and Death stayed a little while longer, just him and me, waiting for the nurse to come. It was . . . On ships the engine stops and suddenly you hear it; in a hospital the machines stop, and suddenly you hear them and it is the loudest thing you've ever heard, and Death sat with me and we were quiet, just the two of us, so quiet.

"Then the doctors came, and Death went about his business, I suppose.

"Sorry. That's . . . you've only just met me and . . . but it's good to tell it, I think. Sometimes I forget, sometimes in this job you see things and . . . Anyway. That's what I do. You have a lovely house."

185

"Thank you. It's small, but we like it. We want to try and find something bigger in the future, you know, maybe if kids . . . "

"Of course."

" . . . but it's hard, housing being what it is, and we don't want to rush into something . . . "

"Get comfortable, get uprooted . . . "

"Exactly. We did the bathroom ourselves. My wife, well, she trained as an opera singer but worked as a plumber to pay the fees, so she really knows what she's doing. I just stand there and hold a hammer and hope I look useful . . . "

"And the tiling . . . ?"

"We did that too, all the spacers, actually really came to enjoy it, and it wasn't hard, just getting the tools; you need to have the right tools for the job otherwise it's a nightmare, the wrong kind of cutter . . . "

Words, rolling on.

Sometimes the Harbinger of Death hears these words, words of house prices and commutes and the price of pasta and the new washing machine and the difficulty of finding a place to dry your wet clothes, and they make him indescribably sad.

Tonight, for some reason, as he listens to a story of a life still being built, and speaks of the ending of all things, he is not afraid, and this world, which seemed to be only ashes, begins again to give him an extraordinary joy.

Chapter 59

And as the world turns into night, the Harbinger of Famine walks through the refugee camp, a blue helmet on her head, and sneezes, and a child runs up to offer her a tissue, one of five in its possession, and the Harbinger of Famine smiles and says no, you keep it, you never know when you might need it later . . .

And as the world turns into night, War himself (for almost no one in this world has ever seen War as a woman, not since the days of fallen Troy) careens around the outskirts of Washington DC, slams his fist into the horn of his reinforced Mercedes and screams, *"Fucking Beltway, if I want to fucking turn left then don't put the fucking sign five yards before the turning. I will rain fire down upon you, I will burn the seas beneath your ships, I will . . ."*

And so on and so forth; nothing unusual – not for these streets.

And as the world turns into night, the Harbinger of Pestilence hangs his suit and tie on the hook behind the bedroom door, and changes into trainers and a sweatshirt, and checks the time, and puts his wallet in his left pocket and his keys in his right, and steps out into the cool Berlin dark.

Not on business tonight. He rides the S-Bahn to Halensee, pauses outside the station to buy himself a hot cup of tea, and follows the tinkling of bells towards Kurfürstendamm. A crowd has already gathered, flags flying in the breeze, bright costumes mixing with sedate after-work loafers and suits. A few came here on foot; others by train, but they are briefly outnumbered by the cyclists with green flags who speed towards Brandenburger Tor, wicker baskets on front, babies in tiny helmets staring from the back.

The Harbinger of Pestilence joins the crowd, unobtrusive at the rear. Tonight he is not here for work; tonight is a night that is all his own. The numbers grow, people bumping and smiling, many taking photos, of themselves, of each other, standing on tiptoe to film over the heads of the assembled people. A man, a headdress of bright red feathers wobbling high above his skull, sparkling huge-heeled boots on his feet, bends down to kiss the Harbinger gently on the cheek, not for any particular reason, merely because he was there, and smiled, and seemed alone. Two women holding hands, one with a crucifix around her neck, ask if he will take a picture of them, defiantly holding each other close. A pair of fathers with their son hoist him onto their shoulders, so he might see over the crowd, and at last, with a whistle and the blaring of pop from someone's loudspeaker, the rainbow flags are unfurled, and the marchers begin their long walk, to the applauding of the crowd.

Words flutter on the pennants, as they move through the shopping streets of Berlin.

Peace.

Love.

Justice.

Friendship.

The Harbinger of Pestilence is given a glow-stick, decorated in silver tassels, which he waves side to side in time to half-heard music, not sure what else to do with it, and walks on, singing a song of freedom.

And as the world turns into night, Death listens to the last words of an old man dying alone, far from home.

". . . women . . ." he whispers. "Made one a president! President of my country a woman, they should stay at home, they should stay at home, know their place, never have happened in my . . . in my day . . ."

The last of his breath leaves his body, and Death closes his eyes. Because here too is something worth saying goodbye to, in its own, quiet way.

Chapter 60

"The future . . ."

" . . . the past . . ."

" . . . my opinion is . . ."

" . . . what's wrong with the world . . ."

" . . . the righteous path . . ."

" . . . our children . . ."

" . . . our parents . . . "

" . . . our hopes . . . "

" . . . our suffering . . . "

rat rat rat human rat

Charlie starts awake in the night, screaming.

Emmi holds him tight, and after a while they both lie there pretending to be asleep, so that the other doesn't have to worry about them.

"How'd you keep your trousers up, Gav?"

"Don't know what you mean, miss."

"You know exactly what I mean. They're practically around your knees."

"You got a problem, miss?"

"I'm just wondering how they don't fall down."

"You want to know a secret, miss?"

"Probably not."

"I got my nan to sew my trousers to my underpants."

"I see."

"It stops them falling down."

"Right."

"You won't tell, will you, miss?"

"I don't think anyone would believe me."

In a windy, rain-washed land . . .

. . . in a land of sun and snow . . .

. . . in a land of green, of slow river and prickling hedgerow . . .

They ate scones with clotted cream by the sea, and at last Charlie said, "Thank you," and Emmi said,

"For what?"

He gave a half-shrug. "For . . . everything. For you. For everything."

She smiled, and squeezed his hand tight, and again, for the thousandth time, wondered whether this relationship was giving her more than it was taking — more joy, more time, more laughter, more delight, more strength, more confidence in herself – and realised, to her surprise, that it was.

Chapter 61

An email arrives on Patrick Fuller's phone.

He opens it immediately. Usually his secretary filters such things, but not these, not any more. They're too important, and besides, the content was making her uneasy, though she'd never say so.

. . . cordially invite . . .

. . . politely request . . .

. . . to bear witness to . . .

. . . the end of a world . . .

For the first time, Patrick hit reply. He'd never done so before, even though the emails had been coming thick and fast, faster even, over the last few years – but until now there had never seemed a need. What had changed? Perhaps he had merely reached his critical mass.

Why me?

An answer came back within a few minutes.

Because you are one of the men of this time.

Whatever the hell that meant.

He flicked through the email chain, noting things that interested him, things that bored him, and finally closed the program and phoned his secretary.

"All right," he said, as she answered, tired and bewildered at this late hour of the night. "Let's go see another."

Part 6

LAUGHTER

Chapter 62

"Of course he is a dictator, but look at the results! Clean streets, good schools, a soaring economy. Yes, journalists vanish and none of us say what we actually think, but do we need to? He's given us a new hope, a new vision for the future, and the moment he dies, there will be ethnic genocide again, just you wait and see . . . "

"An economist, a physicist and a mathematician are asked what two plus two equals . . . "

"The UN special reporter, in saying all of this, I do not think he has the right information. I do not think he has been told the correct things, he has gone to the sites but only heard the stories of the victims. He cannot be trusted, I think; the UN is not a reliable witness to these events."

"The world is jealous of us, jealous of Russia, they want us to fail and that is why they accuse the President of all these things . . . "

" . . . so the mathematician says two plus two equals four . . . "

"It is not the role of the Church to offer mercy to those who wilfully sin, but rather to save the sinners from the sin itself."

"We have been occupied, we have been invaded, we have been LISTEN TO ME we have been invaded and everyone pretends that it isn't war!"

"More tea, Vicar?"

" . . . and the physicist says, well, given a certain variation in measurement and the speed at which you perceive the equation, I would also suggest that two plus two equals four . . . "

" . . . the decree provides inter alia: 'Any person who publishes in any form, whether written or otherwise, any message, rumour, report or statement being ... calculated to bring the federal military government or the government of the state or public officer to ridicule or disrepute shall be guilty of an offence under this decree.' Section 1 of Decree No. 4, 1984, passed by then military dictator Muhammadu Buhari of Nigeria."

"If you want to defeat the extremists then you've got to let Russia keep the Crimea, and I know that's hard for Ukraine but this is so much bigger now ..."

"And the economist leans in, checks no one is watching and whispers: 'How much do you want it to be?'"

"They're not a bit like us, not at all really – but they do like Mr Bean."

Chapter 63

Charlie nearly missed the flight to Lagos because of the visa. Usually Milton Keynes handled such things, but no, this time he had to go in person to the Nigerian Embassy in London, where he queued for forty minutes before finally being told the relevant official had gone home and he'd have to try again tomorrow.

He tried again tomorrow, and after waiting for an hour was led into a room where he filled out all the paperwork and signed the forms, while a smiling, patient woman talked him through customs regulations and asked if he was harbouring any infectious diseases, and the next day he got an email from the embassy saying that, given the nature of his visit, he'd filled out the wrong visa declaration after all and could he come back in again.

"Eh, relax!" said a woman swathed in green who sat next to him in the reception area, waiting for her interview. "It's like a little bit of the home country, right here in London!"

*

In the end, he received the visa eight hours before his flight was due to depart, and having assumed it would take even longer than that, didn't bother to go home, having all his luggage ready with him.

Emmi said, "Have you been to Nigeria before?"

"Not Nigeria," he replied. "But I've been to other places in Africa."

"Where?"

A list; struggling to remember, so many flights, airports, customs, security, luggage, travellators, escalators, terminal bus services, coffee, chairs, gates, arrivals, departures, arrivals, departures, so many . . .

Here. A few memories, surfacing like the tip of the jumbo jet from thick grey cloud.

Democratic Republic of the Congo. A whirlwind tour to half a dozen villages with no name, depositing talismans of ancient gods, maps of the local area, a vase that made one old man weep to behold it. The destruction of the villages by who knew what faction fighting for God knew what cause were not noted in the international media; even the local press was too tired to make very much of it.

Sierra Leone, Liberia, Guinea. On that trip, he'd crossed paths with the Harbinger of Pestilence many, many times, but the Harbinger of Pestilence's work had kept him in a hotel near the largest Médecins Sans Frontières team, his shoes stinking of chlorine, a rash developing on his belly from too much time in a sealed white suit; whereas the Harbinger of Death had crossed into Mali, heading for Bamako, then further north to the temples that would soon burn, though no one really understood why.

Botswana. The Harbinger of Death hadn't expected to be asked to deliver anything to the wild, to the places where no living thing roamed, but there he was in the dead of night, laying out an offering of fresh red meat from the butcher's shop on the grass.

The lions came once he was gone, and the brown elephants

lingered another night by the dried-up riverbank, and perhaps they too saw Death, in whatever fashion such things appear to creatures of the long grass.

In Eritrea the Harbinger of Death had been arrested, and thrown into a tiny room too narrow to sit, too low to stand, and remained there, hunched up around his own body, waiting for the best part of a day, his feet swollen and the floor soaked in piss – his, someone else's, the dried-up stench of a hundred men's – until Milton Keynes made a phone call and got him out.

Death had not been impressed by this treatment of his Harbinger, who had after all been sent as a courtesy.

Death, when unimpressed, will make her feelings known. But the journalists who would have told the world of all they saw that night, the night when Death came with a flaming sword, blood in her mouth, were already dead, and the corpses were buried without name.

Durban, the day the school in Glenwood ceremonially tore the last remnant of a low brick wall down. "Once," said the head-mistress, "this wall was built so that the black children learned on one side, and the whites learned on the other. Some walls fall slowly, but in time, they do fall, and our children are the ones who make that future bright."

Angola, the day the women came to the still waters of the lake, with their glass tubes and their rubber gloves and their carefully cooled medicines in the back of the truck, and took water samples and said yes, today yes, there is no more guinea worm here.

Do nematodes behold Death?

swim swim eat reproduce swim swim eat reproduce

Kenya. "I shot the poacher so the rhino might live. There are five hundred rhino left alive on this planet. There are more poachers who will come, and I will shoot them too."

Kigali. "We will live. We will make of this land something better, and something new. We will remember the past. We will look to the future. We will build Jerusalem."

Ghana, a gift from Death to the generals of a book on the history of the French Revolution, the Terror, and all that followed.

That year elections were contested and the monitors turned round and proclaimed that the outcome was democratic and fair, and the soldiers stayed home, and the people sang in the streets.

For these things too, Death comes, and some said that on that day, Death too sang and danced, and that night only the old died.

The night before he flies, he brings Emmi flowers, and cooks her dinner, and she's getting better at accepting both these things, getting better at believing someone might love her, and that's okay.

The Harbinger of Death flies to Lagos.

Chapter 64

A man met him at the airport. The man was not an inch over five foot, and if he turned sideways he was an almost perfectly thin, straight line. He had a polished shaved head, a little flat nose, perfectly oval eyes and a smile that stretched out so far towards his ears that it seemed to pull his neck out with it, straining muscles in places muscles should not have been strained in their vigorous exercise of friendliness. He clutched a cardboard placard in both hands. On it was written in large black pen: MR HABRENGER.

"Ah you are the Harbinger of Death welcome welcome welcome I am Yomi welcome please come this way let me take your bags thank you your bags did you have a good flight not too long not too hot people complain it's too hot but this is mild mild really please come here is my car – go away boy go away make you no vex me – sorry the children they always annoying here, here, sit down let me move that you like music, I have the best music you like One Direction?"

"Um . . ."

" . . . *you should stay tonight!* Hey! You see that guy, the pylee they no good, go slow, go slow . . . "

"Is the traffic always so . . . ?"

"Hold on, I see a way through!"

"Are you supposed to drive on the kerb?"

"Everyone does it – look, he's driving the wrong way!"

"So he is."

"You okay?"

"I'm . . . I'm not in a hurry, I think, I think that's what I mean to say, there's no need to rush on my behalf . . . "

"Eh, this is how you get around in Lagos, you're in Naira now, you gotta learn how these things work!"

"I suppose you're right."

"Hey – you here to kill anyone big?"

"No, I don't actually kill . . . "

"There's bad blood, bad blood flowing now, people are scared and when people are scared, big kasala, it all feeds itself, fear and fear and fear and fear feeding itself hey, if you could make an engine that worked like fear there'd be no more pollution, no more stink in the air but only fear, only fear you know, beats entropy, till Death she comes. But eh – you live, don't you? You live while you are alive and that's how the fear stops, so hey hey, live, that be all, live!"

Yomi chuckled at this thought, then slammed his fist into his horn as a car scraped along the side of his own.

A hotel in Ikoyi, Lagos Island. Huge pride was taken in the place feeling like it was anywhere in the world, except, per-haps, in Nigeria. The floors, polished by a rotating machine on the end of a pole pushed by a woman who'd been told to leave her hooped earrings at home; the potted plants, rubbery with dark grey grit like cat litter all around the base of the stem. The reception desk, with a brass plaque on it that said *Reception*; the red uniforms, far too heavy and hot for the climate, the bright smiles, the man who stood by the elevator and leapt, as if stung by a cattle prod, to press the button before you could and – now this was the impressive part – didn't demand a tip for his service: was this Lagos?

The Harbinger of Death stood in the window of his room on the seventh floor, and looked out across the lagoon towards the fume-smothered brown-grey shimmering horizon, heard the car horns blare in the street, felt the rattling of the local generators buzzing behind the houses, and for a moment wasn't sure if he hadn't been here before. Maybe he had – or rather, maybe another Harbinger of Death had been here, some few years ago, and he was remembering her thoughts, all the memories of the Harbingers blurring into one, arrivals, departures, arrivals, departures . . .

(For a moment, Charlie closed his eyes, and thought he knew how it felt to soar above the walls of burning Rome, eagle wings and yellow eyes, and found absolutely nothing strange in this thought.)

(Jet lag can be a funny thing. Just jet lag.)

Lagos, in the evening, walking along the inland shore. The air around the lagoon is skin sticky. Even on the water, where cooler breezes should blow away clinging sweat and the smell of stagnation, the heat seems to break up from the bottom of the boat as if being cut free from the sea. It is hard to find a place where there aren't other people, except in the hotel room. At the side of the busy roads stand women with great vats and platters balanced on their heads – moin moin, akara, ewa agoyin and bread, fried plantain, beef stew, black beans and vinegary nibbles, barbecued meat to burn to the pit of your belly, sacks of boiled peanut and charcoal-grilled croaker fish covered in orange sauce that tingled on the ends of Charlie's fingers long after he'd licked them clean. He toyed with buying green eggplant from a man in shorts and flip-flops who stood outside a shop that was 99 per cent mobile phones to only 1 per cent air to breathe, and decided against it. Traveller's sickness was almost inevitable, and there was a certain argument in getting it over and done with, but he wasn't in Lagos for long; maybe this time, maybe, he could dodge that bullet.

A police car in the distance, and the women squatting by their sizzling tin-foil stoves vanished like morning mist, no fuss, just a part of business. Oyinbo, oyinbo, called the children as Charlie wove his way through the deadly, yield-none traffic. Oyinbo, oyinbo, foreigner, white man! Sometimes there were pavements on the side of the roads. Sometimes there weren't. Sometimes there were shallow muddy paths where a pavement had been intended, but no slabs had arrived. Sometimes there were giant advertising hoardings offering American burgers or redemption in the bosom of Christ. There were very few beggars. Even the old widows, stooped and toothless, waddled up and down the road trying to sell bruised fruit or toy guns, their bodies swathed round with purples and blues, yellows and greens, scuffed at the hem.

Power goes out, again, again, the people groan, curse, mutter, how can we work this way? In the sprawling shanty houses that press against each other in every nook of Lagos, that crawl to the edges of the white mansions where the superstars and the pop stars and the God stars and the military men live, the cables are tugged every which way across the sky, and the electricity company curses and says, "How can we provide you with anything, when you steal it all?"

"You don't even have anything for us to steal!" comes the reply. "You don't even give us that!"

And so it goes on.

Morning, Charlie had a long appointments list. Yomi met him outside the hotel gate. Charlie had to run down to vouch for his fuming driver − the security guards wouldn't let him in, until Charlie appeared.

"Where you wanna go today?" asked Yomi.

"I need to pick a few things up, then drop a few things off."

A shrug. "It's your job, abi!"

They drove through the chugging Lagos traffic, horn blaring sociably. Yomi, after some persuasion, flicked the radio on, rolled through the stations.

"And I say Jesus, Jesus, Jesus!"

"*Oh Barbara Ann, take my hand . . .*"

"Fighting in the north . . . "

"I'm talking about the environmental consequences of . . . "

"Difference is, Yoruba, I'm talking about the nation now, the Yoruba nation . . . "

"*The time is twelve, midnight my brother . . .*"

"God don butta my bread."

"*Our country dem wan repair . . .*"

"Eh, that sounds like you've got a serious problem, caller, a serious problem, let's ask our listeners at home what they think."

In the end, they settled for what Yomi assured Charlie was mildly acceptable Yo-pop and Afrobeat, if you liked that kind of thing.

Charlie did. Charlie liked hearing the music of the places he went. It was something that always stuck with him, a thing he remembered and cherished. If he got the chance, he'd like to visit the Africa Shrine, but Yomi tutted and said no no, if you want to hear real music, proper music, I'll take you to Ikeja, you can hear the new bands play, the new songs!

Is it like One Direction? Charlie asked, his heart sinking.

Yomi glared at him, a sudden fury in his gaze so hard that Charlie swallowed, fought not to look away. "All that is music for the driving and the working," he replied. "Naira music is music for the people, the justice and the soul."

Charlie said he thought that sounded perfect. In the day they drove out of Lagos, a hundred miles there, a hundred miles back, to deliver a bucket and spade to a family deep in a muddy river delta, where distant plumes of flame turned the sky black and orange. Then they went at night to listen to the new music being made, and Charlie ended up getting slightly drunk with a very drunk Yomi, and the two of them shared a taxi back to Lagos Island with an educational technologist ("technology can change the way our children learn") and a nurse ("the reason the rural nurses don't turn up for work is because the work they're being asked to do is ridiculous").

*

The next day, they drove again through the too-bright, belching wide Lagos streets, beneath the growing towers of the banks and the telecom companies, past the heavy palm trees and round the endless growling byways and highways. Charlie checked his phone for the list of names he had to visit, and doubted they'd make it to all of them, not through a city so wide, so dense, through a place of concrete and tar, iron and dirt, of weaving cars and shouting hawkers, of buses bursting to the seams, of billboards and markets, shops and docks; he'd need to add another day at least, maybe two – but that was okay, these things happened, and in an odd sort of way, through the heat and the sweat and the grumbling and the noise, he was having a good time. The wet heat of the city was burning something of the dryness of the Syrian desert from him, and now when he closed his eyes at night he only sometimes – only when he permitted his mind to wander – saw the eyes of a hundred corpses staring back at him. Only sometimes. Then he felt guilt that he didn't see them more. Then he saw them again. Then he turned on the light and washed his face to drive their glares away. Then, eventually, he slept, and the world moved on, and the music played and the voices chattered and the earth was piled upon the bones, and sometimes he remembered, and sometimes he simply lived, and sometimes – very occasionally – he was okay with doing both.

Busy busy busy. There were times when Death liked to work like this, many appointments in one place, all at once; Saga had warned him to keep an eye out for such things, be sure to get his flight back home. "Earthquakes, tsunamis, intense local shocks of that sort, keep an eye out for Pestilence, usually a sign of something if she's around ... " Then she'd thought about it again, and added, "Or maybe it's just Milton Keynes. Do a job lot on a single airline ticket, visit as many people in one place as possible, economise, be efficient in your harbingering – after all, it's hell getting through immigration in Moscow these days, and visits to Israel or Cuba almost always need a separate passport."

*

202

A shopping mall, anywhere in the world, families having fried chicken on plastic chairs as the shoppers moved around them, brilliant pinks and ruby reds on their bodies, eager to buy the latest black-and-whites from the designer outlets. Kitchen goods, children's books, video games, DVDs of the latest Nollywood hit, travel agent, pharmacy megastore complete with deluxe nappies. The dapper men stared at the gold watches in the windows, their silk handkerchiefs folded immaculately in their jacket pockets, leather shoes polished to perfection – by day he sells washing machines, and at night to supplement his income he teaches a little maths to some of the children in his street, where he still lives with his wife, his mother, her mother, their two sons – but you will not tell this from his clothes, not him, not this perfect gentleman!

In an international chain that sells international makes of baby buggy, made in China, the Harbinger of Death gives a woman with bright red lips and deep black eyes a book of laws bought from a shop near the university. She takes it nervously, then looks up and says, "Is it Boko Haram? Are they going to shoot this place up, like they did in Nairobi?"

Charlie doesn't know.

As they headed towards Mushin, Yomi's phone rang. "You appear to be heading into Mushin," said the polite voice on the other end of the line. "Are you all right?"

"Yes yes," barked Yomi briskly. "I'm taking my client there!"

After he hung up, Yomi looked briefly ashamed, then blurted, fast, "My wife. She insisted I got the car fitted. Just in case, you know."

Charlie didn't answer.

"She wants to move to Abuja," he added, into the silence. "She says it's a better place, but I visited Abuja once, and it was boring. Boring boring boring, no good, not like here, not like Lagos, Lagos is the magic place, that I swear, that I swear until the day I die."

His honour a little restored at this proud declaration, they drove on, to the sound of the radio.

*

Unpaved streets between unlicensed houses. The first time Charlie visited a shanty town, he'd imagined dark, Dickensian alleys, leering faces. The first time he visited a shanty town, someone had tried to sell him a Coca-Cola and had wanted to know which mobile phone network he recommended. That man had lived in a single room the size of Charlie's kitchen, which he shared with seven others. The roof was corrugated iron, the walls were patched with card. They watched football on a TV 30×30 cm, stole the power from the big development next door, and Charlie had wondered what team they supported, and where he could get the shirt. They squatted in a gulley dug in the road out back to shit and piss, but what the hell, the man had said, it's a roof, it's family, it's home, you know?

Now he comes to Mushin, and gives a woman and her three children a trowel and a tape measure. The woman smiles and says thank you, and her children stare and say thank you also, because that's what good manners ask, and Charlie gets into the car and drives away again, back onto the belching bypass that swings above the streets of blustering, waiting men.

In an expensive condo on the shores of Victoria Island, the Harbinger of Death passes through two security men and a PA to reach a boss who sits with his feet up on a polished glass desk, a man who made something big in telecoms a few years back, and has now got so rich he's forgotten what it was like to run a business and doesn't realise how little of his own profit he really sees. Charlie gives him a small brush, of the kind used for cleaning the inside of tight-lipped bottles, metal fibres spiking off the side, and the man stares at it then laughs and says, "It is for the gun, no?" and pulls from his desk a revolver, brand new, elephant-tusk handle and heavy silver, almost too heavy to lift, the kickback hard enough to break the hand if you're not paying attention. "I got it for the streets," he explained. "The streets, the people, uch, the people, so jealous!"

Charlie said, "I'll take your word for it."

"Will you stay for afternoon tea? I can do cucumber sandwiches."

"That's very kind, but I must be going."

A policeman. An impromptu roadblock, he swaggers round in mirrored shades and white gloves, collecting a little dash, the fee, you see, the policeman's fee for passing this point, and what if you haven't committed a crime, he's the law, he'll find something you've done, you wait and see.

Charlie delivers to him three thousand US dollars in used notes.

The policeman stands on the side of the road, door to his car open, music playing loud, mouth hanging wide.

"You don possess? I no sabi."

"It's from my employer," explained Charlie, Yomi hovering uneasily behind, now afraid – it's hard to say whether of the policeman, or of the large sum of money changing hands in public view. "He requested that I give you this gift, as a courtesy. Or as a warning."

The policeman doesn't understand. He takes the money home, and hides it – of all places – under the bed, and doesn't tell his wife.

A church.

There are five thousand people packed into a hall that was perhaps designed for conferences. In the afternoon, there will be five thousand more, come to witness a different preacher. Today's pastor is small, in his late sixties, dressed in bright purple polyester, a choir of five swaying behind him, a drummer and guitarist largely doing their own thing. He prowls up and down and calls out Jesus, Jesus, Jesus! Jesus spare us, Jesus redeem us, Jesus, Jesus!

Women have brought their underpants for him to bless, to help them get pregnant. He sells sanctified sanitary pads and holy children's T-shirts and sacred bottles of vegetable oil, guaranteed to keep the demon gluttony away. As the pastor cries out his judgement upon the world, men with yellow buckets move between the rows of weeping, joyous, ecstatic people, hope in their hearts and music in their lungs, and collect naira in large-denomination notes.

"Jesus! Jesus Jesus!"

A woman with a lump in her breast falls to her knees before him, and weeps and weeps, and he presses his hands to her forehead and cries, "Begone, demon, begone! Begone to the void, begone!" and she writhes and screams and talks in tongues and her daughter also cries, alone at home as the preacher does his work, because her daughter is a doctor and knows what will come, has seen her mother's fate writ large and cannot convince her to take the chemo, no matter how hard she tries.

"Jesus! Jesus commands you! Jesus heals you!"

The Harbinger of Death sits in the front row, and doesn't realise that the Harbinger of Pestilence is also there, thirty-two rows further back.

At night, golf clubs swing in Ikoyi, the expats drink with other expats in an expats' hotel. The music plays along the shores of the lagoon, the jet skis bounce across the water, the moon rises, the supermarkets clatter with the sound of trolleys on grubby floors, meat sizzles on the red-hot pan, the croakers croak and the boats move through the thin-legged shacks that sit on the water, away from the landlubber's laws, and Charlie listens to music by the beautiful, stinking, litter-laced sea, and closes his eyes to hear it more, and is, for a little while, at peace.

Chapter 65

Finding Isabella Abayomi was surprisingly hard.

He hadn't been given a home address by Milton Keynes, only a time and a venue. The venue was a nightclub in Yaba, the door unmarked. He walked past it twice before finding it, and knocked with a great sense of unease. The door was answered by a woman, who glowered and exclaimed, "Yes yes? Wetin dey happen?"

"I'm looking for Isabella Abayomi ... "

"Fifteen hundred naira!"

"I'm sorry, I ... "

"Gi mi!"

He hesitated. Isabella Abayomi was the last person on his list, and though this felt a little like extortion, he did have a job to do. He handed over the money. The woman gave him a stub of paper with a number on it, and stamped his hand with the inky image of Minnie Mouse. This done, she finally stood aside, and he walked through.

A long corridor, lit by erratic bulbs. The walls were lined with posters – some cartoonish, some of faces, men and women striking heroic poses or leering or grinning or glowering at the camera, bright reds and yellows, blues and greens bursting around their names, times and dates on the bottom. The woman shooed him to the end of the corridor when he paused to look, to where it opened out into a wider room, circular, around which were nailed long wooden benches pressed, like square pegs into round holes, erratically against the wall. A stage was in the middle, lit by two bright lights inside rusting cans nailed to the ceiling. A microphone stood in the centre. Of the hundred or so possible seats, seventy were filled, and music played from a boom box on one side of the stage. Charlie opened his mouth to try and explain again, Harbinger of Death, you see, not really here for this, have to find ...

... but the woman was gone. He looked around, bewildered, and having no better idea of what to do, sat down in a corner by himself. A couple in front of him whispered and giggled, swapping photos on their mobile phones. An earnest old man read a newspaper alone. A group of teenagers, too young for the intense beer they were drinking, whooped and shrieked happily in a corner.

Charlie waited.

At last, the woman who'd answered the door marched down to the stage and turned the boom box off. This seemed to mark a ceremonial event, for the room fell silent now, waiting as one.

Then another woman walked on stage. Her face was narrow, drawn down to a pointed chin. Her hair was wound up tight in a great blue and purple turban. Her eyebrows were two perfect half-circles above her small oval eyes. Her lips were painted blue, her fingernails were violet, as were her toes, visible where they popped out between her silver sandals. She walked up to the microphone, took it off its stand without a blink and said,

"Last night a thief tried to mug a policeman. The policeman was alone, didn't have his badge, but as the thief stole his wallet he shouted, 'Hey, give me my money back, I'm a policeman!' 'You're a policeman?' replied the thief. 'In that case, you should give me *my* money back!'"

Chapter 66

"A rabbi, an imam and a priest walk into a bar . . . "

"Knock knock!"

"So listen to this, he says, *he says* . . . "

"My religion, explains the imam, is the greatest religion in the world!"

"Who's there?"

"Doctor doctor, I think I'm insane!"

"What's the difference between English football and a tea bag?"

"No, says the priest, my religion is the greatest in the world!"

"Fuck."

"The tea bag stays in the cup longer."

"You're both mistaken, explains the rabbi. My religion is the greatest religion in the world, let me tell you why . . . "

"Fuck who?"

"And it's the final round of the jungle football!"

" . . . needed to repair the roof of the synagogue . . . "

"Tsk tsk. Fuck *whom*."

"What do you call an American who'll do the jobs that no one wants for little money and not complain?"

" . . . but it was a Sabbath! The money was right there, I could have taken it, but on a Sabbath I can't handle money . . . "

"There's the elephant again, running down the middle, the insects are scattered to every side, he shoots, he *scoooorrresss!*"

"Putin can't stand homosexuals, but the Bolshoi Ballet on the other hand . . . "

"An immigrant."

" . . . so I closed my eyes, and I prayed, I prayed with all my might . . . "

"What does the cheese say to itself in the morning?"

"Suddenly the elephant stops. He freezes in the middle of the field. He drops the ball!"

"Halloumi!"

"And finally they see the centipede, it's the centipede who's been crawling up the elephant's leg . . . "

"And suddenly, my prayers were answered! I opened my eyes, and all around, for a radius of about ten yards, it was Thursday."

Chapter 67

Isabella Abayomi was a comedian.

It took Charlie a few startled minutes to realise this. She didn't tell jokes, and her references were to a news cycle that he wasn't part of, but as his ear adjusted, he began to hear the meaning behind the names she named, the stories she told, and without noticing when, he started laughing.

". . . and the policeman said, 'But you're not Jesus, I know Jesus, and besides, Jesus was Igbo!'"

The laughter was slow to come, as she gently built up her matter from the most mundane to the bizarre. A trip to do her washing evolved into an alien gunfight over the skyline of Lagos; dinner with her mother grew into a diatribe on corruption in the military; a mission to get her shoe repaired evolved into a quest to found a religion.

"Three dollars cheaper! Three dollars cheaper and I'm saying, I don't care if it's twenty dollars cheaper, I don't care if it's a thousand dollars cheaper, there's no way I'm wearing it after what he did!"

Only once did Charlie laugh and realise that he was the only person laughing.

"So he said, 'Fuck this, fuck this, I've got democracy to defend, I've got a new world to build.'" (The room laughs.) "'I'm a big believer in democracy now, I always was in fact, the dictatorship was such a learning curve'" (laughter), "'and the first thing I learned was kill the fucking comics!'" (Charlie laughs. No one else does.)

"Anyway . . ."

He thinks: Emmi would love this. She'd get it instantly, and think it was great.

He doesn't laugh for a moment, even though the jokes are funny, as that thought passes by.

". . . and I say, no, not Yoruba, you're *barred* . . ."

By the end of it, one woman to Isabella's right was laughing out of control, a high shriek that distracted the rest of the room. If everyone else hadn't been primed to find the thing funny, her ear-popping voice would have been an irritation, but as it was Isabella merely acknowledged the sound with a wry smile and kept on going, and the laughter of her audience fed itself, until even Charlie's face began to ache.

One man didn't laugh. Charlie didn't spot him, in the shallow darkness of the audience, and if Isabella did, she showed no sign. White trousers, white suit, he sits in the furthest corner from the

210

stage, left leg crossed over his right, hands in his lap, and he does not laugh, and he does not smile.

The set lasted an hour and a half. When it was done, Isabella Abayomi bowed once, and as briskly as she had arrived, walked away from the microphone. The old woman scurried forward, the boom box went back on, people, smiling, chattering, more alive than they had been when they arrived, stood up, and began to walk away.

Charlie scurried down the stairs, edged round the side of the stage, somehow feeling that it would have been violating a religious law for him to walk on its surface, looked over his shoulder guiltily, saw no one watching, and followed Isabella through the back door of the theatre, out into a courtyard behind.

The courtyard was square, a floor of dirt, a couple of chickens, their feet tied together, sitting placidly in a basket by the back gate. A single light burned yellow above the blacked-out window of the club; Isabella had her mobile phone in her hand, checking a message, other hand on the gate, ready to go.

"Miss Abayomi?" he called out.

She stopped, head rising fast, almost fearful, took in his skin, his clothes, his expression. "Yes? Can I help you?"

"Miss Abayomi," he repeated, shuffling closer as she angled her body round to see him better, back to the door to the street. "I've been sent to give you . . . " He reached into his bag for the little envelope of cards, sealed with her name on it, but she raised one hand as he did and barked,

"Stop there! What have you got?"

"A gift, it's from . . . "

"I don't want gifts, who are you?"

Strange, a woman who'd been so funny now so defensive, angry even, glaring at him.

"My name's Charlie, I'm the Harbinger of Death . . . "

He was still holding the envelope out to her, and was surprised at her speed when she knocked it from his hand, slapping it to the floor. He stepped back, then awkwardly, when she neither moved nor spoke, bent down to pick it up again, muttering his

211

usual words, here as a courtesy, here as a warning, don't know which, my employer, courtesy, courtesy, he is . . .

"Fuck off." Her voice cut through it all. She turned, struggling for a moment with the gate, which didn't fit squarely into the wall, before dragging it with a creak of metal and dust open, and striding out into the street. Charlie scurried after, envelope in hand.

"Miss Abayomi, I understand that you probably don't want to see me, but I'd really like to give you this gift, it's part of my job, and you don't have to take my presence as meaning . . . as necessarily being . . ."

She ignored him, marched chin high, shoulders back. He tried following her, but didn't want to physically grab her, not in the street, quiet though it was, and though he'd met people who didn't want to hear from him, usually they took the gift that was proffered, as much out of surprise as anything else, and he wasn't sure if his employer would be pleased to learn that Isabella had not.

"Miss Abayomi . . ."

She rounded the corner at the end of the road, into a dirt alley that ran between houses back towards the main street, the rattle of generators and the smell of petrol rising up from behind the dry beige walls.

"Miss Abayomi!"

"Hey, oyinbo!"

The voice came from straight ahead, where a man stepped out from the shelter of a door into the street. Two more men followed, but the one who'd spoken waved them to a halt, flanking him, one either side. The two men wore dirty vests and baggy shorts. The man in charge wore white suit trousers, white shirt, seven gold rings and a gold crucifix, encrusted with diamonds, which bounced gently around his chest. "Eh, oyinbo," he said, head on one side, curious, "how now?"

The man from the club; the man who had not laughed. Maybe he was a disgruntled customer? Maybe a reviewer who took his work too seriously?

212

Charlie considered both these thoughts as a patient, faced with a picture of their own tumour, may sometimes say 'Maybe the scan was wrong' or 'I'd like a second opinion' – in all earnestness, believing none of it.

Isabella stopped dead, and so did Charlie. He looked at her, and saw fear again in her eyes, the starting, jumping thing that had turned her from funny to angry in a bare second. She stared first at the man in white, then at the Harbinger, and for a moment he thought she saw Death as she saw him, and the two were briefly one.

Then the man said, "Wetin wasala, yansh babe?"

"We no go tumble you," she replied, quick and high, then blurted: "Oyinbo Harbinger of Death!"

The man raised his eyebrows, looked at Charlie again, wasn't impressed. "You wan try me?" he mused, and to his surprise, Charlie felt Isabella's hand slip into his own.

"Does Death come tonight?" she whispered, her lips barely moving with the sound.

"I . . . I don't think so."

"Then run!"

He only ran because she pulled him; even then it took him a few stumbling moments for his feet to move, for the realisation to sink into his mind that yes, he was now running, and yes, the men were following, two men in grubby clothes running flat out, and their boss in his shiny shoes following at a more sedate pace, confident in his boys, sure of himself.

If the men hadn't followed, Charlie would have found the whole thing hilarious.

But perhaps it was, even now, even with the suspicion growing on him that he might be running for his life. Perhaps there was something laughable in the entire thing, perhaps . . .

They rounded a corner, heading back towards the comedy club. Isabella shoved her shoulder into the metal door that they'd come through, nearly falling into the dirt as it gave way reluctantly beneath her, pulled Charlie in behind, slammed the door shut. One of the running boys got his shoulder against it, and

Charlie heaved and pushed with Isabella, throwing all his weight against the metal as they struggled to force it closed.

For a moment they balanced there, in a tug of war; then the door slammed shut and Isabella rammed a bolt across. Charlie pressed his back against the door still, as it shuddered and bounced beneath the force of kicks and fists, as Isabella ran to the door to the club's rear entrance, heaving on it hard.

The door was locked; the music was silent.

Isabella cursed, reaching again into her pocket for her mobile phone, as the door against Charlie's back screeched and rocked, the bolt rattling in the wall, screws loose in the metal.

"Are you calling the police?" gasped Charlie as the straining metal knocked against his spine.

"Police no good," she snapped. "You dumb?"

"But you're calling someone good?" he whimpered hopefully.

She silenced him with a gesture, though the kicking against the door continued. Held the mobile to her ear, waited for the connection, taut now, a professional doing a job. When she spoke, it was Yoruba, fast and sharp, and Charlie didn't understand. She couldn't have spoken more than ten words before the call was over. She hung up, moved towards the door to throw her weight against it too.

"You know that gentleman?" asked Charlie, head wobbling with each blow to the metal.

She spat in reply.

Before Charlie could ask anything more, the banging stopped.

For a moment, the two stood in silence, eyes locked, waiting for the next thing.

They waited.

Outside, the sound of something moving.

Isabella held her phone tight in her fist, a weapon ready to strike. Charlie didn't move, still hauling down breath, still pressed against the door.

When the first boy came over the wall, he did so in a flop, rather than an acrobatic explosion. He was hoicked up by his colleague on the other side, and nearly missed the top altogether, balancing for a moment precariously on the thin ridge, not sure which way he was going to fall. When he did jump down into the courtyard, Isabella was already there, trying to push him up, knock him back the way he'd come, but the net result was he landed almost on top of her, the two of them falling in a tangled heap to the ground. At her cry, Charlie broke away from the door, instinctive, and tried to grab the boy, pulling him off her, punching him around the head and chest awkwardly, inept, the worry growing that all this activity was hurting his fists far more than it hurt the overgrown kid, who didn't seem to care but flapped and pushed at Charlie like he was an irritating bee at a picnic. He moved straight for the door, but Isabella caught him by the ankle and held him tight, and when he tried to kick back at her, Charlie wrapped his arms around him and pulled him off-balance, so his foot went wide. Isabella let go, and the entire edifice of scrambling boy and bewildered man toppled again, falling to the earth.

A moment of hands and fingers, clawing in flesh and dust. There was no dignity, no skill, no finesse in anything to do with this fight; just one body moving one way, and another trying to hold it back. Charlie didn't even notice the shank – it wouldn't have been fair to call it a knife – until the boy stuck it into the top of his right arm, and even then he assumed it was something else, just a nail catching or a muscle being pulled, until Isabella called out, "Knife!" and he looked down and saw the little blade buried in his flesh.

Realisation of the thing made it at once both painful and terrifying. He rolled back, horrified and fascinated, and the boy leapt to his feet, punching Isabella in the stomach as she tried to grab him. As she fell to the floor, he slid the bolt back and opened the metal door.

His friend ran in at once, and seeing Isabella doubled up and Charlie staring at his own arm in bewilderment, chose to make himself useful by kicking Charlie happily in the kidneys and punching Isabella once in the face. Then, pleased that he'd earned his keep, he turned to his breathless, gasping friend, exclaimed

215

something in cheerful Yoruba, and stood back to give the boss room to work.

In came the boss, white trousers, gold rings. There was a red silk handkerchief in his pocket, Charlie noted dimly from the floor, folded to a perfect triangle. He looked down at Charlie and wasn't impressed; looked at Isabella and curled his lip in absolute contempt.

"Yansh babe," he breathed. "Kwat nkpe."

She replied something in Yoruba; he answered. She said something more, a rattle gun of words, angry, bitter, hateful, begging.

He shook his head, a disappointed pastor.

More words; his taut and contained, hers flying with higher pitch now, higher fear.

He undid the belt of his trousers.

A moment as Charlie tried to understand, or perhaps, more fairly, tried not to understand, to reject comprehension altogether. He looked up at the man, and saw something in his face he thought he'd seen before, a kind of smile, a thing that reminded him of . . .

(A bed studded with broken glass; a crater full of dust and the beams of torchlight; a man on the edge of it all, one hand in his pocket, the other holding a cigarette, and he had smiled and he had been . . .)

And he looked at Isabella, and saw that she knew exactly what this was, everything that this moment meant, and there wasn't any doubt in her mind, any polite inhuman voice saying *I say, but no, but really, don't you think that* . . .

And he looked at the two boys, and saw that they were kids, not even out of their teens, and one had a flick knife and the other – the one whose face was covered in dirt, clothes were torn from the fight – was watching him, and there was something in his eye that Charlie also knew, a look he had seen a thousand times, a memory of

a pale figure against a blasted tree

and it seemed to Charlie that all the world withered in this moment, like embers in the fire and he wondered, if that was what he saw, what Isabella saw too.

(She sees the man in the white suit, and knows who he is, and what he intends. His name is Jonah, he is the son of a judge whose salary is paid for mainly by the drug runners of Navy Town, and the people smugglers from the north, why only last weekend they played golf together and wasn't the weather fine ...

... but Jonah, Jonah has no interest in the law, so he makes his money taking over the businesses of men his father imprisons for no notable crime, and stealing the lives of people who the law has declared dead, even though they haven't died, and one day he saw Isabella doing her stand-up, and thought she was magnificent and said, will you be mine, and she said no

she said *no* and no one says no to Jonah, not here, not ever, not in his town.

And what was worse, she said no and she tried to make it funny.

She laughed *at him*.

All this, Isabella sees.

All this she has seen coming for so many years, so many years of refusing to be afraid, and in refusing, giving life to her fears, for it is an act of will to be fearless, and an act of will requires contemplation of the facts.

She has played out this moment a thousand times already in her imagination, and now it is come, she has only one rule, only one, which she will repeat to herself through every second of what is to come: she will *fight* and she will *live*. She will live.)

Jonah said again, a curse upon her head, undoing the button of his trousers, "Yansh babe," and she refused to flinch.

Then Charlie said, "I am the Harbinger of Death."

His voice was weak, knocked from him by a kick to the kidneys, a blade still lodged in his arm. For a brief moment he wondered if the blade was sterile; then he thought that perhaps he was an imbecile, so repeated again, "I am the Harbinger of Death. When they locked me up, my employer came in the night, and when the sun rose, even the crows were dead, black

217

feathers on the floor. In Belarus, when they took me to the rich man's house and put a gun to my head, I called on Death and he answered, he always answers, you see, the fire, the flood, our lady all in white, Santa Muerte, he's coming, always, always in your shadow, he's—"

The boy who hadn't been in the fight, enthusiastic, eager to make a good impression, kicked Charlie again in the soft bend of his stomach, and he collapsed, gagging over his words, which had indeed made no more dent upon the moment than a butter knife on diamond.

What was Death, here?

Nothing to get worked up about really.

But the man, Jonah, was perhaps a little more circumspect, and with a gesture of his fingers, Charlie was picked up from the floor and held in the boys' arms for his attention. Trousers half falling down, no bother to him, he shuffled over to Charlie, looked in his eyes, turned his head this way and that, examining every feature of the Harbinger's face. Charlie tried to look away, and couldn't. Then the man reached up with his left hand, and hard, pulling at skin so it stretched and compressed like rubber, ran his fingers across every part of Charlie's face, pressing into his eyes, tweaking his nose, pulling at his lips so that his fingers bumped against Charlie's gritted teeth, and seeing Charlie flinch and try to pull away, he smiled.

He smiled, for he was God, and Death was something for the old and lesser men.

He half nodded, and Charlie was pushed back to the ground, held, facing Isabella. Jonah walked back to her, enjoying himself, slapped her once across the mouth, and when she didn't fall, slapped her again, holding her down with one hand around her throat.

Isabella glared at him, biting her lip until it bled, better blood than tears . . .

Then a woman's voice said, from the still-open door of the courtyard, "I will kill you."

She said it very calmly, steady and flat. Eyes turned to her, this new guest on the scene. She held a pistol in her hands, a double grip around the handle, and at the sight of her, Isabella nearly choked with relief. Her hair was tight cornrows cut to beaded ends at the back of her neck; her skin was paler than Isabella's, but still deep, dark and warm. Her high cheekbones were set against wide, bright eyes. She wore a yellow long-sleeved top and a green wraparound skirt. Two large hoop earrings hung down to the sides of her neck, and a mobile phone was lodged in her bra.

She pointed the gun at Jonah, and for a moment, he didn't seem to believe it.

"You no happen," he hissed. "You no dare."

"I don't think you believe that," replied the woman firmly. "Comot!" And again, when they didn't move. "Comot!"

She stepped aside, leaving the door free for them to move, and kept stepping, guiding by the motion of her weapon the two boys, suddenly children again, and the older man, towards the street beyond. "*Comot!*" For a moment, her voice, so calm and flat, nearly rising to a shriek, her control wavering for just a second, the gun shaking in her grip.

Perhaps it was that, more than the calm, which made them run. Perhaps then, for the first time, they saw that her fear should make them afraid.

Jonah did his belt back up, pulled it tight, murmured, "You dead, bitches. You dead."

And he too walked away. Not running; not him. He never ran.

"You dead," breathed Jonah, and grinned. He stood a few inches from the gun, and spat at the woman's feet, and walked away.

Chapter 68

Isabella cried.

Charlie thought he might cry too, but as the adrenaline

drained from him, the awareness of the blade in his arm occupied all his attention, deadened everything else.

The woman with the gun held Isabella as she rocked and shook and wept, held her tight as tears and snot seeped into her shirt, held her and held her and whispered words in Yoruba that Charlie didn't understand – my love, I love you, I'm here, I love you, I came, I came, my love, my love ...

There wasn't any shame in her tears. This wasn't sorrow, or grief, or fear. This was a letting go of a resolve that had been three years in the making; this was the release after the storm. Charlie knew it, remembered how it felt, the moment the terror stopped.

Until Isabella cried no more.

In a land of forests ...

... in a land of lakes ...

At last the woman with the gun turned to Charlie and, gesturing uneasily, said, "Who's the oyinbo?"

At this, Isabella, her eyes still red, began to laugh, the tears that had shaken her body a minute ago now transforming to something different, something high and wild that came easily from a place near the screaming part of her soul.

"He's the Harbinger of Death, abi! He's the Harbinger of fucking Death!"

The woman's name was Kemi.

A group of kids surrounded her car as the three of them approached, said miss, miss, we guarded it, even though you parked it here, we guarded it well – and she gave them five hundred naira without looking, and they whooped and laughed and ran away, and there was much rejoicing.

Kemi drove. Isabella sat in the front seat, Charlie in the back. If he didn't look at his arm, the pain was easier to ignore. He could imagine that it was merely a nasty insect bite, perhaps, or maybe the consequence of a particularly savage bit of tennis. True, he couldn't quite grapple with the latter fantasy, but it was absurd enough to make him smile, and smiling also served to numb the pain.

Isabella, sitting up front, one hand pressed tight into Kemi's, seemed to feel the same way. She talked, without much meaning, a babble of words, and sometimes stopped and laughed and exclaimed, "You, with a gun!" and then, "Harbinger of Death," and laughed and talked a little bit more and sometimes cried, but every time she cried she made it a joke and said, "Tsk, look at me, with my fat red eyes."

Kemi gripped her hand tighter, and was silent as she drove them to the hospital.

They went to the emergency door, but the nurse took one look at them and snapped, "You can walk, can't you?" so they went to minor injuries.

The queue at minor injuries was six hours long, and as a junior doctor, eyes huge behind his owl glasses came to inspect them, he pointed at the blade still sticking out of Charlie's skin and said, "Only that, yes?" and Charlie wasn't sure how he was supposed to answer.

Then a much more senior doctor saw Charlie huddled in a plastic chair next to Isabella, and barked, "You are a foreigner! What are you doing here?" and sent them off to a hospital for Americans and expats instead.

At the American hospital, they asked Charlie if he had insurance.

He did, pulling the policy from the bottom of his bag. Then they looked at Isabella and said, "You?"

She shook her head, hand still clutched tightly in Kemi's fist, and Charlie blurted, surprised to hear himself speak, "I'll pay for her treatment."

"Don't be—" began Isabella, but Charlie cut her off.

"I'll pay."

Isabella looked for a moment like she might argue, but Kemi squeezed her fingers hard, and she fell silent, and looked at the floor, and there were tears in her eyes again, the tears that only ever come when kindness appears after a long stretch of darkness, and she nodded, and they took her inside.

*

They gave him a local anaesthetic when they removed the blade, and enough injections and vaccines against he didn't want to think what diseases that they decided it would be easier to put a cannula in than bother with individual shots.

So he lay there, alone, in this pristine, quiet, strange little bubble of foreign wealth in the middle of the teeming city, a needle in his hand and the light white and bright in the ceiling above his head, while Milton Keynes sorted his insurance and nurses in bright blue scrubs padded quietly between the empty beds. Nothing like the hospital Kemi had taken them to, where every walk was a run in disguise; where the injured and the bleeding, the bereaved and the scared wept in the halls. Here was a place for the oyinbo, the white men, the ones come to Lagos to experience sun and spicy food and Afrobeats by the sea, preferably without ever having to leave the safety of the world they knew.

What was the world Charlie knew?

(Something someone had said, breaking into his mind. A world is ending. A world is ending. Breathe out, let it go . . .)

He closed his eyes, and the after-image of the fluorescent over-head lights stayed in his vision, a moving, out-of-focus rectangle that seemed to sink through the ink of his eyeball of its own accord, pulled down by gravity.

After a few hours, he said, "Can I go?" and the doctor said yes, and they'd call him a cab.

He sat in the waiting room, and felt . . .

. . . nothing.

The clock ticked and time passed and he was

just here.

Sitting.

Then his phone buzzed, and it was Milton Keynes, confirming that the insurance was all fine and that his flight was booked for the day after tomorrow back to Dubai, and could he send details of any follow-up vaccinations he might need so they could get that sorted, and he looked at the message, and thought of Isabella, and thought for a moment that this might finally be his time to cry, now that she had probably stopped.

He put the phone back in his pocket without replying, and felt something warm and papery inside. He pulled it out. An envelope, still sealed, *Isabella Abayomi* written on the front.

He stared at it for a while, like a cat suddenly offered an unknown bowl of food after twenty years of happy eating.

Then he stood up, shuffled to the reception desk, said, "Is the woman I came with still here?" and when the receptionist pointed down the hall, he followed her gesture with mumbled thanks, and walked on, head down, a votive shuffle in a sanctified hall.

Isabella and Kemi were sitting outside an office in the imaging department, waiting for results. Isabella stood painfully when Charlie approached, and Kemi followed, reluctant. Isabella said, "You shouldn't pay for this ... "

But Kemi cut her off with a simple "Thank you. I don't know why you are here, Harbinger of Death, but for what you are doing for Isabella tonight – thank you. But may I ask: did those men come tonight because you were here, or were you here because those men came?"

Charlie hesitated. There was no malice in Kemi's voice, just a calm enquiry from a reasonable woman. A reasonable woman, he mused, with a gun in her handbag. He took a deep breath, and it hurt, so he let it out quickly and, from a more shallow breath, blurted, "I don't think those men were anything to do with me. I come before Death, and I didn't see him tonight."

He held out the envelope, and saw Isabella flinch.

"Please," he said. "Please. I ... I don't know if it's ... but my employer isn't ... he's not ... sometimes he can be but I don't think that ... There was once a house in Belarus and these men came and they were ... Please. Will you take it?"

Isabella shook her head, almost hiding behind Kemi's stiff, upright frame. Kemi drew in her bottom lip, then puffed it out with an expansion of her cheeks, and took the envelope.

"Thank you," said Charlie.

"I don't want it," snapped Isabella.

Kemi shrugged. "Nevertheless, it has come, and so has Death. These things are here, whether we want them or not."

She slit the envelope open with one long, sharp nail, and pulled out the cards inside.

Pictures.

Bright pictures, oil paint, photographed and reproduced.

A cottage by the river.

Elephants in the long grass.

A lion's head, roaring.

Mountains where the wild baboons roam.

Women with children clutched to their bright robes, walking through fields of plenty.

Sunrise over the savannah.

On the back – a place for a stamp, lines drawn for the address.

Picture postcards of another place, a different kind of paradise.

Kemi flicked through them in silence, and Isabella watched, and when they had seen them all, Kemi put them back into the envelope, tapped the envelope twice against the wall to square up its contents, then slipped it into her bag.

"Thank you, Harbinger of Death," she said politely, offering her right hand to shake, the handbag with the gun in it dangling from her wrist. "Thank you for everything."

He shook her hand, eyes still fixed on Isabella's face, then smiled and began to walk away.

He made it to the door, then stopped, and looked back.

"Miss Abayomi?"

Isabella didn't look at him.

"You were very funny. I watched your show. It was really good. I enjoyed it. Thank you."

Her eyes flickered up, met his, then turned away.

He took another step, then turned back and blurted, "Sometimes I come as a courtesy, sometimes a warning, and today . . . which one am I? Do you know?"

Now Isabella's eyes flew to him, and there was rage again, burning fury, a thing without a name.

But Kemi smiled. "Oh," she breathed. "By now? A courtesy, I

expect. Maybe a warning? More likely a courtesy. Things being what they are."

"You think Death is coming for you? That it is inevitable?"

"Yes. Probably. The man you saw today, the man who . . . His name is Jonah. His father is a judge. He is a millionaire. He owns other people's lives, their businesses, their everything. He wanted to own us, but we . . . have each other. It is illegal, of course, for us to be together. It is a vile sin. If we are ever arrested – and Jonah will make sure we are, if he doesn't simply kill us – we will be imprisoned. In the northern states, we could be stoned to death. These . . . postcards are very whimsical, but they do not change a thing. We are Nigerian. This is our home. We will quite possibly die for it, and each other. That is why you are here, Mr Harbinger of Death. What you witnessed tonight . . . was not the first. There have been others, and there will be more to come, and one day, we will not be there for each other, and maybe, by your presence, that day is sooner than we thought. Don't look so shocked – you cannot be as we are and not consider the possibility. If you kill a yansh babe, you do not kill a human being, not really."

human human human rat rat human rat rat human

Charlie shook his head, a pounding against his ears, a drum-beat in his skull

human rat rat human rat

Kemi's head tilted to one side. "You are . . . are you all right?"

"I . . . I'm fine, yes. Thank you. I mean . . . I'm sorry."

She shrugged. "We chose our life."

"And tonight? Tonight doesn't change it?"

"No. As I said: this is not the first."

He looked past Kemi, to Isabella, silent behind the woman she loved, and wondered where was that wit now, where was her humour, her laughter that could infect others. No sign of it, away from the stage, but perhaps that was to be expected, perhaps laughter was just another part of the performance too.

He looked down.

He didn't move.

225

They waited.

Then he looked up and said, "Is it safe for you to go home?"

They didn't answer.

"I'm staying in a good hotel. Actually – I'm staying in an over-priced bad hotel, but it's good enough."

"We don't need pity," hissed Isabella. "Our lives are our own."

"No," he retorted, sharper than he'd meant. "Death is coming. I have seen him. I saw him on the ice, I saw him on the edge of the pit; I saw him in the street where the rich men drank champagne, I saw him by my father's side. Death is coming for you, he's coming and I came before. Now in the name of everything, for the sake of all that matters, please, just . . . just please. For one night only. Please let me do something good."

The two women looked at each other.

Words, Yoruba, gentle, fast.

Then Isabella said, "Okay."

Chapter 69

"I want to go to Africa."

"What we like about him is he's reduced his dependency on foreign aid by nearly seventy per cent. I know this will be his fifth term in office, but from a financial standpoint . . . "

"White people were slaves too, you know! Why do they have to make it such a big thing, like it was just so . . . "

"Tuareg, Zulu, Bantu, Masai, Ashante, Hutu, Tutsi, Shona, Hausa, Luba, Fula, Berber, Mande . . . "

"Where in Africa?"

"Coffee bananas pineapples oranges mango maize sugar mahogany ebony diamonds uranium . . . "

"Did you know that technically, Egypt is in Africa? I mean I always assumed . . . "

"What did the British ever do? I know that there were some massacres, but actually the bureaucracy we left behind . . . "

"They don't want it. Well it's not their culture. I know that that's what they liked in Ethiopia, but thing is, Angola is five and a half thousand kilometres away . . . "

"The play is set in Greece. Yes I know it's about recovery from war, but why does that automatically mean it needs to be . . . ?"

"Do I look like a victim to you?"

"I just don't understand why these places can't be like everywhere else."

Chapter 70

In the land of sun . . .

. . . in a land of oil . . .

. . . on the edge of a lagoon where the city grows . . .

Isabella and Kemi had to have two separate rooms, because that was how it worked.

Kemi snuck into Isabella's room and held her tight, squeezed up close to her on the single bed. It will be a long time before Isabella feels safe again. The eyes of strangers are full of bullets now.

Charlie lay on his back, in his bedroom by the sea, and stared at the ceiling, and did not sleep.

Knock knock knock!

Knock knock knock!

Charlie opened his eyes, and perhaps he had slept after all, because the sun was high and the day was hot, and someone was knocking at his door. He pulled on the hotel's complimentary dressing gown, thin-soled slippers. "Who is it?" he called, resting his aching, bruised back against the wall.

"Police!"

There wasn't a spyhole in the door. He opened it on the chain. Two men, wearing scuffed white shirts and black trousers, stood in the corridor. One waved an ID at him through the narrow gap, said, "You are Mr Harbinger of Death?"

"What do you want?"

"We need to talk to you about an incident last night."

"Can you give me five minutes?"

"Yes. We'll wait here."

"Thank you."

Charlie closed the door, and wondered if he had any clean pants.

They sat in the hotel bar. No one was serving alcohol, not at this time of day. Charlie ordered fruit and yoghurt. The two policemen ordered coffee. For a while the three of them sat, waiting for their orders, saying not a word, as if the ritual of conversation could not begin until bellies were full, caffeine flowing. Charlie made a show of checking his phone, and wondered how bruised his face was. In the rush to put clothes on, he hadn't looked too closely in the mirror, and now his shirt was done up out of order, one rogue button sticking up at the top, nowhere to go; one loose eye hanging unloved at the bottom. His jaw, when he moved it, creaked. His stomach ached. His arm throbbed, and for a moment he wondered if the hospital should have discharged him.

Tsk tsk, muttered a junior doctor, owl-eyed, kicking up from his memories. Is this all that's wrong with you? Don't waste my time, there are people with real injuries to deal with, you know?

A bowl of yoghurt; a bowl of fruit. The yoghurt tasted metallic in his mouth; the fruit was the fruitiest, sweetest, richest thing he thought he'd ever eaten.

The policemen drank their coffee, watched him a while. At last the senior officer, a man with hair turning grey around the temples and a small constellation of dark moles beneath his right eye, said, "We want to talk to you about an incident last night, in which we are told you were involved."

"You want to know about the attack?"

"The attack. Yes. Do you know this man?"

A picture, put on the table in front of him. He recognised the face, the diamond-encrusted crucifix. "Yes. He attacked us."

"Attacked . . . who?"

"Myself and Miss Abayomi."

"The three of you were involved in a confrontation?"

"If you want to call it that."

"Where was this?"

"Outside the comedy club where Miss Abayomi performed."

"Why were you there?"

"I was . . . I was there on business."

"What kind of business?"

Charlie hesitated, the spoon drooping in his hand, yoghurt dripping off it back into the bowl. "Well. I'm the Harbinger of Death. I was . . . I was there for that."

"Whose death?"

"It . . . doesn't work like that."

"Doesn't it? You arrive, and people die; that's how it is, abi?"

"No, it's . . . sometimes it's that, but sometimes . . . I'm sent for an idea. In Greenland I was sent for a man, but I think I was sent also for the ice, because it was melting and the world will change, and in Syria the dead were dead already and I was sent for a poet who had become . . . Sometimes I am sent for an idea, as well as a person."

"And what idea were you sent for this time?"

"I don't know." Even as he said the words, he stopped himself, stared down into his bowl, then blurted, "The world is ending."

"What?"

"The world is ending. No – a world is ending. I think . . . I think I am sent for that."

"That doesn't make sense. What does it even mean?"

"I, uh . . . I . . . It's a thing like . . ." The words trailed away. Charlie closed his eyes, tried to find words, the ice, the dust, the fire, the dead, the songs in the mountains, the . . .

Opened his eyes again, saw faces that he suddenly feared would

229

never understand, saw for a moment the whole world staring at him from these policemen's eyes, the human race peeking at an occluded, obscure star. He looked away. "I can't explain." Wished Emmi was by his side.

The policeman shrugged while his junior colleague made notes on a yellow pad, sucking in his lower lip as if displeased at the things he was now transcribing. "So here you are, at the club, harbingering away, and there is Miss Abayomi, and here is this man ... " He tapped the picture of Jonah again with his index finger, twice. "How did the argument begin?"

"It wasn't an argument. He stopped us as we were trying to leave. He threatened us."

"He threatened you? What exactly did he say?"

"I ... I don't know, exactly, the words were ... but he had two boys with him, two men, I can describe them, they were ... "

"Boys like children?"

"No, like ... like young men, and it was obvious that he was threatening us ... "

"But you don't know what he actually said."

"No, but look, we ... we ran, back to the club, tried to lock ourselves in, away from him, and one of his boys came over the wall and he ... Look, he did this ... "

Charlie pulled up his shirt, suddenly hot, panting for breath. The bruises across his belly and ribs were glorious purple and red, sweeps of yellow and brown – everything he could have hoped for as an impressive display.

The junior policeman stopped writing, raised his eyebrows, pen still poised to strike.

The senior sighed and shook his head, a tired old man who'd seen too many gloomy mornings after the weatherman promised sun, and said, "Cover up, Mr Harbinger of Death, you're in a public place."

Charlie pulled his shirt back down, feeling suddenly ashamed.

"So these boys ... they want to talk to you, and you say you feel threatened, but you're not sure why, and at what point did Kemi Afolayan draw her gun?"

Charlie opened his mouth, and closed it again.

He sat back in his chair, and realised that this was perhaps how puppets felt, when their master let go of the strings. He licked his lips, tried to find some words, eventually mumbled, "That man . . . was going to . . . he was . . ."

"Yes, Mr Harbinger? What was he?"

"He took his belt off. He . . . he was going to . . ."

"Ah, this is more of your being threatened without actually knowing why. Is it possible that you get frightened easily? Maybe you misunderstood the situation?"

"No, no, I was there, I . . ."

"The gun: when did Miss Afolayan draw it?"

"I . . . He was going to kill us."

"Are you sure? Did he say so?"

"Of course he didn't say so," spat Charlie. "Of course he didn't fucking say it. You know, I know, I've seen . . . Kemi saved my life."

"That's not what I heard. I heard that she and Miss Abayomi verbally and physically threatened this man, that they threatened to kill him. The words were . . . What were the words?"

The junior policeman cleared his throat, and with the aplomb of a singer at the opera intoned, "You're dead, you're dead, we're going to kill you, you're dead."

"I didn't hear them say that, I heard *him* say that, I heard this man . . ."

"Have you ever seen Miss Abayomi and Miss Afolayan kiss?"

"What?"

"Have you ever seen them kiss? Touch each other in a sexual manner? Rub each other's breasts? Lick each other's necks, perhaps — something of this sort?"

"No."

"Are you sure?"

"Yes."

"But they are lesbian."

"I . . . I wouldn't know that."

"Do you think they threatened this man because he knew?"

231

"No."

"Do you think they threatened to kill him because they were afraid of being exposed?"

"No."

"Do you think . . ."

"*He was going to kill us!*" Charlie's voice rang round the room, a scream of fury and despair. "*He was going to rape her and then he was going to kill us both!*"

He was half out of his chair, resting on his fists, gasping for breath. The room turned to look, stared, waited, turned away. The two policemen sat, quiet and calm. The older had one leg folded over the other, hands resting on his knees. The younger held the pen tight in his right hand, a wading bird ready to strike.

Tick. Tick. Tick. An old-fashioned clock, eight minutes slow, tick tick tick on the wall.

"Please sit down, Mr Harbinger," sighed the policeman at last.

Charlie lowered himself back into his seat, shaking from ears to toes.

"You don't know much about our country, do you?" breathed the older man, not unkindly. "That's all right. Not many people do. They talk about this continent – Africa – as if it was one big place, as if your Scotland was the same as Greece. It's Africa, they say, it's just how Africa is. You have come here, perhaps, with certain preconceptions, with a certain sense of your own importance, of privilege. Privilege – an interesting word, privilege, you as somehow above it all, and from being above, perhaps able to judge? Height is the key, morally superior, intellectually superior, a white man come to a black city, yes? Mr Harbinger of Death, don't look so ashamed, it is very, very common amongst your kind.

"Let me explain: Lagos doesn't give two fucks about you. Lagos doesn't care what you saw, or what you think you saw, or what you're going to say, or who you're going to say it to. You could be the most important man in the world and who would care, not us, not here, the city . . . this city . . . we are ours, ourselves, we are the tellers of our own stories. There are certain parts of my job that require paperwork; that is all. And the paperwork will tell the story that the city needs to be told. Once I was angry about it, do you believe that? Once I thought it was some sort of injustice, this thing that happens, this way things are. I do not think that way now. I imagine that if this was New York, I would advise you to get out of town, but honestly, leave, stay, it's all the same to me. I don't care."

So saying, he stood up, threw a few notes onto the table, smiled, and offered his hand to Charlie to shake.

Charlie sat dumb, and stared at the floor.

The policeman smiling, head on one side, then, thoughtful, pulling his lips in and rolling them between his teeth for a moment: "Mr Harbinger . . . what is Death?"

"What?"

"What is Death? Do you think?"

"I . . . Death is Death is . . . "

"But – I have often wondered this – why do good men die? Is it luck? Is there destiny? If there is destiny, is there a God? What do people see when they die? Do they go somewhere else? Is Death kind? Is Death cruel? What is Death?"

Charlie shook his head, looked down at the polished hotel floor.

The policeman shrugged, and with a flick of his wrist to his partner to follow, walked away.

Chapter 71

Here: a story told.

Once, said the Harbinger of Death, I was sent to visit a dying man.

(Most of Charlie's stories begin this way.)

This man, he lived in Belarus, and he had been Stalinist when it was a good idea to be Stalinist, an admirer of Khrushchev's secret speech back when that was in vogue, a fan of Brezhnev, an ardent supporter of Yeltsin, an advocate for the EU and closer ties to Moscow and a big pal of Putin's, all with equal commitment, all of the time.

And his name was . . .

. . . his name was really rather long, and besides, it's not my business to talk about these things; there's a certain . . . confidentiality, a certain respect that you should have for these matters, for the dead, so we'll call him Rodion and leave it at that.

Rodion, through his stalwart commitment to pretty much anything, was a very rich man. When the USSR collapsed, he became even richer by buying up state enterprises — the road building, the hospitals, the schools, the factories, you name it — on the cheap and turning them into vast, profitable businesses. This was, in its way, an admirable thing. It was a less admirable thing when he entered politics and conducted this business by a) turning up on election day with free TVs for anyone who voted for him and b) shooting journalists. But these were the times, that was the fashion, what's a guy to do?

In a land of forests . . .

. . . in a land of endless sky . . .

I was sent, said Charlie, to bring him a jar of honey. It came from a small village in the south of the country, and was, he said, exactly like the honey his mother used to make. He was dying, of course. My visit was not a warning — he had cancer, everywhere. My visit was a courtesy, an act of memorial from my employer to a man who, in many ways, embodied something that was worthy of note.

It was a long drive to his mansion, in the hills north of Brest, a beautiful place, incredible. Ancient oak trees that had survived the passage of so many armies; a constant chorus of birds; still blue waters around the lakes where the wild horses roamed. Spotted deer grazing on the side of the road, sunlight bursting through the forest, the smell of it — leaves and blue skies. I was still new to the job and I had no idea, I'd just assumed, Belarus, prisons and factories, and of course there is that too, but the land . . . I felt hope that something this beautiful had survived so much of humanity, I really did. That there was still something in humanity that appreciated this. Does that sound strange? I'm tired, forgive me, I've had this headache for a while now, it's been . . . but you want to hear the story.

To the north of Brest, then, up an unmarked road. His mansion was all white, high above a lake, with those ice-cream rooftops you see on Orthodox churches sprouting from all four corners, and granite flagstones and potted plants, a little sliver of paradise. But he was also a very rich man who'd come by his money through questionable means, so there was a security gate and men on guard, blue shirts tucked into their trousers, big sunglasses and friendly smiles, who still smiled even as they patted me down, and took my phone from me and said, in bad English, "Harbinger of Death, yes? Yes yes, Death comes, you come, come come come!"

They didn't seem surprised to see me. Sometimes people are resigned, sometimes they're even pleased, but they weren't just expectant, they were delighted. Before I could even see the boss his men had thrown together a sort of feast, platters of rye bread and caviar, cold meats and salad, all perfectly prepared. I ate with a man I took to be his chief enforcer, Malcoim, who had better English than the rest and talked, talked, wanted to know everything about me, where I lived, places I'd been, whether I'd met my employer, what he was like. I didn't satisfy him. There was something about this situation, this strange place in the hills, that made me quieter than I might have been. None of this was normal, none of it felt right – who is pleased to see the Harbinger of Death?

"What is Death?" he asked, and I didn't really understand the question, so he made it a joke. "These things we wonder," he exclaimed, "they grow old, yes?"

Finally, once they'd fed me and invited me to use the bathroom, freshen up, they took me upstairs to see Rodion. I knew he was an old man, but the cancer had made him so much older, a bundle of bones tiny in a giant bed, his face already a skull with some skin taped to it, his hair all gone, eyebrows gone, tubes up his nose and in the corner of his mouth, a urine bag against the side of his bed.

I said what I had been taught to say, in Russian first, which I was told he would speak better than English. I am the Harbinger of Death, I am sent as a courtesy, I bring a gift. He had a nurse, although I'm not sure if she was qualified; there was something ... let us say she was beautiful in a sort of ... magazine way ... and very uninterested in the machines that were sustaining his life – anyway, he asked her to pour a teaspoon of honey out for him, and put the spoon in his mouth, and it seemed a great effort for him to swallow, and when he finally did, I thought, this is it, he's going to cry, he's going to tell me all about his mother and his childhood and the terrible things he's done and how he regrets it, because Death has that effect on people – I don't mind, really I don't, it's good for people to talk, it's good for humans to listen, it is a very ... very humane thing, and humanity is ... But he didn't. He said the honey reminded him of home, and he was grateful for it, and he didn't really say much else. Then Maksim announced that was it, our time was done, we shouldn't bother the old man, and out we went.

My job was done.

I went downstairs towards the car, making sure to thank Maksim for his hospitality, but he stayed with me, still smiling and beaming bright, and when I got to the front door of the house he caught me by the sleeve and said, still as pleasant as a summer's day,

"So what will it take, eh?"

"I ... don't understand."

"Come on. Five years, maybe ten, what will it take?"

"I don't know what you mean."

Still smiling, always smiling. He tilted his head back towards the way we'd come. "The boss, the boss, what will it take? I heard Death sometimes plays games; we can play, if you like. You want life? I'll give you life. Say ... one life for every year?

You can choose, young, old, pretty, stupid, virgin, mother – it's all the same. Just name your price."

"I'm sorry, I think there's been a misunderstanding . . . "

He held a little tighter now to my arm. Smiling. "No, there is no misunderstanding. That man up there, the man you just met? He is not my father, but he is greater than my father. He is a father of his nation, he is a father of a great new world. I would die for him; if you wanted my life, I would give it, of course, my life for him, no doubt. You think I'm joking? I'm not. Not about this. Not about him. So tell me – name your price."

I swallowed, and wished he wouldn't smile. "You are . . . attempting to negotiate with me for your employer's life?"

"Yes yes yes," clicking his fingers in the air, impatient now, "come on, what price?"

"I'm sorry. I am not authorised to negotiate for my employer."

Maksim put his arm around my shoulder now, pulling me away from the door, flicked with the tips of his fingers at a scuff in my shirt that I couldn't see. "Hey, Charlie, I know you have to say that. For the ordinary people, maybe, for the little people, but this is Mr Rodion, this is the boss, he is the king of this country. I know your boss respects that, so don't treat me like I'm one of them, eh? Don't put on that act for me." Still smiling, but only with his mouth.

"You have been . . . very courteous," I replied. "I know that these things are important to my employer, and I'm grateful, but you see I just can't . . . I don't have that sort of authority."

"But you can find someone who does?"

"I . . . No. I'm the Harbinger of Death. It's me and then it's . . . I'm sorry, I thought this was all understood, I thought that . . . "

"You can talk to your boss, tell him not Mr Rodion, not yet, name the price."

"No."

"No?" Still smiling.

If he'd been shouting, screaming, crying, I felt sure I would have known what to do, but not this smile. I wondered if he'd seen Death before, if he knew what Death looked like, and felt like maybe he hadn't. Maybe he'd sent other people to do that bit of work for him, maybe he'd been away when his parents died. Maybe he'd just never looked.

"Charlie . . . " He had this way of saying my name. The first part goes down, Char, a disappointed sound, then up again, Lie, like we were a married couple bickering over whose turn it was to hang the laundry out: *Char*-lie. "Charlie . . . why don't you get your boss on the line, hm? Why don't you just give Death a bit of a call, tell him that it's important, that we're willing to pay, ten, twenty, a hundred lives, or something else, anything he wants, you name it, we can do it, that's how things work, yes?"

Mouth dry, but there weren't any other words. "I can't. That's not how it . . . "

His fingers dug into my shoulder, hurt, I gasped, mostly in surprise, but he still kept on smiling. "Call your boss. You call him. Tell him it's important."

"I can call Milton Keynes . . . "

"Are you taking the piss?"

"No, I mean, it's, it's the office, it's where . . . "

"What the fuck do I want with Milton fucking Keynes?"

This is a question many people have asked, and I tried smiling too, thought maybe I could make a joke out of it, make something funny, find something between the two of us that mattered, say something like . . .

"I'd die for the boss, Charlie," his voice, still pleasant, cutting through my thoughts. "I'd die for him. I'd make other people die too."

"I can't, it's not my . . . "

He hit me round the side of the head. It was an oddly playful thing, an open slap, the kind of thing old friends do when they've been caught doing something ridiculous – except this had power, knocked me to one side. Still, it was absurd enough that I found when I straightened I was smiling too, not understanding, thinking maybe it was just some sort of gesture, some laddish prank going wrong.

Second time he hit me, still like a kitten playing with its dozy friend, I stopped smiling.

Third time, I tripped over my own feet, fell to the floor.

He stared at me, surprised and friendly, offered me one hand to get back up, which I took, because it was there, because that's what you did, you accepted hands that offered to help, that was how the world worked.

"Oops," he said, dropping me as I climbed to my feet, and then offering me his hand again, which again I took, and again he dropped me. "You seem to be having some trouble there, Charlie. You seem to be in difficulty. Do you need me to get help?"

"No, no, I'm . . ."

When do you stop making these things a joke?

He was smiling, so I was smiling.

I thought I was going to die, and I was smiling because it was absurd, I couldn't die here, there was no reason to think I was going to die here, and of course I was, it was as clear as day and utterly unbelievable.

I've got better at recognising the truth of these things, I think, as the years go by.

"Hey! Charlie keeps falling down!" he called out, to the house at large. "Come give him a hand!"

Others came. The other servants of their dying master, Mr Rodion's boys.

They were eager to help.

I think . . .

. . . looking at my job . . .

. . . that I have been kidnapped eight times in total.

I have been imprisoned five times.

Held at gunpoint twelve times.

My travel insurance is nearly sixty pages long. Milton Keynes handles that.

Milton Keynes – what the fuck does anyone want with Milton Keynes?

One time, when I was trying to cross into Uzbekistan, the customs official managing my documents just flipped out when I told him my job, he just lost it, he pulled a gun and started shooting – not really at me, just around the room, shouting and shooting until one of his own guys hit him with a chair. I didn't understand why. Afterwards they said his daughter was ill, and he had been coping very well. I don't know what happened to the daughter. I imagine she was fine. You imagine that kind of thing, don't you? You imagine a normal life, a reasonable outcome, that's how . . .

Departures, arrivals, departures, arrivals

being reasonable is how you get through US Customs. I have been detained eleven times by US Customs, and every time they ask the same thing – what is the purpose of your visit?

I've got the visa, I've been into the country many times before, but

"What is the purpose of your visit?"

"I'm the Harbinger of Death."

"What does that involve?"

"I am the one who comes before the rider of the Apocalypse. Sometimes I come as a warning, sometimes as a courtesy."

"Yeah, but what's your actual job?"

When I interviewed for the job, Harbinger of Death, one of the most important attributes it highlighted on the form was interpersonal skills.

I found that odd, at first.

If you're going to travel the world, bringing news to those who are about to die, surely it makes sense not to care.

It took me a long time to realise why that was wrong. You have to care. It's your job to care. You are the human, you are the . . . you are the thing that is imaginable, that comes before, you are . . .

real.

Where Death isn't.

Death is real, of course, Death is . . .

I always try to be reasonable. And I make sure there's at least

240

two hours between my arriving and any connecting flights, especially when changing planes in Atlanta.

The men in Belarus – they were not reasonable.

It wasn't reasonable to beat me.

It didn't make any sense.

That's what I struggled with, more than anything, I think. It just didn't make any sense. What would hitting me achieve? But they hit me anyway, I think that was how they knew to negotiate, I mean, that was how their world worked. They'd never come up against a force which couldn't just be pummelled into defeat, they'd never met a thing that didn't simply curl up in fear.

Death doesn't fear.

Death doesn't stop.

As Harbinger, it's part of my job to be . . .

. . . when I filled out the application form, I was asked to list an example of a situation where I had demonstrated strong communication skills. I chose writing for my university newspaper, though I'd only ever written three articles and they'd all been about concerts. Saga – she was the Harbinger before me – said she wasn't sure it counted. I said she was probably right, that I only did it because I liked listening to music.

What kind of music? she said.

And I told her. I figured, I'm not going to get this job, I might as well be honest, so I told her about music, about the way it made me feel, not just listening, but singing, all these voices, every voice unique, every sound that comes from every throat on the planet a unique, incredible instrument and how it was a language we all spoke, how it was a truth that every human born shared and it was . . .

so in Belarus they beat me, a lot. I wasn't so worried about dying, but I thought, I'm going to be a cripple, aren't I? I'm going to have to retire and have false teeth that I need to glue onto my gums every morning and never be able to walk properly ever again because something will be severed in my spine and never use my hands or speak clearly or see, I'll be blind by the time

241

this is done, I'll be blind and why are they beating me? What the fucking hell is the fucking point of it?

Anyway.

They stopped, eventually.

There wasn't any point killing me. There wasn't any point to any of it.

They gave me a phone and Maksim said, "Call your boss. Tell him. Tell him we'll fucking rip you to pieces. Tell him he doesn't come here. Not for ten more years. You tell him."

I couldn't hold the phone properly, I kept on dropping it. The boys all laughed at that, but in the end Maksim held it up for me and I dialled the number.

Saga had given me the number on my first day, her very last. She said, "Don't use it. Death will answer."

I didn't want to, I didn't want to but they put a gun against my head, right here, they put it against my head and I didn't want to die, couldn't believe, didn't understand, knew that they meant it, didn't know why, what could possibly make people be this way

(human human rat)

(sometimes people don't see other people the way they see themselves)

so I dialled the number.

The phone rang a very long time. I started to cry, because I thought I'd got it wrong, that this was it, the end of me, that there was nothing reasonable and nothing mad I could do to live, and I wanted to live, even if it meant being in pain for the rest of my life, I wanted so badly to try and live

Then Death answered.

His voice is . . .

. . . everyone sees their own Death, their own way. Everyone hears Death in their own manner.

I hear him as soft, quiet, a man, English, like me, rich, perhaps, I think he's rich, but also . . . like someone off the TV. Someone who reads important books and says important things and knows that he's right. Death knows that he's right, when I hear him speak.

And Death said, hello?

"Hello, sir, it's Charlie."

Tears and blood on my face, he could hear me crying, but seemed like he didn't care.

Ah yes, Charlie. Of course. How are you?

"Not so good, sir. There's ... I'm in Belarus, sir, for Mr Rodion ... "

Mr Rodion, of course, I went driving with him once through the streets of Prague, a long time ago.

"I ... I am ... thing is ... " I couldn't get the words out, my voice sounded strange, my tongue didn't fit in my mouth.

Take your time, Charlie. Take your time.

"He doesn't want to die, sir. And ... they've got me in this room and there's ... this man, he's ... "

Are they threatening you?

"Yes, sir."

Have they hurt you?

"Yes, sir."

Are they going to kill you?

A gun against my head, I can tell you exactly where it was, though at the time it felt huge, it felt bigger than my whole skull. "Yes, sir."

I see. That displeases me.

"I'm ... I'm sorry, sir."

Oh Charlie, don't worry so – this isn't your fault at all, this is rather an unpleasant reaction of discourteous people to what I am confident was an entirely professional and civilised visit on your part. Look, I am rather in the middle of things right now, but do you mind putting one of Mr Rodion's men on the line?

"Yes, sir ... "

And Charlie?

"Yes, sir?"

Close your eyes, and count backwards from one hundred.

"Yes, sir."

Now hand me over.

I handed the phone over. "My employer wants to speak to you," I stammered.

Maksim beamed, a proud son fulfilling his father's wishes, and took the phone. The gun was removed from the side of my head. I closed my eyes, buried my head in my hands, curled up into my own knees, and counted.

One hundred

ninety-nine

ninety-eight

When your eyes are shut, you hear the world differently. Maksim's voice, speaking Russian, loud, bluster. The creak of his shoes on the ground. The tick-tick-tick of hot pipes cooling. The rush of water somewhere else in the house. The buzz of the bulb.

eighty-nine

eighty-eight

eighty-seven

Once, I was sent to give a box of chocolates to a woman whose husband was beating her slowly to death. She had a sweet tooth, but he told her that chocolates made her fat, so we ate the chocolates I bought her together, secretly, on a bench near her flat. I asked her why she didn't go, why she wouldn't just run away, and she said you don't understand, you don't get it, I know he still loves me, this thing he does, he still loves me really, it's just ... it's just he's going through a hard time. When he stops he's so gentle, he's the gentlest, kindest man you'll ever see, he's just ... We made our life together, we made our home, he knows me so well, it's just he gets angry, that's all. He just gets angry. And then it stops.

I was a warning; I was a courtesy.

I said, miss, if that's what you believe, then today I am merely a courtesy, nothing more.

She moved into a shelter that night, and Death passed her by.

Once, I met a journalist who'd been kidnapped in Pakistan, and nearly died when the Americans accidentally dropped a bomb on his position in Kandahar. He was in a wheelchair, and still trying to get back to the front lines. I said, why, why would you do that?

And he replied: I lived. I lived and it is a miracle I lived, and my life is a miracle, a miracle, do you see? Every breath I draw is a miracle!

fifty-five

fifty-four

fifty-three

The world is ending. Oh God, Patrick told me on the ice, he said the world was ending, a world, the world, what does it matter, and I didn't listen I didn't understand please I didn't understand . . .

The pipes creaked, the bulb buzzed, but Maksim wasn't talking any more.

I visited a woman up a mountain in Japan. She lived alone, dressed all in grey, no hair on her head. She said, "Is the game over, then? Is the dance done?"

I gave her a scroll, ancient, fragile, I'd carried it so carefully up the mountain, handled it with cotton gloves, but she took it briskly, unfolded it, smiled, nodded, gave it back to me, told me to set it on fire as the sun went down.

"It's for you," I replied. "It's a gift."

"It is not a gift," she explained. "It is the contract we signed together, a long, long time ago. I have enjoyed the years, but I am not sure the price I paid was worth it."

She shooed me back down the mountain, and I did as she asked, and burned the scroll as the sun went down, and I think I heard Death's footsteps on the path as he climbed up to her cottage, and she died. Only the curious thing is, when I told the people in the village below that she'd died, no one would believe me.

"She's been in that place for nearly three hundred years!" exclaimed one woman, who I assumed was mad, but her son corrected her. "Only two hundred," he chided. "She wandered a lot more before that."

Does Death make bargains?

Does Death play dice?

I hear this ticking sometimes in my mind, like the clock that counts down to Armageddon, tick tick tick tick . . .

I listened, and maybe Maksim was listening too, or perhaps he wasn't, perhaps he was just quiet. I couldn't hear the sound of voices on the telephone. I couldn't hear his shoes shuffle on the floor.

thirty-nine

thirty-eight

Something else I couldn't hear. Something else I had heard since coming to this place, what was it? It was hard to describe, a sense of an absence, but I couldn't put it in words.

A miracle. Every breath I draw is a miracle.

Then I heard footsteps on the floor.

Click. Click. Click. Click. The door didn't open, the door didn't close, but sharp footsteps, not the creak of Maksim's leather shoes or the shuffle of trainers, but bone-hard heels on stone, click, click, click. They stopped. They turned. They walked. They stopped again. And they didn't move any more.

Silent now.

Quiet now.

The wind had stopped, and the birds were no longer singing in the forest.

Five.

Four.

Three.

Two.

One.

There was blood running out of my mouth, down my neck, into the collar of my shirt. There was blood behind my right ear, and from a cut in my cheek where a man with a gold ring had hit me. There was blood on my shirt, where a pointy shoe had kicked hard and something had torn.

I opened my eyes.

The men in the room. They just lay there. One was in a chair, another sprawled across a leather couch. Maksim was on the floor, curled up, his hands underneath his head, his knees pulled to his chest, like a child, sleeping. Just . . . sleeping, all of them. Only they slept with their eyes open, the sockets full of blood,

246

and their tongues lolled and there was a look on the face of one man, one man who I think had really wanted to kill me, a look like he had seen ...

They were dead, of course. All of them. Six men, sleeping forever in a nightmare. The phone was next to Maksim's hand, like he'd carefully positioned it before lying down, so gently, to die. I picked it up; the line was still open, the signal strong.

Death said, Charlie?

"Yes, sir."

Charlie, I'd like you to contact the office.

"Yes, sir."

Tell them what's happened. Don't worry about next week's appointments; you need to rest. Take a bit of time. Get your ticket upgraded to first class for the return flight. There's a wonderful spa near Leighton Buzzard, if you feel like that sort of thing, the office will carry the cost.

"Thank you, sir."

Do look after yourself, Charlie. You are very important to me.

Death hung up.

I walked through the house.

A few birds tried singing again, but their voices were weak and far away.

Everyone was dead. The cooks, the cleaners, the nurse by the bed. One man was slouched over his desk, head on his keyboard, napping, not breathing, no pulse. A woman lay on a recliner by the pool, hat over her eyes, ankles crossed, a bikini and false tan, going cold. I don't know why I walked through the house, dripping blood as I went. I don't know why I needed to see, needed to know. Perhaps something compelled me, something that ... but I doubt it. I think I looked for my own sake, too frightened to get into my car until I knew they were all dead, every single one.

Not quite every one.

Mr Rodion was still alive.

Taped into his machines and tubes, still alive, still breathing, the nurse resting on the end of the bed, blood running out of the corner of her mouth, head turned towards him. He was still alive, mute and trapped in that morgue.

He lived for five more years, just like he had wanted. Everyone he had known and loved – they died. But he lived. Death does not take kindly to being ordered around, you see.

I didn't go to the spa near Leighton Buzzard, in the end.

I listened to music.

I listened to requiems for the dead.

And one day, when I was still healing, I went to this park in Streatham, just by chance, just because I needed to walk, needed to move, needed to not sit and think. They were having a kite festival, all these kids and ribbons and colours and music and barbecue food, and I sat and watched it, and until that moment all I had seen was death

death in my dreams

in every face in the street

death in the sky and in the earth

but that day

watching the kites

I saw life, and understood that it was a miracle.

Life is a miracle.

My life is a miracle.

That feeling, that sense of . . .

. . . how could anyone ever walk away from that?

How could I ever give this up?

Chapter 72

"Charlie?"

Leaving the hotel, Lagos, bags packed, body aching, a voice.

"Charlie?"

Charlie looked up.

"Patrick?"

Patrick Fuller. Straight back, steady eye, heels together, straight dark hair. Today he wears a coal-black suit that seems unrumpled from his time spent on the plane, and an assistant stands behind him, auburn hair, bags around her eyes. How has Patrick kept his own eyes so fresh? What is it about business-class ginger beer?

"What are you ... why are you ...?" Charlie is tired; so, so tired. He knows he's slept, but he can't remember, he isn't sure if that sleeping was ... There's a place he knows somewhere where the pain in his body stopped and the sleeping began, but it all blurs, everything seems to blur these days, he's got a headache you would not *believe*, but anyway ...

"Business," replied Patrick. "I have some work here, I've been ... You look terrible."

"I'm ... fine."

"Charlie," tutted Patrick. "Are we ... may I consider us friends?"

"I ... hadn't thought about it. But yes, I suppose."

"Then as a friend, let me tell you, you look terrible. Can I get you a drink? Something to eat? The restaurant in the hotel is ..."

Charlie shook his head quickly, a little too quickly, fluids sloshing around inside his ears. "Thank you, but no. I have a plane to catch and I have to ... I have to persuade someone else to catch a plane."

"Are you sure? When you're back in England, call me, I'm serious, call me and we'll ..."

"Thanks. I'll do that," replied Charlie, and knew he was probably lying.

Chapter 73

Death comes to Lagos.

Perhaps the policeman was right: this is not a city that gives a damn about the world beyond it, this city, this city! It is life and joy and pain and suffering and beauty and kindness and wonder and care, all unto itself, a universe of its own devising; what does it care for the world beyond, what does it care for the laws of men, it is Lagos! Lagos laws, Lagos rules, the city lives!

And yet.

Even to Lagos he comes, he comes, Death comes to us all, in the end.

A shopping mall like any other, a woman with bright red lips and deep black eyes. The Harbinger of Death gave her a book of law, and she was fearful because, even though she does not fear terrorists, because fearing terrorists means you have lost, she is afraid of terrorists, and will never admit it. "Is it Boko Haram? Are they going to shoot this place up, like they did in Nairobi?"

Maybe they will, but not today. Today she will go home safe, and tomorrow too, and in a few months' time she will discover that her husband has been stealing money from her, all her meagre savings gone, and when she goes to the police they laugh her away and say so what, he's your husband. Then she looks at the legal code; then she understands, and that day, a dream fades for ever, and Death sits by her side and hands her a tissue as it dies.

Death visits Mushin on the back of a mildly illegal okada, a motorbike taxi, clinging on to the driver as they weave through the endless go-slow of Lagos streets, until they come to the slums. It's a long and uncomfortable way for Death to travel, but he feels it is appropriate, necessary, to take the path that others walk. There he finds a house where a woman was given, of all things, a tape measure and a trowel – or rather, he finds the

250

ashes, for the house has burned to the ground, and so did nearly a hundred properties all around, the fire engines never coming, for why would they come to Mushin? But just this once – in a rare moment of unity – the people come together, all of them, all at once, and build something new, something with bricks and mortar, not timber panels and rusted nails, and the swaggering area boys chip in some of their stolen cash and only mug and hijack travellers in other districts, for a little while, because the people of those streets are their people, and this is their home, and there are some things that matter more than money. And the woman found the trowel in the burnt-out remains of her life, and realised it wasn't meant for gardening, but for smoothing cement. And for a little while, the old world dies, and the new world is born, and for this sort of business Death likes to put in an appearance, and spends a few hours happily hauling concrete. Here too is the ending of a world, in one way or another.

A rich condo on Victoria Island. A wealthy man who loves his new gun, his beautiful silver gun, so good, so right, no one lays a finger on him, not him, he's protected, he's sweet, he's safe, he's . . .

. . . while cleaning his gun, whispering sweet nothings to his favourite toy, the man accidentally blows his own brains out, and Death tutted and rolled his eyes, before moving swiftly on.

A policeman who runs a roadblock for no good reason. He received three thousand dollars, and had no idea what to do with such a sum, so having no idea, he carried on doing what he's always done, taking dem dash the day after, and the day after that, and the day after that, until one day he's gunned down by a thirteen-year-old kid who's trying to impress the local gang with his bravery, who has dreams of being Robin Hood and saving the lagoon from corrupt and evil men, and he dies of his wounds in the middle of the street, the ambulance stuck in traffic, no one in a real hurry to save him.

Funny thing, he muses, as he bleeds out. With three thousand dollars, he could have stopped for a while, maybe found some other path.

Maybe that was the point.

Ah well, too late now.

Death holds his hand as he dies, and smiles without reproof.

Nine months later, his wife finds the money, still untouched under his bed, and thinking that it came from corrupt doings, gives it away to charity.

"Jesus! Jesus commands you! Jesus heals you!"

A mother dies in a hospital bed, her daughter asleep from too much weeping.

In the end she took the chemo, because she wanted to live, after all this, she wanted so badly to live, but the drugs were too little, too late.

Death sat down beside her, as she breathed her last.

"Jesus ... loves me ..." whispered the woman. "Jesus ... protects me. I feel ... his love. I am not afraid."

Death smiled, and kissed her lightly on the forehead.

She died quietly, aged forty-one, and the church held a fund-raiser in her name.

The pastor didn't specify where the money would go.

And Patrick?

Patrick Fuller has come to Lagos, for business, certainly. He is building condos by the edge of the lagoon with a business partner (who unfortunately blew his brains out, but it's okay, an accident, not a sign of financial irresponsibility); he is attempting to develop land for a new factory near Mushin, the locals don't want it, say that the chemicals will poison the water, but Patrick knows when to give and when to take, and in his gut he feels that this one is a winner.

He's shopping in a mall like any other in the world, buying designer clothes priced like any other, Louis Vuitton; he once tried to move into luxury goods, but LVMH has the market sewn up good, and like he said, Patrick knows when to walk away.

He attends a church, and listens to the music. He is not a believer, and the entire thing leaves him utterly unmoved.

He visits a comedy club, but the place is silent, and his security don't like the look of the area, so no sooner has he arrived than he goes away. He'll admit, maybe not to Charlie, though he can't say why, that these last two visits have nothing to do with work. An email came, inviting him to see the end of a world, and so he came, and he wasn't very impressed, and so he moves on, to make the next deal, and doesn't understand what it is that has made Death so interested in such things.

And Isabella and Kemi?

Isabella said: this is my city, my country, my home, this is my life, my battle, my war, my world. This is my struggle to be seen as a person, to be human, this is my human body, this is my human life, this is my everything, this is my all, this is . . .

And Kemi said: this is my city, my home, my life. And here is the woman I love.

For a long time, they'd sat silent, the three of them. Isabella, Kemi and the Harbinger of Death, waiting in the foyer of the hotel.

Then Isabella said: if we run, then who will fight these battles? If we leave, who will speak for our people, in this country? The conservatives will win. There will be no freedom to choose who you love, there will be no safe place for people like us. There will only be the law and lies. We should not run. We must not run.

Kemi stared at the ceiling for a while, then down at the floor. Finally she looked at the Harbinger of Death and said, "What would you do?"

"That's not important. Your choices are what matter here."

"Don't be an idiot; I'm not asking for instruction, I just want to measure some opinions."

"I would live," Charlie replied. "More than anything, I would live."

"There is great cowardice in abandoning a cause."

"I don't think you're abandoning it. I think you abandon the cause when you abandon the will to live."

Silence, for a while.

Then Kemi reached into her handbag, and pulled out the envelope of postcards. She shuffled them quickly behind her back, turned them upside down so only the white could be seen, fanned them out in front of her towards Isabella and said, "Pick one."

Isabella picked one. Kemi turned it over, revealing a picture of high cloud-striped mountains above glowing blue lakes. "Tsk," she muttered. "Rwanda; out of the frying pan, abi?"

Charlie said, "Let me help with the tickets. I've got a lot of air miles."

Isabella and Kemi leave their life behind.

Death watches the plane go, and is perhaps, in as much as she is ever pleased by anything, satisfied with the outcome. In the departures hall, grubby, noisy, a mess of a place, she thinks she glimpses a figure, bruised and aching, but walking proud, heading for the security line.

The man does not see Death, and they pass each other by.

And later that night, Death goes to the comedy club where once Isabella played, and sits on the empty seats in the dark, and listens to the silence.

Part 7

SCUBA

Chapter 74

"Describe a situation in which you were at your best."

"My greatest strength, I think, is my people skills. I just really like people."

"What would you say you bring to the company?"

" . . . looking at a whole-market rationalisation, a restructuring from the bottom up, by which I mean to say . . . "

"Describe yourself in one word."

"Strong."

"Confident."

"Passionate."

"Dedicated."

"Penguin."

"Did she just say . . . "

" . . . of that forty per cent, ten per cent will be phased out through retirement, and the remaining thirty per cent induced to leave by redundancy incentives. The higher-level management will receive a redundancy package equal to . . . "

" . . . a substantial leakage of urine or faeces – such that there would be a requirement for the person to have to wash and change their clothing. The descriptors do not refer to minor degrees of leakage that could be managed by the use of pads and not necessitate a full change of clothing . . . Urgency . . . will not usually meet the criteria . . . "

"I'm a winner, I'm a winner, that's what America needs, America needs winners, I own – now get this – I own assets up to a value of . . . "

"Describe your weaknesses."

"I care too much."

"Once I'm committed to an idea, I find it hard to let go."

"I need to use the toilet every forty minutes."

"Did he just say . . ."

" . . . in every case, the diagnosis history/nature of the condition must be carefully considered and the true risk of loss of control considered on the balance of medical probability and evidence. Medication, specialist input and aids used must be documented."

"Tell me what your goals are for ten years' time."

"This is a commissions-based industry."

"A right to terminate within three months."

"We're not sacking them. We're just informing them that unless they can move back to London when the office moves, they'll no longer be of use to us."

"At the moment I take home eighty per cent of what he does, and he still expects me to cook on a weekend!"

"The claimant may show you pads or extra change of clothing which they carry with them when they go out. The claimant may have to leave the room during the assessment to visit the toilet. Any such information should be documented in the relevant sections of the report . . . Risk of incontinence . . . should only apply if the likelihood of loss of control is very high *for the majority of the time.*" (Training and Development Handbook for the Department of Work and Pensions, last revised February 2015)

Chapter 75

Charlie said, "Saga's in London."

"Who is Saga?" asked Emmi.

"She's . . . she was the Harbinger of Death. She had the job before me. She hired me, taught me … She asked if I wanted a drink. I said yes. Do you want to come?"

"Will it be in a noisy pub? I don't need noise."

"We can go somewhere quiet."

"Then I think … yes. I think I would like to meet her very much."

Three days later, Saga whooped, rocking over her empty plate, " … 'But why would anyone want to know that they're going to die?!' He asked that! Can you believe it? Our Charlie, sat there in this terrible suit, *terrible* … "

"It was a friend's."

" … just the worst suit you've ever seen, and I said, do you have any questions, and he asked that! Incredible, I just thought … Oh, things were so different back then, weren't they, you were such a … but look at you now, and Emmi – Emmi, you have to tell me – does he still get carsick?"

"Carsick? No, I've never seen … "

"First time, took him to see a woman in Cornwall, a master craftsman, stained-glass windows, a skill, you see, a skill dying out, and we weren't five minutes onto the M4 before *blurgh* … "

"He doesn't really get carsick ,,, "

" … I don't really get carsick."

"And I thought, really, is this it? Really? This is the man we're hiring as Harbinger of Death? Some of the applications we got – Harvard, Beijing, the Sorbonne … "

"University of Birmingham," muttered Charlie, taking refuge in his beer.

" … but those kids, the high-flyers, they've always got the same problem. Why do you want to be Harbinger of Death? 'Because I want to understand what Death is' or 'Because I am passionate about mortality' or – I once heard this, I swear – 'Because the Apocalypse is coming and I wish to ride before the flame' – he was London School of Economics, I think. I just laughed. 'You already know what death is, or have you been living under a rock!' Or 'You care about mortality? Surely life is too short!' Emmi, your glass is empty, let me get you another . . . "

"That's very . . . "

"More, please! Another one of this – what is it? It's very good – another, please! Thank you! The mail you get, the office is just inundated, people send their knickers, which I've never understood, send their knickers to Death and I'm just astonished, really, shouldn't be, but it's so . . . I mean, you come in one day, you take your pants off, you don't even wash them, and you're like, I shall now find out the address of this celebrity or that horseman of the endless night, and I shall send them this bit of lingerie still hot from my sweaty skin and . . . well, I can't fathom it. I just find it very odd."

"Can I ask . . . "

"Emmi, you're wonderful, have I told you that, you're just the most wonderful . . . "

" . . . why did you hire Charlie?"

"Ah. Sweet sweet Charlie. Sweet Charlie in his stupid suit, he can't spell 'principal', do you know that? Principal, principle, he gets the two mixed up, typos on an application to be Harbinger of Death! I said, 'You might be kidnapped. Sometimes Harbingers are.' And do you know what his answer was?"

"No . . . "

"He said, 'That's okay. It's a people thing.' That's the answer, Emmi my love. To your question. I hired Charlie because the most important thing when you're the Harbinger of Death, the thing that matters more than anything else, is seeing people. Not corpses, not killers or victims or soldiers or criminals or presidents or anything like that. You have to see . . . people. People who are afraid. People who have lived their lives, in their ways. You are the bridge. Death stands behind you, but you look forward, always forward, and humanity looks straight back at you. And that's a wonderful thing. A toast! To Charlie."

"To Charlie."

"May he one day buy a better suit."

*

And at night, as they lay together with the curtains open, watching the sweep of car headlights across the ceiling, Charlie said, "She's right."

"Hm?" Emmi, half asleep, head buried in her pillow.

"What Saga said, about people, looking. Humanity, looking. She was right. There's more to it, there's more than . . . Did you know she teaches scuba diving now? She retired to an island and she . . . Emmi?"

"Uh-huh." Mumbled sound from far away.

"Death stands behind, and I look forward, and the world looks back and I see it and . . . the world when it sees me sees only Death. That's the truth of it. I am not . . . Emmi? What do I look like, to you? What do you see?"

Emmi was asleep.

Charlie held her close, and closed his eyes.

Chapter 76

A standard check-up . . .

Of course, I understand.

You've been having headaches . . .

Long days.

Recurring nightmares. Panic attacks?

I wouldn't call it an attack . . .

Milton Keynes insists . . .

It's fine.

So. Shall we begin?

Okay.

On a scale of one to five, where five is strong agreement and one is disagreement . . . do you find it difficult to get out of bed in the morning?

Um . . . so I give it a number?

Yes.

Well, it depends, doesn't it, I mean, it depends on the day . . .

Just a general number will do.

I suppose . . . two. No, maybe . . . two.

Do you find yourself feeling sad for large parts of the day?

Two.

Do you find things which gave you pleasure don't give you pleasure any more?

Two. No. Three. But I think that's just because with the travel, I mean, you change, you feel . . .

Do you ever consider harming yourself?

One.

Do you agree or disagree with the following sentence: "my life is balanced and fulfilled, and I am confident in the course I'm taking"?

Uh . . . three.

You only need to agree or disagree.

Oh. I guess . . . I agree?

"I have a good work–life balance."

Do I have to agree or disagree?

Yes.

Probably not.

"I am looking forward to the future and all that it brings."

I . . . It's kind of hard, actually, I mean, these are all binaries . . .

Charlie. Don't worry about it. This isn't something that will be fed back to Milton Keynes, it's just an assessment for your benefit, for your welfare.

Yes, but I mean, to assess . . . because sometimes I wake up and Emmi's there and she is . . . and on other days I have a plane to catch and I love it, I mean, I love to travel, I do, because in Lagos there were these women and I . . . and sometimes I have this . . . it's not a panic attack, I mean, I don't need a paper bag or anything . . .

You've been hyperventilating?

No! No, I mean . . . I mean you don't know, do you? You just don't know. Some days I'll go to the mountains of Peru, and the

262

sky is so . . . and the land is so . . . and I met a woman who was dying, and her death was sad, of course it was, but she was . . . she was ready. The world was ready, the world was ready to move and there wasn't . . . I was there to honour her, it was good that she was honoured. And sometimes I am sent to other places, and there is nothing but pain and grief and death for no reason, stupid, it's just so stupid so . . . so unreasonable, and there was . . .

I think we're losing track of the . . .

. . . look. I was kidnapped once in Mexico. I had no idea what was going on, but I didn't think I was going to die, because I am the Harbinger of Death, I have seen Death, I know what Death looks like and this wasn't . . . Not just seeing Death in person, but seeing the shape of Death, the shadow he casts, I can recognise that, and it wasn't there. This was a kidnapping and I was terrified, but somehow not of that. Not of the end. And even if I had been, I didn't fear it. I didn't fear Death, that day, I didn't fear the world stopping – shit, does this count as suicidal? It wasn't, I swear, it wasn't, it was just . . .

They took me to this place, and they had some sort of religious ceremony. There was singing, and this priest – priestess, I mean, but Catholic, sort of, she sang and they put a gun to my head and I had no idea if it was loaded, none at all, but I wasn't afraid, not there, I wasn't afraid because it was so alive, it was the most alive I think I have ever been, it was as if I could feel every cell in my body, every part of me bursting with life and it was . . .

. . . so I'm not going to be good at answering these binary questions, you see. Because sometimes I am so terrified of getting out of bed, because I don't know what the world will bring, or what I'll see. I am terrified because there is such darkness out there, there is such cruelty, I am terrified when the phone rings that someone will tell me that Emmi has been hurt or someone I love will have died or the world I thought I knew will be gone for ever and I dread it, I dread the day, I dread what it will bring.

And sometimes I cannot wait for the sun to rise, because the world is full of people, of human beings singing their songs and telling their stories, of life and passion, glory and wonder, and Death is not a thing to fear, but is life's mirror, reminding us to live, live, *live*, and I am honoured, I am so honoured to travel the world and see that the world is a place of people, and to be alive with them, living with them, even at the end.

Does that make sense?

Does that answer your question?

. . . I'm not going to lie, Charlie, it answers the questions, but is piss for my paperwork.

Chapter 77

humanhumanratratrathumanratratratrathumanrat

Charlie!

"The Shan people trade in opium, carrying it across the Chinese border. Military action against civilian populations has grown since the death of their leader in an air raid on . . . "

Char-lie . . . .

"I'm not lazy, I'm not given any opportunities, how dare you say I'm lazy, how dare you, I do my job and I do it right, why should I do more, why should I give a damn about anything more than . . . "

HUMAN HUMAN RAT RAT RAT RAT RAT RAT HUMAN

" . . . executed in China, their organs removed and shipped to a donor for immediate transplant . . . "

CHARLIE!!

Wide awake, soaked in sweat, staring at the ceiling and the ceiling stares back the world stares back the whole wide world is staring, staring staring but not at him not at him but at *he* that comes behind, at the shadow thrown against the dust he comes, he comes he comes he comes always he comes he comes comes comes comes

Breathe in, breathe out.

Breathe in, breathe out.

Charlie.

Put the headphones on, listen to music.

Music is a miracle.

Your life is a miracle.

Slower, now, slower.

The world isn't watching you now.

You're safe here.

Close your eyes.

Listen.

Sleep.

All this will pass, by itself, in time. Everything does.

"Charlie?"

"Emmi?"

"I'm worried about you."

"About ..."

"Not about us. About you."

"Oh."

"The nightmares, the ..."

"I did a good thing, in Nigeria."

"Yes, you did."

"Not part of my job, but ..."

"The nightmares ..."

"I'm fine."

"You're not. People who say they're fine like that, they never are, everyone knows, it's just a thing everyone knows, I mean, it's like a post-English thing, now we know that when the English say they're fine they mean they're fucked, can you be that, can you be post-English, anyway, you're fucked. You're not fine. You wake shaking in the night."

"I ... There was this time in Mexico and I ..."

"Have you considered a holiday?"

"Sounds good . . ."

"Have you considered a new job? Charlie? I won't tell you what to do with your life, I'll stick by you and be there for you whatever. You once told me that as Harbinger of Death you couldn't make this about you. You mustn't go to the dying men and say 'I saw a man die, and it really affected me.' Their story is not about you. I won't ever make you quit your job. I am not suffering to see you suffer; these things . . . these things are not about me, or even us, but you . . ."

"I love my job."

"I know."

"I had no idea how wonderful the world was."

"I know."

"Two women left Lagos, and Agnes Young has buried her grandfather and I . . ."

"You honour life."

"Exactly."

"And sometimes I find you crying, when you thought you wouldn't be found. Charlie? Charlie. These things . . . Think about it. When you can. Just think about it."

"I will. I promise."

Part 8

ROAD

Chapter 78

Is this it?

Is it time to quit?

How long has it been? Three years? Four?

Quitting after four years in any ordinary job, that would be . . .

. . . and he loves the work, he loves it, he just . . .

Maybe.

The booking comes in.

A long, rambling trip.

There'll be driving along an empty road, maybe thousands of miles, just him with the window down.

Emmi sees him off to the airport, kisses him goodbye.

He'll think about it on the road, he promises, he swears, and this time, he is telling the truth from the bottom of his heart.

They detained Charlie at Miami airport, but that was fine. Many customs officials felt this way about his work.

"So, you're the Harbinger of Death."

"That's right."

"Business or pleasure?"

"Business."

"And how long, may I ask, are you planning on spending in the country?"

"About three weeks."

"So you've got a lot of business."

"Yes."

"I'm going to need a full itinerary."

"I can't provide that."

"Why not?"

"My employer hasn't yet sent me details of the trip."

"But you do have a return ticket from JFK."

"Yes."

"But you don't know what you're doing in the meantime."

"No."

"Sir, you understand that under these circumstances I am allowed to deny you entry to this country."

"I understand that."

"And you understand that any appeal against the decision is likely to result in it being upheld."

"No."

"No?"

"You may wish to deny me entry to your country, but the State Department will let me in."

"You're sure of that?"

"Yes."

"Why?"

"Because once I'm in, they can have me followed, and they can put FEMA offices on high alert at every urban or industrial centre I visit. And if they don't let me in, they'll never know where I might have gone, and Death will come regardless. Death will come, Officer. As I explained to your colleague – sometimes I am a courtesy, as well as a warning. You do what you must."

They let him enter the USA.

"Have a nice trip," said the man who stamped his passport. "There's a shuttle to Disneyland from right outside the terminal."

Chapter 79

In a land of freedom . . .

. . . in the land of the mountain and open plain . . .

Lying on his belly on a bed in Miami.

The bed was hotel normal.

The hotel was international chameleon.

The city was a sprawling void.

The plane, as it descended over Florida, had flown over swamp. Sometimes straight roads cut through the swamp, running from nowhere to nowhere. Sometimes a swimming pool, cartoon blue, appeared for no discernible reason out of the muddy waters. Sometimes, not nearly as often as Charlie had expected, there was a town, low, metallic, small, clinging to curves of reclaimed land like a scorpion to the back of a crocodile.

Palm trees. Wet, car-fume-enhanced heat. The constant whoosh of air conditioning. Mickey Mouse ears – on heads, on posters, on the tops of cars, and on the electricity pylons as they wobbled their uneven way through the twisted trees.

The woman who cleaned his hotel room spoke Spanish.

The receptionist spoke Spanish.

The man who called a cab for him.

The cab driver.

The woman behind the counter of the shop that served him a giant pastrami sub, the taste of onion and pepper overwhelming everything else, jaw labouring mightily against the weight of bread.

On the side of the highway, billboards.

Illegal immigration – it's everyone's problem.

XXX Supermarket, next left turn!

Discount gun and ammo fair, this weekend only.

Been in an accident? Scott and McKaw will fight for what's justly yours.

Aged 5–18 and want to be a model for Jesus? Apply now.

Talk Radio, for all your news and gossip.
Bill's Motor Repair, trusted for 35 years.

"Illegal immigrants are criminals, they come here, they're criminals ..."

"They're criminals because they come here?"

"Yes, they cross the border illegally! If I'm hit by an illegal driving a car, I can't sue them, not like I could a US citizen!"

Once, the first time Charlie came to the USA, he thought he'd travel by public transport. But the trains were creaking and crowded, crawling slowly down narrow routes, not so much a spider's web across the continent as a spider's thread. Then he thought he'd take the Greyhound bus, listen to Bob Dylan songs and have interesting encounters with old-timey wise folk who lived on the side of the road; but the bus only ran twice a day, and his flight got in at the wrong time, and he had places to go, people to see.

So he hired a car.

"Miami is full of New Yorkers now, they all retire down here, come south, it's been ruined, the whole place, ruined."

Charlie had ice cream by the beach, with extra sprinkles on top. The sand was soft yellow, mown flat every night once the swimmers were gone and the beach was closed. The women in bikinis and boys in Hawaii shorts danced and raved until the sun came up, and then slept until the sun set again, ready for another hard night by the sea. The old folk tutted and turned their heads away and said it wasn't right, not right at all, and moved to Tampa, where they could do their crosswords in peace.

"Hi there! Come stay at the Pleasance Motel!"

A video, men and women staring at a cheap camera. "Hi there! Welcome! Hi there!" They waved awkwardly, and then the next video played, advertising Sally's Crab Shack and the best place to hire jet skis.

Charlie drove.

At night, he checked his itinerary, and every evening something new would have appeared, a growing list of names and days, appointments and gifts required.

To an old woman on an island over the long bridges beyond Tampa: a gift of a photographic film showing DNA markers. She smiled, an oxygen line taped to the side of her face, and said, "I still recognise it, you know? I still remember the day we isolated the gene."

"What was it?"

"It caused the body's immune system to attack the kidneys. You could still sustain life with dialysis, but that's not living, not really, not when . . ."

A hacking cough. Charlie sits and listens and waits. She is near the end, Death comes, Death comes, but first the Harbinger comes before.

"The whole team got prizes. Except me. I was a junior research fellow, and the only woman, and at the time I didn't think, but now . . ." She smiled, laid the image carefully on her bedside table, and pressed Charlie's hand between her own. "We changed the world; I don't need a medal. I'm ready for Death now," she mused. "We talked a few times, when I was doing the overseas work. She would come and sit with me when the medicines ran out, when Pestilence was doing her thing. We'd look at the empty cabinets together and wonder how many people would die tonight from easy things, easy, easy things – dysentery, diarrhoea, cholera – all because the money had stopped. She was always polite, was Death, always had time to talk to the medics in the front line. I'm glad she remembers me, now the time has come."

Charlie smiled back, and squeezed her hand tight, and was happy – so happy – to be here, for this moment. "Sometimes I am a courtesy," he replied. "I am honoured to have met you."

They talked a little while longer, as the sun went down.

On the drive back towards his Tampa hotel, Charlie stopped at a red light, and five men and women with no clothes on except flip-flops on their feet crossed the road in front of him, bags of shopping in their hands.

This highway, said the sign a little further down, *is sponsored by nudists.*

At the convenience store where he bought a bottle of water, a woman in pearls and nothing else waited patiently by the door, while the smiling clerk brought her a dressing gown to wrap herself in, lest she upset the other customers.

Chapter 80

In a vast and beautiful land . . .

. . . in a land where the law sets you free . . .

In Washington DC, the Harbinger of Famine slammed her fist into the horn of her car and, in an unexpected moment of honesty for a woman so generally professional and austere, roared, *"Fucking Beltway why the fuck can't you just fucking take me where I need to . . ."*

In a forest in the drooping southern Carolinas, the Harbinger of War held her mobile phone up and said, "I thought the coverage would be better out here."

"Ma'am, we don't need good coverage for what we do."

"But your business . . . "

"Conducted from an office. This place here is for training."

"I see. Well that does explain . . . "

"Our clients expect the highest standard of private security."

"Of course, of course. Tell me – do they provide the bazookas, or do you?"

"The outbreak isn't . . . "

" . . . we can't take responsibility for . . . "

" . . . the virulence is off the scale for . . . "

"The WHO just need to get off their asses!"

"The question is of course one of risk to the population and I really think . . . "

Atlanta, Georgia. The Harbinger of Pestilence has spent so much time in this city that he's thinking about buying a flat. He folds the top sheet of the report into a perfect origami swan, and leaves it on the table as the argument rages on.

A tower block in mid-town Tampa, one of the largest, crawling up from between the pink and beige houses towards the sky, a logo on the top, reflective glass windows. A woman who her whole life has sold health insurance, and now sits and cries in the arms of the Harbinger of Death and weeps, "Shit shit shit fuck shit! Shit fucking shit I thought they'd pay I thought they would but they refuse say he's not covered not covered after all I did how can he not be covered we've already sold everything we've already sold . . . "

The appointment in Charlie's book was for a ten-year-old boy, and Charlie did go to the hospital, and did give him a stuffed dinosaur, because he loved that sort of thing, but the mother's name appeared too, and Death gave her a dinosaur as well, so they could share in stories of Jurassic adventures, while there was still time.

By the Gulf of Mexico, an ancient man on a yacht, waiting for the storm.

"There may not be an El Dorado," he laughed, "but there's still the ocean! There's still the seas and the skies and the storm!"

Charlie drank bourbon, and marvelled at how great and black were the veins that protruded from the man's hands, such fragile things, a pinprick might burst them. Sometimes he coughed, emphysema, maybe something more, but with his shorts flapping around his high, craggy knees, and thin remnants of his comb-over lashing in the wind, he wasn't going to let such things get in the way.

"I seen Death many times," he chuckled, at Charlie's polite expression of interest. "I met him once in the eye of the hurricane, paddling a raft made of whale bones, all lashed together, like there weren't nothing in the world could trouble him. His skin was the colour of the drowned men, his eyes were fish grey, but we talked, as the world turned all around us, and he said he'd come find me again, another day. They say there's gonna be a big blow up from the south in a few days' time, and I was never one for dying in my bed!"

At this, he laughed again, and rubbed his skinny, rope-worn hands together in glee, and looked up towards the sky, willing the clouds to thicken.

An appointment, strange this one, not what Charlie had expected at all.

He drove to what he imagined was the edge of Orlando, though in truth, the edge of the city was hard to find; it stretched and sprawled and sprawled again into another roadside community, another bend off the highway, rolling past trimmed lawns of hard-biting crab grass and crooked pools of stagnant water where by day the crocodiles rested, sheltering from the heat, and where at dusk a drifting log perhaps blinked at the dog walkers passing by. In a community with its own basketball court, matching porches and identical two-car drives, all the houses the same, the American flag flying outside every other door, the red flag down on the post boxes, Charlie got briefly lost as he tried to find number 22319 in the midst of identical, nameless roads. When he did, he was not the first person there.

Boxes sat on the concrete drive. A sofa waited on the white kerbside. A dining room table was being loaded into the back of a lorry already bursting with goods. A man sat on a rocking chair, while all around, neighbours peaked through their blinds and tutted and said wasn't it a shame, and some came outside with iced lemonade and asked if there was anything they could do, and stood by awkwardly when it turned out there was nothing.

A lady decked out in beige offered the man in the rocking chair a slice of key lime pie – extraordinary, delicious, the limes grown in her own front yard – and when he was finished eating like one in a dream, not even the sour zing enough to stir him from his contemplation, she said sweetly, "It'll be all right, hon,

I truly believe that," and prised the plate away from beneath his fingers, and shuffled back indoors before her skin could burn.

Charlie parked in the street, a few metres down from the largest of the loading trucks, aware that no one else was parked here, no one else was in the middle of the road, every car neatly stashed in its neat drive by the door to its neat single-storey white house. He climbed out into sticky, storm-promising Florida heat, just as the final box was loaded into the lorry, the door slammed shut, the last worker in his blue shorts and stained brown vest climbing up into the passenger seat, leaving behind the man, the rocking chair, a single brown suitcase, and nothing else.

Charlie approached as the trucks turned their engines on, the men inside glancing down, curious at him from their high perches. He stood in front of the rocking chair as the trucks drove away, and said, "Um . . . "

The man didn't look at him. His age was hard to guess at. A gentle tan through layers of sunblock had left his skin robustly pink, telling perhaps of a genetic lineage from a land where rain was more common than sun. Lines beneath his eyes and around the corners of his mouth hinted at the passage of time. His hands were huge, swallowing the arms of the rocking chair into their grip. The hint of grey at his temples was perhaps premature, and had been dyed back to the same sun-brown as the rest of him. His eyebrows were great sweeping brushes above huge blue eyes. He sat and moved the lower part of his jaw from side to side, back and forwards, and was otherwise perfectly motionless, staring at nothing at all.

Charlie coughed, tried again. "Mr Robinson?"

The man didn't move. He wore a white shirt, sweating profusely down the spine and under the arms. He wore pale linen trousers, and a pair of bright green running shoes, muddy and worn around the sole. A silver ring was on the little finger of his right hand, and there was a bend in his nose where once it had been broken in a football match and reset oddly, and a notch in his chin like the Grand Canyon, shaded beneath his lower lip.

"Mr Robinson?"

He looked up slowly, and saw the figure of Charlie without taking anything in, as if the Harbinger of Death was merely a shadow blocking the view, not a person at all. "Mr Robinson, my name is Charlie, I'm the ... the ... "

The words, easy and familiar, faltered.

The man waited, squinting against the brightness of the day, motionless on the rocking chair.

"I'm the Harbinger of Death."

A long silence.

Robinson drew his lips in slowly, as if he was going to chew them, while his jaw worked side to side, back to front, before finally letting them flop forward, and, turning half away, said, "Is it time, then?"

"It's ... No, Mr Robinson, I'm ... I've been sent by my employer, as a courtesy, sometimes as a warning, I've been sent to ... Is this your house?"

Staring at nothing, the man shook his head. "No, sir."

"It's ... "

"Taken away. Debts. All gone. Wife gone too. She left before, few years back, but the money was what did it for her too."

The flatness of this, the blank statement of truth, left Charlie silent, uncertain. "I'm ... very sorry to hear that."

The man shrugged. "Been a long time coming. Comes a moment you can see it, when all the lies drop away, but by then there's no stopping the thing."

"Are you ... Do you have a place to go?"

Now Robinson raised his head again, seemed to see Charlie clearly, took in his clothes, his face, his posture, and said at last, "You're the Harbinger of Death?"

"That's right."

"You're late. You shoulda come before the bailiff."

"The bailiff isn't ... that isn't ... " Banal comforts tickled the end of Charlie's tongue. He felt the gaze of the neighbours on his back, watching, wondering what they should do, could do, would be safe to offer to do, all things considered, and swallowed the words. "I was told to give you a lift."

"A lift?"

"Yes. My employer . . . likes to give things to people. It is . . . it's part of . . . I'll admit I've never been asked before, but I was told . . . Look, I'm going to New York, eventually. I have to make a few stops on the way, but . . . "

"Are you mocking me?" Soft, quiet, huge hands around the ends of the chair. A gentleness that reminded Charlie of the slow way a wolf moves across snow, eyeing prey.

"No. I'm . . . I'm very sorry for your predicament."

Silence. Usually Charlie was comfortable with silence; a great many people he visited, on discovering the purpose of his mission, had either everything to say or nothing at all, and he didn't mind either response. But this silence, midday hot, eyeball-burning, the smell of the swamp on the edge of his nose, the Spanish moss dripping in the trees, a line of sweat suddenly released and rolling down the inside of his arm. He looked at Robinson and wondered why the man didn't move, didn't speak, didn't cry, didn't punch him. He waited, curious to see where he would go, surprised to find he didn't mind either way.

At last: "New York?"

"Yes."

"You been told to give me a lift to New York?"

"I've been told to give you a lift."

"My brother's in New York."

"Oh?"

"We never got on much."

"I see."

"And you wanna give me a lift?"

"It's . . . That appears to be my job."

Robinson nodded at nothing much, then stood up. He was almost a foot taller than Charlie, his shoulders hunched in the way of many tall people, his chin pushing forward, challenging some unseen future. He jerked his head to the side, indicating Charlie's car. "That yours?"

"Yes."

"You hire it?"

"Yes."

"It's small."

"When I hired it, your name hadn't yet come through on my itinerary. I didn't realise it'd be . . ."

"You know what Death is?"

"I . . . I know there are many ways to die."

He nodded, slow and sure. "True that." Stared again at the car, as if trying to puzzle out so strange a thing in a land of monster trucks. "Think we can fit the rocking chair in the back?"

Charlie hesitated, looking back at the white-painted seat that the man had just risen from. He wondered what exactly he was meant to say, how far this particular part of his job should go. "I suppose we could try."

Chapter 81

"I think he's right, I think that if even one terrorist comes out of a mosque then they should all be monitored . . ."

"Build a wall!"

" . . . you want to protect the students then you gotta arm the teachers . . ."

"It wasn't like this just ten years ago; this isn't the world I knew."

"These guys. They behead. They rape. They torture. They don't see their victims as human."

"This year, give the gift of love to your family and friends, to those who mean the most to you . . ."

"I am proud to have served my country, and I am proud to say that I am also . . ."

"That's right, huh, that's right, then what about the fucking churches because there's more guys go to church on Sunday and blast their wives on Mondays than have ever come from a single mosque in this nation . . . "

"Women-on-men violence has been rising steadily and the law doesn't protect the rights of men when it comes to . . . "

"Sweetie, New York is *not* America."

"Gas for only one seventy-nine a gallon, yes, I said one seventy-nine, you won't get better prices this side of the state line . . . "

"These guys. They behead. They rape. They torture. They aren't human."

"I am *not* afraid."

Chapter 82

They rode I-75, heading towards I-10 and Alabama.

Charlie drove cautiously, a man used to speed cameras round every bend.

Robinson, when they swapped, drove at 85 mph, skimming down the inside lane, half an eye turned to the traffic coming from the opposite direction. "You're looking for guys who flash their lights, that means there's a patrol car ahead, it's a warning."

"I see."

"The patrol cars – they ain't about enforcing the law, people drive at the speed people gotta drive at to get where they need to go, I mean, seventy miles an hour are you kidding me, country this size? They're about making cash. Some poor sucker doing seventy-five, boom, that's a fine, that's court fees, that's the city making a packet. You know there's some cities make nearly most of their budget from taking people to court?"

"I didn't know that."

"It's a tax, man, it's a tax. The rich can pay it and the poor get burned. 'Cept this is tax that's also a lottery, you hear me?"

"I think so."

"The roads are fucked. They're just fucked."

So saying, Robinson fell quiet, and they kept on driving north.

Glimpses of America out of the window.

The Spanish moss is a light grey-green, old woman's hair draped off pale trees. Occasionally flowers bloom and burst, sudden eruptions of purple, orange, pink and blue in front of the courthouses and lovingly cleaned white wooden homes that line the interstate. Sometimes the eight-lane behemoth slows for traffic lights at a crossroads where stand two competing garages, a sandwich joint and a shop selling doughnuts and ammunition. Tiny churches line the roads out of town. Baptists, New Baptists, Evangelical Baptists, Methodist Baptists, Methodists of the New Church, New Anglican Methodists, New Anglican Methodist Baptists, etc. Some are next door to each other, separated only by muddy parking lots. They compete with signs in black letters pinned to white boards, like something from a 1950s movie.

JESUS LOVES YOU ALL

THE REDEEMER AWAITS

And Charlie's personal favourite:

ISN'T JESUS GREAT?

Outside Tallahassee, they leave the interstate and crawl through bouncing backland roads. Endless shallow bridges cross nameless waterways, the wetlands too inconsistent to ever be mapped or claimed. Houses stand empty, a hundred yards back from the road, walls falling down, windows cracked, no one home. And sometimes, a house that looks as if it should be empty, isolated, away from the world, has an SUV parked outside, polished and loved, while the porch lists at an angle and the American flag wilts in the breathless air.

*

A delivery to a farmer in fields of ragged grass – an old French textbook.

He weeps when he sees it, and says it was his when he was a child, this is what he learned French from, but he went to work on the farm, because it was his, his home, his life, his love, and now it was all over, all of it, didn't matter how hard you made the land to grow, the prices kept on falling and there was nothing to be done except sell everything that seven generations had fought to build.

Robinson had got out of the car to watch Charlie speak to this man, but as he wept and Charlie held him, Robinson retreated without a word, and sat, grey stone, in the passenger seat, waiting for Charlie to return.

A motel. Two storeys, pink walls, a smell of damp, best not to look too closely at the mattress beneath the faded blue sheets.

Charlie wasn't sure he was budgeted to pay for two rooms, but then ... Death had said to give Robinson a lift, and it seemed rude to not pay for a hotel room too, so he handed over the extra dollars without a word and Robinson took the key and held it until his knuckles were white, the veins throbbing on the surface of his hand. Charlie wondered if he should offer to buy him a drink, go down the pub, whatever it was you did in motels on the side of the interstate. But Robinson just went to his room and double-locked the door, and when the motel's Wi-Fi loaded, slowly, so slowly, he discovered the nearest likely venue was fourteen miles away.

Fourteen miles, he was beginning to realise, was nothing in American terms, but the idea of getting in the car again made his whole body hurt.

A flick through TV channels.

"This woman was brutally raped before she was strangled, her naked body thrown into the storm drain to be found by ... "

"What I love about cheerleading is it's like a really amazing way to express myself!"

"Police shootings of . . . "

human human

"Tornados in central . . . "

"Abortion . . . "

"Gun control . . . "

"The Confederate flag . . . "

human human!

Charlie turned the TV off, closed his eyes, saw for a moment a hollow in the earth, eyes staring back, heard the flies, smelt liquid flesh, saw the stares of the children gunned down because they weren't

human human

A drumbeat in his head, he sat up gasping, went to the bathroom, washed his face, looked in the mirror, heard the drums, took a shower, stayed under the thin hot water until the little cubicle was lost in steam, felt a bit better, remembered in that moment why he had needed to feel better, and remembered again

rat rat

In the end, he turned the radio on, and fell asleep to the sounds of either country or Western – he could never work out which was which.

Chapter 83

Robinson drove for the first three hours as they headed towards Mobile. At a pair of traffic lights he pulled a sudden U-turn, swinging round into a medley of high-speed gulching traffic to head back the way they'd come, crossing three lanes in a few moments to pull up in front of a shack selling boiled peanuts and home-made jelly.

Charlie, clinging tight to his seat belt, bit his lip hard as they parked, but without a word, Robinson got out of the car, went up to the shack and knocked on the door. As soon as it was opened by a woman with skin the colour of midnight and nails the colour of tangerines, he began bartering fast and urgent.

A few dollars changed hands, and he returned to the car with a plastic bag, within which were more plastic bags containing the promised goods – nuts, jam, and a few thick slices of bread to spread it on.

"For you," he said, passing the bag to Charlie.

Charlie's irritation at the stop, made worse by the wet heat, the long road, the roar of the traffic tumbling past, faded to immediate shame. He took the bag, and wondered how many dollars Robinson had left, having bought it. "Thank you."

"You'll never have tasted nothing like it," Robinson promised him, and indeed, as they rejoined the road, driving five miles back to the next turning before swinging round again to resume their route, Charlie had to admit that it tasted like heaven.

A grand mansion house on the edge of Mobile. At one point it had fallen into disrepair, the roof crumbling, the glass in the old gas lamp posts cracked, the moss and the vine creeping into every scar and tear, pulling it apart until it was on the cusp of becoming a ghost house. Then an investor from Massachusetts bought it and the surrounding marsh, put a new, bright red roof on, a swimming pool round the back, redid the iron work to its original 1890s condition, repaired the windows, pulled down the vines, cleared back the scrub, trimmed the trees, restored the murals and the crystal lamps in the great rooms inside, laid gravel paths and, after nearly three years of careful, loving labour to bring it up to scratch, reopened the entire thing as a stately home specialising in weddings, corporate events and luxury parties. The money he made from the venture he divided between his four children, of whom one became a doctor, one a computer programmer, one a glass-blower at a workshop in Michigan, which surprised everyone, and one who vanished in Tasmania without a trace, and was never heard of again.

In a land of freedom . . .

. . . in a land of dreams . . .

Robinson and Charlie drove up a gravel path as the sun went down, pink and golden light through the curled, clawed branches of the trees. Torches burned either side, bright yellow flame and shimmering distortions to the air where invisible gas burnt away. The extensive car park, reclaimed from the wetland all around, was nearly full, Alabama and Mississippi plates, a few Florida too, three from Louisiana. Some of the cars were hired: gold stretch limousines that had struggled to make the tight turns up to the front of the mansion; six-door adapted sedans with padded leather seats and minibars inside; cars that lit up the road beneath them with magenta and cyan light, signs draped across the back: PRINCESS ON BOARD.

Charlie's grubby little hire car felt tiny and obscure as he parked, and an attendant all in black, save for a pair of white cotton gloves, came up to him as he was locking the door and asked if he wasn't meant to be in the staff car park round the other side.

"I'm a guest," he replied. "In a manner of speaking."

His British accent perhaps did more work here than his crumpled clothes, his smell of too-long at the steering wheel. Robinson stretched, bones creaking, huge hands reaching up to the sky as he unfolded. The attendant frowned, then nodded, waving Charlie by.

They walked across a wooden bridge spanning a lake heavy in green lichen, the mosquitoes humming around their faces, citronella candles burning brightly in glass jars every five feet. The trees around, dark against the brilliant open sky, sang with the sounds of life, chittering, scampering, leaping, falling. Robinson paused on the bridge to listen to it, head on one side, and Charlie stopped too, and for a moment they stood and smelt the air and heard the fat-bellied fish leap in the water and the tree frogs sing, and it was beautiful.

Then a grey-haired man in a tuxedo and a young woman in a baby-blue gown, her train held aloft by a Latino woman in a dark purple cocktail dress, came along, and her gown was a little too wide for the bridge and she struggled to get by, so Charlie and Robinson pressed themselves flat against the railing, then followed on behind.

As they neared the house, the sound of music, a ten-piece band in full swing, waltzing, slow numbers for dignified people to dance demurely to. A man, also in black, also wearing white gloves, bent at the hips as they approached, in a manner that, if Charlie hadn't known better, he might have called a bow, and asked them their business.

"My name is Charlie," he replied. "I'm the Harbinger of Death. I'm here to see Mrs Walker-Bell."

"Are you staff?"

"I'm the Harbinger of Death," he repeated with a patient smile. "That's all."

The man nodded, seemed almost to bow again, then turned his back on Charlie to pull a walkie-talkie from beneath the long curve of his black frock coat, a strangely modern, clumsy object in this seat of elegance. A few words were exchanged, an answer given. He returned again to Charlie, smiling now, relaxed. "Mrs Walker-Bell requests that you wait inside, and asks if you would like some champagne."

They waited inside.

Charlie had champagne, because he thought Robinson might like some, and because Robinson wouldn't have any if Charlie didn't. The two of them sat in a room where perhaps happy married couples had breakfast the morning after their celebratory feast; a bowl of potpourri between them, flowers bursting up from thick green stems set in clear glass vases on the table against the wall; crisp white tablecloths, high-backed white leather chairs.

They waited, as through the half-open door shadows flitted, voices were raised in laughter, and the music played. They waited. Robinson toyed with his champagne, looking at Charlie's untouched glass, waited. Waited. Music played, shadows moved, they waited.

In a moment almost of irritation, Robinson picked up his

champagne glass and drained it down in one gulp, wiping his lips with the back of his hand.

Charlie looked at him wordlessly, then pushed his glass across the table.

Robinson took it, rolled it between his fingers.

The two men sat, and waited.

Slower, Robinson sipped his champagne.

After thirty minutes, a man dressed in black came to the door. Frock coat, trousers with buttons on the front, white gloves, cravat. Skin rich and dark, hair cut close. It occurred to Charlie, not for the first time, that nearly all the members of staff he'd seen thus far had been black.

"Mr Harbinger of Death?"

Charlie rose to his feet.

"Would you follow me, please?"

Charlie followed. Robinson half rose from his seat, not sure whether to come or stay, and Charlie smiled, shrugged. Robinson shuffled after them.

Through white corridors lit with warm tungsten lamps and scented candles. Fresh flowers were woven into wreaths and hung from every door; bouquets of pinks and purples had been laced into swagging scarves that drooped from the ceiling, some so low that Robinson had to duck to pass beneath them, sweet petals dropping onto the floor to create a scuffed, shuffled cascade of perfume beneath their feet.

Voices, drifting through doors.

"Presenting . . . Mr Dwight-Lee and Miss Dwight-Lee!"

" . . . it's such a good opportunity to see my old friends, we've moved so far apart but now here, together . . . "

"Used to be you could only wear white, but they said the dads wouldn't pay for another white dress so now they've changed the rules, pastels, but see she's got a new style, she's got . . . "

"Can you play 'Smells Like Teen Spirit'?"

"A throne, gold leaf, platinum inlay around the . . . "

"Beautiful beautiful! A little bit . . . you know . . . high school prom . . . but still so beautiful!"

"I know you're a baroque group, but it goes like this ... *here we are now ... entertain us ...*!"

"It's about celebrating who we are, about celebrating our families, our love for family, our love for ... "

"Real pearls."

" ... wanted a glass slipper but actually the *blisters* ... "

"Is it ... has she worn that dress before?"

A sudden drumming in his head, it came so hard that Charlie stumbled, caught his balance against the wall. Robinson, surprised, came up short behind him, reached out to help, didn't touch, uncertain. "You ... okay?"

Charlie nodded, the pain fading as quickly as it had come, as if every vein had tightened and then relaxed, blood squelching through his skull with the relief of it.

"Fine," he muttered. "Fine."

They walked on.

In a room decorated duck-egg blue, soft cobalt flowers painted across the walls, couches pressed against bookcases of unused, unloved ceremonial leather books, gold lampshades and a portrait of someone – probably no one knew who – with huge whiskers and a crooked top hat beaming down from above the unused – this was Alabama – utterly unused fireplace, a woman waited.

She was small – the word diminutive might not be unfair – and had the energy of a tiny hedgehog that has realised that the tiger fears getting spines up its nose. She bristled, she brimmed, she paced a few steps this way, then a few steps that, fingers clenching and unclenching at her sides, gold on her wrists, chain mail of gold around her neck, her white hair pulled back tight from her high forehead, her thin pained brows arching in expectant fury. She wore cream, a knee-hugging skirt and a careful, conservative top, covered over with a padded jacket. At the back of her skirt, clipped beneath her jacket, was a radio. Two gold earrings in the shape of seashells hung on her long lobes; her lips were crimson, and so were her nails, and she probably wasn't a day under seventy years old, going on twenty-two.

"Well?" she snapped, banishing with a flick of her hand the

man who'd accompanied them to this door. "Which one of you is the Harbinger of Death?"

"Me, ma'am," replied Charlie, putting his bag down slowly on the floor, lest fast movement set his head pounding again. "My name's Charlie."

"I didn't think you'd have a name."

"I've been told that, sometimes."

"Why do you have a name?"

"I'm from Birmingham."

"Alabama?"

"England."

"There's a Birmingham in England?"

"Yes."

"And you're from there?"

"Near there, yes."

"Huh." A reconsidering sound. The woman had had some expectations, these were now being threatened; she didn't approve of changing her mind. Then a fast shake of her head, discarding the danger. "I thought the Harbinger of Death would be skeletal. Glowing eyes, that sort of thing."

"I think you might be thinking of Death himself, ma'am."

"Aren't you part of Death?"

"No, ma'am. Like I said, I'm from Birmingham."

"*Huh.*" Challenge her perceptions once – shame on you. Challenge them twice ...? She stepped forward quickly, one hand sweeping up like a castle drawbridge, fingers out. Charlie shook it, smiled wanly, went into his prepared speech.

"Mrs Walker-Bell, I've been sent to give you—"

"There's nothing wrong with me, you know that, don't you?"

"I'm sure you're right."

"You think I'm gonna be shot? Get hit by a car? Fall out of a plane?"

"Sometimes, ma'am, I'm sent as a courtesy, and sometimes as—"

"Spare me the talk, get to the point."

"Sometimes my employer comes not for people, but for ideas."

290

"Ha!" This time, the first sign of humour on her face. "Then you tell your boss he'll have a long time waiting! The world here is not for turning, thanking you very much."

Charlie smiled again, picked up his bag, opened it, carefully handed her the folded package from within. She sniffed, peeled away the edge of the grey plastic wrapping that surrounded it, saw a peek of scarlet, a corner of midnight blue, pulled the wrapping back fast.

"You were sent to bring me this, boy?" Her face, diamond hard, rugged, an unpolished eternal stone.

"Yes."

"By your boss?"

"Yes."

"You know why?"

"No."

"You know what it means?"

"No."

"You know anything much?"

Charlie hesitated, drawing in his breath, head on one side. Then, "No."

A moment in which she didn't know what to make of that reply. Then something moved in her face, a shift in her shoulders, and for the first time she smiled, a smile that might almost have been human. She held the package tight to her chest, said, "Follow me."

She began walking, and so they followed. "Who's your friend?" she asked, jerking her head back at Robinson as they scampered to keep up with her.

"I'm giving him a lift."

"Boy, you taking a lift off the Harbinger of Death?" she exclaimed, half turning now, feet still sure of their direction, to look properly at the tall, tanned man.

"Yes, ma'am."

"Wouldn't it be easier to fly?"

"No, ma'am."

"You got cancer or something?"

"I don't think so, ma'am."

A little half-nod with her chin; she knows about these things, she knows about cancer, it's one of many things in life she has already decided won't be laying a finger on her.

Through a door to where the music played, then, to Charlie's surprise, up a ladder, Mrs Walker-Bell gesturing at them to go first, "Because I'm wearing a skirt, why do you think?"

They climbed the ladder. On the top of the ladder was a platform, raised on steel scaffold poles, disguised beneath draperies of white and powder-pink fabrics. On the top of this platform, her head nearly grazing the ceiling, on whose surface plaster horses galloped, teeth bared, manes wild in the wind, stood a woman. She wore black – black long-sleeved top, black trousers, black shoes – and was standing next to a long-barrelled light whose bright white beam shone down into the ballroom below, illuminating an arch of white roses, through which now paraded proud dads and beautiful daughters, long silk gloves up their elegant arms, faces bursting with joy, the room clapping and waving as each new belle entered the ball, the music playing, petals beneath diamond shoes, black-clad waiters sweeping round the hall with silver trays, dancing, laughter, champagne – more champagne!

Mrs Walker-Bell arrived at the top of the scaffold tower, didn't seem to even see the girl with the light, who looked befuddled at these interlopers to her world and wasn't sure whether to throw them off or not, and exclaimed, "Have you ever been to a debutantes' ball, Harbinger?"

"No."

"Don't do that sort of thing in Birmingham, England?"

"No, not really."

"You?" One eyebrow shot into the attack position as she glowered at Robinson.

"No. But I went to prom when I left school."

Her nose crinkled a little at that, but she restrained herself from further judgement. For a while they stood, three strangers and an awkward, confused technician, watching the hall turn.

What did they see?

Robinson: wealth, beauty, elegance, grace. Once upon a time he was young, and smoked pot, and dreamed of owning his own motorbike and a black leather jacket with studs in. Then he was older, and married, and she bought home these magazines with pictures of pastel houses with thick pale carpets that the kids didn't ever seem to get mud on, and glass tables and marble bathrooms, and he indulged her fantasy, even though they could never afford it, because it made her happy, and one day she made friends with a lawyer ("Don't call him an ambulance-chaser!" she snapped) who lived in a community gated off from the highway, where every garden was a golf course, and he had that life, he had that world, and as he showed Robinson round the garage (manly tools, never touched) and the living room (beautiful books, never read) and the kitchen (every convenience, stainless steel, never dirty), Robinson had felt a thing that was . . .

. . . envy.

And in time envy had whispered in his ear, *this is ridiculous, this is obscene, no one needs* . . .

. . . and now he looked down into the ballroom and saw the beautiful women, so bright and talented and graceful and charming, and their wealthy dads, perfectly turned out in white shirts and black tails, and there it was again, no matter what he did, there it was and it was . . .

. . . envy.

He saw a beautiful life, and it was not for him.

Mrs Walker-Bell: beauty, elegance, grace, of course, absolutely. But these were not merely aesthetic attributes; in this moment she looked down and saw a moral value, a way of living that was, fundamentally, *better*. Because animals struggled, animals sweated and groaned and growled and fucked and pissed and suffered; but humans knew how to dance. Humans raised themselves to something higher – another good word, *cultivated*. The cultivated man, the old values, gentlemen and goodly ladies, the world was so much simpler then, the world now could learn so much from the meanings that lay underneath the concept of elegance. And tears glimmered in the corner of her eye to behold it, to look down and see, here at last, humanity, fulfilled.

And Charlie?

Charlie looked down and saw people, dancing, and felt too tired, too weary of looking, to see anything else. Then his eyes skimmed the hall again and he did see something else, and his fingers tightened hard against the scaffold railing of the tower, and he looked again, and the figure looked back, and raised one hand from where it had rested in the crook of its folded, champagne-nursing arm, to wave, just once.

Charlie said, "I need to ... There's someone ... " He made to move, but Mrs Walker-Bell caught his arm as he did, held it tight.

"Death won't come, will he?" she whispered. "Not for my girls?" Tears were rolling down her face, suddenly old, a soft belly beneath her spines. "Tell him that we've been changing, making it more ... modern. I know the world can't ... that things change and that you have to ... but three of our girls this year are black!"

Charlie pulled his arm slowly free from her grasp, and climbed down the ladder.

Robinson stayed a while, to watch the dancers, and listen to the music.

Chapter 84

Charlie found the man he knew round the back of the hall, standing on the rear porch where it rolled down towards the marshy, tree-draped land. The sun was down, the candles burning in their dozens around the freshly lichen-scoured stonework. The heat of the day was fading to something drier, more bearable, a thing that softened muscles rather than made them shudder with sweat.

Charlie approached, closing the double glass doors to the

house quietly behind him, cutting off the sound of music. Now he wished he'd had his champagne, that he wasn't wearing the same shirt he'd driven five hundred miles in, that his head didn't ache and his eyes weren't sticky and dry.

"Patrick," he said quietly, drawing level with the man with the glass.

Patrick Fuller smiled, not looking round from his contemplation of the stars growing brighter in the stained night sky. "Charlie."

Patrick, wearing a frock coat and bow tie, the only other English accent in this corner of the Deep South, the champagne barely sipped from his glass.

"We never did catch up after Lagos, did we?" he mused, head tilted up to the turning sky.

"No. I'm sorry, I was ... Why are you here?"

"I received an invitation."

"From Mrs Walker-Bell?"

Patrick glanced over at Charlie, mouth curling in wry reproof. Charlie looked away, nodded at his shoes.

"Did it invite you to see the end of the world?" he sighed.

"The end of *a* world, Charlie. The end of a world. I looked more closely, and that was definitely the phrasing. Even in Alabama, it seems, Death will come for the debutante balls; for the cat-string violins and the ol' guitar. I imagine the tradition will continue for a while, but changing, always changing."

"In tarot," mused Charlie, "Death usually means change, rather than destruction. I don't buy into that thing, though, it's not ... So you were invited."

"Yes."

"And you came."

"Yes. When Death asks you to bear witness to the end of a world, I think it is impolitic to turn the invitation down. What did you give Mrs Walker-Bell?"

"I'm not at liberty to say."

"Of course. Very proper. Professional etiquette, I imagine."

"Something like that."

For a while the two of them stood together, staring at the sky. Then Charlie blurted, "Back in London, the Longview Estate, there was a woman you introduced me to, there was ... Some things were said that were ... "

Patrick waited.

"In Lagos I was ... I had seen something and I wanted to make it right, do something right, but the police, you see, and it wasn't as simple as... it wasn't my story or my choice to ... "

Charlie fell silent.

Then quieter, staring flat at the horizon now, seeing nothing much at all, "Do you think you'll miss this world, when it's gone? The ballroom dancing, the gold slippers, all of that?"

Patrick sucked in his breath slowly, exhaled in a cautious puff. "No, I suppose not. There will always be an elite, and there will always be events which celebrate the aspirations and the possessions of the elite. Celebration ... perhaps also demonstration. A well-turned-out daughter used to be the demonstration of a possession you were willing to barter with, a child you were prepared to sell into the market, and these sorts of occasions were an opportunity to put up the shop window. The dance has changed, but now you're illuminating different attributes. Yes, that your daughter is highly educated and beautiful, but also that you can afford these things, that you have embedded value in ... in a certain way of doing things. A proper way, a way that is respectful of the past, proud of the present. If Death is coming to Mrs Walker-Bell's ball, he won't come with fire and thunder, but with trouser suits and coding courses, with MBAs and an attitude towards wealth and the display of it that values ... other modalities. The ball will go on. But it will also change."

Silence a while.

Then Charlie said: "She told me that there were three black girls dancing this year."

Silence.

At last Patrick murmured, "When I came to the ball, I thought I'd see you here. I hoped I would. Do you know why

I have been invited to be a witness to all this? It's been a long time since we met on the ice, I've been thinking about it a lot – do you know?"

Charlie shook his head.

"I believe it is because I am part of it. It is immodest to say so, of course. No one man shapes the world, we are all part of systems, wheels within ... but that's a lie, a fallacy we create to justify our own meagre lives, or lack of vision, or failure to take control. I do shape the world. I shape it with money, and ambition, and my use of both these tools is determined, yes, by my skills and my learning, but even they are refined through the prism of who I am. The world would be different if I were different. I am ... I am invited to witness, I think, not the death of a world, not the old falling off, but the new being born. We two, we are ... we are essential, I think, to this process, both you and I. One of us comes to mourn, the other to rejoice. I think that's what this business is. I think that is why I came."

Silence.

Patrick sipped his champagne.

Charlie stared at the darkness.

"Charlie?"

He didn't answer.

"You have the harder task, I think. In Greenland, the old man died, and it was sad, but I do not mourn what he represents. In Nigeria, the world changes and the old passes by and I am proud – truly, I am – to say that I am part of its future. Here, the girls grow old and the old rules change and I for one celebrate it. Three African-Americans at the debutantes' ball – you strike me, Charlie, as a man who could rejoice in this new thing, marginal as it is. And yet it would appear that you are sent to honour the past, not the future. To ... to listen to the stories of dead men. To carry their memories, and find something human in them that others might not perceive. I think it must be ... a difficult job. Not one I'd take. Charlie? Charlie?"

No reply.

Patrick sighed, another gulp, deeper now, draining the pale

liquid down. Then, "I'd better go inside. Mrs Walker-Bell is a very generous host."

He started to walk away, hesitated, looked back.

"I would be your friend, if you'd let me. I do genuinely believe . . . we are called to much the same business, in our ways."

No answer.

He sighed, faintly, and turned towards the house.

Charlie looked up. "I don't mourn," he said, sharp. Then, louder, "I don't mourn. That's not what I do. You're wrong. I . . . am sent for something else."

"Do you know what?"

"I think so."

A half-chuckle, waiting. "Are you going to say?"

"No."

A shrug. "Fair enough. If you're sticking around, you should try the whiskey. She only gets the best stuff."

"I'm not sticking around."

"Then I'll see you at the end of the road."

Patrick walked back inside, to where the music played.

Chapter 85

Driving through the darkness, looking for a hotel.

Charlie drove, Robinson pressing his head against the glass of the window. The air conditioning was up too high, but Charlie didn't mind, and Robinson didn't complain. Headlights, headlights, white towards, red behind, the sodium lights at the crossings, no sidewalks for pedestrians, is it legal to turn right at a red in this state? Charlie doesn't know and Robinson isn't certain. The signal on Charlie's phone is very bad.

Headlights, headlights.

Very few street lights in the USA, Charlie is beginning to

learn. Even on the major highways, it's all headlights. Even in the cities, the towns, fewer than he expected.

They find a hotel. It's overpriced, for what it is, but has two single rooms, breakfast thrown in. Robinson says they should stick around for the breakfast – sausage gravy, proper andouille too, a taste of real food.

Charlie sets an alarm on his phone, lies down to sleep to the roaring of the hotel air conditioning, and wonders if this is what spaceships sound like, as the fans rattle and blare into the night.

Breakfast. Sausage gravy; andouille.

It is the best meal he's had so far. Charlie wonders if it would be rude to lick the plate.

Heading east, towards Atlanta, Charlie drives, then Robinson drives, and after two hundred miles, it seems like Robinson is going to keep on driving and doesn't want to stop.

And just before midday, without any warning, Robinson starts to talk.

"I never got on with my brother as a kid, but in New York he runs a tool hire company, you know, power tools, and I was always handy and that's a business model that's not gonna fail, not ever, 'cos people always need tools, but they're so good these days that they gotta be expensive, I mean, if it was just a stick with a nail in, anyone could make that, but some of the tools they make these days, like diamond tips, you try buying a diamond-tipped drill bit, and carbon fibre and titanium and all these different kind of steels, it's incredible, material sciences, you never really think about material science, do you, but if I was sent back in time, I'd be like you can build machines and cogs and gears and change the world, but unless you got the basic knowledge of how to make steel which don't crack, iron which don't rust – even getting aluminium, that's electrolysis, do you know how much of the world is aluminium these days? Maybe I shoulda done geology at college."

And as abruptly as he'd started talking, he stopped, and they drove in silence for another thirty miles.

Then: "Are those girls gonna die? The ones at the debutante ball?"

"I don't know. I mean . . . everyone dies."

"That's not what I'm saying."

"I'm just the messenger."

"Shit, man. Shit. I been waiting for you to say that so I could tell you to your face that that's shit. Surprised it took you so long to say that crap, not that I ain't grateful for the lift, but shit."

Silence, another ten miles.

Then Charlie said: "I don't think the girls are going to die."

"You gotta feeling? That something you do? I mean, if every time you visited everyone, like, kids – you visit kids?"

"Sometimes."

"Like every time you visited a kid, if you knew they were gonna die, die young, I mean, die before they'd ever lived, you'd be . . . I mean, I couldn't imagine it, you wouldn't be able to, you'd have to be . . . and you don't strike me as being that kind of man. I don't think you'd be the kind of man could look a woman in the eye and know that tomorrow she'd be dead, not all the time, not every day."

"You're wrong." Charlie stared out of the window, watching the trees run past. "Sometimes that's exactly what I do."

"And you're okay with that?"

"Sometimes. Sometimes . . . sometimes knowing is a curse. And sometimes it's a blessing. Sometimes if you know, you have a chance to do the right thing."

"So those girls, that place . . . am I gonna turn on the news and see that it's been flattened?"

"I doubt it. The . . . the situation wasn't . . . I was sent to see Mrs Walker-Bell, I wasn't sent to talk to all of them, it didn't feel like . . . I gave her the Confederate flag." Robinson raised his eyebrows, but didn't look away from the road. "I'm not meant to tell you that, please be . . . There is etiquette, you see. But as you ask. That's what I gave her. And based on my experience of these things, I don't think that's something you give a dying woman. It's an idea. Death comes for ideas too, you see. Flags

300

change meaning, the idea, the thought that pops into your head ... Where I'm from, the cross of St George was once a symbol of the pride of England. Plucky defiance and noble character, stiff upper lip and brave defiance against the odds, fight them on the beaches – that sort of thing. We kinda gloss over how it was a flag of colonialism too, I guess. Now it's become a symbol of the political right wing, who wave it as a weapon against anyone whose skin colour they dislike. It's a flag of ... of *us*. Of us who are English, of us who are *not* Scottish or Irish or Welsh or European or ... It's become a flag that makes those who wave it ... "

human human human

He stumbled on the words.

rat rat rat

Robinson picked up where Charlie's words failed, didn't seem to notice the Harbinger of Death flinching in pain, pressing his head against the cold glass of the car window. "I know what the Confederate flag is. It's a flag of slavery. It's the flag of brave free men."

Charlie nodded at nothing much. "Time changes meaning; history gets rewritten. For a while it was the banner of racists and bigots, sorry for saying it, but that's just how it reads. Then time changed, and it was again the flag of individuals who died bravely, and that bravery was true whatever their cause. Now murderers who believe that race war is both inevitable and desirable wrap themselves in it, and that's not the flag, that's not fabric and colour ... it is what people see. It is the idea it becomes. It may not be that for everyone – for Mrs Walker-Bell I imagine it is still the flag of her people, of their culture, their pride, their history and their fallen men. But elsewhere ... it has changed. One world dies. Another is born. The ball goes on."

One of us comes to mourn, the other to rejoice.

"So ... you think Death is coming for a flag?"

"I think Death is coming for an idea."

Robinson thought about that a long, long time. Then he shrugged. "That's not so bad, is it? I mean, people live, that's

301

what we're saying, right? People will live, those girls will live and if an idea ... an idea isn't life, you know? An idea isn't people."

Charlie stared out of the window, and didn't reply.

Chapter 86

Georgia.

The first thing they saw when they crossed the state line was a giant billboard showing a happy, smiling bear. Beneath it was a warning:

HAPPY BEARS DON'T
START FOREST FIRES!!

The second thing they saw, about a hundred yards later, was a police car, waiting in an obscured turn-off between the two lanes of the interstate, speed gun pressed against the windscreen.

A few seconds after they passed it, it turned on its siren, and went screaming after a sedan that was doing 87 mph and hadn't killed enough of its speed as it approached the border.

A computer coding class.

Female teacher, female students.

The youngest girl was ten, her dark hair plaited into cornrows, her bright eyes laughing in the reflected light of the screen.

"I been learning HTML and CSS," she explained, as Charlie sat by her side in the crowded classroom. "But I wanna learn Java next, and when I grow up, I'm gonna make computer games but also programs that make the world better, like tools that people can use in their lives to help them do things and fight poverty and stuff like that."

On the screen, a tiny animated turtle was drawing an

ever-tighter spiral towards the centre point, pausing every now and then to explain how far into its journey it had got, and for its shell to change colour from green to blue.

"On Sundays," added the girl brightly, "I make robots."

Charlie gave her a book on web design, and then went outside, to sit on the bonnet of the car with the girl's mother and grandmother.

To the mother he gave a USB flash drive on a chain, 12GB, to carry her daughter's work. The daughter didn't need it, but her mother carried it anyway, because it made her feel close to her, gave her a little piece of her child in her hand.

To the grandmother, he gave a silver brooch shaped like a dove taking wing, and the grandmother said, "My mother was beaten by her husband, because of the drink, and because of the poverty, and because of the shame. My husband, he didn't beat me, but we weren't never really in love, and when he left me I think it were a good thing for the both of us. I never got out of the place where I lived, though, never got a proper job, had to raise my daughter so cheap, so tight, like as how you wouldn't believe – you remember?"

And the mother nodded and said, "I don't remember much about my dad, but Mom always did the best she could by us. It was hard, you know, hard, but we had some times, didn't we, we always found something to laugh at, and me ... well I got pregnant when I was fifteen. They told us at school that abstinence, it was the way you kept yourself safe and all, but you tell a teenage girl to be abstinent, you make her do that, and of course they didn't tell us about condoms or anything like that, and now my daughter ... "

She shook her head, smiling at the squat classroom, dropped between sushi bar and rib joint off the rushing highway.

"For her, the world will be different. For her, the stories we tell will just be funny stories, and she won't have to laugh to take the sadness away."

Charlie smiled, and chatted to them a while longer, about the things they'd seen and the lives they'd lived, and Robinson

303

watched too, and as the women laughed and their daughter worked, even he began to smile.

"Death," said Charlie, as they drove away, "sometimes he comes for a change in history. Sometimes he comes for the end of something that you never thought would stop."

Robinson nodded, and that night they had Cajun chicken and spicy rice, and for the first time Robinson chatted, gossiped even, about people he'd seen and places he'd known, about politics and his love of baseball, and about how, if you hung on in there another twenty-something years, the Chicago Cubs would get over that time they were cursed by a man with a goat, and win every season coming, just you wait and see.

"When I get to New York, I'm gonna start again," he exclaimed, as they shuffled, dozy and full of food, towards the hotel. "I thought my life was over, but it ain't, it ain't at all, this is something perfect, this is something good, this is the new beginning I always needed. You know how you sometimes feel like your life is just playing a part, being who you need to be, because you think that's what you oughta? It's like my whole life I been pretending, pretending to be this guy with this house in Florida, and now . . . now I'm me. Now I'm something new. Will Death come soon? I wanna talk to him, I wanna know how he sees the world."

Charlie shrugged, a little tipsy. "I guess . . . Death will come when he's called. I think . . . sometimes it's that too."

"What is Death? What's he like?"

"He's different for everyone."

"But everybody dies."

"Yes."

"So how can Death be different?"

"He's . . . sometimes he's . . . sometimes he's a storm, and sometimes he's a kindness and sometimes he's . . . sometimes he is pain without end and sometimes he is . . . As a child, there is a moment when we see him for the very first time, and he has always been there but finally we know, but as an adult, we never believe, we close our eyes because we are too afraid and he is ... I'm very tired. I'm sorry. There's this ... "

Tick tick tick tick ...

"I think I need an early night."

"Good night, Charlie."

"Good night, Robinson."

They swayed their separate ways to bed.

Charlie drove.

He gave a gift of fresh flower seeds to the last engineer left in the coal plant as it closed its doors, and the man shook his head and said, "What am I gonna do with this? I'm out of work now, my boys, we're all out of work, it's over, it's all over for us ... "

And it was, and Death came to wave them off as they headed into an uncertain future, and stayed a little while longer as the men in hard hats came to pull the coal plant down, never to be rebuilt, because on the hills a little to the west, there was now a field full of solar panels instead; and in the torn-up desert of their lives, fresh flowers grew.

And Charlie drove.

In a town on the edge of the Georgia–South Carolina border, a man behind the counter exclaimed, "Bicycle helmets kill you, why you giving me a bicycle helmet, my friend, he wore one of these and he's now paraplegic, I mean, you should see him, he can't even feed himself, he can't even ... like bicycle helmets destroy lives, I'm telling you!"

But on the way home that night, he didn't have enough space in his bag to put the helmet, and it *was* from Death, and it wasn't in his nature to leave these things behind, so he put it on his head and cycled home, and was hit by a speeding car driven by a fifteen-year-old, and spent the rest of his life with a limp and a pain in his leg, and lived.

He lived. In pain, struggling with mundane tasks, he lived and he loved and the man he loved loved him back just as much, such an intensity of commitment that sometimes he couldn't believe that the human brain had such strength within it to love so hard, and he lived.

And Death, heading the other way in his four-wheel drive, passed him by.

Chapter 87

A bar, in a seaside resort in South Carolina.

The Ferris wheel was motionless outside, but on the crazy golf courses the children putted their balls into the gaping mouths of crocodiles, down the side of plastic volcanoes, and on the sand the bathers stretched their pasty bodies out beneath the sun, and drank cold beer from the cooler box, and listened to the roar of the ocean.

Charlie and Robinson walked along the seashore, and it was beautiful; the smell, said Robinson, the smell from the Atlantic is nothing like the smell back home, it's a different sea, going to a different place, you can tell, you can feel it in the air.

Returning to the hotel, there were two men waiting for them by the reception desk, rolled-up shirt sleeves, black trousers, one greying and friendly, one young, blonde, stiff and tight, thick wrists and bulging arms, a body bordering on comically, inhumanly buffed.

They stepped forward as Charlie approached, said, "Excuse me? Are you the Harbinger of Death?"

"Yes," he replied politely, causing the hotel receptionist – to whom this was new information – to flinch away. "Can I help you?"

"We'd like to buy you a drink."

"Thank you, but I'm ... "

The younger man pulled a leather pouch from his pocket,

opened it up, revealed a badge. "Sir," he repeated. "We'd like to buy you a drink."

Charlie hesitated, running his tongue round his lower lip, the good spirits of the evening slowly dissolving. Robinson murmured, "Want me to stick around?"

The man answered before Charlie could. "Sir, we'd like to talk to the Harbinger alone, thank you."

"It'll be fine," Charlie replied, half turning his head towards Robinson, a little grateful nod. "It'll be fine."

"I'll knock on your door in an hour," grunted Robinson, and pushed – a little too close, a little too hard – between the two men, stomping towards the lifts that went up to the guest rooms.

They had a drink.

Charlie had orange juice, which turned out to be mostly orange acid with sugar in it.

The older man had a Bloody Mary, the younger, soda water.

They sat in the low, warm lights of the bar, as the traffic trundled by outside, headlight, headlight, great lorries heading to far-off places, huge family growlers high off the ground, kangaroo bars on the front, children watching TV in the back.

The men introduced themselves. The older was Stanczak; the younger Nelson.

The younger did all the talking, while the elder leant back into the curved couch of their booth, one leg crossed over the other, smiling.

"Mr Harbinger of Death ... "

"My name is Charlie."

"I saw your passport."

Charlie half shrugged. "So that's my name."

"Why do you have a name, may I ask?"

"You know, you're the second person to ask me that in the last week. I have a name because I'm a person. I come from Birmingham."

"Alabama?"

"England."

307

"Is that the place with Sharia law?"

"No."

"But you are employed by Death, as his Harbinger?"

"Yes."

"So you are, as well as a British citizen, a person?"

"Yes." Charlie has been in this business too long to take offence at this sort of thing.

"Mr Harbinger ... "

"Charlie."

Nelson's mouth twisted with distaste, but reluctantly: "Charlie. What is the nature of your business in South Carolina?"

"I go where I'm sent."

"And where is that?"

"I'd rather not say."

"Why not?"

"Lawyers and doctors have confidentiality. My employer considers that his work, being often so pertinent to theirs, should also have a degree of professional discretion about it."

"His work is Death."

"No. He *is* Death."

"Do you know the location of Death at this time?"

"Everywhere."

"Are you being obstructive?"

"No. Death is everywhere."

"I think you and I both know that I was referring to the individual known as the reaper, the bringer of darkness, the rider of the Apocalypse."

"You want to know where my employer's current physical incarnation is?"

"Yes."

"Somewhere behind."

"Behind?"

"On the road behind me. That's how it works. I go before ... he follows behind."

"But he tells you where to go."

"Yes."

308

"So if you were to deviate from that path – if you were to, for example, return to Georgia . . . "

"Death would still come to South Carolina, but would perhaps be annoyed that I had not fulfilled my function."

"And what is your function?"

"To go before . . . Gentlemen," Charlie leant forward suddenly, folding his fingers together between his knees, still smiling, without humour, "I have been asked these questions a thousand times before. So have my predecessors. In the time of the revolution, when Death and War both stalked these lands, I imagine the Harbingers that were then sent to America were also asked these questions, and also gave the same replies, which have been documented for all to see. You are asking questions you could find the answers to in your local library, or Wikipedia. This is . . . this is nothing. Death comes, and the world turns, and that is how it always has been, and always will be. So forgive me for asking: why do you want to have this drink?"

The younger man sat back, impatient perhaps, or maybe only huffing to hide his uncertainty. For a moment, the three sat there, looking at each other, reading each other's waiting eyes, before the older man, putting his glass down, said, "Does Death barter?"

Charlie eased deeper into his chair, relaxed, another familiar question. "No. Not really."

"Not really?"

"I'm told there was once a queen . . . and once a mother of a very ill child . . . and once a soldier somewhere in the south . . . but that was a long time ago. The last Harbinger told me that Death was once challenged to a battle at Laser Quest, and the idea was so delightful that he took the bet – but that might just have been my predecessor's sense of humour, she's a bit like that, you see. She's got a name, and comes from a place too. I don't know who won the battle, if it was real."

He waited. The older man, his question asked, resumed drinking, casual as a sunbathing lion, his belly full, his work done.

The younger glanced at the older, then leant forward again, shaking his head a little, impatient with both his colleague and Charlie.

"America can offer—"

"No."

"The people of America demand—"

"No."

"Are you authorised to speak for—"

"No, but I know how this works. Everyone knows how this works."

"You've been tracked, as you say, you're human and we can—"

"You can't manipulate Death. Threatening me, turning me out of your country won't stop him coming."

"There are things we can offer."

Charlie shrugged.

"I'm told that Death will come for ideas, as well as people."

"Yes, that's true."

"There are ideas we could preserve, there are concepts that are—"

"No. The world changes, and that is all."

"You say that everyone knows how this works, but your boss—"

"Everyone does. You do. Even as you sit here talking to me, you know that it's meaningless. You've known your whole life."

Nelson, leaning a little further now, sitting right on the edge of the couch. "What is Death?"

Charlie nearly laughed, glanced over at Stanczak to see if the question was a joke. The old man's eyes sparkled with mischief, but he said nothing.

"You know the answer to that," Charlie chuckled. "Everyone knows the answer to that."

"Do I? They say that Death stalks the earth, but what is he? What is Death, what does it mean, why does he come, why does he choose who he chooses? Is it luck? Is it fate? Can we choose, or is our time just ticking down? Is there ... is there God? Is Death God?"

"Death is Death," replied Charlie with a shrug. "That's all there really is to say."

"That's no good. The people I work for ... "

"He knows." Charlie gestured with the tips of his fingers at Stanczak. "You could save yourself a lot of time, and ask him."

310

Surprised, Nelson looked round to his colleague. Stanczak pushed his lips out in a kind of facial shrug, shifted a little in his seat, didn't unfold his crossed legs, didn't put his near-empty glass back down. "These questions ... always mean something different to different people," he mused at last.

Nelson's face crinkled into a scowl. He turned back on Charlie, faster now, halfway to his feet. "We can make things difficult for you ..."

"Deport me, if you want. You wouldn't be the first."

"You think your country will have you back?"

"Yes."

"How do you live with yourself? How do you do that?"

"I am the Harbinger," Charlie replied. "I honour the living."

For a moment, he thought that Nelson might hit him, and wasn't sure why. He'd seen the look before, seen it come from nowhere, from a human experience that hadn't yet been explained to him. But Stanczak got to his feet before the younger man could move, laid a gentle hand on his shoulder, said, "I think we've said all that needs saying here."

Nelson, a rubber band waiting to snap, poised for a moment on that moment of tension. Relaxed. His head rolled down. He nodded at nothing much, and let Stanczak lead him away.

The next day, a black Toyota followed them all the way to the state line.

If Robinson noticed, he didn't say, and Charlie felt no need to remark on it.

Chapter 88

In a land of freedom ...

... in a land of mighty rivers rolling inexorably to the sea ...

A dead armadillo on the side of the road.

Charlie was surprised, but Robinson wasn't.

"You should see Kansas," he mused. "A man could feast off roadkill in them parts."

Billboards.

Divorce lawyers for men only.

Vasectomies.

Weigh stations for the lorries ploughing up and down the road, checking that they weren't carrying too much without paying their fee, tyres ripping up tarmac.

Mobile homes, dragged along at 70 mph.

Shattered, tattered limbs of torn-up black rubber strewing the side of the highway.

Bridges named for soldiers dead in war. Private, sergeant. A trooper, dead too young, his name now guarding an overpass in the middle of empty green.

A set of traffic lights through a town whose name Charlie missed.

As they waited, a train rumbled by, yellow carts, blue writing. It moved at about 30 mph, and for nearly twenty minutes they rumbled beside it, trying to find the end. Charlie wondered how long it was, couldn't imagine it being less than a mile.

Robinson said: "Do you take trains much?"

"Yes. Sometimes."

"In Britain? I mean, I know you've got like, the metro . . . "

"There are a lot of trains in Britain."

"For anyone to take?"

"Yes. Assuming there aren't the wrong kind of leaves on the line."

"What does that mean?"

"It's . . . it's a British thing."

"Like British humour?"

"Like that."

"America used to be the land of trains, you know."

"So I've been told."

"You been round the world?"

"I guess so."

"What do you think of it? Of America, I mean?"

"I think ... it's very beautiful."

Robinson's lips twitched, words suppressed, and they kept on driving.

Chapter 89

"Defender of democracy, that's what we are; when the shit hits the fan, who do you call, you call America ... "

"The peoples of the free world ...!"

"Climate justice means that the burden for the carbon-neutral programme should not have to fall upon developing nations ... "

Tick tick tick

"New baby born every second in the state of ... "

"Our good friends and allies, Saudi Arabia ... "

"American values, American freedoms ... "

"Korea, Vietnam, Afghanistan, Iraq ... "

"Where were you for Crimea? Where were you for Rwanda? Where were you in the Democratic Republic of the Congo, where were you at Srebrenica?!"

"One day set foot on Mars."

Tick tick tick tick

"National Service will teach those kids what it means to be citizens, citizenship should be earned ... "

"What about the women?"

"No religious test shall ever be required as a qualification to any office or public trust ... "

"For poor, read: black."

Tick tick tick TICK TICK TICK

"Of course I mean Christian values, America is a Christian nation!"

313

"A well-regulated militia being necessary to the security of a free state, the right of the people to keep and bear arms shall not be infringed."

An evening, sitting on the coast of the Atlantic in North Carolina, watching a storm.

Inland, maybe thirty miles away, pink and yellow lightning forked down to the earth, a far-off rumble of distant drums, faint, washed out by the sea.

Over the ocean, moon-white lightning danced through the clouds, casting the shadow of itself against the overhung sky.

Robinson drank beer in a surfers' bar down the beach.

Charlie sat on the sand, and listened to the waves, and watched the storm.

"Yeah. I'm with the Klan."

Robinson had fluctuated as to whether he wanted to meet this man, sitting on the porch of his wooden house, legs crossed, sunglasses huge, folded round his face. "The KKK?" he hissed. "You're giving what to the KKK?"

"French chocolate."

"What the fuck?"

Charlie shrugged. "It's just my job."

After much agonising, Robinson had come, figuring, perhaps, that he would be more comfortable in the company of Death's servant than alone, waiting in the car at the end of the drive.

The old man, bald beneath his straw hat, white ironed shirt and pale green shorts, leather sandals on his feet, had watched them all the way up the mud path to his door, waiting, and when they'd got near, a dog on a chain had started barking and howling from the side of the house, where it was lashed to a hosepipe, and his daughter and granddaughter had come out-side to see what the fuss was about, and now stood there, arms folded, glaring.

"Harbinger of Death, you say?" He made a hiss-pop sound between his teeth, puffed out his cheeks, then smiled. "Well, it's good that Death sends these courtesies, I suppose. And would you be Harbinger of War, or no?"

"No, sir," mumbled Robinson, standing a little behind Charlie, glancing up at the high branches of the sun-soaked, heat-cracked trees as if fearful of being spotted in these parts by friends or strangers. "I'm just ... catching a lift."

"Death gives lifts now, do he?"

"I do," corrected Charlie, handing over his bag of chocolate. The old man answered with his eyebrows and opened up the package, his face splitting into a triumphant grin when he saw what was inside.

"Hey – Daisy, Magda, he brought chocolate!"

"Don't want it," grumbled the girl, pink dress, blonde ponytail, hiding behind her red-faced mother, still glowering at Charlie as the dog barked and bounced.

"Don't be like that, sweetheart, it's the good stuff, it's the best stuff, you won't have tasted anything like this before. Now come here and try a bite, don't be foolish. Come here. Come here!"

Pushed a little by her mother, the girl came forward, angling herself to keep as much of her grandfather's chair as possible between her and Charlie, and took the chocolate, shoving it into her mouth and running away before she had a chance to chew.

The old man, slower, ate a piece, then another, closing his eyes to savour the taste, humming and umming in appreciation before declaring, "Boy, that is the stuff, that just hits the spot. You know, back in the day, I was posted to Berlin, back with the boys, and that town, that place ... but the coffee and the chocolate, I always remembered that, always stuck in my mind."

"I'm glad to have brought you some."

"But he's not the Harbinger of War?" added the man, shooting another glance at Robinson.

"No, sir. The Harbinger of War is a woman."

"You don't say? Maybe that's right. The things menfolk will do for their ladies, you know? Hey, you guys wanna stick around, have a drink?"

"Thank you, but ... "

"Magda! Hey, Magda, get these boys a drink."

"We've got a long way to go ..."

"A lemonade. You'll have a lemonade, right? I mean, you are the Harbinger of Death, ain't you supposed to be courteous and that?"

"I ... A lemonade would be very nice, thank you."

"Magda, lemonade and like, some of those cookies, you know the ones, the best ... You like cookies? Sure you like cookies. Daisy, be a sweetheart and grab a coupla extra chairs will you? Bless you. Here – sit, sit!"

They obeyed, and drank lemonade as the sun drifted over the trees.

"Figured you'd be the Harbinger of War, what with the way this country's going," mused the man, as his family flanked his wicker chair, and they drank lemonade together. "Racial war is only a matter of time, and it's the job of the Klan to make sure folk are ready for it. Because the nigger, when he fight, he gonna fight like a dog, and folk are complicit, they're complicit in their own destruction here. Well not me. I got a beautiful daughter, I got a beautiful granddaughter, who I love, and I gotta protect them from what's coming. But I guess if you're from Death, not War, that's something too. Funny, though, funny. I always figured it'd be War."

Charlie said nothing. Robinson's feet, shoulders, back, all angled away from the man, his head down, said nothing.

"You been long in these parts?"

"No, but I've visited before," Charlie replied.

"You seen the way things are going? The white man, he's being oppressed. The blacks have got everything sewn up, they got the schools, they got the colleges, they got the jobs, they got the benefits, they're just living off the state now, living off the thing that the white man build. You just look, you'll see it, I promise you."

"I ... haven't seen it, so far."

"You look. It's there."

"I'm afraid I don't believe that."

316

The man tutted, and shook his head, and his grandchild glared. "Boy, you gotta open your eyes. If you read the Bible, you'll see, only way it coulda happened is if . . . in the Bible . . . if humans bred with monkeys, I mean, that's what we're saying here, that's . . . "

A pain in the side of Charlie's head; he rocked forward, grasping, eyes squeezing shut.

"Hey, you okay?"

A ringing in his ears, eyes staring into his through the darkness. He squeezed his own eyes shut until they hurt, and still the faces were staring.

"Son – you okay? Magda, get the boy some water, will you, he's come over peculiar."

Slowly, slowly, the pain fading. He opened his eyes again, the world too bright beyond, forced himself to relax, one finger at a time, put the lemonade glass down. Magda gave him a glass of water with ice in it, which he drank, slow and grateful. Robinson watched him, silent.

"You not used to the heat?"

"I'm . . . I'm fine. Sorry. I sometimes . . . I'm fine."

"You should go inside if you're not used to the heat. I imagine in Britain you don't get much sun."

"I'm . . . It's not that. I'm . . . I'm fine. I think. Maybe we should go. Thank you for the lemonade, and your hospitality."

They stood up, Robinson moving quickly towards the car. The old man watched them, then blurted, "You know . . . the Klan's still going strong. People say that we're not, but we are. Magda's been making new member outfits all the time, and Daisy, she's real good with the sewing machine. We're still to be reckoned with. We still matter. You know that, don't you?"

Charlie smiled faintly, and didn't reply. Robinson was already marching down the path, fists tight at his sides.

A few paces more, then the man called after him, and there was fear in his voice.

"Day before yesterday, I got this pain in my belly, like this pain it were . . . Hospital's a long drive, though, a long drive, and my pa, he died when he were . . . but we're strong. We're all strong. We gotta be, for the people we love."

Charlie stopped, turned back, saw the old man in his wicker chair, the two women either side, backs straight, eyebrows drawn. He thought about waving, and didn't, and walked away.

In the car, Robinson silent, knuckles white where he held the steering wheel.

They stopped at a shopping mall on the side of the road, and Robinson prowled through the garden store, the hunting store, the outdoor-survival mega-mall, before finally realising he didn't have enough money to buy a coffee.

Charlie bought coffee, without a word.

They drove on.

At last Robinson said: "He might have killed people. He might have fucking lynched people."

"Possibly."

"And you gave him chocolate?"

"Yes."

"*Why?*"

"Because soon he will die."

"But he's *scum*, he's a fucking bastard, he's a fucking racist, he's . . . "

"Once he was a child, and now he is an old man, who looked at the world and chose to be mad, and frightened, and see other people as . . . as rats. As . . . as less than human. My job," a pounding headache, he forced out the words, "is to see everyone as human. Even him. When a man kills another, Death comes. We all see him in a different way, we all see . . . something of ourselves, but Death comes anyway. He comes. He is coming. Seeing is all."

Robinson said nothing.

The road.

Always: the road.

Chapter 90

A dinner party in Wilmington.

He didn't want to go, but the woman he brought Russian vodka to – "Ah, my childhood! You brought me my youth again!" – was, in her own words, "Three or four days from the long goodnight but no one believes me when I tell them, you stick around, you make them understand that this time, it's real."

Charlie said, "I'm not sure . . ."

But she raised one yellow, shrunken hand and barked, "Don't be ridiculous! It is eight p.m., there is dinner waiting, my sons and nieces and nephews are all downstairs, I love all of them, you must meet them, stay, eat! I insist, I insist that you stay and eat, I won't hear of you going another step without sitting down at my table!" Then she grinned and reached in closer to whisper in his ear. "Don't tell the in-laws, but I'm leaving most of it to charity. They're all fine as they are, but urban literacy rates need so much work."

Charlie stared, surprised, into her bright, mischievous blue eyes, and wondered why Death came for her, of all the people who were dying that night.

(Death came to honour her, for she had built her world from nothing, made an empire where others would have dug a grave. When the college had said no, no, business was not for gals like her, she had done it anyway; when her husband had said babe, babe, I love you, but I just don't get that feelin' in bed with you any more, she had thrown him out and he had been astonished, when the divorce came through, to find that he had no more and no less than his just deserts. And when the world turned and time moved on, she had sat in her mansion by the river, and considered the future, and decided that it would be very different from the past. And on this subject, Death is inclined to agree.)

"My kids," she chuckled with a little, bone-thin shrug. "They've had love, milk, education and a decent starter package out of me. In this country, you can do anything, and I did. The rest is theirs to make, they just don't know it yet! Go meet them – have some dinner. I insist."

In the face of her insistence, it would have been rude to refuse. Her joyful laughter followed them down the hall.

Tick tick tick goes the grandfather clock, and around the dinner table the voices say:

"Oh my God, the Harbinger of Death, that is just like so ... so ... you know!"

"I'm just saying that if we are to uphold Christian values then we have to consider the value of the unborn child ... "

"I know it's not politically correct, but someone's gotta say what everyone is thinking!"

" ... it's just so, like, you must ... it must be *amazing*, like so totally ... totally *real*."

"The free market is democracy! Well, it is, isn't it?"

"Health insurance is so important, I mean, I know that I'm sounding like a boring old man here, but actually, when I look at my contract I think ... "

"And you have a girlfriend? Oh my God, and she must be like 'I'm dating the Harbinger of Death' and I bet she's beautiful, is she beautiful?"

"Yes. She also teaches chemistry ... "

"Oh God, she's a teacher? I always wanted to be a teacher, but you know, it just didn't work out that way ... "

"Hybrid technology, actually, with hybrid technology I think the debate on fossil fuels is ... "

"Aid just supports corrupt regimes, it doesn't make any difference – if you're paying for an economy then that economy isn't working!"

"Charlie, you'll know about this. In England, you guys don't pay for hospitals, but like, the death rate is really high, isn't it?"

"Actually I don't think it's—"

"There's these death committees, where they literally sit there and decide who's gonna die."

"That's not how it ... "

"Oh my God, I'm just like, yeah, I can pay for it, you can't, so what, you gonna sue me?"

"Me? Shopping, mostly. Mostly: shopping."

After, Robinson and Charlie stood by the waterside, the lights of the battleship cold against the night sky, the traffic roaring over the bridge high overhead, strings of bulbs slung between the iron lamp posts. A horse and cart clopped away through the town's tourist streets; fresh ice cream dripped from the cone clutched by a pair of giggling children onto the floor.

At last, Robinson said: "She's leaving it all to charity, huh?"

Charlie nodded.

Silence a while.

Then Robinson began to laugh, and after a little while, Charlie joined in.

Chapter 91

The long road, going north.

In the mist-soaked mountains of Virginia, down a dirt track framed by aluminium silos, a hot-water bottle to a woman with faded yellow hair.

She took it, and cried silently, and didn't say why.

Beneath the rustling trees of the mountains, a box of different-flavoured jams for an old man who had once walked the Appalachian Trail, and who knew which berries were good and which were bad, and whose little house was about to be demolished to make way for a 7-Eleven, and who said, as they drove away, "A man can lose himself on the path, if he wants to. Sometimes losing yourself is the only way to find out who you are."

On the track through the mountains, an offering of incense before a face carved into stone, no humans in sight, no words to be spoken, but it seemed for a moment that the wind was still and the animals were silent, and the light moved strangely upon the water.

A one-way system into the city.

"Fucking Beltway!" roared Robinson, slapping both hands, open-palmed, against the wheel. "Fucking Beltway with its fucking signs in the fucking ... "

In the end, they ended up being sucked into a car park outside the Pentagon, before finally crawling their way across the Potomac river.

A hotel full of men come to Washington for conferences.

Three different kinds of walk along the National Mall, Charlie observed.

Natives – jogging and plotting on Bluetooth earpieces, or marching at brisk high speed, next meeting to get to, faster to walk than grab a taxi.

Strangers come for work – tired, eyes popping and red, too flustered to stop and look at the sights of the city, but still drawn upwards, proud of themselves for having arrived here, awed at the place where now they stand, worried that they won't make the three p.m. session on Intra-Committee Communication Strategies Pt.2.

Tourists.

They queue around the Washington Monument, stare down at the sculptures of raincoated men who died fighting in Korea. They circle the great sweeps of stone raised in honour of the men who died in the Second World War, they stare upwards, upwards, through the great halls of the Smithsonian.

"See?" Robinson declared, as they gazed into the still waters of the pool. "America fights for democracy."

Charlie bit his lip, and Robinson glared. "What? What is it?"

Did America fight for democracy?

(Once upon a time, War stood on Omaha Beach as the bullets flew, put his hands on his hips and laughed as the men fell, the water turning red with blood. "Shit!" he exclaimed, as the last parachute opened over northern France and the tanks rolled over the limbs of the brave and the fearful who had died in the sand. "Just listen to the music now!")

The Museum of the American Indian.

Charlie gives a small carved statue to a woman who waits outside. It is shaped like a sea lion. She holds it tight to her chest, and through wide, horrified eyes whispers, "You go inside, and it's like my people never died."

A beggar, shooed away from the centre of the city by the Washington police; can't have such people sullying their streets. He holds tight to the cup of tea that Charlie has provided, as if he'll never let go.

"I tried the VA," he whispers. "But they said they were all full up."

Charlie bought the tea because the man was cold, and the tea was hot. He is not in the appointments list.

A Congressional aide, jogging along the river. She stops so Charlie can give her an audiobook, to play on her next run. She takes it as jet fighters roar overhead, patrolling the skies, then leans in and whispers, "It was me. I authorised it. I gave the command." And doesn't explain, puts her headphones back in, and keeps on running.

Tacos, on a floating platform in a marina. The plate, when it comes, is nearly a foot high. Charlie and Robinson plough through as much of it as they can – chips and avocado, sausage and meatballs, onion, melted plastic cheese and tomato – before yielding and letting a group of American football players, come to celebrate with their girlfriends, finish off the rest. As they leave, Charlie looks up and thinks he sees someone familiar, getting out of a car with two women and a man. Dark straight hair, carefully cut suit . . .

He thinks about going to say hi, but Patrick doesn't seem to see him, and looks busy, and he has no scruples about walking on by.

"Oh my God, you're in Washington, I'm in Washington, we should have ..."

The Harbinger of War carefully laid her goods down – three beers in high frosted glasses – smiled her brilliant, white-toothed smile and said, "Bombing, of course. Americans are such pussys these days when it comes to putting boots on the ground, they think some of their people might get shot so they just bomb from above, neater, safer – unless you're on the ground! – but you know how these things are, bombs bombs bombs, just a few map co-ordinates, a grainy target and boom! Job done. Fucking senior management."

She slurped her beer, grinned, enjoying the white moustache that formed around her top lip, then turned to Robinson.

"So you're travelling with Charlie?"

"Yes. To New York."

"Seen Death yet?"

"No, ma'am."

"You will. Charlie doesn't just give lifts to people – although maybe he does – but if he was told to give you a lift, then Death told him to do it, and Death's following behind. He'll come for you when the time is right, don't you worry."

"I'm not worried, ma'am."

"Good! That's the spirit! Why fear the inevitable? *Salut*, all, *salut*!"

They drained their glasses down.

Afterwards, sitting by the river, a strange quiet after all the roads, Robinson said, "I'm sorry I called you out, when you said you were just the messenger. I'm sorry I said ... what I said. About it being crap."

"Don't worry about it."

"This job of yours. This fucking job. I think I get it. I think I get that thing you said, about life. I think it's ... I dunno, there was the KKK guy and there's kids and there's old women crying and there's the road, this long fucking road and I don't even know if I know where it's going any more and I just think ... sorry, man, I gotta say it how I find it ... I just think what kind of guy could put up with this shit?"

Charlie was silent for a long while. Planes landed and took off on the other side of the water; a couple rollerbladed by; an old man leant against the statue of a high court judge, and wondered if he'd left his keys at home.

Finally Charlie said, "I went to Mexico ..." And stopped. Then started again. "Can I tell you this? Discretion, I mean ... can I tell you?"

Sure, Robinson replied. Tell me. I wanna understand. I wanna know what it means.

I don't know if I can answer that. These questions, what is Death, people always seem to ask ... but for me, for myself ... Once I was sent to Mexico.

Chapter 92

Once ...

... it's important to be delicate about these things, like a doctor, you don't want to go discussing intimate personal details, but as you ask ...

Once the Harbinger of Death was sent to Tijuana, to give a bottle of maple syrup to a journalist working the crime desk. This was many months ago, before Nigeria, before the rats and the humans and the craters in the dust, but after the ice. A long time after the ice, Christ, that felt a long time ago, was that even Charlie who beheld a pale figure against an endless sky? He doesn't think so. Not Charlie at all.

But look, anyway, the point of all this is . . .

Charlie gave a bottle of maple syrup to this journalist, yes, and she stared in horror at first him, then the bottle, when he laid it down on her desk, before blurting, "Already? But there's so much I had to do!"

He muttered his usual generic comfort for these times – sometimes a warning, sometimes a courtesy, blah blah blah . . .

But she stopped him, mid-flow, grabbed him by the sleeve and pulled him to the longest wall in the office. There, framed in cheap plastic polished to metallic brightness, were hundreds of headline pages from the newspaper, selected for the significance or the horror of the story, stretching back over three years of labour. On the front page of every one, two recurring themes – a picture of a woman, huge round breasts thrust to the camera and a tag line inviting you to meet [cheeky/flirty/luscious/lovely/celestial/bashful/timid/fiery/sensational] [Maria/Juana/Margarita/Gabriela/Rosa/Alicia/Yolanda/etc.]

and above this, a full-page spread of corpses.

Corpses in the back of trucks, their still-open eyes staring at the camera. Corpses thrown three-deep into open pits, lit up garish white by the photographer's flashlight. Corpses carried by policemen in blue shirts; corpses in the morgue; corpses left on the side of the road; corpses on the floor of a shop; corpses with their limbs cut off, their bleeding torsos printed in full colour for all to see.

"You think you are a warning?" snapped the journalist. "My whole life is a warning, my every waking breath is a warning! Do you know how many times I have seen Death?"

(Five is the answer, but Charlie does not know this. Once on the edge of a mass grave after eleven teachers vanished; once outside the police station. Once Death sat at the back of a small huddle of migrants, starving and weary as they prepared for the desert crossing to the north; once Death helped her mother walk to church, the day the stroke happened; and once Death paraded with the street boys and the men of violence, swaggering down the middle of the street while the coppers looked on, silent and afraid, and she took Death's picture, incredulous at the arrogance of all these men who knew they owned the city and paraded with the Lady of the Night in their ranks – but the photo came out blurry, and she wondered if only she had met the eternal one's milky eye.)

Now she berated the Harbinger of Death, shouted at him like a schoolteacher, demanded to know what he was thinking and how he could be so crass, and Charlie stood, head bowed and toes pointed together, and let her shout, because he'd learnt that as the Harbinger there wasn't much point arguing back, and that it was all part of the process to let people get these things off their chests. He wasn't there to make her story about him. He knew this now. He revelled in it. It was a freedom, of a sort.

She shouted for nearly five minutes, and on the sixth minute stopped as suddenly as she had begun, aware that the whole room was staring at her and that the object of her wrath hadn't said a word, hadn't argued or tried to justify his being there, but was merely waiting patiently for more.

Instead, she grabbed him by the sleeve and dragged him from the office, and took him straight to the nearest bar and bought a bottle of tequila and said, as they got catastrophically drunk together, "I will never leave this city. I will never give up. I will never betray my country or my people. There is a fight here – a fight that must be won, and no matter what, I will win it!"

Charlie, looking up through a haze of cheap alcohol, had exclaimed, "You ... are an inspiration ... to your people!" He frowned; something about these words on his slurred tongue hadn't seemed quite right, but she was nodding forcefully along, and it did seem to him at that moment that she was truly magnificent, a goddess of truth and justice, swathed in light.

"When people go across the border," she exclaimed, "it is because they do not think things here can be made better. The schools, the medicine, the police, the corruption, always the corruption. But this is a beautiful country, there is so much promise here, we have risen up before, we the people, we will do it again, we will find our voice, we will tear down the old walls, we will build Jerusalem."

"I think ..." Charlie murmured, pushing his empty glass across the bar towards the near-empty bottle, "that might be one of the best things anyone has ever said."

And when she finally staggered home that night, someone had killed her cat and left its corpse in her bed, and the next day her boss was stabbed to death, fifty-two times the knife went in, and the killer, as they marched him off to jail, chuckled and chatted merrily with the cops who took him down, not a care in the world, and was bailed fifteen hours later, and vanished without a trace.

Twelve hours after that, the journalist left Mexico, hiding in the boot of an American friend's car as it crawled across the border, trusting to all the gods that he, being a journalist too and a holder of US citizenship, would not be searched.

And as the car cleared customs, a chauffeured car drove the other way, the passenger obscure in the back. She did not know it, but the passenger knew her, scrutinising the hot trunk where even now she cowered – and this once, having sent the Harbinger before as fair warning, Death passed her by.

She's working as a cleaner now in a New York hotel, and sometimes she is given leftover pancake after breakfast by the chef, with maple syrup on top – her favourite – but you won't find her name on the books; in fact, it's a miracle how much these big chains achieve with so few employees. She shares a flat with five others, all illegals, and the landlord accepts payment in cash, and a little bit more for keeping quiet, and on Sundays she helps do the garden for a rich lady across the river in Hoboken, who always makes her coffee and cupcakes, and who believes that immigrants bring crime – drugs and crime – to her beloved country.

One day, she will go home.

One day, she will build Jerusalem.

Not that Charlie knew this. He had delivered his message, and caught a late flight down to Mexico City to deliver good wishes and a bottle of scented oil to a former Cuban executioner, now dying in a hospital ward. "Ah," murmured the man, as Charlie sat by his bedside and listened to the whir–click of machines. "It is good that your boss remembers his own."

Then Charlie had sat and listened, temples pounding with an almighty hangover, mind lulled and hypnotised by the steady beating of the hospital equipment, as the executioner had talked of men he'd killed and things he'd seen, of the stories told in the prison yards and the crimes committed. He'd spoken softly of the dictators who had preceded Castro in Cuba, of what treachery meant, of what reason was, of the good men who'd died for their beliefs, and the bad men who'd died with just the same conviction for theirs, and of the courtesy he had always striven to uphold, courtesy, courtesy for the soon–to–be deceased, for he was the taker of lives, and after he had done his work there was no hope of redemption, no chance to be converted or see the light, but only darkness. It is not the dead who lose hope when a death sentence is passed, he breathed. No no – it is the living.

Then, on that trip to Mexico, Charlie had loved his work, for it seemed that he was a confessor to these men and women, a stranger come without judgement or agenda, to warn and to inform, a courteous listener to the stories of lives lived, lives coming to an end. Sometimes the confessional was a raging, shouting, alcohol–soaked affair; sometimes it was a quiet murmuring by a hospital bed, but always, he listened, and found in it a kind of wonder. If he had been Charlie, perhaps he would have wept, but he was not. He was the Harbinger of Death. He stood between this life and the next, and he was honoured, so honoured, that the living spoke to him at their end.

Then he left the hospital, the last person to go as visiting hours ended, and as he stood outside drawing breath, a blue van pulled up at terrific speed, and three men in white vests and bright shorts leapt out and put a knife to his throat and screamed, "Move, *move*!!" and threw him into the back of the truck with a bag over his head.

Chapter 93

Not afraid.

Funny, that.

Lying in the back of a truck in Mexico City, bag smelling of tomatoes on his head, a boot in his back, kidnapped by who knows for God knows what, Charlie wasn't frightened. He thought about being held prisoner, chained to a wall, and found the idea strangely harmless, a kind of quiet for a little while, a chance to think without the disturbance of the next flight, the hotel maid coming to clean his room, the normality of life. Sure, if it went on too long he'd probably go mad, but that was okay too, wasn't it? He thought about being ransomed, and decided that Milton Keynes would probably pay, and hoped they had insurance in place to cover the cost, and the excess wasn't too high. He thought about being killed, a bullet to the back of the head, and decided that if it came, he wouldn't look. He hoped he would live, and it seemed then that the idea he might die was so remote, so ridiculous a thing as to be strangely alien, a ghost glimpsed in the mirror, a ghost with his face, a thing he watched and that watched him back, and that was all there was to it. The living watching the dead, the dead watching the living, and he looked his ghost in the eye, and he was not afraid.

The truck jolted hard, stuck in traffic; he could hear the buzz of angry engines through the rattle of the wheels, smell the fumes coming up through the floor. Then it moved again; then it stopped, the harsh bump-bump of the endless commuter roads of the city. Someone in the middle of the road outside offered to clean the windows and the driver screamed in Spanish, "Fuck off, fuck off or I'll fucking kill you!" and the woman with the bucket and sponge snarled something about the driver's mother and a donkey, and moved on.

When the truck cleared the traffic, the driver revved the engine for all he was worth, honking and swerving along the faster roads, the centre of gravity lurching from side to side. None of the men in the back spoke, except for one, who asked once if they knew where Serge was, and the others didn't, and that was the end of the conversation.

How long had they driven, and to where? Charlie had no idea. Perhaps, if he was a more experienced kind of man, the kind of man who knew how to fire a gun or build a bomb out of glue and a tin of tomatoes, he'd have kept track of the seconds since his kidnapping, the turns of the car, orientating himself by some . . .

. . . some cunning technique . . .

. . . that he simply didn't know.

He was a stranger in a strange land, at the mercy of the strangers he met, and so far the strangers he'd met had all been kind, considerate, generous people, and tonight they'd kidnapped him at gunpoint, and all things considered, it had probably needed to happen some day.

When they stopped, they were in a residential street, somewhere that could have been anywhere. Mexico City's suburbs began and stopped, began and stopped a dozen times as the city had expanded, wiping out its new furthest border every five years until, in a very little time, outer edge was inner city, and inner city was vibrant heart, and vibrant heart was in decline as the centre of gravity swung towards another new commercial project, built on land that was once a swamp, and where the bones of the Aztecs now made for a stronger foundation bed beneath the soil.

The houses were reasonably new, blasted concrete painted the colour of cooked shrimp; tiles giving way to greedy weeds curling for the sun; graffiti sprayed across one long, flat wall, images of great green monsters leaping upon their prey, of comic-book heroes with swords longer than their flying bodies, of hands reaching upwards to a blood-red sun, fingers grey with dust and cracked with age. A zigzagging power line that swayed across the street had been tapped and re-tapped a thousand times, spider lines spinning away from it into open windows where TVs

331

played. There was no tarmac on the roads, and a shallow gutter ran away down the middle towards a square hole in the ground where one day a drain cover would be fitted. Through an open door, a woman laughed, a huge high sound like the smashing of violins, before, hysterical at a joke Charlie could not hear, her laughter dissolved into the gasping hiccups of a body too contorted with merriment to breathe.

Some of this Charlie could faintly perceive as, still with a bag over his head, he was dragged stumbling up the street. A man passing by crossed over quickly to the other side, looked away. A teenage girl, glancing out of the window, gasped, and immediately called her best friend, demanding to know what to do – she said call the police, and the girl did, but they thought she was a prankster, and no car came. Not that it would have made much of a difference if it had.

Round a corner, through an open door. A low hubbub of voices, a change in the air, heat, dryness, the sound growing of folk rock? No – listen again a little closer, and through the sound of acoustic guitar, light drum kit and electric keys:

" . . . I give myself to you, I give myself to you, you are my creator . . ."

Voices getting louder, music getting louder, the light through the bag on his head not quite right, not electric, not car headlight. A hand on an arm pulled him to a sudden stop, the bag was removed and Charlie beheld

Death.

No – not Death.

A face of white bone, no eyes, no tongue, teeth grinning wide. On her head was a hood of sky blue, ringed with little white flowers. Round her shoulders and down into her body, which was a mere four foot high, swathes of blue and pink cloth, circled over with plastic wreaths and loops of string, on which were hooked scraps of paper and gifts of money, safety-pinned peso notes and pictures of loved ones, grinning children, absent husbands, sick partners and wives waving from hospital beds. At her feet a shrine of candles, beer cans, tequila bottles and plates of rice and beans; burning incense in little black bowls, thick spliffs gently filling the room with grey–green smoke. In one hand she held the world, a plastic thing with the holes still visible where it had been removed from its frame; in the other, a gun, the barrel pointed towards the floor.

The room had perhaps once been a living room or a kitchen, a wall knocked through to make it wider, scaffold columns shoved in to support the sagging floors above. Now it could hold some forty people; some kneeling, some with hands crossed over their chests. In a corner, two old ladies and a man sat in their wheel-chairs, having been carefully positioned to get a good view. On the floor near his feet, a smear of blood. Charlie's heart climbed into his throat, and stayed there when he saw the headless chicken, its body still dribbling the last drops of life into a yellow washing-up bowl, near the door through which he'd entered. Some of the people held candles; others made do with cigarette lighters, and the light spun and spat, distorted with the moving breath of worshippers lost in their own muttered prayers, offered up to the Lady of the Night, the White Daughter, Santa Muerte herself, glory to her name.

Charlie was at the very front of the congregation. No one moved to threaten him, no one paid him much attention. If he wanted to, he could have reached out and put a finger through the empty eye of the icon in front of him. The men who'd brought him to the house were already departing, except for one, who paused to kneel and cross himself, kissing rosary beads before scurrying after. The music had changed, still twangy folk, but now with a stronger rock tempo.

"... only he make the schools, only he bring us gold, only he, only he ... "

Charlie risked a half-shuffle, a glance round at the worshippers rocking and swaying in this giddy candlelit mass. The old, the infirm, nodding along to a song only they could hear; the young, a child of five, playing with a crucifix between her fingers. Women, black leather skirts squeezed tight around their buttocks, scraps of shirt opened wide, bright lipstick, small handbags; some men too, in little cocktail dresses, high heels giving new curves to their calves, hair long, piled high, curling or permed around their heads. There, rocking on his heels, a taxi driver, and a pair there of musicians, eyes wide and pupils wider. A small gathering of street boys, white vests and low jeans, hips thrust out, faces set to glare, guns tucked proudly in their belts, a sign of identity, a sign of power, all that they were, some with eyes half closed as they whispered their prayers. A cluster of garbage collectors, the stench of their work clinging still; a policeman on his knees near the door, crying for an unknown sin, as a woman rested her hand on his shoulder to comfort him.

Here, to this shrine in the dark, came the children of the night. The dispossessed, the believers too strange for the high cathedral and stiff-necked bishops to welcome into the fold; the lovers who hid the truth of their affections; the prostitutes and the night-shift men, the women who had toiled in tasks without a name, the men who knew that no other god would answer their prayer. They all came to worship at her feet, the last saint who would love them, she who had been Mictlantecuhtli, the Skinny Lady, the Holy Girl, Death in flowers.

Charlie looked back at the image of the saint, and for a moment thought he might laugh, and heard the whispered prayers of the congregation all around, and knew he wouldn't.

Then a woman, five foot tall and nearly two foot wide, stepped between Charlie and the statue of the skull-faced woman, glaring, and there was a kitchen knife in her hand, stained with blood, and when she spoke, the room fell silent all at once, and some sank to their knees, pressing their palms against their foreheads, then their fingers against their hearts.

"Hail Mary, full of grace. The Lord is with thee. Blessed art thou amongst women, and blessed is the fruit of thy womb, Jesus. Holy Mary, mother of God, pray for us sinners, now and at the hour of our death, amen."

"Amen," whispered the room.

"Hail Holy Queen, mother of mercy, our life, our sweetness and our hope. To thee we cry, to thee we send up our sighs, mourning in this valley of tears . . . "

"Amen."

"Soul of Christ, make me holy. Body of Christ, be my salvation. Blood of Christ, let me drink your wine."

So saying, the woman removed the corpse of the chicken from the yellow wash bowl, tossing it to the side like an old tissue, lifted the bowl with one hand, put it to her lips and drank. Then she held it out to Charlie, who realised with a start that he was the only person besides her still standing at the front of the room. He shook his head, and wordlessly she held the bowl towards him again, eyes bright and dark. She wore no ceremonial robes, just a plain green T-shirt, jeans and flip-flops. He could even see the shape of a mobile phone in her pocket. She pushed the bowl towards him again, and his eyes drifted to the bloodied knife at her side. He took the bowl, closed his eyes, raised it to his lips. The blood was still at that perfect temperature where it made no impact on his sense of heat, and only when he felt a thin dribble of liquid along the line of his tongue did he realise he'd let some of it into his mouth. The urge to gag came fast and strong; he pushed the bowl back into the woman's hand to hide the sudden arching of his shoulders, the bending of his belly, and looked away. His mouth flooded with hot saliva; he washed it round his teeth, diluting the blood, and, the woman still watching, swallowed.

She nodded, satisfied, laid the bowl back down.

"*Dies irae, dies illa.*" Her voice, a strong mezzo-soprano, filling the room, a sudden power that surprised Charlie as it rose from her chest. "*Solvet saeclum in favilla . . .*"

Still standing, blood on his lips, fighting with every fibre of his being the urge to wipe his mouth clean with the back of his sleeve, Charlie felt the music enter some part of him that had long since detached itself from all other senses, a still, sacred place that now rose up to murmur at the back of his throat:

"*Mors stupebit et natura . . .*" Death is struck, and nature quaking, all creation is awaking, to its judge an answer making . . .

The woman's voice, holding him now; she seemed to sing just for him, and he wished he had something to record her

335

with, to hold this sound for ever, and then he was glad he didn't, glad that only he and she would have this moment, this song, a magical thing sung to a skull-faced saint, to a silent god, to a church that had failed, to a congregation in the dark, to him, to Death.

As she sang, he wanted to join in, add the harmony line, he could feel it within him, catching on the tune, and so he sang it in his mind, and wondered if she too heard how beautiful it was, and thought perhaps she did. Were there other churches, he wondered, where a woman could sing this song?

"*Judicandus homo reus . . .*" The guilty man who will be judged, spare him, oh God, merciful Lord Jesus, grant them rest, amen.

"Amen."

His lips shaped the word, but no sound came. Then the woman took the knife and held the tip of it against his throat, where the windpipe joined his chest, and he drew in breath, involuntary at the touch of the bloodied metal, and met her eyes and found he could not look away.

She moved the knife down, touched it to his heart, to his chest, to the base of his sternum, a cross in blood.

"In the name of the Father, the Son and the Holy Ghost . . ." she breathed, and this done, gently put one hand on Charlie's shoulder, and guided him to kneel with the rest.

There he stayed, kneeling on the floor before the statue of the skull saint, as prayers were said for a missing child, and a sermon was given on charity amongst neighbours, and songs were sung, some just the woman, some all the room.

"*My heart will fly up to Jesus,*" Charlie rasped, his singing voice gone, tongue stumbling over the sound. "*My soul will soar with the dove . . .*"

When it was done, a line of penitents came to the front of the room, knelt in a line in which Charlie found himself now the centre. The woman took the gun from the hand of Santa Muerte, and starting at the left end of the kneeling supplicants, put the barrel to the head of each man and woman in turn, and pulled the trigger.

The trigger snapped on empty, and Charlie's body jerked, though all the others remained still.

To the next praying figure the woman went, and rested the gun against his skull, and pulled the trigger, and Charlie found that there were tears brimming in his eyes and his breath was coming fast, too fast, and the woman went to the next man, and pulled the trigger, and Charlie thought that the saint was staring at him, her eyes not empty, but a living blackness, a living, spinning blackness that stared straight into his soul and saw his beginning, his ending, knew the day and the place and laughed to behold a thing he could not know.

The woman pressed the gun against the skull of the girl who knelt by Charlie's side, pulled the trigger, and the girl bowed her head in gratitude at this, and her tears were tears of joy.

The woman put the gun against Charlie's head, and there it seemed to linger a while. When she spoke, it was in English, heavily accented but clear. "And I looked, and behold a pale horse: and his name that sat on him was Death, and Hell followed with him."

She pulled the trigger.

After, a couple of people helped Charlie to his feet, the tears still rolling down his face, though he couldn't say why. They stood him by the door, and put a large green laundry bag in his arms. Then the congregants filed out, and as they went, they nodded to him and murmured a few words of thanks, and put in the bag rolls of grubby pesos wrapped in rubber bands, and cans of beer and a few bottles of tequila, and watches, ranging from a woman's watch in bright plastic pink to an underwater-safe titanium thing from off the wrist of a man with a gun. And they put in bottles of water, and pictures of loved ones, and copies of old newspapers, and a child's doll, and two men put in flick knives, and a woman put in a lock of hair wrapped in paper, and soon Charlie's arms were aching with the weight of gifts in his bag, but he held on tight until the last congregant was gone, and the house was dark, and the woman who'd led the prayer was the last to go, the headless chicken in a plastic bag at her side, her cheeks puffing as she blew the candles out, until they stood together by the glow of a cigarette lighter clutched in her fist.

She looked long and hard at the Harbinger as they stood on the porch, her head turning from one side to the other. His face was streaked with tears, his mouth stained with blood, his skin grey from grease and dirt from the bag that had been pulled over his head. The tears were still hot in his eyes, and he didn't know why, and he clutched the green laundry bag to his chest like a mother holding a newborn child.

The woman saw all of this, and seemed to approve. For the very first time, she smiled, then blew out the flame. This done, she wound the plastic bag with the chicken three times round her wrist, and walked jauntily away up the street.

Later, she plucked the chicken and fried it with white beans and tortilla chips.

Charlie stood alone, arms aching, knees sore, and wondered if there was anywhere nearby where he could get a cab.

Chapter 94

"What is time?"

"When we talk about wave-particle duality, there is a fundamental misconception in how we define these concepts ..."

"Positive attracts negative, yes, but how? And don't tell me electromagnetism, what does that even fucking mean?"

"The model holds so long as ninety per cent of the mass in the universe is invisible to us."

"Personalised medicine is the future, but the latest DNA testing technology seems only to make people worried for their health ..."

"Why has Daddy gone away?"

"So you're saying if you're not baptised . . . but then what about people who never even heard of Christianity?"

"Imagine a swan taking flight through your third eye . . . "

"I suspect we'll find out that it's merely an extension of the strong nuclear force, once we've got the tools to examine it more closely."

"If God is all-merciful, why would he let this happen?"

"I saw it! I saw the atom! It looked sorta flooshy."

"Last year I had a heart attack, and I nearly died. This year I finally made peace with my son, and moved to Portugal to be nearer to him. I can't fucking believe it took a triple bypass and two hours of CPR for me to get my fucking head straight."

"Why'd we jump? For the fall. Dude, always, obviously – for the fall."

Chapter 95

Prayer to Nina Blancha, Lady Death

Lady Death, right hand of God
Commander of the seven angels
Mistress of the four elements
She who knows the secrets of every heart
You who laid with me in the crib
Pressed your finger to seal my lips
You who carried me through danger
Put the gun in my hand
Called me man
Our lady Death, lady of the white robes
Lady of the silver sword
Pluck a grey hair from my head
Pull the skin softly from my eyes

Let the blood run thin in my chest
All this is yours, as was promised
Only spare my child a little while more.

Chapter 96

The road, heading north.

Charlie wakes, and knows that this is the last time he will travel this road, and that is good, and he is at peace.

Baltimore.

"Black power!" shouts the woman.

Charlie says, "Excuse me, I have——"

"*Black power!*" she roars, turning the loudhailer towards Charlie's face so that the noise of it pops in his ear. He struggles to keep up as they march, a group of maybe thirty strong, she in the middle, crop top and skinny jeans, hoop earrings and green eye shadow, roaring, "*Black power!*"

"Ma'am, I was sent to give you——"

"*I don't care what you were sent to give me!*" blaring down the loudhailer again, forcing him to flinch. "*I don't want nothing from you white trash! Get out of my way, and get off my streets! Black power!*"

In the end, he gives it to the much more pleasant man who walks three steps behind, and who promises he'll pass it on. It's a soldering iron. Charlie doesn't speculate as to what it means.

"You saw the marchers?" A white woman, clutching to her a curly-haired daughter with almond skin. Two others from the march, dark skin, bright clothes, faces ashamed, comforting her. "I tried to walk with them, to show solidarity, show my child that she can be mixed race and still part of this, that all races are equal and together we are something good. But that woman – the

340

one with the loudspeaker – she just shouted at me till we went away. How can I teach my daughter that we're all human if that's how people behave?"

In the distance: drumming, and the sound of voices, amplified.

Charlie gave the woman a hug, and the child too, and said, "The world will change. Just you wait. The world is always changing."

In Philadelphia, a mother holds her teenage daughter as she cries.

"I can do all the moves, I did a perfect splits and a perfect double backflip and I can do the lifts and I can do . . . "

She pauses in her recitation to blow her nose in a snotty handkerchief.

"Sweetie, maybe it was just the competition, maybe next year . . . "

"No, Mom! Next year I'll be too old, they'll never have me, this was my only chance to make the team!"

A pair of sparkling blue pompoms lie by her side. Her bright red hair is tied up in a bun behind her skull, her pink crop top clings tightly to her toned belly and breasts.

"It's my thighs. I know it – and you know it too! It's my thighs, they look fat, he practically said it, the others, some of them, they've had surgery and it's just changed everything, you can see it when they do the kicks, but I'm fat. My thighs are fat, my butt is fat, but what else am I supposed to do? That's just who I am!"

Her mother gives her another tissue.

Charlie gives her a stethoscope.

New Jersey.

"Dilute it a thousand times, that's still a very strong solution for us, very strong, so we then dilute again and at this point the water is remembering the herb, it's remembering the potency of that initial ingredient and this is good for indigestion, but also for colon cancer . . . "

Charlie listened to her talk, and when the lesson was done, he stayed behind in her clinic, the walls covered with boxes of herbs and images of the human body, divided by energy and chakra and a dozen other things he couldn't name.

"You're ... the Harbinger of Death? But I ... I feel fine."

Charlie smiled, and gave her a copy of her own business card, much travelled, well thumbed, now returned at last.

"What is this?" she demanded, fingers trembling as she turned it over in her hand. "What is this?"

Charlie walked away.

"*What is this?*" she screamed after him, face opening like a cave. "*What is this?!*"

At the hotel, two policemen were waiting.

They showed no interest in Robinson, but asked to see Charlie's passport, his entry visa, proof of where he was going, where he'd stay.

One said: "What you do is disgusting. What you do isn't right."

Charlie didn't answer.

The other said: "There's no point talking to him. He's not even fucking human."

Charlie looked away, and that night, not even painkillers could dull the throbbing in his head.

They drove north.

Chapter 97

New York came upon them slowly, peeking round New Jersey's towers before finally blooming onto the horizon between the smoking chimney stacks and low industrial fog.

They dropped the car off at Newark airport. Robinson's rocking chair was still in the back. The two men stared at it, awkward in the car park.

"Could take it on the train," suggested Charlie wanly.

Robinson didn't grace the suggestion with so much as a dry look.

"Call your brother, maybe see if . . . ?"

Robinson shook his head.

"We can't just leave it, I mean, the car is . . ." Charlie gestured, futile, round the kerosene-scented tarmac.

"I'll see if the boys in the hire shop want it," Robinson said at last, and marched into the office.

A few minutes he came out, a young man in a suit in tow. For a little while they argued at the back of the car, soft and cordial, before the man hefted the rocking chair out, and took it with him back into the office.

Now they were just two men with suitcases.

After a little while Charlie said, "Let's see if we can find a train."

Robinson hesitated, then followed.

The train clattered and screeched towards Manhattan. Charlie bought Robinson's train ticket. It would have been rude to abandon him in Newark. The rolling stock felt old, on the verge of cracking apart, but it ran, and when they emerged at Penn, the roar of the city and the pace of the people flooding by hit Charlie like a padded punch to the face.

Robinson stared up, craning his neck towards the tops of the buildings, as the traffic honked and the taxis blared and the people marched and shoved their way into the subway, and Charlie let out a sigh of relief, feeling, perhaps, a little closer to home.

"Well," he said, at last. "Here we are."

"I guess so."

"You gonna be okay?"

"Yeah." Robinson let out a long, steadying sigh. "Yeah, I reckon . . . new life, new start. New . . . everything, I guess. I'll build again, I'll make something new, I reckon . . . This is a good place to begin, you know?"

"You've got my number, if anything . . ."

"Thanks, man, I appreciate it. But seriously, I got a good feeling, I got ... You know when you can smell that dream? I know it's New York, everyone always feels that way in the Big Apple, but me ... I smell it. I think your boss, I think when he comes, he'll be coming to kill the old me, the guy down in Florida, an' sure, he worked hard, but he'll be dead and I'll still be livin' and that's for the best, I think. I think ... that's for the best."

"Goodbye, Robinson," said Charlie, holding out his hand.

"Goodbye, Charlie. Thanks for the ride."

A moment, then they turned and went their separate ways.

Visits in New York.

An ancient old man, his head twisted to one side, who says, through a machine, "They said I would die forty years ago but still I lived. I lived and now I will finally die but in living I proved them all wrong."

He will not fear Death, when Death comes, but will smile proudly into the eyes of a long-time-coming friend.

A cop, pacing up and down, one hand on his gun.

"I felt it coming a long time now, a long time coming I've been feeling it, my end, the end, it's coming, always it's coming, I know that, I've always been ... "

Charlie gives him a stress-busting candles and aromatherapy set.

"What the fuck is this?"

"I think there might also be a CD at the bottom with the sounds of nature."

The cop throws him out for taking the piss.

A different cop, staring at him too long and too hard as he rode the subway back to the hotel.

A guy in a black suit who he thought he'd seen before, walking along 33rd Street.

He ate pizza in Harlem with an old woman. "It's all changing," she tutted, gesturing at the street. "It's all changing, gentrifying, that's what they call it, gentrification, when I was a kid it weren't nothing like this . . . "

He listened to jazz in Washington Square.

"For the first time ever, from Cuba, on the trumpet . . . !"

Three hours passed beneath the shade of the trees, playing pigeon-poo bingo on the benches along the paths, and he listened to music, and hadn't noticed the sun move.

He wondered where Robinson was, thought of calling him, having a drink.

Decided against it. There was still an appointment waiting for Robinson, and Charlie wasn't sure it was his place to interfere.

From an internet café off 44th Street, he called Emmi.

The first time, he didn't get through.

He went back later that afternoon, bought frozen yoghurt, tried again.

This time, when the call connected, he nearly wept with relief.

"Charlie?" Tired, late at night for her. "Charlie, where are you?"

"New York. I'm coming home soon, my flight is booked for tomorrow."

"I missed you."

"I missed you . . . so much."

Trying to hide the sound of salt on his face, what the hell is this? He hasn't been gone so long, he's always travelled alone, why is he crying to hear her voice, what the hell has happened?

"How's America?"

"Good. Tiring. Good."

"You meet anyone interesting – I suppose you can't talk about it."

"No, no, it's . . . it's fine. I met a lot of people, some really good people, really interesting, really . . . really kind. Also met a leader of the KKK . . . "

"You're kidding me."

"Seriously."

"Is he dying?"

"I think . . . maybe yes."

"I . . . don't know how I feel about that."

"Death is always sad," he replied, faster than he realised. "Sometimes life is sad too."

"Charlie?"

"Yes?"

"You okay? You sound . . . "

"I'm just tired. Really, really tired."

"I've talked to you when you're just tired, you sound . . . "

"I'm fine. I'm fine. I'll see you very soon."

"Okay then."

"I . . . I'll call when I get back."

"Good. Let me know what time your flight's due in."

"I will. I love you. Bye."

"Bye. I love you too."

He didn't hang up, and neither did she, and for five, ten seconds, the line remained open, before, awkward in the silence, he ended the call.

He walked through Central Park, because it was there.

In a wide space of open grass, six hundred people were doing a yoga session. The speakers, relaying the instructions from their leader to the rest of the crowd, were badly set up. The sound from the first arrived a microsecond after the sound from the second, which arrived a microsecond after the sound from the third, creating an echo that rippled down the field and made it hard to hear much of anything at all.

He walked around the reservoir, watching the reflected city in the water.

At the top of a mound clustered with dry, drooping trees, a tall, pale man with a shaved head in orange robes was practising hitting the air with a quarterstaff. Another man, tanned skin, gym-built arms, watched hypnotised before finally walking up and asking if he could join in.

The taller man smiled patiently, said, sure, why not, and proceeded to execute wrist locks, armlocks, takedowns, to kick out his leg and hurl him from the hip and shoulder to the ground, twisting bone and muscle until the man cried out in pain, at which point he let go.

Having been released from agony, the man bounced back up to his feet and exclaimed, *that was totally awesome* let's do it again!

They did it again.

At the end, the man in orange gave the stranger his staff and said, "Jump over my staff."

"Uh ... "

"Hold the staff in both your hands, and do a tuck jump over it."

"Oh I don't think I ... "

"If you believe you can do it, you will."

The man nodded, took a long, deep breath, held the staff in both hands. He tucked his knees to his chest, leaping as high as he could, swung the staff beneath his buttocks, caught one foot on the passing wood and fell over backwards, groaning on the grass.

Half a mile further down, a Jedi knight swung plastic light sabres patiently at the air, while a small crowd watched but didn't get involved.

"It's a martial art," he explained, when Charlie asked. "I am learning the ways of the Force."

"Are you ... an actor?"

The Jedi stared at him, patient, frustrated, already bored. "It's a martial art," he repeated. "I am learning the ways of the Force."

A TV studio.

Bright lights, security checks on the door – no guns beyond this point. Three cameras, raked audience seating, a long curved desk, a comfortable couch for guests to sit on, bottled water and tall, sturdy glasses. Security men around the edge of the stage; a background composited from various city skylines, meshed together into a neon glare.

He saw Patrick a second before Patrick saw him.

"Why are you ... ?"

"I was invited," Patrick replied, clean and bright. "And I know the host."

"You do?"

"Yes. She interviewed me once, a few years ago. About a project I was part of."

"I didn't realise you were famous."

"Expert," he replied, with a flash of a smile. "Not famous. Sit with me."

Charlie sat with him, as the lights went down.

The host: bright dyed hair, straight teeth, brown eyes, dazzling smile, charming, funny, her long, thin legs visible beneath the structure of the desk, her speciality the open question: "And how did that make you feel?"

First guest: sports personality.

"Yeah, like, it's been like, a real good season, yeah, and like, I think if we like, do better next season then it'll be really great."

Second guest: minor politician.

"The problem with the schools – now let me finish – I'll tell you the problem with the schools, people always get this wrong, always, they always think – I'll tell *you* . . ."

Third and fourth guests: a wannabe Senator and a scientist.

"Climate change is hokum," exclaimed the wannabe, tilting her head back in derision at the thought. "It's just left-wing hokum, the scientists don't agree, they don't get it right, the last few years the world's got colder."

"Actually," murmured the scientist, early fifties, polite, badly dressed, awkwardly shiny in poor make-up, "I think you'll find that—"

"You know what it is? It's an attempt by the rest of the world to stop America reaching its full economic potential, that's all it is, it's an attempt to . . ."

Charlie's head, aching. He leant forward to press his fingers into his skull, to drown out the drumming.

Tick tick tick tick . . .

"If you have evidence for that . . ."

"Evidence, I don't need evidence, I've got my eyes, I've got my common sense, when did ordinary Americans give up on believing in themselves, that's what I want to know, when did . . ."

"But if you look at the data . . . "

"Scientists just try to blind us, they just try and confuse us with their long words . . . "

Tick tick tick tick . . .

"The shrinkage of the ice caps . . . "

"And even if it is real, even if it's happening, I say, so what! I wanna grow grapes in Maine, I think it sounds amazing, less winter, yes please . . . "

In a land of ice . . .

. . . in a land where no trees grow . . .

Charlie must have grunted, because Patrick was now looking at him, leaning over, whispering in his ear, you okay, you okay?

The scientist, getting flustered. "I don't see how you can reasonably state—"

"Look, you're just one guy, I'm just one woman, but I'm speaking about what people want, not about some hypothetical model that you people can't even get right. I mean, wake up and smell the gravy, it's time to get real about . . . "

Tick tick TICK TICK TICK TICK.

"Professor Absalonoftsen went onto the ice, now listen to me, he went onto the ice and he never came back and that was—"

"Why should I sacrifice my lifestyle? Why should I be forced to make these choices? I know who I am, I know how I live, I know what my values are and you . . . "

"Will you let me speak?!"

" . . . come here telling me what to do with my life? I mean screw that, screw that, it's just a load of nonsense it's just—"

"Let me speak, you ignorant, stupid woman!"

The scientist's scream, loud enough to cut through the room, caught somewhere between rage and tears.

Silence.

The host, who had let it run, loved to let it run, revelled in it, cleared her throat. "Okay, guys," she breathed. "I think it's time to just calm it down and . . . "

"Did he just call me that?" whispered the woman, eyes wide, face white. "Did you just hear what he said, did you hear, I want

349

an apology, I demand an apology, that was just ... Are you a misogynist, are you a bigot, did you just hear what he ... "

Charlie was aware that there was a security guard next to him now, and an assistant with a headset on, helping him to the door. Patrick followed, as they led him into a backstage room, white light and a couch, a storage cupboard converted for first aid, how prescient, Charlie thought, how thoroughly well thought through.

They sat him on a couch, and the woman with the headset said she was a first aider, and was he diabetic? No. Epileptic? No. Did he have pain in his chest? No. Did he get migraines?

... yes. Maybe that was it.

She looked relieved. Her first aid course hadn't had much to say beyond these basic questions, and it was good that of all the answers, his took the problem largely out of her hands.

Patrick sat by Charlie's side as Charlie drank a cup of water, and said, "You're not okay."

"I'm ... just over-tired."

"Charlie. I've seen you on the ice. I saw you in Lagos. I see you now. What's happened to you?"

"I ... I think I've seen ... There's this sound in my head, this ... I walk and sometimes I hear ... I hear people talking, I hear the world talking and it's ... I'm fine. I'm fine. Thank you, I appreciate this, I appreciate you ... I'm fine."

"You're not fine."

"I'm fine."

"I didn't come to New York to see you die. That's not the world I want to end."

"What is it, then?" he breathed. "What world are you here to see die? Which world are you making today?"

Patrick thought about it a while, then said, "I think ... I think I am looking for a world without fear. I think the ice is melting, and the old gives way to the new, and in America they shout and argue and scream at each other over the airwaves, and when it's all done, when the world has turned and we have made something new, I think it will be ... maybe not better ... but I think

350

it will be honest. I think we will be honestly who we are. Who we are now. Death said that a world was ending ... and with that world, a way of life dies, and a way of being dies with it, and I think when it is done that this new world ... it will be better. I know you don't think so, but it will be ... I am looking forward to living in it. I am honoured to see it grow."

Charlie shook his head. "I've gotta get out of here," he growled, dropping unsteady to the floor, finding his feet. "I've gotta ... I have a job to do ... "

"Don't be ridiculous. Even the Harbinger of Death needs a break."

"No, I've ... The job is more than a job, it's ... There's a bridge, there's a goodness, there is ... I've got to ... " He staggered, and nearly fell. Patrick caught him under the arm, held him up.

"You're a bloody idiot," he muttered. "Where do you need to go?"

He helped Charlie wobble to the backstage dressing rooms. Corridors packed with clothes and props, busy men and women with tools and radios, a buzz of noise, the sound of applause from the studio, muffled by bricks. Charlie asked for a name, explained his purpose, was directed to a door.

Knocked once, twice.

After a moment, the door was answered.

The scientist, his tie ripped from his throat, his face contracted and pale, stood in the doorway.

"What do you want?" he spat, hands shaking by his sides, knees knocking in his trousers, breath fast and hard.

"I am the Harbinger of Death," Charlie replied, leaning hard against the wall, as Patrick watched. "I was sent to give you this ... "

He handed over a small cardboard box. Slowly, the box wobbling in his jelly-fingered grip, the scientist took it. Opened it up.

A tie, blue and purple, lay inside. He lifted it slowly on one finger, holding it in front of his now-bare neck. Tears began to well in his eyes, and quickly, he put it back in the box, held the box close to his chest.

"I . . . " he began, and then looked down, liquid curling round the lines of his cheeks. "I . . . I fucked up totally, didn't I?"

Charlie didn't reply.

He raised his head now, faster, staring hard, first at Charlie, then at Patrick, and seeing nothing in Patrick's face, looked back at Charlie, grabbed his hand, held it tight, bent in to hiss in his ear. "*Reason is dead*. Reason is dead. We killed it, and reason is dead."

So saying, he let go, and holding the tie box against his heart, stepped back inside the dressing room, and slammed the door shut.

Patrick gave Charlie a lift back to his hotel.

How had it got this late?

"Can't I take you to a doctor?" he asked, as Charlie got out of the car.

"No. Thank you. I feel okay."

"You've got my number."

"Thank you. For . . . for tonight. I appreciate it. Thank you."

"Call me. I mean it. And get some rest."

So saying, Patrick gestured to his driver, wound the window up, and the car drove on.

On a scale of one to five . . .

That's meaningless.

On a scale of one to five . . . sleeping well?

No.

Eating well?

No.

Do you feel sad in the day?

Yes.

Are you worried a lot of the time?

Yes.

Why?

Dying.

Dying?

All of it.

All of what?

All of it. It's the end of a world. It's the end of a world.

Are you listening to me?

Are you there?

Can you see?

It's the end of the world.

Charlie, tired, dishevelled. Been a while since he last shaved, must have not noticed, didn't really care. Slipped his keycard into the door of his room. Door unlocked. Stepped inside. Keycard into the holder inside the door that turned the electricity on.

Lights snapped up around the bed, drowning out the glow of the city through net curtains. The air conditioning whooshed, his eyes prickling in the sudden dry air. Went to the bathroom, had a piss, washed his face, stared in the mirror, wasn't sure he knew the face that stared back. Walked to the bed, lay down, fully dressed, thought about turning the TV on, didn't move.

Didn't move.

Didn't move.

Voice outside, distracting. Rolled onto one side, reaching for his phone, and over-reached, pushing it to the floor. Flopped onto his belly, crawled to the edge of the bed, fumbled around in the carpet to pick it up. As he rose, someone knocked on the door. He staggered out of bed, still holding his phone, and answered it.

Three men stood outside. They wore white shirts, black trousers, leather shoes.

One said, "Mr Harbinger of Death?"

Charlie replied, shouted, nearly screamed it, "*My name is . . .*"

The man who'd spoken drove a syringe, thin and white, into the side of Charlie's neck, and caught him as he fell.

Chapter 98

"There is a curfew on the apartment, so if I'm not back by ten p.m. I can get locked out, and I want to know how is that safer for women, how does that make me safe. I am being imprisoned and they say it is for my own protection . . . ?"

"I have always loved the BBC, but I cannot support an organisation that has biased its every guest towards big business and right-wing commentary, instead of offering a balanced, expert view . . ."

"Some people are better off dead."

"Oh my God, so this handbag, it's just the most perfect and I was like, I need to have it and she was like, sweetie, you just got one but I was like, you don't understand, you don't understand, I *need* . . ."

"People are dumb. You wanna get ahead in advertising? I'll tell you the secret: *people are dumb*."

"The bubble will burst, just you wait, it always does."

"I don't think the internet's changed all that much, really."

"So I'll have the katsu, with extra chilli flakes and some . . ."

"The problem is that it may not be accessible for all our readers, and we really think that with a little work you could make more people feel more comfortable with . . ."

"Boom bust boom bust boom bust . . ."

Tick tick tick tick tick . . .

" . . . eighty per cent of my time answering emails and I'm like, what even is this shit and then I don't read it 'cos I've got better stuff to do and then everyone's like, 'but I sent an email', I mean *shit* . . ."

"If you've been affected by any of the issues raised, then please . . ."

"I left her, because with her, I wasn't really me."

/*your comments here*/

Chapter 99

The sun rises, and Death comes to Manhattan.

Death has been here many, many times before.

In the good old days, she came with her brothers and sisters. Pestilence and Famine have always had a soft spot for crowded places, and War loves the music of the marching band more than any song.

"Parp parp parp, parp parp-te-parp!" hooted War, as they watched the boys march by.

"You're embarrassing yourself," Pestilence muttered, stretching out her dull, aching bones.

Let it play, Death replied, as the ticker tape fell. Let it play.

That was long ago, and since then even Famine has moved with the times, and sits in board meetings and says things like, "It's not about the quantity; it's about the method of distribution."

Death has moved with the times too. Witness her choice of Harbinger. Once – once she chose her Harbingers to strike terror into the hearts of men, once they were demagogues who raged against the rising sun, who walked through fields ploughed with salt and shook their fists at the raven and the moon . . .

. . . but now.

Now Death comes to Manhattan, and she stays in a four-star hotel off the Avenue of the Americas, and will be taking advantage of the complimentary face mask treatment, thank you, because who wouldn't really, if given the chance?

Times being what they are?

In Harlem.

"I knew you'd come," whispered the old woman. "When I'm gone, no one will remember how this street was, before the world changed."

I remember, Death replied, as the woman's eyes slipped shut.
I always remember these things.

At the precinct.

"I shot him," whispered the cop. "I shot him. I was so fucking
scared. I was so fucking scared and he was just a kid and I shot
him. Jesus. Oh Jesus."

He didn't just shoot the kid – he shot him three times in the
head, five times in the chest, then switched rounds and shot him
another three times in the chest and twice in the leg, before his
colleagues managed to restrain him. The boy was trying to pull
out his wallet with some ID. He was drunk; he didn't really
understand what was happening.

Death holds the boy's mother as she cries. Death walks with
the funeral procession on a day too bright, too blue for a child's
mourning. Death sits with the policeman as his world falls apart.
You've been so scared for so long, she breathes. You've been so
frightened of me your whole life. Now we're here, you don't have
to be scared any more.

At the nursing home.

"Doctor said I would see you when I was just a young man.
But they were wrong and I lived. I have been stuck in this chair
and I have not used my hands for so many years but I lived. I
lived."

Death kissed the man on the forehead. You lived, he replied.
And you were wonderful.

At the university.

"Professor, will you apologise for the remarks you made on
the show, will you resign, what do you say to the threats of legal
action against . . . "

The scientist, slamming the door shut, cutting out the noise,
pressing his back against the wood, dragging in breath.

Death waited on the other side of the room, one leg slung
across his desk, the other perching on the floor.

For a while, the two faced each other, the scholar and the end, until at last the scientist said, "Reason is dead."

Death shrugged.

"Was there ever a time when to be human meant we valued these things? When the height of humanity was invested in these attributes – logic, thought, reason, enlightenment, the betterment of society, the good of the whole, the . . . " He stopped, half choking on the words, then took a deep breath, and tried again. "As a boy, I grew up in a time of invention, of aspiration and wonderful dreams, and to be a scientist, a doctor, an engineer – these things were considered the greatest paths man could take. We walked on the moon and the world as a collective creature breathed a sigh of wonderment and delight, one species, one dream, a dream of . . . or did I imagine it? Was I in fact living in a fantasy, in which I saw only what I wanted to see? Have I made the past something romantic, and in fact it's always been this, we've always been this species, and everything I believed, I believed to make myself feel better? I made this dream of reason my form of God? Is that the truth?"

Death didn't answer.

The man staggered towards him, until they were just a few feet apart, stared deeply into Death's eyes, saw a thing he could not look at, shuddered and turned away.

His hand, on the desk, knocked something in a small cardboard box. He hesitated, then picked it up, opened it.

Inside, a garish blue and purple tie.

He lifted it up, turned it this way and that, feeling the silk, watching the light play on the colour. Then slowly, he flicked his collar up, threaded the tie through the cotton, and began to tie the knot.

Death watched him.

When the last loop was tight, he stood stiffly to attention, shoulders back, chin level, and said, "Reason is not dead. Not while I fight for it."

Death smiled, slipped down from the desk, and without another word, passed on by.

*

One last call, before her work is done.

She finds Robinson on her third day, sitting in the sculpture garden of the Cathedral Church of St John the Divine.

Inside, prayers written on pieces of card: *We pray for social equality. We pray not to judge people by their skin, creed or colour. We pray that we might respect all people, whatever their sexual choices* . . .

Candles burn, and a haze machine pumps thin mist into the high, high ceilings of the place, so that it seems that shafts of light are spearing the vaults of heaven, and Robinson sits outside. He smells of sweat and the street, of dirt and the corners of doors. He smells of rotten cheese, and when he leaves a shop, having begged for a drink, a bite to eat, his stench lingers after him, like dust in the air.

In these few days, his beard has grown and his body has shrivelled, and he sits now, knees curled to his chest, holding his suitcase, scuffed, the top bent by the weight of his head where it has been his pillow.

Death sits down next to him, and Robinson raises his head, slowly, so slowly, to see her at last.

He smiles, teeth furry and aching. "Wondered where you were," he breathed. "Wondered when you'd come."

Wordlessly, Death held out the packet of peanuts that she'd been munching, and with shaking hands Robinson took the proffered plastic, tipped a few nuts into the dirty palm of his hand, and began to eat, one at a time, popping each salty treat onto his tongue and chewing as if it was medicine.

"Brother's business failed. Few years back, never told anyone. Too ashamed. I didn't tell him neither what had happened to me. Think he saw that I was ashamed too. He does construction now. Works on the sites. Don't think he's any good, but he knows a few people, gets shifts where he can. Who'd have thought it'd fail, business like that, men always need tools, always, it's how you know you're doing something right, being a man, making something and . . . anyway. It went down. I was close to paying off the debt, back in Florida, back south. I was down to twenty-four thousand dollars. Twenty-four thousand! I was at eighty five years ago, if they'd just waited, if they'd just given me a chance ... but that was on top of the mortgage, I guess, so ... When you're poor, banks don't lend. Poor people ain't as safe a bet as rich ones, so if they do lend, the rates, well they're more than your projected profit so you can't start nothing new, not on rates like that, so you have to go to someone ... different. More flexible. I shouldn't have, but it were the only way I knew to make it so that ...

"... anyway. I guess you know all this, don't you?"

Death offered him a slurp from her bottle of water, to wash the salt down. He drank, deeper than he'd meant, nearly choking on the clear, cool fluid. Wiped his mouth with the back of his hand, shifted his position a little, shoulders back, staring at the sky.

"How's Charlie doing?" he asked at last. "I really liked Charlie, by the end."

I haven't heard from him for a little while.

"He's a good guy."

Yes. He is.

"I appreciated the lift. For all that ... I appreciated the lift."

You're welcome.

"Am I gonna die?"

No. Not today.

"But ... why are you here?"

Death sighed, creaking her head from side to side, working out an old ache. What did Charlie tell you?

"That everybody dies. That everybody sees death, but the looking is all." He thought about it a little longer, then added, "That sometimes you come for ideas, as well as people."

Silence a little while. Then Death said, There is this dream, in America. There is this wonderful dream. I remember when I first understood it, it was so incredible, I nearly wept, and I am not renowned for my sentimentality. It said that if you worked, and if you cared, and if you believed in yourself, you could do anything. There was no bar to the potential or the achievement of man, there was nothing that stood between him and fulfilling his every aspiration.

I went to Georgia and I held the hand of an old woman, and she died so proudly because her granddaughter is learning how to work in new technologies, and will not live the life that she lived or be what she was, and she was laughing, at the end. She was laughing with joy to think of it, even as her heart stopped. This dream. Who knows what the daughter will be, but this dream, it surrounds her in a halo of light. In North Carolina a woman made her world, and having made her world she made this world a better place, and when she died she spoke of the future, even though her life was gone, but always, still, the future.

I am with a man now who rides his last storm, we will meet in the eye and he will rejoice in all that he has done, and it was mighty, and he is beautiful. All those who now I touch, they are so beautiful, and so many of them are lifted up and given light by this dream. This incredible dream. It is a dream of freedom, and like a flag, freedom has many meanings. The dream is in the hands of the men who buy assault rifles from their local store; it is in the eyes of the surfers as they ride before the wave. It is on the tongues of the men who run beneath the monuments in Washington; it is in the prayers of the churchgoers of this cathedral; it is in the eyes of the child who learns to read, in the whispers of the father watching his son grow up. It is a dream worth honouring. It is a dream that is most fit for the living.

Robinson nodded, holding his suitcase tight, and didn't meet Death's eye.

"I got nowhere to go," he said at last.

I know.

"I got nothing. No money. Don't know anyone here. No bank will respect my name, I ain't got no security, no healthcare. Last night some dude pissed on me, 'cos I was there and he felt like it. He pissed on me like I was nothing, like I were . . . "

A rat?

Words failing, Robinson nodded.

Death waited until the man's tongue could speak again.

"I believe in that dream," he whispered. "I believe in it. I believe in the potential of every man, woman and child. I believe that we can all make something of ourselves, that the world is there waiting to be ... waiting to be seized and that ... that ..." His words faded away again. He looked down, at dirt.

Death waited.

"I ... I just need a helping hand," he whispered at last. "I just ... I just need someone to see me, waiting here. That's all I need, and then I'll rebuild again. I swear to you, I'll rebuild, I just need someone to see!"

Death smiled, put her hand on his shoulder, squeezed it tight. Good luck, Robinson, she said, and stood up to go.

He scrambled to his feet after her, uneasy, reaching out. "No! Wait! Please – don't leave me!"

Death shook her head, perhaps a little sadly, and walked away, and didn't look back.

Robinson stayed standing there, alone, as Death moved on, and the world passed him by.

Chapter 100

"The problem with the French ..."
   "The problem with the Jews."
   "I don't have anything against Muslims, I'm just saying ..."
   "Ha, the Welsh! Best punchline ever to ..."
   "日本人, 他们不好人, 他们不好 ..."
humanhumanhuman
   "Defend the Russian people!"
   "Sunnis aren't like Shias in that ..."
Ticktickticktick
   "The clock now stands at ..."
   "Not my fucking problem."
   "Well the Germans, if you have to trust a German!"
humanratrathuman

361

"If that's what the Greeks want then it's their economy."

"Nationalists today . . . "

"Freedom fighters!"

humanratratratrat

"All we want is security."

"All we want is peace."

"All we want is food."

RATRATRATRATRAT

"All we want is a better world for our children."

Tick.

Tick.

Tick.

Tick.

Chapter 101

Charlie woke in a box.

Knees to chin, one arm pressed beneath his body, the other wrapped around his chest, neck bent, feet against the wall, lying on his side. He opened his eyes and saw wall, he moved his knees and felt wall, he shifted his aching back and hit wall, he opened his mouth and thought for a moment he might scream, but instead, without bidding, an animal sound, a trapped, shouted gasp came from his lungs and he pressed with the palms of his hands against the walls of the box and shook from side to side, and thought for a moment that the box might tumble.

It didn't.

He called out for help, and no one came.

He begged for someone to let him out, and no one came.

He cried for a little bit, and then shouted some more, and then cried again, and no one came.

He lay burning, sweating, gasping for breath, a foetus in a wooden box, and wondered if this was how Death came, and if his shadow was catching up with him at last.

He couldn't breathe, and knew that would mean he would die.

He didn't die.

He wept.

He had no more tears.

No one came.

He waited.

Tick.

Tick.

Tick.

Tick.

The box was flung onto its side and he rolled with it, banging his head; the top was pulled off, bright white light flooding in; he was lifted bodily out by his armpits, then dropped on the ground, grovelling with relief and gratitude, only for more hands to grab him by the arms and pull him to his feet. A bag was put over his head, his hands were cuffed behind his back, dogs growled and barked, he felt them press against his legs and cried out in new fear even as the blood rushed back to his toes. He fell, staggered, was pushed onto a chair, someone hit him round the side of the head, why, there wasn't any reason for it, then hands straightened him up, the bag was removed, a light, brilliant white, hurting his eyes, a face in it, hard to see features, big face, he thought, huge face, roaring, spitting in his own.

"*What is Death?!*"

Gasping, dizzy, bewildered, he reeled away from the breath, stinking of mint, from the voice, loud enough to make his ears pop, from the light, and blinking tears from his eyes whispered, "W . . . what?"

A hand — not that of the man in front of him — slapped him, puppy-like, round the back of the head again. The man in front of him caught him by the chin, great fingers creasing and stretching his flesh, roared, *"WHAT? IS? DEATH?!"* and shook him like a glow stick.

"I don't know what you mean!"

Again they hit him, harder now, knocking him sideways. Picked him back up.

"You are in the shit, there's no way out of here, do you understand that, there's no way out, no one is coming, no one knows where you are, so you tell me, you tell me, what is Death?"

"Death is Death! Death is Death, it's just . . . "

This time, the slap was a fist. He fell off the chair, and again they picked him up, and hit him, and again he fell and was picked up, he didn't understand that at all, what was the point of it? Why not just leave him on the floor?

"Why is Death?" hissed the man, turning Charlie's face so his mouth was right against his ear, so close he thought he could feel teeth nipping at the flesh. "Why is Death?"

"Why is Death what? Here? Death is everywhere, Death is . . . "

This time, when they hit him, they let him stay down, which seemed to make sense, and kicked him, which made none at all.

He lay hoping that if he curled up around the pain, the posture would swallow sound too, rolling into his knees, pressing his head down, feet twisting as if he could push the fear and agony out of the soles of his feet by will alone.

The man with the big hands pulled him up by the hair. "What is Death?"

Hit him.

"What is Death?"

Hit him.

"What is Death?"

Hit him.

By the time he blacked out, his mouth was so swollen, he didn't think he could have answered anyway.

A white room.

Too white, too bright.

Padded walls.

The light came on and burned, and with it came sirens, roaring, the sounds of screaming, blasting through his brain.

Then off.

Silence.

All silence.

Darkness, complete, nothing, no way to know where up was, or down, or where the world began or ended in this infinite void.

Then light again.

Then dark.

For a while, Charlie lay on the ground with his hands over his ears, but in time they fell away, and the screaming was just sound without meaning.

He closed his eyes, and in the darkness someone came through the door and threw iced water on his head, and he tried to sleep with his eyes open, and couldn't.

An eternity.

They put him back on the chair.

Softer now, the man with the great round face – Charlie decided to call him Bubbles, found the idea funny for all of a microsecond – leaning back against his chair, framed in the light, chewing gum.

"What is Death?" he asked, and when Charlie didn't answer, someone else hit him. They didn't need to hit very hard now – you could shove your thumb into any number of soft places on Charlie's skin and the agony would send him to the floor.

"What is Death?"

"Death is . . . the end . . ."

Something hot and sharp, maybe electric, across the small of his back. He thought he smelt burning, hair sizzling.

Bubbles squatted down in front of him, still chewing, and, not very interested in the question: "What is Death?"

"Death is . . . is a rider of the Apocalypse . . . is . . ."

Again, pain.

Again, curling, sobbing, burning.

365

Bubbles finished his gum, stuck the used remnants to the bottom of the chair.

"What is Death?"

"Death is . . . the end of physical processes. The brain's activity . . . "

Whatever it was that burnt burnt too much, and Charlie decided to count this blackness as blessed, blessed sleep.

A different room.

They took the bag off his head and there were books, a table with clawed wooden feet holding globes at their base, a marble top. A tray of fresh green salad, a glass of white wine, a white sofa carefully covered with a blue plastic sheet. He was sitting on the sheet. He supposed it was to prevent blood from getting on something that would stain.

A priest sat on the couch opposite him, hands folded on his chest. He wore a black robe and a dog collar, but who knew if that counted for anything? Charlie thought he had an unkind face.

"Has your employer ever spoken to you about Heaven?" he asked, his accent something European, familiar, a comfort even, as Charlie blinked bewildered in the light of the low, warm bulbs.

"No." The word came awkwardly through bleeding gums, torn lips.

"Has he talked to you about the hereafter?"

"No."

"Do you believe there is an afterlife?"

"No."

"Why is that?"

"I . . . I . . . " For a reason Charlie couldn't fathom, he started to cry. He put his head in his hands and sobbed, like a child. The priest sighed, stood up, straightened his cassock, crossed over to where Charlie sat, and very gently put one hand on his head.

"There there," he sighed. "Don't let it get you down."

Slowly the tears faded, and Charlie fought the urge to wrap his arms around the man's legs, to hold him tight for ever.

The priest returned to his seat, cleared his throat

self-consciously, crossed one leg over the other and said at last, "So why don't you believe in an afterlife, Charlie?"

"I . . . haven't seen any evidence."

"But you've seen Death."

"Yes. But I think . . . I think most people have."

"But most people don't receive a pay cheque and regular pension contributions from him, do they?"

"No."

"So would you say you are an expert in this field?"

"I . . . I just . . . I just go before."

"Yes, that's what I'd heard. Is it just the lack of evidence that means you don't believe, or has he said something?"

"I go to people. Sometimes they live, and sometimes they die. And . . . and sometimes an idea dies, a dream and . . . and Death comes and . . . sometimes they are frightened, they're so afraid and I think that . . . and sometimes they aren't, and they are ready and I go before because . . . "

"Charlie . . . "

"I go because . . . "

"Charlie, focus on the question."

"*I honour the living!*" He nearly screamed the words, half slipping from the plastic-coated couch, clinging onto it before he could hit the floor. "*I go for the living, I speak to the living, I honour the living I honour life I honour life I honour that they are living before they die to see death is to see life the life that lives how dare you fucking . . .*"

He fell, dropping now to the thick carpet, dragging plastic with him, hauling down breath.

The priest sighed, leant forward, fingers steepled, looking down at the Harbinger of Death. "The thing is," he murmured, "these questions are a matter of some very serious policy."

Charlie raised his head slowly, looked the man in the eye, and then spat, blood and spittle, in his face. The priest flinched, drew back slowly, pulled a tissue from his sleeve, wiped the fluid away, got to his feet, nodded at someone behind Charlie.

He closed his eyes, and let the arms carry him away.

*

"Why does Death come?"

"Death always . . . comes . . . "

Pain.

Fall.

The ground was Charlie's favourite place. He liked the ground in this room. If he fell, the light wouldn't burn his eyes, just for a little while.

Up, again.

Again.

"Why does Death come here?"

"Death is everywhere."

Pain.

Fall.

Ground. Beautiful, cold ground.

Again.

"Why do good people die?"

"Luck."

Pain, harder now, more; this was an answer that displeased especially.

"Why do bad people live?"

"I don't know."

This time they hurt him so bad they had to stop a little while, for the doctor to check him over, before carrying on.

"Is Death the same as chance?"

"I don't know."

Pain. Fall. Again.

"Is there a God?"

"I don't know."

Pain. Again.

"What is Death?"

"I don't know."

"Why are men mortal?"

"I don't know."

"Why do we age and die? Will humanity live? Will humanity die? What will be our children's destiny? Does Death know the secrets of the dead?"

This time, the doctor called a stop before they could finish beating him senseless.

Lying on a white floor in a white room.

There was some scarlet there now — that'd be him.

The doctor put ointment on, he found that funny, funny word, ointment, funny, funny men.

He thought about Emmi, and knew she'd be frightened, worried senseless, where was he? The thought of that made him want to scream, though the burning was less now.

Men came.

Bag over the head.

Carried.

Pushed him into

the back of a car.

A woman in a trouser suit, a briefcase open on her lap. The engine was running, the car was in a car park, empty, yellow sodium lights shining all around. She didn't look at him as they spoke, but stared straight ahead. She had a face like a bar of soap in which someone had poked a couple of eyes and the thinnest, thinnest pretence of a mouth.

Her accent was British, clipped and steady. She said, "Mr Harbinger, we would be prepared to negotiate with your employer for certain services rendered. The geopolitical situation being what it is at the moment, we are reaching out to all the riders of the Apocalypse to discuss terms of mutual benefit. How would we most conveniently reach Death?"

Charlie would have laughed, but something was broken inside, so he didn't. He let his head roll to one side, staring at her over his crooked shoulder. "Drop a bomb. He'll come."

"We *are* dropping bombs," she replied calmly. "We require the discussion of terms."

He grinned, bloodied teeth in a broken mouth. "Humans summon Death," he whispered. "They summon Death and they summon War. With drum and with sword they summon them,

369

and bid them obey the call to arms, and they will come when called and being summoned, they will not obey."

"Mr Harbinger . . ."

"They were summoned to the trenches, over by Christmas they said, and forty thousand men died in a single day, can you imagine it? They were summoned to Stalingrad, the Apocalypse upon this earth, and the men who called them were so proud of their mighty machines, so proud, until they looked into the eyes of the monsters they had unleashed . . ."

"Mr Harbinger, this is not what I am—"

"Death is waiting for you," he hissed. "He's waiting with the nuclear warheads, framed in radioactive light. He's in the place where the ice melts; he's in the pit of the volcano. He's always been waiting. You just didn't know how to see."

"This is unproductive," she muttered, gesturing at a figure outside the windows. "This is clearly not the way to conduct business in the modern world, and as such . . ."

Hands pulled him from the car, and back to the darkness.

"What is Death?"

No more hitting. Nothing left to hurt.

They made him squat, and if he fell, they picked him up again and stabbed him with something hot, until even stabbing didn't make him stay, at which point Bubbles just sat cross-legged in front of him, chewing gum, speaking.

"What is Death?"

"Cancer and mitochondrial decay and . . ."

"What is Death?"

"A drunk driver behind the wheel, the man with the gun . . ."

"What is Death?"

"Dirty needle, protein shell and RNA . . ."

"What is Death?"

"Bad decision at the wrong time, the ending of a world . . ."

"Which world is ending?"

"The old world. All the time. Always ending. Change. Change and end. Close down one, make something new, always, always turning, nothing sad, always sad. Sad to die, sad to live, men who lynch, men who die, all of it sad, and the world turning."

"What is Death?"

"The way by which we live ..."

"What is Death?"

"The light and the dark, the reason we save, the reason we fly ..."

"Why does Death need you?"

Charlie opened his one good eye, peered through its blurred surface up at Bubbles, and thought he perhaps saw something on the man's face that was, for the first time, real. An actual question that came from a human being, rather than the litany that had gone before.

"I am ... the bridge."

"What does that mean?"

"I am ... what makes you see."

"Explain."

"I'm tired, please I'm ..."

"Explain!" Bubbles slammed his palm into the floor by Charlie's head, making him jump.

"I ... Death comes and it is all that it is. It is the ending. It is all things stopping. You know him, you have seen it coming your whole life, but you did not see, you could not imagine, not you. Smoke twenty a day and you know Death comes, he comes, he comes, but you still smoke because life, life, life. Build on the side of the mountain, jump without a parachute, you say you might die, but these words have no meaning. Death is not–living. Death is not real, until the day you meet his eye. I ... am the bridge. I am the one that comes before. I am living. I am ... what makes it real. No one believes in Death until they look him in the eye. I am the belief. There needs to be something mortal for it to have meaning. I am ... the living. I am alive."

"You're a monster."

Charlie shook his head, pressing his forehead into the cold, lovely ground.

"You love to tell people that they're gonna die."

"I love life," he whimpered, the tears coming again, he'd given up worrying about why or trying to stop them. "I see life, the whole world, so alive, so alive, please let me go please please I want to live please just—"

"What is Death?!" roared Bubbles, and Charlie cowered, curling away from his words. "You tell me! You tell me what Death is, you tell me!" Shaking him now, rattling his head on the thin stick of his neck. "*Tell me!*"

"Please!" wailed Charlie. "Please please let me go you'll bring him here you'll bring him he'll come just like he did before he'll come for you please please live I want to live you want to live I love life if you see life truly then you see death see life see death see life death life death please let me go please . . ."

Bubbles dropped him back down, watched him lie, grateful, on the ground, then spat on him, and walked away.

A businessman in a suit.

He pulled out a yellow notepad and a pen, which he licked the end of before hovering it above the paper, ready to strike.

"Mr Harbinger," he began. "What is your date of birth?"

Charlie told him.

"And your home address?"

Again he answered.

"Your parents . . . father is deceased?"

Yes, he was.

"No siblings?"

No.

"And your sexual orientation? Are you hetero, homo, bi . . . ?"

Charlie didn't answer.

"It's just for the files."

"I've had girlfriends."

"Do you have one now?"

He didn't answer.

"Mr Harbinger . . ."

"My name is Charlie."

"Yes, of course. Mr Harbinger . . . the sooner we're done here, the sooner I can go home. It's my daughter's birthday tonight, I really don't want to be late."

"What day is it?"

"Do you have a girlfriend?"

"No."

"There. That wasn't so hard. Now: why did Death choose you?"

"I don't know."

"Her birthday, really very important . . . "

"There was a job interview."

"Describe it for me."

He did.

"There were other applicants?"

"Yes."

"But Death chose you."

"Yes."

"Why?"

"I don't know."

"Why do you think he chose you, and not someone else?"

"I don't know."

"Mr Harbinger – I can see that you're tired, but I need you to focus. Would you say that Death has a nationalist bias?"

"No."

"And yet the death rates in certain countries . . . ?"

"Hospitals. Doctors. Car safety. Gun laws. Wealth. Life expectancy . . . "

"You are saying that death is merely a facet of human civilisation?"

"Yes."

"A thing that we generate ourselves, by living?"

"Yes."

"If that's the case, then let me ask you this: why aren't all societies better? Why isn't humanity better? If Death is, as you say, merely an adjunct to human processes, then it stands to reason that humanity can command Death, can control him,

373

and by their actions shape the meaning of mortality. If this is so, then why doesn't Death obey our command? Why isn't Death, if you pardon me saying so . . . merely a footnote to the act of living?"

human human rat rat human rat human rat

"Because . . . people aren't perfect."

"And because of chance?"

"Yes."

"And because sometimes fathers kill their children, and the children of other men, and wives shoot their husbands, and planes fall from the sky and people throw themselves off bridges, yes?"

"Yes."

"Why?"

"I . . . I don't . . ."

"Why do they do these things?"

"I . . . because that's life, because that's . . . that's . . ."

"Why is there Death?"

"You . . . you know this, you all know this you all know the answer to this there is . . . why would you . . . there is nothing that I can . . ."

"Why is there Death?"

"Why is there life? Why is there birth why is there . . ."

"Focus, please, Mr Harbinger. Just this question: why is there Death? Why must people die?"

"Because they age and they . . ."

"Why must they age? Where is it written that this is inevitable? Why is there Death? Is not Death the enemy of humanity, the enemy of life? Are you not serving the enemy of—"

This time, Charlie had enough energy to throw himself across the desk, and did a reasonably good job of nearly strangling the man before the men who were always waiting managed to pull him off him, and kick him to the floor.

Chapter 102

Tick tick tick tick tick tick tick
    Charlie?
    tick tick tick tick tick
    Charlie?
    Are you there?
    I'm here.
    What are you doing?
    Waiting.
    For who?
    For my boss. He's coming, he's coming. I need him to come now.
    Tick tick tick tick tick tick

A shower, tepid.
    Fresh clothes.
    The doctor examined him.
    Put him on a drip.
    Let him sleep in a bed.
    He thought, maybe they'll let me go.
    A day later, they took him back to the room, the chair, the light.
    And they started all over again.

What is Death?
    What is Death?
    Why is Death?
    Why do good people die?
    Why do bad people live?
    What is on the other side?
    Can Death be bargained with?
    Can Death be banished?
    Why does life have to end in Death?

Is Death a patriot?
Can we summon Death?
Can we control him?
What are you?
Why are you?
Why is Death?
Why are we dying?
Why are we not better?
Why are people flawed?
Why is life finite?
Why do people kill themselves?
Why does joy vanish?
Why do we bring children into this world?
Why is there life?
What is Death?

Bubbles sat on the edge of the desk and said, "Between you and me, now that the tape has stopped, I think this is a fucking waste of my fucking time. What the fuck is the point of it? Some guy in some office wants me to ask these questions and I'm like, sure, I'll ask the fucking questions but it don't mean nothing. I know what Death is, just like you do. I seen him, back in Kabul, I seen him when my old man passed away. I seen Death and Death seen me and that's all there is to it. Death is, just like the sun is, the sky is, Death is what you get at the end and that's all the fucking point of it, but shit. Here we are, you and me, and until you come up with something better, Harbinger of fucking Death, we're gonna go this merry-go-round again."

At that point, Charlie thought maybe he'd misjudged Bubbles, and that actually he was a nice guy after all.

Once, he woke and a woman was holding him tight. He thought perhaps he was hallucinating, as she pressed herself close to him and stroked his hair and kissed the side of his neck and said it's okay, it's okay, you'll be okay, and gently pushed his head away so he couldn't look at her, and still held him tight.

He believed her for a little while, and thought this was a fantastic dream, until she whispered,

"Is Death God?"

Then he closed his eyes, and closed his lips, and didn't say a word.

Then he was lying on the floor, and one of his teeth had fallen out, and Bubbles said, "What is Death?" and he screamed, he screamed, blood flying from his mouth in Bubbles' face,

"*He is you!* He is you, he is me, he is all of us, Death is in all of us in every man who killed in every child who was ever born he is us he is humanity he is in every second of every clock he is in every atom of the universe he is *you*!! You are Death, you are Death and so am I, you kill and I kill and the world changes and we all die, we all die and we run from it, you hit me because you're so fucking scared so hit me! Hit me! Fucking hit me because you don't understand because you won't understand so hit me! Hit me if it'll make you not afraid hit me! Hit me because you've known your whole fucking life what Death is and never had the courage to see!"

He fell back, no breath left, and for a while Bubbles stood silent, chewing, eyes flickering to an unseen observer. Then, at a signal Charlie couldn't see, he bent down and lifted the Harbinger up, put him on his seat like a loose-limbed toddler, said, "Gum?"

Charlie shook his head.

"Some folks are gonna be in to talk to you in a bit."

Bubbles headed for the door.

Charlie half turned in the chair, trying to watch the shape of him against the light. "Do you see him yet?" he whispered, as the blood rolled down his chin. "Do you see him? Can you hear him coming? Do you see?"

Bubbles stared back at Charlie, and for a moment, he seemed to flinch.

Two men and a woman came through the door. One had an East Asian accent; the other sounded French.

They pushed papers across the table.

"If you sign here ... Have you got a wet wipe, he's getting blood on the ... Thank you. So sign here and also here and ... Yes, well, don't worry about that, I'm sure it'll be fine. Now: do you need to use the restroom? No? Are you sure? Can we get some more wet wipes, he's a bit ... Thank you. No allergies to plasters? Or latex? Good. Well, thank you very much, that's about it, so ... good luck."

So saying, they left.

A man in a white shirt, flecked with Charlie's blood, turned off the floodlight that had been in his eyes, turned on the overhead fluorescent. Charlie cowered from the change, saw that the room was small, so much smaller than he'd realised, with a fire exit sign above the door. The man smiled uneasily, held out a lumpy white object in a plastic bag. For a moment Charlie didn't understand, and then he saw.

"Your tooth," the man explained, with an uneasy smile. "I think if you keep it in milk, or something, it'll last better."

Then the bag was pulled over Charlie's head, for what felt like the very last time.

Chapter 103

"This world, I look around and I see so much love ..."

"We're sceptics, but that doesn't mean we need to mock people's deeply held beliefs."

"I am not in a position to pronounce on an individual's sexuality."

"We are all the people of this world, all of us, together."

"We will make a new Jerusalem."

"Marriage is not the only choice. When I choose to express my love, I express it for myself, for us, for each other ..."

"Exploration teaches us as much about ourselves as it does the universe ..."

"The time has come for change."

"There is a value in beauty; beauty expresses something human."

"It's a new beginning."

"Look how far we've come."

Chapter 104

Charlie

opened his eyes.

Lying on the side of the road.

That was fine.

He'd come to enjoy lying on things, in his way.

Insects chittered nearby.

He smelt leaf mould.

Saw darkness.

Felt tarmac.

Leaves whispered, titillated by a cool night breeze.

He thought about rolling over.

Didn't.

A car swooshed by, somewhere nearby, a junction, perhaps, slowing for a corner, then heading off in the opposite direction.

Charlie

waited.

Another car. Headlights blinding, slowing to a halt, stopping, the engine still running, a door opening, thunk, footsteps, a woman's voice, joined by another, *Jesus*, is he dead? Are you dead, mister, is he ...?

He's not dead, thank Christ, Jesus, call an ambulance, dial 911,

Jesus, okay, let me look at him, don't move him, his neck might be broken, mister, mister, can you . . . ?

Charlie closed his eyes, smiling at the dark.

A hospital room.

When he could speak, he gave them the number for Milton Keynes, having to mumble it dumbly through broken lips.

They gave him water, small sips, small sips now.

When he could speak again, he asked for a phone, and one of the two girls, both students, who'd picked him up said he could use hers, and he said it was international, it'd be pricey, and she shook her head firmly and said, "If there's someone waiting at home who loves you, you need to let them know that you're all right."

He called Emmi.

The phone rang, and rang, and rang, and she didn't answer.

He tried again.

No answer.

Shaking, he gave the phone back to his rescuer.

"You can try again later," she promised. "You can try again."

He nodded, and closed his eyes to sleep, and thought of another number, and asked if he could try that instead.

Patrick arrived at nine the next morning. The two women who'd picked Charlie up refused to leave until he came. "Mister, you're in trouble, we don't just leave people who are in trouble, that's not the way of things round here."

Patrick brought flowers.

"Jesus," he breathed, walking into the room. "You get hit by a train?"

"Kidnapped," Charlie replied. "Got kidnapped."

"You know who by?"

"No."

"What'd the doctors say?"

"I'll be all right. They didn't want to kill me."

"They look like they wanted to kill you. *Jesus*," Patrick

380

murmured, settling uneasy into the chair by the bed. "I thought I told you to take it easy?"

"You also said I should call."

"Yeah – I'm glad you did. Look, apart from being ... you know ..." a long gesture, taking in Charlie's bandaged body, "are you okay? Is this room, are you ...?" A shrug.

"Milton Keynes sorted it."

"Glad Milton Keynes is good for something. How long are you going to be in here?"

"They think they'll let me go today."

"Seriously?"

"The doctors say that everything was meant to hurt, not cripple."

"You were ..." Patrick drew in his lips slowly, looking for the word, then briskly, finding no alternative, "tortured? Was that it? Because of your job?"

"I was wondering if I could get a lift."

Patrick gave him a lift.

To his surprise, Patrick drove a hired estate car, no chauffeur, the windows down, instead of the air conditioning on. Charlie turned the radio on, tuned it to something classical, no words, let his head flop against the back of the seat, face turned towards the sun as it danced through the trees.

"What did they want?" Patrick asked at last, as they headed towards Madison Avenue Bridge.

"I don't really know."

"They didn't ask you anything? They did this shit to you and they didn't ...?"

"They wanted to know what Death is."

"Really?"

"Yes."

"That's an insane thing to ask."

"No it's not."

"Sounds insane."

"It's not."

"You're the expert."

They drove.

Music. Barber's Adagio for Strings; when a good man dies, said the conductor, every nation has a song they can sing to honour his passing. Here, we have this. Listen.

Charlie listened. Maybe Patrick did too; he wasn't sure.

The wind through the window, the smell of the motorway, traffic thick, the trucks roaring by, the sun high overhead.

At last he said, "What is Death?"

Patrick mumbled, don't dwell on it, don't think about it, not important now ...

But Charlie cut him off, repeated: "What is Death? It's the oldest question; maybe the very first question ever asked. The dead can't tell us, the dying don't have the language to explain. The only guaranteed part of our lives is the one thing we cannot express, control or command. It comes and we are ... so afraid. Too afraid to look. Too afraid to understand. We think we know, we think we prepare, but we don't. Like a man tied to the train tracks, we see death coming, all our lives we see it coming, and we cannot name that light, but know exactly what it is. To see life, to honour life, you must know that one day it will end, that it has ended, that it will begin again, that all things change, that change is death. These words, too big, too big to understand, too big, too frightening, and so we ask ... it's one of the most human questions anyone has ever asked. It's a question everyone can answer, and no one ever will."

Patrick contemplated this for a while, steady in the centre lane. Then: "Still sounds insane to me. Not worth beating the shit out of you, I'll say that for sure."

"I'm glad you came."

"I wanted to. I think ... I think that maybe I was meant to."

"Meant?"

"Do you believe in God?"

"They asked that too."

"I'm sorry, I didn't ... "

"No, I don't believe in God."

382

"But the world . . . no . . . *a* world is ending, and I was called to witness, yes? I was called to witness because I am part of the ending. My actions . . . I am the change. I am the future, and it is fitting, I think, that I should see the past too, yes? Is that . . . what you think?"

Charlie closed his eyes, pressed his head against the glass. "I suppose."

"The men . . . the ones who took you. You really don't know who they were?"

Charlie didn't answer.

"I think that's the world too," breathed Patrick, nodding at nothing much. "Maybe that's why I'm here, as well, to see this. To be here for . . . you. I think that in my world, the powerful will always get away with it."

The road was long, and stretched all the way to the horizon.

Part 9

MUSIC

Chapter 105

A hotel room in Manhattan.

Charlie tried calling Emmi, and there was no answer.

He had a hot bath, and the water filled with floating beads of jelly-like clotted blood.

He tried calling Emmi: no answer.

He called Milton Keynes.

No answer.

He hobbled to the pharmacist to get more painkillers. Their smallest bottle was fifty pills, their largest two hundred.

He bought fifty.

At the counter, a daughter, arguing with her mother.

"Size eight is how you get ahead, it's what the agency want and so it's what you need to—"

"Mom, I'm sick and tired of it, I'm sick and tired of trying to be—"

"Do you want to grow up poor? Do you want to be a nobody? God has blessed you with good looks, missy, and you will use them, you will take your pills and you will ... "

Charlie limped away.

The street.

The noise.

God please make it stop please make it stop the noise the

" ... if you're fat why would you wear tight clothes, I hate having to look at all that ... "

"Get that load of ass."

"Look, I'm not saying she's not good at her job, but the head-scarf is just so ..."

" ... fell five points but we're gonna clean up when Tokyo comes back, just you wait ..."

"No! Tell him that I'll get the money, I'll get it and ... you just fucking tell him!"

"I'm not sure I like you hanging out with those guys any more ..."

"God, the area's really gone down, like you should see the bums on the street corner ..."

"Taxi!"

"Who the fuck does the Pope think he is, telling him he's not a Christian ...?"

"I don't watch the news. It depresses me. It's so ... "

RAT RAT RAT RAT

The pain came so hard that Charlie nearly fell, catching himself on a wall, gasping for breath. People flowed by. A couple stopped to look; most didn't. A woman, Filipino, wearing a bright green T-shirt and jogging bottoms, stopped and said, "Mister? You okay?"

He nodded dumbly, and staggered on.

Make it stop please please make it stop it's too

Into the hotel foyer.

"Tipping these days is just another kind of robbery ..."

"Yes, but there was a mark on the sheets ..."

"Commute in from Hoboken ..."

" ... dinner with them but they're just the most repugnant ... "

"I said three extra large!"

"Women who cut their hair short are just trying to be ugly, like that's some kind of victory for them ..."

"These days they let anyone in, like we're just victims of our own generosity ..."

"I don't think he's really trying, do you?"

Made it to the lift, head pounding, body burning.

The floor

Step step step

388

tick tick tick
the door. Pushed it open. Electricity
snap
same hotel room, same everywhere, same the world over
arrivals, departures, arrivals, departures whoosh the plane
takes off and it lands somewhere exactly the same somewhere
new somewhere different somewhere full of people who were just
human human human
TV through the walls, please God, please God, make it stop . . .
"The value of your investments may go down as well as
up . . ."
"Take out a payday loan!"
"With my new microfibre cloth, cleaning the kitchen has
never been easier or more fun!"
"I mean is the guy even American? His dad was born in Kenya
or wherever . . ."
He soaked his face in cold water, fell onto the bathroom floor,
stayed there because it was cold, the cold pressing against his
body, lay flat on his back.
Lay there.
Heart beating.
De-dum de-dum de-dum.
Time passing.
Tick tick tick tick tick.
World turning.
Lay there.
Didn't move.
Somewhere outside, the city passed him by. The world buzzed
and hummed and the music played and the young were born and
the old died and some who weren't old died too and the bombs
fell and the dust blew and the ice cracked and the buildings tum-
bled and the world
changed and changed and changed again
tick tick tick tick
And Charlie lay on the floor.
Tick. Tick. Tick. Tick.

One of us comes to mourn, the other to rejoice. I think that's what this business is. I think that is why I came.

Charlie?

I walked the ice, as a boy I came here and I walked the ice, me and your mother, and saw so much life, life clinging on where you would have thought it would die, life that begets life that begets life that . . .

Char-lie . . .

This is my city, my country, my home, this is my life, my battle, my war. This is my struggle to be seen as a person, to be human, this is my human body, this is my human life, this is my everything, this is my all, this is . . .

CHARLIE!

One day we will build Jerusalem.

Something in his pocket.

He became aware of it slowly, as pain settled into a background ache.

A little pot, which rolled free when nudged with his fingertips. He caught it before it could slide off into a corner, and held it up.

Fifty painkillers, in a white plastic jar.

He stared at it for a very long time.

Then, slowly, rolled onto his knees.

He opened the pot, counted ten pills out in a row round the edge of the sink.

Stared at them.

Counted out eight more, laid them above the ten, forming the beginning of a pyramid.

Didn't have enough room to put six more above, so instead put another eight below, turning the pyramid into the beginning of a diamond.

Stopped.

Stared.

Counted.

Tick tick tick tick.

He put the lid on the pot, laid it to one side, reached out with the tip of index finger and thumb, and picked up the first pill of the middle row of ten, moved it towards his mouth.

There was a knock on the door.

Knock knock knock.

He hesitated, waiting for it to go away.

Knock knock knock.

And then again, when he didn't move: *knock knock knock.*

He put the pill down slowly, crawled to his feet, and with the chain still on the door, opened it an inch, flinching as he did so, remembering pain, needles, falling, a memory so intense it was almost like reliving it, clutching at his body.

Through the door, an eye, brown, heading almost for black, a hint of pale skin. For a moment he thought it was Patrick, there was something so familiar in the shape of that face, the cut of that suit, a figure that he knew.

Then he looked again, and it wasn't Patrick. Not Patrick at all.

Hello, Charlie, said Death. May I come in?

Chapter 106

Death sat on the end of Charlie's bed.

Charlie stared at his hands. Death looked round the room, curious, as if he'd never been in a hotel like this before.

For a while, neither spoke, until at last, having concluded his study, Death looked at Charlie, and leant in, almost nudging him with the side of his body, and declared, I thought we should have a little chat.

Charlie didn't move, didn't lift his eyes from the floor.

We're overdue for a review, Death went on absently, eyes wandering again round the room. And there's a new employment directive that counts travel time towards working hours, and

391

Milton Keynes seems to think this will affect your contract and wanted to have a word about it.

Silence.

So, Death went on, gaze returning to Charlie's swollen, bloodied face. How are you finding it all?

Slowly, Charlie raised his head, and met Death's stare. "Honestly," he answered, "I'm having some difficulties."

Death nodded, understanding, and patted Charlie on the shoulder. Kidnapped and tortured, yes? Been a while since that one, but sometimes these things do happen.

"Are you going to kill them?" Charlie asked.

Kill ... who?

"The people who did this to me?"

Charlie, tutted Death. I don't kill people. I merely ... show up for the event.

"But ... in Belarus ... "

I'll grant you, I have a bit of a temper sometime, and I dislike ... rudeness, particularly to my envoy. But the gentlemen in Belarus were attempting to manipulate me, and arguably in doing so they only invited their destruction. Haven't they read *Frankenstein*? Haven't they been to the movies? Don't they know how these things turn out? But in answer to your question, no, I doubt there will be any ... overt repercussions for the individuals who have so recently abused you. A daughter might die, perhaps. A birthday party might be the last, but in the end, they will live because, you see ... that is the world we live in. That is how things go, these days. I am not justice, Charlie. I am not logic, or law, I do not even up the balance of things. You know, I was once called capricious and I said, "I'll show you capricious," and then I went and changed my mind!

He chuckled, looked at Charlie to see if he'd laugh too, stopped quickly when Charlie did not.

Anyway, he went on, shifting a little on the end of the bed. Do you want them to suffer?

"No," answered Charlie thoughtfully, and was surprised at his own words. "No, I don't."

Good! That's good. You know — it's that sort of attitude that makes you so good at your job. So important to see the value of these things. So important to recognise the human underneath the bluster. I've had people in the past who just saw corpses, talking corpses, and they were never what I hope for, never as generous or thoughtful with their words or their time as would be wished, but you are ...

Charlie put his head in his hands, dug his fingers into his skin as if he might try and tear down to the white surface of his skull. Death stopped, surprised, looked a little closer. Charlie? Are you all right?

He shook his head, and had no words.

Charlie, *Charlie*, tutted Death, rubbing him on the back. Oh Charlie, this won't do! Come now, you've got to talk to me, I can't stand to see you in this state.

"I ... can't," he whispered. "I can't. What you said ... I can't. I went round the world and I saw ... the end of everything. The ice cracked and the professor died, he fell and left his son behind because the world was ending. Agnes and Jeremiah, they screamed and screamed and screamed and no one listened, because they were weak and the rich were strong and that world was torn down and for what? Isabella made people laugh and she lives, she lives and that is good, but when the policemen came they pretended it had never happened, because *he* had power, and sometimes people live and sometimes people die but the laughter stopped and the war was not won and Qasim ... he called them rats. You gave him a pen and the ink was dry. They died because they were not human, and I came to America and here ... people suffer and the world turns and the dream ... the dream does not die, it changes into something new, something that lets the good men fade, all because people *are not human!*"

Words, half shrieked from a broken voice. A gathering-in of shuddering breath, trying again, slow.

"And now I look at the world and I was honoured, I was so honoured to be your Harbinger because I honoured life. I was everything you wanted me to be, I went and I did honour to the living before the end, and it was a privilege. It was the greatest privilege that can be bestowed. And now I look and all I hear is the beating of the drums and all I see is a world in which to not be one of us is to be something else. The scientist was right, reason is dead; the dream is dead; *humanity* has changed into something new and it is brutal. It is ugly. Life is ugly. And it is obscene. And I look. And all I see is you."

A shuddered gasp; he rolled forward again, pressing his head into his hands.

Death nodded, taking the words in, hand still resting on Charlie's back. Then he exclaimed, Come on, and got to his feet.

Charlie looked up at him, confused, eyes burning, jaw slack.

Come on, repeated Death, chipper brightness. There's an appointment we ought to keep.

"I don't . . . "

Come on. It's not far. We can get a taxi, if you like.

Death marched to the door, pulled Charlie's keycard from the slot, plunging the room into gloom, waved it cheerfully at Charlie, smiled a mischievous smile. Come on, he repeated. Just this one. Just for me.

He held the door open.

Charlie followed him, into the light.

Chapter 107

A cab, only a few blocks, but Death declared that Charlie didn't look like he should be walking.

A porch, covered over with a long green awning. A reception desk, manned by a woman with huge hair wearing a bright pink dress. A waiting area, sofas, fresh flowers, old men and women waiting in wheelchairs, some with relatives, kneeling down, holding their hands, talking. Some were sad; some were smiling.

Some were in some other far-off place, but even the oldest and the most confused looked up as Death passed, and seemed to recognise his passage, though they couldn't recognise the faces of their nearest friends.

Come on! Death kept on exclaiming, pulling Charlie through the halls. He seemed to know this place well, dodging and turning round the passing staff, nurses with clipboards, a doctor marching busily along, porters wheeling the old folk to and from the little café out back, relatives on their phones. Come on!

They headed up a flight of stairs, avoiding the queue of wheelchairs for the lift, and as they marched through another hall, decked with flowers and semi-arid pot plants, Charlie thought he heard the sound of music. Violins, cellos, a hint of piano in the distance. It was clunky and out of tune, but as they walked it grew louder, filling the corridors, until at last they came to a pair of double doors, which Death eased open so that Charlie might peek inside.

A large room, filled with chairs and flanked with Zimmer frames and wheelchairs. Some – many – of the old folk who sat there were asleep; some were snoring. An old man had a yarmulke upon his head; another was doing a crossword in his lap, not bothering to watch the creaking musicians.

Charlie looked.

A group of children, fifteen or twenty strong. Their average age was maybe twelve, their skin colour ranging from fair Persian, subtle and easily burnt in the sun, to dark Indian, the colour of autumn. Of the musicians, three or four were girls, and two of those, along with their teacher, wore headscarves to hide their hair.

Charlie glanced at Death, and Death smiled and said, I think they're going to try their hand at Bach next. Don't judge them too harshly.

He eased away from the door, letting it close softly, and then turned again, and pulled Charlie through the corridors, round and round, to where an old man sat alone, staring out of a window at the street below, a book open in his lap, his head on one side, eyes yellow and faint.

A woman was sat opposite him, writing notes on a clipboard, but as Death approached she rose quickly and said, "Oh . . . it's you."

Good afternoon, Death replied brightly. How are you today?

"I'm . . . fine, thank you."

This is Charlie, he's my Harbinger, explained Death, as her eyes flickered to Charlie's face. Don't worry about him, he was hit by a certain amount of human anxiety dressed up as a runaway train.

"I . . . see." She did not, but who quibbles semantics with Death?

We very much enjoyed the music.

"The . . . ah, the school. Yes, they've never played here before, but I think the old folk will like it."

They're a Muslim institution?

"Yes."

Playing for a Jewish nursing home?

"Yes. Some of our old ones were a bit . . . they weren't very happy about it, the politics, it's all tied up, isn't it? But I said that half our staff are Muslim and the other half are Hindu or Christian, and if you can have your ass wiped by someone who believes in a prophet other than yours then you can definitely listen to a bit of classical, can't you? And the school were very enthusiastic, they said it'd be a delight, that we were all the same really and . . . anyway. You've come for . . . " A gentle nod towards the dozing, distant man.

That's right.

"I see. And, um . . . well, if I come back in, maybe . . . an hour?"

That sounds good.

"Okay. Well then. I'll, uh . . . I'll be back in a bit."

Thank you. You're a dear.

The woman nodded, and scurried away.

Death knelt down in front of the wheelchair, put his hand in the man's own.

For a moment, Charlie wondered what the woman had seen,

or what she'd even heard, as Death spoke. Did she hear the same words Charlie had; did she see the same figure? Or had some other, personal, private conversation happened between her and his employer, some secret thing that only they would share?

And the old man?

He opened his eyes at Death's touch and he beheld . . .

. . . what he beheld was his secret, and only his to know, but he smiled.

"Oh," he wheezed. "It's you."

Hello, Isaak.

"Been a while."

It has, hasn't it?

"You haven't changed."

Ah, but in my way . . .

"Where was it last . . . ?"

Sobibor.

"Sobibor," he breathed. "I remember. You were there. You helped me, you said you'd never tell, and I never told either. Sobibor – you had to survive day after day in the camp, and you were there and together . . . "

Death squeezed his hand tighter, smiling up into the ancient, blurred eyes. I remember. I was always there. You lived for the day, and you lived for the day after that, and one day the days would end, but you would live until that very moment. I remember.

The old man, with great effort, laid his free hand on Death's own, and squeezed back. "I wondered when I'd see you again, my friend. There were many times when I thought . . . but you came for someone else, not for me. I didn't know if that was because of what we'd done, what we'd seen together, whether you wanted someone to witness, to remember."

People will remember, Death replied quietly. I remember everything, but I have a Harbinger too, and he remembers as the mortals do, and he remembers for the living.

The old man craned his head to see Charlie, who moved round

397

to be better in his view. He smiled at Charlie, who tried to smile back, then the man's gaze returned to Death.

"Do you think they're waiting for me?" he asked.

I don't know.

"I always thought they would be."

Then that's what matters.

"This man ... together ..." He pointed at Death, but looked at Charlie. "I never told, and he swore he never would. But you should know. You should know because ... the living must know. You had to live. You had to live, even if it meant betraying your people, even if it meant ... I lived by closing the doors. They went into the chamber and together we closed the doors, didn't we? We always closed the doors."

Charlie bit his lip, looked at the man, looked at Death, then knelt down by the man's side and added his own hands to the tangle of flesh folded across his knee. Charlie's fingers were hot, the only warm thing in that grasp, a beating heart. "You lived, Isaak," he whispered. "You lived."

The old man smiled, and the smile stayed on his face forever.

Chapter 108

Our Father, who art in Heaven, hallowed be thy name ...

Om mani padme hum ...

Allah, the All-Merciful, the All-Compassionate ...

Give us this day our daily bread, and forgive us our trespasses ...

Let us worship the supreme light of the sun, the god of all things ...

Om mani padme hum ...

On earth as it is in heaven ...

There is no god but God ...

Lead us towards peace, guide our footsteps towards peace ...

May he rebuild Jerusalem ...
Grant us grace, kindness and mercy in Your eyes ...
For ever and ever ...
Amen.

Chapter 109

After.

After the silence.

Death said: I'm going to stay here a while, until the carer comes. Do you want to stay?

Charlie replied, "Thank you, but no."

Death nodded, head on one side. You are ... very important to me, Charlie. I do hope you understand that.

"I do. Thank you."

When you get home, once you've had a bit of a rest ... we should talk about this new travel directive. We have to be scrupulous about these things.

"Of course."

Then, almost as an afterthought: A woman called Emmi has been trying to get in touch. She threatened to kill a rabbit. I'm not sure what that would have achieved – something to do with blood and invocation or something of that sort – but she was very insistent. Milton Keynes flew her out here.

"Emmi's here?"

Oh – yes.

"In New York?"

Yes.

For a moment, Charlie's face broke into something that might have been the beginning of a laugh, and which Death misunderstood, adding hastily, Don't worry about it. These things ... one must do what is proper, mustn't one?

"I . . . Thank you."

I'll stay here a while, until someone comes. Where will you be?

"I think . . . I'm going to go and make a phone call."

And then?

"Then . . . " Charlie thought about it for a moment.

Only a moment.

"Then," he said, "I shall listen to the music. For a little while."

Death nodded and smiled, and Charlie walked away.

And the world turned.

War peers through the binoculars at the South China Sea, well wrapped up despite the high summer sun, and says, "Oh I can't ever tell! It's just another bloody damn bit of rock, if you ask me!"

"But sir, if you look closely," said the captain, "you will see that our people have put a flag on it."

"Oh!" War chuckles, patting his rolling belly within his coat. "Well, that's something different, isn't it?"

And the world turned.

In a mirrored hall in southern England, Famine wiped sweat from her glistening face, and rolling up her yoga mat exclaimed, "Milk is basically pus. You're drinking the pus of a cow. I mean if the ancestors . . . "

"Well this is what I've been saying . . . "

" . . . just on berries and nuts . . . "

"Exactly! I mean, they didn't have all this stuff we have, we evolved to be able to live in the forests and the mountains, we evolved on a diet of very basic foods, vegans think they know what they're talking about but even vegans . . . "

"I've always felt that veganism was just a cover for lack of moral nerve . . . "

And the world turned.

Pestilence said, "So . . . detoxing exactly what?"

"All the negative toxins that build up in your body."

"Such as?"

"Well, there's the food-borne toxins, and the airborne toxins, and there's toxins in the water . . ."

"I see!"

"And our programme will help expel them from your body . . ."

"And the hosepipe up the bum?"

"To flush your colon."

"Of toxins?"

"Exactly! Exactly that! I'm so glad you understand. You . . . you do understand, don't you?"

Pestilence rolled back in his great office chair, a dozen little mechanisms adjusting with a pneumatic whisper to accommodate his form. "Isn't the modern age wonderful?" he mused. "Isn't science simply amazing?"

And the world . . .

. . . turns.

"The shedding of these assets is of course a vital step towards the reactualisation of our financial base . . ."

Patrick Fuller, looking down on the city from a tower block in Manhattan.

Behind him, people talk, but he knows where the words are heading, what the numbers mean.

"The opportunity cost is actually greater if you look at figure five . . ."

Talk talk talk talk. Jabber jabber, as if the conclusion isn't inevitable. As if the future isn't already there to be seen.

One day, he muses, as the presentation rolls, one day the world will be a more honest place. One day people will just say what they mean, and business will be conducted properly.

One day, he too will build Jerusalem.

He raises his eyes to shield them from the setting sun, and watches until the last pinprick of light has vanished below the horizon.

*

401

And the world . . .

   . . . always has . . .

   . . . always will . . .

   . . . turns.

Emmi said: "I came to America you're so fucking stupid I can't believe what happened to you I can't believe it I came to America that's why when you rang no one answered I was here I made them tell me where you were and they didn't know and I called the embassy and they didn't know and no one knew so I came and what happened to you what the fuck happened you're in such a state I can't believe you're even standing you're so stupid you're so stupid I love you I love you you're such a fucking idiot."

And Charlie held her, so tight he thought she might just be sucked into him, become a piece of his soul. She held him rather more gingerly, for fear of breaking something, but even that was meaning enough.

Somewhere in the past, Charlie thought he saw another version of himself, less bruised, less battered, who would have felt the need to speak, to babble words to cover himself, protect him, her, everyone from something, maybe from a thing he might do, or a promise he might break or . . .

   . . . whatever.

But that was then, and this was now, and everything changed, and everything changed.

She held him, and he held her, and there they remained a little while longer, as the world turned.

Chapter 110

"Watch a bit of the news in the morning, you know, while having Coco Pops . . . "

"... well I'm phoning in because I think it's important that people like me, we make our voices heard."

"The way Brexit is being depicted – why can't we find the positives?"

"Ooooohhhhhhhhhmmmmmmmmmm!!!!"

"Oh my God, it's such an honour, such an honour, I'm just ... I want to thank my mother!"

"So for this strike we go stick down, like this, and the reason we do this is 'cos it's the final part of the low block on the ..."

"Aerobic and anaerobic respiration. Can anyone tell me the difference?"

"So these cysts ... they're harmless, right?"

"... listening to the sounds of nature, and all around me, I just felt it, in that moment, I felt my place in the world, and I want to share that experience with you now ..."

"It was our privilege to give these weapons to the martyrs of Gaza."

"With IPv6 and the advent of HTML5, we can expect to see a phased redundancy within the next seven years ..."

"I don't mind being tracked. I like that Google knows me, it's more helpful that way."

"Oooohhhhhhhmmmmmmmmmmmmmmmmm ..."

"We will not be releasing any further updates to the operating system in the foreseeable future ..."

"Now the kids have gone, we're looking at downsizing a bit."

"Online piracy isn't just an insult, it's a fundamental threat to art ..."

"We'll get back to you in ten working days!"

"Ooohhhhhhmmmmmmmmm!"

"Do you want fries with that?"

"It'll be all right in the end."

Copyrights

extras

www.orbitbooks.net

about the author

Claire North is a pseudonym for British author Catherine Webb. *The First Fifteen Lives of Harry August* was her first novel published under the Claire North name, and was one of the fastest-selling new SFF titles of the last ten years. It was selected for the Richard and Judy Book Club, the Radio 2 Book Club and the Waterstones Book Club promotions. Her next novel *Touch* was published in 2015 to widespread critical acclaim and was described by the *Independent* as "little short of a masterpiece". Catherine currently works as a theatre lighting designer and is a fan of big cities, urban magic, Thai food and graffiti-spotting. She lives in London. Find her on Twitter as @ClaireNorth42.

Find out more about Claire North and other Orbit authors by registering for the free monthly newsletter at www.orbitbooks.net.

if you enjoyed

THE END OF THE DAY

look out for

THE BOY ON
THE BRIDGE

by

M. R. Carey

*Once upon a time, in a land blighted by terror,
there was a very clever boy.*

*The people thought the boy could save them, so they
opened their gates and sent him out into the world.*

To where the monsters lived.

1

The bucks have all been passed and the arguments thrashed out until they don't even bleed any more. Finally, after a hundred false starts, the Rosalind Franklin begins her northward journey – from Beacon on the south coast of England all the way to the wilds of the Scottish Highlands. There aren't many who think she'll make it that far, but they wave her off with bands and garlands all the same. They cheer the bare possibility.

Rosie is an awesome thing to behold, a land leviathan, but she's not by any means the biggest thing that ever rolled. In the years before the Breakdown, the most luxurious motor homes, the class A diesel-pushers, were a good sixteen or seventeen metres long. Rosie is smaller than that: she has to be because her armour plating is extremely thick and there's a limit to the weight her treads will carry. In order to accommodate a crew of twelve, certain luxuries have had to be sacrificed. There's a single shower and a single latrine, with a rota that's rigorously maintained. The only private space is in the bunks, which are tiered three-high like a Tokyo coffin hotel.

The going is slow, a pilgrimage through a world that turned its back on humankind the best part of a decade ago. Dr Fournier, in an inspirational speech, likens the crew to the wise men in the Bible who followed a star. Nobody else in the crew finds the analogy plausible or appealing. There are twelve of them, for one thing – more like the apostles than the wise men, if they were in the Jesus business in the first place, and they are not in any sense following a star. They're following the trail blazed a year before by another team in an armoured vehicle exactly like their own – a trail planned out by a panel of fractious experts, through every terrain that mainland Britain has to offer. Fields and meadows, woodland and hills, the peat bogs of Norfolk and the Yorkshire moors.

All these things look, at least to Dr Samrina Khan, very much as she remembers them looking in former times. Recent events – the collapse of global civilisation and the near-extinction of the human species – have left no mark on them that she can see. Khan is not surprised. The time of human dominion on Earth is barely a drop in the ocean of geological time, and it takes a lot to make a ripple in that ocean.

But the cities and the towns are changed beyond measure. They were built for people, and without people they have no identity or purpose. They have lost their memory. Vegetation is everywhere, softening the man-made megaliths into new and unrecognisable shapes. Office blocks have absent-mindedly become mesas, public squares morphed into copses or lakes. Emptied of the past that defined them, they have surrendered without protest, no longer even haunted by human meanings.

There are still plenty of ghosts around, though, if that's what you're looking for. The members of the science team avoid the hungries where possible, engage when strictly necessary (which mostly means when the schedule calls for tissue samples). The military escort, by virtue of their weapons, have a third option which they pursue with vigour.

Nobody enjoys these forays, but the schedule is specific. It takes them into every place where pertinent data could lurk.

Seven weeks out from Beacon, it takes them into Luton. Private Sixsmith parks and locks down in the middle of a round-about on the A505, which combines a highly defensible position with excellent lines of sight. The sampling team walks into the town centre from there, a journey of about half a mile.

This is one of the places where the crew of the Charles Darwin, their dead predecessors, left a cache of specimen cultures to grow in organic material drawn from the immediate area. The team's brief is to retrieve these legacy specimens, which calls for only a single scientist with an escort of two soldiers. Dr Khan is the scientist (she made damn sure she would be by swapping duties with Lucien Akimwe for three days running). The escort consists of Lieutenant McQueen and Private Phillips.

Khan has her own private reasons for wanting to visit Luton, and they have become steadily more pressing with each day's forward progress. She is afraid, and she is uncertain. She needs an answer to a question, and she hopes that Luton might give it to her.

They move slowly for all the usual reasons – thick under-growth, ad hoc barricades of tumbledown masonry, alarms and diversions whenever anything moves or makes a sound. The soldiers have no call to use their weapons, but they see several groups of hungries at a distance and they change their route each time to minimise the chance of a close encounter. They keep their gait to a halting dead march, because even with blocker gel slathered on every inch of exposed skin to deaden their scent, it's possible that the hungries will lock onto rapid movement and see potential prey.

Khan considers how strange they must look, although there's almost certainly no one around to see them. The two men each comfortably topping six feet in height, and the small, slight woman in between. She doesn't even come up to their shoulders, and her thighs are thinner than their forearms. They could carry her, with all her gear, and not slacken stride. It's past noon before they reach Park Square, where the Darwin's logs have directed them. And then it takes a long while to locate the specimen cache. The Darwin's scientists cleared a ten-foot area before setting it down, as per standing orders, but a whole year's growth has happened since then. The cache's bright orange casing is invisible in snarls of brambles so dense and thick they look like tank traps. When they finally locate it, they have to use machetes to get to it.

Khan kneels down in pulped bramble and oozing bramble-sap to verify the seals on the specimen containers. There are ten of them, all battleship grey rather than transparent because the fungus inside them has grown to fill the interior space to bursting. That probably means the specimens are useless, offering no information beyond the obvious – that the enemy is robust and versatile and not picky at all about pH, temperature, moisture or any damn thing else.

But hope springs as high as it can, and the mission statement is not negotiable. Khan transfers the containers to her belt pouches. McQueen and Phillips stand close on either side of her, sweeping the silent square with a wary 360-degree gaze.

Khan climbs to her feet, but she stands her ground when McQueen brusquely gestures for her and Phillips to move out.

"I need to do a quick sortie," she says, hoping her voice does not betray her nerves.

The lieutenant regards her with a vast indifference, his broad, flat face showing no emotion. "That's not on the log," he tells her curtly. He has little time for Khan and doesn't try to hide the fact. Khan believes that this is because she is (a) not a soldier and (b) not even a man, but she doesn't rule out other possibilities. There may even be some racism in there, however quaint and old-fashioned that seems in these latter days.

So she has anticipated his answer and prepared her own. She takes a list out of the pocket of her fatigues and hands it to him. "Medicines," she says as he unfolds and scans it, his lips pursed thin and tight. "We're doing okay for the most part, but the area north of Bedford saw a lot of bombing. If we can stock up on some of this stuff before we get into the burn shadow, it might save us a lot of heartache later."

Khan is prepared to lie if she has to, but McQueen doesn't ask her whether this is an authorised detour. He takes it for granted –

and it's a very fair assumption – that she wouldn't prolong this little day trip without direct orders from either Dr Fournier or the colonel.

So they stroll on a little way to the Mall, which is a mausoleum fit for an ancient pharaoh. Behind shattered shopfronts, flat-screen televisions and computers offer digital apotheosis. Mannequins in peacock finery bear witness, or else await their long-delayed resurrection.

Ignoring them all, Lieutenant McQueen leads the way inside and up to the mezzanine level. Once there, he stays out on the concourse, his rifle on full automatic with the safety off, while Khan and Phillips gather up the precious bounty of Boots the Chemist.

Khan takes the prescription drugs, leaving the private with the much easier task of scoring bandages, dressings and painkillers. Even so, she presses the list on him, assuring him that he will need it more than she does. That's true enough, as far as it goes. She's well aware of what's in short supply and what they can reasonably expect to find.

But it's only half the truth. She also wants Private Phillips to have his head down, puzzling over her shitty handwriting as he makes his way along the aisles. If he's reading the list, he won't be watching her. She'll be free to pursue her secret mission – the one that has brought her here without authorisation and without the mission commanders' knowledge.

The prescription meds are hived away behind a counter. Khan tucks herself away in there and fills her pack, quickly and efficiently. She mostly goes for antibiotics, which are so precious in Beacon that any prescription has to be countersigned by two doctors and an army officer. There's a whole pack of insulin too, which goes straight in the bag. Paracetamol. Codeine. A few antihistamines.

With the official shopping list covered, it's time to switch agendas. She was hoping she might find what she was looking for right here in the pharmacy area, but there's no sign of it. She raises her head up over the counter to check the lie of the land. Private Phillips is fifty yards away, scowling over the list as he pads from rack to rack.

Khan crosses the aisle in shuffling baby steps, bent almost double and trying not to make a sound. Fetching up in front of a display themed around dental hygiene, she scans the shelves to either side of her urgently. Phillips could finish his task and come looking for her at any moment.

The part of her body she's concerned about is a long way south of her teeth, but for some esoteric reason the relevant products are shelved right there on the next unit along. There is a choice of three brands. Ten long years ago, on the last day when anything was bought or sold in this place, they were on special offer. Khan can't imagine how that can ever have made sense, given the very limited circumstances in which these items are useful. You either need them or you don't, and if you do then price doesn't really factor in. With a surge of relief, Khan grabs one and shoves it into her pack.

On second thoughts, she takes two more, giving her one of each brand. Ten years is a long time, and even behind airtight seals most things eventually degrade: three throws of the dice are better than one.

Popping her head up over the parapet again, she sees that Private Phillips has his back to her. Perfect timing. She steps out into the aisle and rests one hand nonchalantly on the pharmacy counter. Here I am, her stance says. Where I've been all along. Where I have every reason to be.

"Done," she tells him.

Phillips doesn't answer. He's looking at something down on the ground.

Khan goes and joins him.

He's found a nest, of sorts. There's a sleeping bag, rumpled and dirty; an open rucksack in which Khan can see the tops of several plastic water bottles and the handle of what might be a hammer or large screwdriver; two neat stacks of clothes (jeans, socks, T-shirts and a few sweaters, nothing indisputably female except for a single pair of knickers and a black blouse with ruffles on the sleeves); a few dozen empty cans laid out in rows, most of which once held baked beans or soup, and a paperback copy of Enid Blyton's *The Magic Wishing Chair*. There's no dust here to speak of, but it's clear that none of these things have been touched in a while. Dead leaves from a broken window somewhere have silted up against them, and tendrils of black mould are groping their way up the lower half of the sleeping bag.

Someone lived here, Khan thinks. The Mall must have looked like a pretty good place to hide, offering food and shelter and an enticing array of consumer goods. But it was a death trap of course, with a dozen entrances and few defensible spaces. This hopeful hermit probably died not too far away from where they're standing. Private Phillips is looking down at the pathetic display with a thoughtful, distant expression on his face. He scratches his lightly stubbled chin with the tip of one finger.

Then he squats, sets down his rifle and picks up the book, riffling the pages with his thumb. He has to do this very gently because the decades-old glue has dried and cracked and the pages have come loose from the spine. Khan is amazed. She can only assume that *The Magic Wishing Chair* must have featured somehow in the private's childhood; that he's communing with some buried part of himself.

Something falls out onto the floor. A narrow rectangle of thin card, pale gold in colour. It bears the single word *Rizla*.

"Knew it," Phillips exults. He tosses the book aside. Pages spill out of it when it lands, splayed like a hand of cards. He delves into the rucksack with serious purpose, throwing aside the half-empty water bottles and the tool (a claw hammer) to come up with his prize: a half-empty packet of Marlboro Gold cigarettes and a second pack that's still sealed. Hard currency in Beacon, but there's no way these cancer-sticks are going to travel that far.

Khan dips her gaze and looks at the scattered pages of the book. One of them has a picture, of two children sitting in a flying chair, holding on tight to the arms as they soar over the rounded turret of a castle tower. There is a caption below the picture. *"Why, our magic chair might take us anywhere!" Peter cried.*

"Got what you need, Dr Khan?" Phillips asks her. He's cheerful, expansive, riding on an emotional high from the mere thought of those smokes.

"Yes, Gary," Khan tells him, studiously deadpan. "Everything I need."

The journey back to Rosie is blessedly uneventful but, like the trip out, it's protracted and exhausting. By the time they're through the airlock, Khan is pretty much done and just wants to lie down in her bunk until the day goes away. But John Sealey needs to greet her and – under the guise of a casual conversation – to ascertain that she's okay. The boy Stephen Greaves is less demonstrative but she knows his body language: he needs even more reassurance than John, and on top of that he needs, as always, to restore their normal status quo through the rituals they've established over the years they have known each other – greetings and exchanges whose importance lies entirely in their being said rather than in any meaning they carry.

"Good day's work, Stephen?"

"Not too bad, Dr Khan. Thank you."

"You're very welcome."

"Did you enjoy your walk?"

"Very much. It's a lovely day out there. You should take a stroll yourself before the sun goes in."

She disentangles herself delicately, first from John and then from Stephen, and now she's free and clear. The colonel is up in the cockpit. The rest of the crew have their own shit to deal with and no wish to get mixed up in hers.

Khan goes into the shower, since Phillips has already grabbed the latrine. She locks herself in and undresses quickly. Her body is slick with sweat but there is no smell apart from the slightly bitter tang of e-blocker. If there had been, of course, she would have found out about it before now.

One by one she unwraps the three packages, stowing the wrappers in her pockets. The boxes, folded down tight and small, follow. In each package is a flimsy plastic wand. The designs are slightly different, but each wand has a window halfway along its length and a thickening at one end to show where you're supposed to grip it.

Squatting on the floor of the shower, legs slightly parted, she does what needs to be done.

The chemistry is straightforward, and close to infallible. Anti-hCG globulin is extremely reactive to certain human hormones, including the hormone gonadotrophin. Properly prepared, it will change colour in the hormone's presence.

And the hormone is present in a woman's urine. Sometimes.

Having peed on the business end of the three wands, she waits in silence, watching the three little windows. A negative result will tell her very little. The protein layer on the prepared strip inside the wands may have degraded too far to catalyse. A positive, on the other hand, will mean what it always meant.

Khan gets the hat-trick.

Mixed emotions rise in her as she stares at these messages from her own uncharted interior, a high tide of wonder and dismay and disbelief and misery in which hope bobs like a lifeboat cut adrift.

Seven weeks into a fifteen-month mission, ten years after the world ended and a hundred miles from home, Dr Samrina Khan is pregnant.

But this is not Bethlehem, and there will be no manger.

THE FIRST FIFTEEN LIVES OF HARRY AUGUST

also by

Claire North

Harry August is on his deathbed. Again.

No matter what he does or the decisions he makes, when death comes, Harry always returns to where he began, a child with all the knowledge of a life he has already lived a dozen times before. Nothing ever changes.

Until now.

As Harry nears the end of his eleventh life, a little girl appears at his bedside. 'I nearly missed you, Doctor August,' she says. 'I need to send a message.'

This is the story of what Harry does next, and what he did before, and how he tries to save a past he cannot change and a future he cannot allow.

Featured in the Richard and Judy Book Club
Featured in the Waterstones Book Club
Featured on BBC Radio 2 Book Club

www.orbitbooks.net

TOUCH

also by

Claire North

Kepler is like you, but not like you.

With a simple touch, Kepler can move into any body,
live any life – for a moment, a day or for years.

And your life could be next.

SOME PEOPLE TOUCH LIVES.
OTHERS TAKE THEM. I DO BOTH.

www.orbitbooks.net

THE SUDDEN APPEARANCE OF HOPE

also by

Claire North

My name is Hope Arden. I am the girl the world forgets.

It started when I was sixteen years old.

A father forgetting to drive me to school. A mother setting the table for three, not four. A friend who looks at me and sees a stranger.

No matter what I do, the words I say, the crimes I commit – you will never remember who I am.

That makes my life tricky. It also makes me dangerous ...

The Sudden Appearance of Hope is the tale of a girl no one remembers, yet her story will stay with you for ever.

www.orbitbooks.net

THE GAMESHOUSE
NOVELLAS

also by

Claire North

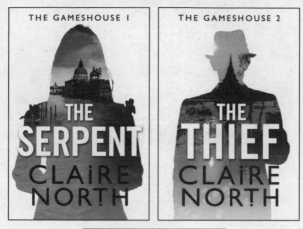

THE GAMESHOUSE 1

THE
SERPENT
CLAiRE
NORTH

THE GAMESHOUSE 2

THE
THIEF
CLAiRE
NORTH

THE GAMESHOUSE 3

THE
MASTER
CLAiRE
NORTH

Three digital and audio-only novellas set in the ingenious and
thrilling world of the Gameshouse

orbit

www.orbitbooks.net